CERWIN'S ORPHANS

CERWIN'S ORPHANS

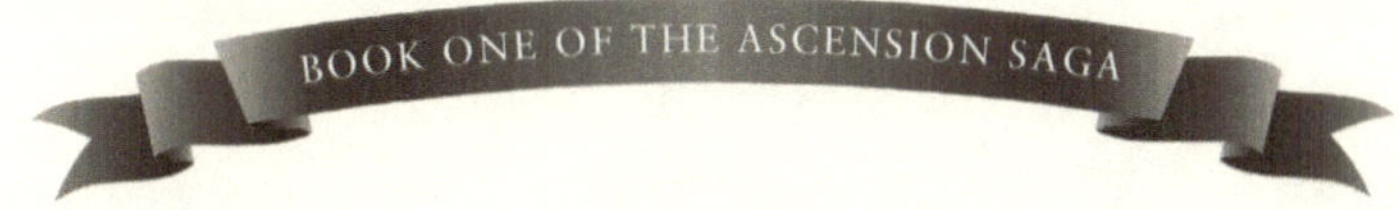

BOOK ONE OF THE ASCENSION SAGA

SCOTT T FERRY

Prologue:

1,340 years ago

The torches lit the room with a dull yellow glow, shadows from the sconces flickering across the stone walls like scampering spiders. The walls were dirty and nitered, showing signs of age and hard use, whilst in the hearth the last embers of a fire spread meagre warmth around the room. The warmth never held, regardless of the number of hearths. Fortress Kingshold, built from cold black granite to withstand assault from any known assailant, was not able to combat a cold southerly wind.

The bay window looked down upon the main courtyard and southern battlements of the mighty fortress standing dark and foreboding on the shoulder of Mount Blackthorn. A company of the Kings-guard were drilling, marching back and forth across the yard, their burnished armour shining regardless of the lack of sunlight. The fortress was abuzz with activity, carts being unloaded in the courtyards, servants going about their various tasks, animals being led to slaughter or their pens, just a normal day at Kingshold.

At the head of an ancient oak table a man sat slumped, with his head in his hands. King Andhonar Blackthorn, the third of his name, was an imposing figure, six and a half feet tall with a mane of peppered black hair, a barrel chest and thick muscled limbs. A vivid pink scar ran from the middle of his forehead across his right brow and ended at the top of his missing ear, courtesy of a Hardite scimitar when he was still a youth. He leaned wearily back in his chair and pushed his platter away, spilling peas and gravy across the tabletop.

The Blackthorn Regency had been at war his whole life, forever expanding its borders, conquering or coercing neighbouring states into submission. Andhonar was named after Andhonar the Magnificent, the king who had forced the six sovereignties to bend the knee over seven centuries ago, the first major expansion of the Regency. As ruthless a conqueror as he had been, Andhonar the Magnificent understood the difficulties of maintaining order over such a vast empire. Autonomous power had been handed back to the rulers of the sovereignties provided they paid homage to Andhonar as their overlord and all acceded. The leaders of their ruling houses became the Lords Dominant, the closest advisors to the Blackthorn Regency.

Andhonar had embraced the traditions of the Regency, aggressively expanding their territory, cherry-picking the lands that offered the richest rewards. The conquest of southern Partia had brought vast mineral deposits to boost the Regency's coffers, the inhabitants either slaughtered in battle or forced to flee north of the newly established border.

He had lived his whole life based on the belief that strength and might of arms was the gift of the gods, to be used ruthlessly to force the weak to bow before the strong. But now? It was as if all he had ever known was wrong, his beliefs a castle built of sand.

Had he imagined it, had any of it really happened? The thought nagged at the back of his mind making him question himself over and over. But he knew the truth, they were all there together and all that remained was to wait. *"If they come everything changes."*

The experience was still vivid in his mind, being linked to so many consciousnesses whilst remaining completely aware of one's individuality. Having instant access to all their knowledge and understanding everything without feeling overwhelmed or unnerved. Even though he and his six Lords Dominant were all mind-walkers, that wasn't what made them aware of each other. When you were there, you just knew.

It was Ascension, the next stage. It had always been and would always be. But for the warning. So, all that remained was to wait. *"If they come everything changes."*

There was a loud rap on the door and a large man in dress uniform entered the room and stood to attention. "My liege, the Lords Dominant await your pleasure."

"Show them in, Berin, and stand guard yourself. No one else is to enter under any circumstances, no one. Do I make myself clear? No one." Andhonar fixed his captain with a firm look.

"Yes, my liege." The captain of the Kings-guard bowed low and then marched briskly from the room. *"Now we shall see."*

The first through the door was Lord Stevan of House Curtess, Lord First Counsellor. A slim, grey-haired man in his sixty-fifth year, impeccably dressed in a red tunic, grey breeches and brown leather riding boots. His family were rulers of Boseland, bonded by centuries of political marriages to the Blackthorn Regency and Andhonar's most trusted allies.

Next, came Lord Orel of House Mensall, Highlord of Harvland, a rotund, balding, bluff, red-faced man in his forties. As was his manner, he was garbed in a plain woollen shirt and leather breeches, a cape fastened at the neck with a brooch bearing the sign of his house, a charging bull. He was followed by Lord Jona Falconer, Lord High Marshall and ruler of Stonebard. Falconer was a giant of a man, over seven feet tall and dressed entirely in black. On top of a quilted tunic, he wore a dinted iron breastplate with crossed sword insignia, the mark of his rank.

Lord Nitem of House Thire and Lord Rumit of House Zoller followed closely behind. They were brothers and ruled over the sister kingdoms of East and Westfall, standing on the northern borders of the Hardite Empire.

Lastly Lord Curlon of House Skar, Lord High Chancellor and ruler of Skarland, sauntered into the room closing the door behind him. He was a tall, elegant man with long straight golden hair, a long thin nose and a haughty bearing. His house was the richest and most powerful in the kingdom, ancient and second only to the royal line, a fact that he knew only too well. So did everyone else.

Of all the ruling houses, House Skar had fought the longest and been the last to bend the knee to Andhonar the Magnificent. They had shown nothing but loyalty ever since, but every generation of Blackthorns knew their ambition and always remained wary.

Andhonar's father had once told him "House Skar may have been loyal for seven centuries, but they would supplant you given any opportunity. They believe in their right to rule and instil that belief in all their descendants, keep them close but never at your back." Those words rang loud in Andhonar's head now, an ancestral warning that picked at his consciousness.

"My friends, please be seated. The fact that you are here means there is no need to stand on ceremony, there is much to be discussed," said Andhonar, gesturing to the table.

The Lords Dominant took their seats, Curlon sitting last and at the opposite end from the king. Curlon slowly pulled off his gauntlets, one finger at a time, carefully regarding his fellow lords.

"It would seem we are presented with an extraordinary opportunity here, gentleman, a chance to create a new world focused on a single goal." He spoke slowly and evenly, radiating a self-assurance that Andhonar found more unnerving than usual. "It only remains to be seen how we go about it." Curlon gave a thin smile as he settled languidly into his chair.

"Trust you to simplify the complex, Curlon. You make it sound like a simple division of labour rather than the most momentous development in human history," blustered Orel. "This is about ensuring harmony and creating equality, not imposing our will. How would that be any different from what we currently have?" Orel exhaled loudly as if to dismiss Curlon's presumption.

"We all heard the warning, that all will be lost unless we unite and come to common purpose. That which has always been and will always be may never exist unless we change and recognise that all are equal and all as important as each other." Lord Stevan Curtess had the respect of all, commoners and nobility alike, and when he spoke people listened. "We have to create a society where all are valued, where all strive to improve our existence. A society where vocation and commitment to the common good are paramount." He looked around the table at his peers, fixing each in the eye. All nodded assent. All except Curlon.

"So, we should what? Give up our titles and our possessions, lay down our power and our armies? Relinquish power and allow any common stock to rise to prominence?" Curlon gripped the edge of the table and leaned forward. He had an intensity in his eyes and a set to his shoulders that reminded Andhonar of a predator. It was beginning to unsettle him. He wasn't quite able to grasp it but something tugged at his subconscious, like an itch inside his head.

"So, what would you suggest Curlon?" Andhonar sat forward and directed his whole attention at Curlon. However, Curlon wasn't cowed at all and that only heightened Andhonar's discomfort.

"My liege, I say we conquer all and force them to follow, unite through strength and destroy all who refuse to join us. Tell the people the truth, give them the choice and mould all to our cause!" Curlon was standing now, leaning forward and shifting his gaze from man to man.

"That is not creating harmony, that is crushing hope and choice." Falconer rose from his seat as he spoke, making it impossible not to pay close attention.

"I am a soldier and have been all my life. You can beat an enemy into dust, but you can never truly break his beliefs through force. You can kill him but no dead man I know can be educated to change his mind. Force will not avail us in this, we must choose a different path." He smiled benignly at Curlon, a strange sight from such a fearful man.

"Our way forward must be taken together in harmony. We have to create something so appealing that all wish to join," said Andhonar, smiling at each man in turn. Each reciprocated until he looked at Curlon.

Curlon gave a thin smile in return and whispered, "I feared you would all want to take some moral high ground, some ideological stance. I'm sorry…"

Suddenly the air around Curlon shimmered and began to pulse. Andhonar watched in horror as Curlon pulled a long dagger from its sheath on his belt and grabbed Lord Rumit by the hair, sliding the blade in behind his ear. Everything seemed to suddenly slow down, but this wasn't the focus of battle fever. At first Andhonar didn't understand why nobody else was moving, nobody but Curlon. And why was Curlon so calm and so assured when he was killing his fellow Lords Dominant? Andhonar's head was swimming but somehow, he shook himself out of it and lurched for his battleaxe, "Nooo!" Curlon screamed. "It cannot be, not you as well!" Curlon clutched a handful of Nitem's hair and held the dagger to his throat as Andhonar closed on him from the other side of the table. "No further my liege or you will lose another of your closest." Curlon hauled Nitem to his feet. Nitem's limbs moved as if under water, grasping for something out of reach and just out of vision.

"Why Curlon? Why betray us now?" Andhonar's voice was a mixture of regret and fury, tears rolling down his cheeks. "There was no need to do this, we hadn't even begun to talk things through." He slowly edged his way towards Curlon, hoping to distract him long enough to create an opening.

"Because I thought I was the only one to have received this gift, because I thought I could end you all and conquer the world with this knowledge, because I crave power. My house is ancient, and I was born to rule, it is my time!" bellowed Curlon.

"You cannot escape Curlon, lay down your blade. Do not force me to kill you." Curlon shifted to his right and pulled his dagger across Nitem's throat leaving a thin red mark. As he did so he threw Nitem bodily at Andhonar, darted to his left and launched himself through the window. Andhonar watched him swallowdive towards the courtyard seventy feet below as he grabbed Nitem's slowly flailing body, dark blood bubbling from his neck and mouth.

Andhonar stood rooted to the spot, Nitem in his arms, weighing strangely little for a man of his size. He tried to focus but confusion reined in on him. He closed his eyes, drew a deep breath and suddenly the whole room broke into uproar.

Chapter One:

The Snap

Main Harbour sat to the north of the White Rush delta which split Great Harbour in two. Great Harbour was the crowning jewel of the Protectorate, a thirty-mile-wide cove enclosed by two gigantic man-made jetties each fourteen miles long and rising thirty feet above the water. It had been a monumental undertaking, the largest engineering project ever attempted, seventy-four years in the building with a workforce of tens of thousands. People had come from every corner of the Known World to be involved in the construction of this man-made marvel and many had perished building it. Many more had lived their whole lives working on the project and were laid to rest in the Great Lighthouse cemetery atop the white cliffs.

It had defensive forts built every two miles, standing like sentinels against unseen foes and held a permanent garrison of three thousand marines, the Silver Shield, who specialised in shipboard combat, close quarter hand-to-hand fighting. The Silver Shield was made up of the most elite soldiers in the Protectorate, fighters of extraordinary skill at arms, dedicated to defending the jetties and Protectorate shipping against any foes. They forged their reputation during the construction of the jetties, most famously defeating the last great Hardite armada, sacrificing over two thirds of their number in the defence of Main Harbour. The Hardite Empire had never recovered from the loss, their fortunes forever on the wane from that day forth.

No force had ever attempted to attack Great Harbour since the jetties were completed, not even the Brotherhood of the Golden Hand, the most feared corsairs in existence. For all their coastal raids and their constant harassment of the island of Santatoria, even they knew better than to risk open conflict with the Shield. The jetties were the most impenetrable stronghold in the Protectorate and its proudest achievement.

The harbour they created was vast and accommodated three separate urban communities, Great Harbour Town, Main Harbour and Summersfort. Trading ships and fishing vessels crowded the docks and piers, jostling with boats and ships from across the Known World. There was always at the very least a squadron of the Mid Ocean fleet at anchor to act as escort to trading cogs or defend the harbour mouth. At least as many vessels found anchorage in the deep calm waters of the massive harbour, safe in the knowledge that no ship had ever been sunk within the jetty walls.

More than one million people lived and worked in the Great Harbour area which was surrounded on its landward side by a ring of hills split only by a valley through which the White Rush flowed into the sea. Main Harbour sat on the north bank of the White Rush and ran northwards to the feet of the white cliffs.

The town was relatively new, expanding to its current vast size almost entirely due to the jetties. As with any modern urban community in the Protectorate, Main Harbour was laid out on straight lines, the intersection of its streets creating squares. Within most squares you would find sleeping halls, dining halls, bath houses, libraries, registries, hospitals, schools and any other building needed to serve the community. It was a pattern adopted and where necessary adapted throughout the Protectorate, and it was a pattern that worked.

For all its wonderful achievements and advances the foremost was surely the medical sciences. The advances in treating infections were stunning, survival rates amongst severely injured soldiers were remarkable. Proof positive that the vocational system worked, a lifetime's dedication to one's passion. It was reflected in all walks of life, every pursuit advancing over time, the knowledge being passed from generation to generation. The school system was almost as impressive, catering for all levels of ability, ensuring every individual received the best vocational support possible. The foremost school catering for the most gifted students was Red Pier Academy.

Red Pier Academy sat at the base of the foothills directly behind the pier itself. It was three stories tall with a tower on each corner of a square, connected by corridors with classrooms facing out on all sides. The towers accommodated the elder students with the eldest situated on the top floors, the sky classrooms.

Jonoh Shipwright leaned gently back in his chair as he gazed idly out of the window of the sky classroom and across the azure waters of Great Harbour. It was a beautiful spring day and the sun reflected off the ripples in the harbour, creating an illusion of dancing light motes.

He had always enjoyed the daily history lessons, fantasising about the heroes of old but really could not see the point anymore. It was only a fortnight until he left for his martial service, two years in the army in a distant exotic land. Or so he hoped. Knowing his luck, he would be stationed on the border of Snowbard, freezing and staring at the Whitecap mountains. But wherever he went it was a time of great excitement, the last step to full citizenship and manhood. So, all things considered, more lessons about the history and expansion of the Protectorate seemed a little pointless.

It wasn't just his looks that made Jonoh stand out, but his long straight golden hair, long thin nose and handsome features did give him a certain bearing. It also added to the impression that he was just a little arrogant. The fact that he had always excelled in life wasn't his fault, and what could he do if it made others jealous.

He'd excelled especially at martial training and games and that had only heightened his expectation, he just hoped he'd be stationed with Garic. Garic Carpenter, his best friend and the only person to ever challenge him in training or games, over six foot of good nature and fierce fighter. But even Garic had never been able to beat him, no one had. They had been friends all their lives, had grown up together, sharing the kind of secrets and in-jokes that only best friends could. Their own private nicknames, ox and doe, they kept to themselves; personal insults reserved for only the most heated arguments. You never knew who you would be stationed with, but he hoped for Garic at least.

Jonoh could hear his teacher Philos Scholar on the edge of his consciousness but was much more interested in the day's activities in the harbour. From this distance the companies of the Silver Shield going through their daily drills looked like army ants swarming backwards and forwards with no apparent destination in mind. He could make out the Mid Ocean squadron ships by their pennants fluttering in the wind, silver falcon on black, a white orchid held in its beak. The trading cogs and various other ships were all recognisable by their flags, Sarjinn golden desert lion on red, Snowbard white eagle on black, amongst many others, all jostled for position at the docks.

Down at Red Pier a whole herd of grassland horses were being ushered from a Sarjinn trading cog, a fat-bellied vessel designed for animal transport. They were magnificent-looking beasts, all the colour of burnished bronze, sleek and haughty looking, as if aware of their aesthetic beauty. Warhorses Jonoh knew, bred for centuries to be strong and durable and far less flighty than other breeds. He wondered what the Sarjinns would be taking in trade, not the coin they craved. Of all the foreign traders, the Sarjinn still complained the loudest that the Protectorate had no coin, but certain products only came from there, so trade they still did.

Jonoh smiled as he remembered the Sarjinn sailing master Xanda who had always said a country with no coin is no country at all. The Sarjinn sailors put it another way – "A country with no coin is like a whore with no cunt, doesn't work." He had laughed along with them, although at the time he did not really know why it was funny.

Twelve years old down at Red Pier with Garic, listening to the sounds and taking in all that assailed the senses. It seemed a lifetime away now, that youthful innocence erased by puberty, drink and most importantly, girls.

Xanda was in his forties and well-liked by all who met him. He had always traded fairly and never represented his goods as any better than they were. The children of Main Harbour would play around the docks and piers during their free time, especially in summer. And Xanda always had treats for them, exotic fruits and strange sweet and savoury pastries from across the sea.

"Jonoh, your name is also Shipwright, yes?" Xanda had asked

one day. "Yes," Jonoh had answered.

"I know a Tamos Shipwright from Main Harbour. Is relation of yours, yes?" said the sailing master.

"Only in the fact that we are all related in Main Harbour, but there are five shipyards here so many shipwrights I think." As young as he was, Jonoh did not realise that Xanda was having a little gentle fun with him.

"I know this Jonoh. I am, as you say, having fun with you. How is it you say? In the Protectorate we are one community? However, the sense of this I do not understand, no family groups, all together in great halls, for eating, sleeping, laughing. This is not natural, is like a country without coin, makes no sense. Which is also what you have, no coin! How can a man aspire to improve his life without coin to buy better things? This makes no sense to Xanda, no sense at all," he had said in his rich eastern accent. The memory of the look of genuine confusion on Xanda's face almost made Jonoh chuckle out loud, but he did not completely muffle all sound.

"Master Shipwright." Garic nudged Jonoh almost making him over balance on his chair. His arms freewheeled wildly as he fought to keep his balance, finally righting himself as his classmates all looked at him with amusement. He could feel the colour rising up his cheeks. Jonoh Shipwright was never one to take embarrassment with good grace.

"Yes sir," he stammered, painfully aware of all eyes on him.

"Are we boring you Jonoh? You seem a little distracted," Philos Scholar asked with a knowing smile on his face.

"No sir, my apologies, although if truth be told I do find my thoughts drifting to my coming service," Jonoh replied.

"Your service will start soon enough, for now try to pay attention to the lesson." Philos smiled benignly at his errant student.

"Yes sir, apologies," Jonoh mumbled back, the redness in his cheeks slowly subsiding.

"As I was saying, the formation of the Protectorate was a long and bloody process. Curlon's forces fought fiercely for over thirty years, ceding ground slowly and at great cost. It was only after the battle of Rush Crossing where Andhonar's forces routed Curlon's that Curlon and his surviving supporters took to ship at Great Harbour and were never seen again." Philos walked across the front of the classroom, hands clasped behind his back.

"I realise of course that this is ground well covered in previous lessons, but it points to the founding principle of the Protectorate. What do you think the single most important tenet of our society is, the principle upon which everything hinges?" Philos looked across the classroom at his students hoping for one of them to come to the realisation on their own. "No? Sacrifice, everything depends upon sacrifice. The willingness to sacrifice all for the greater good, for the benefit of the greater community. Andhonar and the Lords Dominant sacrificed all they had, their wealth, their power, their possessions and even their lives to establish the first Protectorate. To create a society where all are encouraged to follow their vocation, where all actively contribute to the greater community, where all are valued equally."

"Some more equally than others," quipped Jonoh to muffled giggles.

As quick as a flash, Philos Scholar picked up the slateboard cleaner and launched it at Jonoh. Jonoh flinched and started to duck when suddenly the air around him seemed to shimmer. He sat back upright and watched in amazement as the cleaner slowed almost to a stop, moving towards him as if under water. He swivelled to look at Garic only to see his friends face contorted in a look of shock, his mouth forming a curious circle, opening ever so slowly to reveal his crooked teeth. He stood up and stepped forward picking the cleaner out of the air, feeling strangely elated and disoriented. Looking around the room he saw his classmates with differing looks of amazement and surprise, all of them appearing to be stuck in time. He reached across to Garic and touched his face and watched his expression slowly change to one of fear, as if he were in some sort of mortal danger. A slow pulsing started to affect his vision like the disorientation of too much wine. Panic started to creep up on him, so he closed his eyes and took a deep breath.

The classroom erupted into a cacophony of noise, screams, shouts, girls crying. "Silence!" shouted Philos Scholar. "Silence students." There was a slightly reedy timbre to his voice, something akin to fear. Or awe. "By Andhonar's ghost, you have the Gift," he said, his voice still wavering.

He did not know it, but Jonoh Shipwright had experienced the snap. Nothing would ever be the same again.

Chapter Two:

Isolation

Torbin Pale-skin laid back in his bed, sweat beading on his bare chest, the thin linen sheets bundled across his lap. He looked at Jadzia standing naked against the doorframe, her body almost silhouetted against the blazing afternoon sun. She was beautiful, long sleek limbs, full pert breasts, long jet-black hair and smooth nut-brown skin, every inch a native of Lhossa. Ten years together and his desire for her only seemed to increase with every passing day, he could not imagine life without her. Even though he had only spent his seed a couple of minutes ago he started to stiffen beneath the sheets. Always time for another go around.

He got up wrapping one of the sheets loosely around his waist and walked to the balcony door, gently kissing her on the nape of her neck. She half turned towards him, slipping her hand under the sheet and gently grasping his cock.

"Ready so soon lover? It's almost as if you're worried you'll never have sex again," she said spinning away from him and giving his balls a little slap.

"Ow! That was a little too near the mark." Torbin pulled a mock hurt expression and they both fell into fits of giggles.

Torbin walked out onto the balcony and leaned on the wall. The great free city of Lhossa, the last bastion of civilisation, right out on the eastern extremities of the free territories. Its red brick and mud buildings spread out and downwards towards the edges of the Red Desert, safe within the great land walls. With its back to the foothills of the southern Titan mountains it was one of the most defensible places in the southern plains, which was just as well. The fact that it was built with its back to three adjoining mountain valleys, meant that it was self-sufficient. The valleys supported crops of every description and vast herds of cattle and swine, more than enough to feed Lhossa with plenty left over for trade. The city was supplied from the valleys which were inaccessible from any other direction because of the enclosing mountains.

No other outsider had ever been granted domicile in the third tier of the city but Torbin had earned it, holding the southern land wall when the Murgan hoard had nearly over run it. A puckered white scar running from his chest to his groin stood as a constant reminder, not just to him but to the native Lhossan's who revered him and held him as one of their own.

Jadzia was of Lhossan nobility, the daughter of his Eminence Jadwar Sun-blessed, one of the oldest and most venerated families in the city. She had nursed Torbin back to health, never leaving his side even when the healers had declared he would not last another night. It had been months before he was even able to walk, let alone care for himself. He literally owed Jadzia his life and not a day went by when he did not remind himself of the fact.

Torbin loved this city and its people, so full of life, boisterous as an unruly child and wise as the oldest sage. Its people were so warm and welcoming and yet insular and guarded. The contradictions just fed his passion for it. This was home, or as close as anywhere could ever be.

His skin started to prickle in the direct sunlight, so he turned and walked back into the bedroom. Even after all this time in Lhossa he was not a native and even his sun-burnished skin could still blister. Jadzia laid naked on the bed, head propped up on her arm. "Still feeling frisky my love?" she said, smiling shyly up at him. He dropped the blanket from around his waist and slid onto the bed next to her. *"Always time for another go around."*

After they had finished, Torbin washed in the copper basin in the door alcove and dressed himself in traditional Lhossan linen trousers, wide-necked shirt and open leather sandals.

"I'm going to get some meat for dinner and I'm taking Terror with me," he called out as he opened the door to the street.

"Try not to waste all afternoon at the Cleaver," called back Jadzia with a giggle in her voice.

He pulled the door to and squatted down to scratch Terror behind his ear. "C'mon boy, let's go for a stroll and see what trouble we can get ourselves into," he said, rubbing Terror's head.

Terror was the largest bear-hound anyone had ever seen, at least that was the common consensus. Not as tall at the shoulder as a wolfhound but in every other way he was vastly bigger. Massive through the neck and shoulders, with a skull so thick that you were more likely to break a hammer on it than do it any damage. Terror looked like the embodiment of his name, eighteen stone of death. He sauntered along blithely unaware of anything outside his own little world. Threaten Torbin however and you may as well relinquish your life; Terror was not particularly forgiving.

Terror had been with Torbin since he was a pup, seven years of unbroken companionship. Their bond was more than master and obedient servant and closer to father and son. Torbin often thought that Terror understood him better than anyone else he knew, even Jadzia. A strange thought maybe, but not one that made Torbin uncomfortable. It was his most relaxed relationship, uncluttered by verbal communication, just easy.

They slowly made their way downhill towards Market Square, the heat haze rising off the cobbled streets creating shadowy mirages in all directions. The three-storey buildings and narrow streets at least kept the worst of the afternoon sun off you and had the added bonus of generating gentle breezes. One of the things that made Lhossa unique was the fact that there were no windows at ground level, just communal doors into open courtyards. It had evolved that way out of necessity, narrow streets only wide enough to walk three abreast, that much easier to defend against larger numbers. No windows and as few doors as possible on the ground floor to create what in effect were defensible keeps in each building. Having only windows first floor and upwards meant defenders could rain down fire on any attacking force; an innovative and resourceful people Torbin had always thought.

They walked out into Market Square and directly into the full force of the early afternoon sun, a wall of heat descending onto them. Torbin walked slowly across the square, stopping occasionally to exchange pleasantries or look at the wares on offer. You could find almost anything in Market Square, clothes, jewellery, foodstuffs of every conceivable kind, weapons and of course slaves. The slave stalls had people from every corner of the free territories, with the exception of the Murgan. Even Lhossan slave traders were not that stupid. It rankled with Torbin but as the saying went, "When in Lhossa, do as Lhossans do."

Jadwan always set up in the northeast corner as it sat in the shadow of the great temple of Sardis. Shadow meant cooler, always helpful for a butcher. The temple was the tallest building in Lhossa, rising over a hundred feet into the sky, dominating the view in all directions. Worshipping the sun and the skies made as much sense as any other religion to Torbin, at least it was there every day. Even the currency was based on it, Golden suns, Silver moons, Bronze stars and copper clouds.

"Got out of bed early enough for once then, you lazy fucker?" called out Torbin as he walked towards Jadwan's stall. Jadwan was a huge man, not particularly tall but massive around the gut. His jet-black hair and goatee were peppered with white, and he wore his leather cap and butcher's apron over sand-coloured trousers and a short-sleeved shirt.

"Should have worn a hat, you pasty skinned prick," came Jadwan's reply. The two men eyed each other warily then fell laughing into a bear hug.

"So, what can I do for you today Torb? And something for handsome?" asked Jadwan as he hugged Terror around the neck, Terror returning his affection by licking his face. Terror wouldn't let anyone else be so overly familiar, but he did love the portly Lhossan butcher.

"A leg of lamb would be nice if you have one, and you know what Terror wants. What does he always want?" said Torbin, ruffling Terror's neck. Terror looked up at him as if to say 'why ask a stupid question?'.

"Here boy," said Jadwan, pulling an oxen thighbone from under his stall and handing it to Terror. "As if I'd forget about you." Terror looked at him and gave his best dog grin as he laid down and set about his prize.

"How long until you shut up for the day, Wan?" asked Torbin.

"Time for a couple of ales before you go home to an evening of nagging?" he said grinning inanely.

"After all my Zeena's done for you, you would say such a thing? I'm hurt that anyone would say that about such a quiet understanding woman," said Jadwan laughing. "I was just about to start packing up before you two reprobates turned up, so if you give me a hand, the quicker we'll get to the Cleaver."

Once they'd finished clearing Jadwan's stall, the three unlikely looking companions strolled over to the Butchers Cleaver and took up residence in one of the corner nooks. Terror laid down and returned his attention to the thigh bone.

The Cleaver was the social centre of Market Square, granted the honour of being the only inn on the square. It was full of a mixture of local merchants, militia, labourers and all the foreign traders one could ever hope to see. Even Murgan riders would stop overnight in Lhossa and there were some at the bar now, something that always made Jadwan uncomfortable when they made their way to Torbin's local hostelry. They didn't always recognise Torbin but when they did, they weren't always well disposed.

Torbin could see his friend's discomfort. "Don't worry Wan, it's too hot for any trouble today, even for the Murgan. Besides it was ten years ago, old news. The fact that the Murgan freely enter the city for trade and entertainment kind of suggests the war's over." He patted his friend on the shoulder.

"I know but I'm always hearing rumours of those fuckers the Hired Knives. Word has it that even now they still follow the old vendetta. For you my friend I don't believe it will ever be done with." Jadwan shrugged his shoulders and smiled. "But as you say, why worry?" He lifted his tankard and Torbin lifted his in response.

It had been over ten years since Torbin had rallied the fleeing Lhossan militia and held the great southern land wall against the Murgan attack. The Murgan had sworn vendetta and put such a massive bounty on his head that all the assassins and bounty hunters in the Known World had fought for the prize. Vendetta was only lifted by death, natural or otherwise, and the Hired Knives had never given up on a contract. There had been more than a few close shaves, but all that had got close had been sent to the afterlife. Torbin was not easy to kill.

It was two hours later that Torbin and Terror parted company with Jadwan and began making their way back up the hill to the apartment. Torbin loved the late afternoon as the breezes that ran down the streets turned a little cooler, gently blowing against the sheen of sweat prickling on his torso. Terror happily plodded along, thighbone in his mouth, occasionally stopping to have another gnaw.

"Andhonar's lost child do you hear me? Torbin my brother I need you to meet me at the Titan Gate three days from now. A great darkness is upon us and time is of the essence, the very future of the Known World is at stake. I will tell all face to face, do not fail me my brother."

Candor Blackheart, his old friend and fellow Orphan. The urgency in his thoughts hit Torbin like a shockwave, a feeling of nausea almost overwhelming him.

"I will be there Candor of course, but why do you need to meet in person? Would it not be more expedient to tell me all now?" Even as he sent his thoughts, he could sense Candor's unease.

"It cannot be risked my brother, we are no longer unheard, there are mind-walkers other than us, and they are coming."

The shock of the revelation stopped Torbin in his tracks. In millennia of recorded history, no other nation than the Protectorate had ever had mind-walkers. *"A great darkness is upon us."*

Chapter Three:

Surprises

The sound of the blunted spears smashing together echoed around the yard. Marisa Longspear loved sparring, had done ever since she picked up her first staff at the age of eight. It didn't take much in the way of insight to realise that Marisa's vocation would be soldier. She had always been the biggest child at her school, always been the most aggressive, the first to fight. Often as not she had been the one to instigate it, always looking to test herself against bigger and older opponents. She had found it was the only way she could find any competition at all.

Squad leader at the age of twenty-three. Considering her discipline issues, she still found it hard to believe and she was not the only one. Even in the idyllic Protectorate, jealousy could still occasionally rear its ugly head, but reason always won through. She had finally topped out at six feet three, which was a relief. Any bigger and she never would have got laid. No man wants to feel threatened in bed, even though they should. Marisa had not found many who could stand toe to toe with her so when one did, she nearly always wanted to fuck them. Strange how attraction works.

Marisa danced to her left, staying on the balls of her feet, shifting her spear from hand to hand, grinning wildly at her sparring partner. He suddenly launched a wild, two-handed attack at her, switch hitting high and low, swinging in furious wide arcs. Marisa gave ground slowly, blocking each blow high and low, never taking her eyes off him. *"Patience Marisa, patience,"* she told herself. "Allow *him* to *reveal his weakness, let him burn himself out."* He slowed his attack, taking half a step back, warily keeping a high guard, not wanting to be smashed in the skull. Even though the spears were padded at each end they could still leave a bruise and just occasionally a broken bone. Marisa shuffled forward a half step, lightly crouching and rocking back slightly on her heels. He saw his opportunity and whipped his spear round hard and fast at her head, planting his feet and putting his full weight behind the blow. Marisa just ducked under the blow, dropping her shoulder and driving into his ribs with tremendous force. He staggered backwards, desperately trying to keep to his feet but Marisa was already spinning sideways whipping her spear round in a furious arc, cracking into his ankles and sending him flying through the air and onto his back.

"Good spar Tommec but you still need to work on your posture. When you move to attack, your body language always gives your intention away," she said, leaning over to offer him her hand.

"Thank you, squad leader, I'll work on it," said Tommec, rubbing the back of his head where it had cracked against the ground.

It was intake time again, once a year when the new recruits arrived to start their martial service, replacing those who had finished their two-year stint. Marisa looked at her squad's new boy. How this one was only sixteen years old was beyond her. He could already look her in the eye and didn't have a hint of bumfluff on his face, just dark black stubble, the proverbial afternoon shadow. He still had some filling out to do that was for sure, but he was broad through the shoulder and already well-muscled. But one thing she had learned was that brawn did not always triumph in a fight and certainly didn't guarantee intelligence.

"New boy!" she shouted at him. "Let's see what you're made of."

"My name's Garic Carpenter," he called back, stepping forward spear in hand, a surly look on his face.

"I don't give a fuck. You're new boy until I say otherwise. Everyone has to earn their names here and you haven't earned shit," she spat back at him, staring him down in the process. Only he didn't quail, standing his ground adopting a classic half-body defensive stance. "So, you've got some balls then, let's see how big they are."

Marisa sprang forward, feinting off one foot whilst hitting from the other, whistling her spear round at tremendous speed, venom behind every blow. Garic matched her movements, keeping his half-stance defence, blocking each blow in rapid sequence whilst maintaining his distance. Marisa switched suddenly to an alternating attack, thrusting to force her opponent back then arcing sweeping blows low and high. Garic shifted stance, heel to toe, blocking everything she threw at him always keeping his distance, never taking his eyes off her. She switched to staff position, hands apart with two feet of blunted spear protruding outside of each hand. Launching herself into a rapid attack, high and low, unrelentingly fast, she kept the pressure on. Garic didn't back off, instead meeting her blow for blow. For what seemed like an age they hammered away furiously, blow and counter blow, back and forth, until Marisa suddenly dipped her body, spinning to her left whipping her spear round in a low arc, straight at Garic's ankles. To hers and everyone else's amazement Garic spun to meet her and whipped his spear overhand catching her flush on the shoulder knocking her onto her arse.

For a moment there was a stunned silence, the rest of her squad standing with mouths agape. No one beat Marisa Longspear in sparring, let alone a green recruit.

"Where the fuck did you learn to fight like that, boy? You're not a soldier by vocation so your life hasn't been martial training alone. That shouldn't be possible, not against me," said Marisa, gulping in air whilst standing and brushing the dust off her behind.

"My name is Garic Carpenter, not boy," he said, not even trying to keep the testy tone out of his voice.

"Fine, as you wish Garic. I still want to know how you learnt to fight like that," said Marisa. "I'm still your superior even if you did knock me on my arse." Marisa offered a sly grin and the tension subsided. She wouldn't underestimate him again.

"I fought every day of my life against Jonoh Shipwright up until three weeks ago. We are bonded brothers and best friends." Garic looked around at the faces of the assembled squad to gauge their response. He expected the same as usual, a mixture of wonderment and disbelief. Fame by association followed by endless questions and fawning sycophancy, everybody wanted to find out more about the prodigy. One thing about the Protectorate was that news travelled fast, almost instantaneously, a natural by-product of having mind-walkers in every walk of life.

"Well good for you Garic," said Marisa, "but that doesn't carry any weight here and until you earn it, you're bottom of the pile, new boy." She slapped him on the back smiling and the rest of the squad followed suit. He was accepted as himself, possibly for the first time in his life. It felt good.

"Right, no slacking you lot," she snapped. "Tommec take training, half an hour of forms, then one-on-one sparring. Five minutes per match then swap round." Tommec nodded and drew off the rest of the squad to continue training.

"Garic with me. We need to bring you up to speed with the way of things," she said gesturing for Garic to follow her. They walked across the parade ground and into the communal barracks, stopping at a door into a sleeping cell. "After you," she said waving him into the room.

The room was sparse with a table, two chairs and a basic bed. "Sit down Garic, I need to give you the orientation briefing." Garic nodded his ascent and sat on one of the chairs.

"As you can imagine there are a lot of soldiers with the same vocation names. For instance, there are four Longspears and two Shortswords alone in our squad, so for training, drill and battle we use a simple number system. Ten men squads and your number is ten, alright new boy?" said Marisa with a wicked grin on her face.

"Yes squad leader," replied Garic, the tension now gone from his voice.

"Good then listen up. It's important that you understand the structure of the army, so this is it. Ten soldiers per squad, ten squads per century, ten centuries per battalion and ten battalions per army group. Each battalion is made up of five centuries of infantry, one century of archers, two centuries of cavalry and two centuries of auxiliaries. You are number ten attached to squad seven, attached to century five from battalion four. And as you know this is army group Partia, stationed on the northeast border of the Protectorate.

This is as hard a posting as you could find in the Protectorate, cold, inhospitable and only matched by army group Snowbard for enemy contacts. The wasteland mountain tribes are fierce, independent warriors that do not fear us and continue to raid for provisions and plunder. It's important you understand this, life here is not easy and our training keeps us alive. Do your part, defend your own and stay alert and you'll do fine, OK?" she said, fixing Garic with an intense but sympathetic look.

"Yes, squad leader," replied Garic showing no sign of concern.

"Good lad," she said, sliding her chair across the floor until their knees touched each other. "The thing is, getting beaten at sparring warms me up." Her hand slid up the inside of his thigh coming to rest on his crotch "Do you know what I mean?" she asked, giving his cock a quick squeeze.

"Yes, squad leader," stammered Garic, for the first time seeming to lose his composure.

"Marisa, for now, call me Marisa," she whispered leaning forward, pressing her lips to his.

Strange how attraction works she thought, always surprising.

Chapter Four:

Decisions

Jonoh always used to think that people who complained of being saddle sore were just angling for sympathy. Three weeks on the Rush highway had taught him otherwise. There wasn't a saddle in creation that would relieve the ache in his buttocks, so he'd massage them every night to try to return them to some kind of normality. It just heaped more resentment on him. He knew that these weren't the thoughts of a reasoned, mature man but he was only sixteen years old. He didn't exactly blame anyone in particular, but to be pulled from martial service and summoned to Kings Town to stand before the Elder Council was not what he'd planned for. His escort was pleasant enough, a young officer named Bergin Shortspear. But Jonoh had always found vocational soldiers a little limited, so conversation was not exactly stimulating.

The Rush highway followed the White Rush westwards inland, to the point where the Great Rush split into two separate rivers. The White Rush flowed to Great Harbour, while the Blue Rush took a more northerly route through Partia. They both flowed from the Great Rush which had its source in the Blackthorn mountains. The rivers split at Falconer's Rest or Rush Crossing as it was once known. They had stopped overnight at Falconer's Rest and Jonoh had visited the site of Jona Falconer's tomb, drawn to it for some reason he couldn't explain. It was a simple cairn of stones with a plain headstone bearing the inscription 'Here lies a son of the Protectorate who gave all he was for his fellows'. Jonoh couldn't explain why, but he'd been moved to tears and had stayed there silently for an hour, just staring at those words.

Falconer's Rest had been by far the most comfortable and extended stay upon their journey. Word had spread well ahead of them, so upon their arrival in every community along the way a welcoming committee of sorts was either waiting or else hastily arranged. Jonoh was finding it hard to adjust to the degree of notoriety attached to him; everybody wanted to meet the prodigy, shake his hand or just say they had met him. In a society of equals it was almost unheard of that someone would be elevated in such a manner, but understandable. He was after all the first fully gifted for over twenty years, a genuine celebrity if such a thing existed. However, as was the way in the Protectorate, once met he was treated the same as everyone else. No one person stood above anyone else, as it should be.

Outside of Great Harbour, Falconer's Rest was the largest community Jonoh had ever seen, nestled in the angle of the White and Blue Rush. They were billeted in the northwest quarter of the town and their sleeping cells were more than comfortable as guest hall accommodation always was. The dining hall was a low single-storey wooden building, brightly painted and well appointed, with long wooden tables and benches. For their daily community service Jonoh and Bergin spent their hour peeling vegetables for the evening meal, always the best way to familiarise yourself with the locals. By mucking in you became quickly involved in the banter and local gossip, basically an information goldmine.

It was sitting down to dinner that finally allowed Jonoh to relax, the novelty of his presence having subsided somewhat. He and Bergin sat with two of the members of the town's Elder Council, amongst others and slipped easily into the free-flowing conversations.

"Jonoh, do you know the history of Falconer's Rest? I'm not sure how much detail is taught nowadays," asked Torbut Mason. He was a well-built man in his late forties, with dark slightly receding hair and unusual grey eyes.

"Only that it was established after the battle of Rush Crossing and the Lord High Marshall's death," replied Jonoh trying not to drip the sauce from his capon onto his lap.

"True, it was sad circumstances indeed from which to inaugurate a settlement but an honourable way to commemorate a great sacrifice," said Torbut in a manner that gave extra weight to his words. "This you may not know. Jona Falconer sacrificed himself in the defence of his own personal guard who'd had the misfortune to come into contact with Curlon himself. With his forces on the verge of a catastrophic defeat, Curlon had entered the fray for the first time in over thirty years of conflict. Using the Gift, he had cut a swathe through the front ranks of Andhonar's vanguard which was commanded by Lord Falconer. Andhonar had trained his forces to defend against the Gift, had drilled it into them over and over, but Curlon was desperate, and I don't believe anyone realised just how much power he wielded." Torbut fixed a now rapt Jonoh with an intense almost hypnotic look. "Curlon had reached Falconer's personal guard, the elite forces in Andhonar's army whilst behind him his forces had regrouped and were smashing into the van. Destroy the cream of Andhonar's forces and maybe the battle could still be turned, something that Falconer knew only too well. So, he forged to the front of his men and stood against Curlon in person. As well as Falconer had been trained to combat the Gift and as mighty a man as he was, he was no match for Curlon. But instead of finishing Falconer quickly Curlon wished to make an example of him in order to cow his men, hoping to break their spirit. It was nearly a fatal mistake for in his dying act Falconer used the last reserves of his legendary strength and dealt a devastating sword cut to Curlon's torso. Curlon fled the field to save his own life, leaving his own forces to fend for themselves, which they did, refusing to surrender and fighting to the last man." The look on Torbut's face was one of genuine sadness. "They were brave men even if they fought for a damned cause. Falconer's surviving guard buried him on the spot where he died and established Falconer's Rest and here you are." He smiled gently at Jonoh.

After a brief silence Jonoh looked up at Torbut. "I visited his tomb earlier and it had a profound effect on me that I couldn't explain. I believe it has something to do with the Gift, as if there is an actual physical link to certain things. It's only a feeling and I can't substantiate it, but it feels true. The only thing is, apart from when I snapped, I haven't been able to enter into that state again. It seems as if having the Gift doesn't necessarily mean you can call upon it at will." Jonoh sighed resignedly, looking down at his half-empty plate.

"Jonoh come, take a walk with me," said Torbut, gesturing towards the door. Jonoh nodded and got slowly to his feet, a look of sadness lightly etched onto his face. They went outside together, heading nowhere in particular, just slowly walking, taking in the crisp night air.

"Jonoh, let me ask you, do you think I was born a member of the Elder Council?" asked Torbut.

"Of course not, that's a ludicrous question." There was just a hint of exasperation in Jonoh's reply.

"Of-course it is," said Torbut. "It took years of work to come close to mastering my vocation and I was helped and encouraged along the way by many people. Eventually I was considered worthy of a place on the Council and was elevated by my community." Torbut smiled as he spoke, gently resting his hand on Jonoh's shoulder. "You have an extraordinary gift, something that few others could possibly comprehend, but you've only just discovered it. Do you not think that with practice and experienced advice you may eventually grow to master it?"

Jonoh looked at the floor, too embarrassed to look Torbut in the face. "Yes Torbut, thank you, you are a wise man."

"Not yet, but I am trying. Jonoh there are far wiser men than me on the Elder Council, men who can guide you and help you with the Gift. Put your trust in them and the Protectorate, as we all do and I'm sure your doubts will leave you."

Jonoh thought about how much he'd enjoyed Torbut's company, especially as the end of their journey approached.

"How far do you think we have to go now, Bergin?" he asked over his shoulder to the young officer.

"Only a mile or two Jonoh, Kings Town should be just around the corner of this valley. I believe that's Mount Blackthorn there," he said pointing at the vast dark monolith rising above the hill on the right-hand end of the valley.

The rain was coming down steadily making the ride even more uncomfortable, moisture settling into their clothes, adding to the chaffing on their skin. Jonoh thought to himself that if he never had to ride again that would be just fine. As they approached the end of the valley, the Rush highway had turned into not much more than a rutted cart path. Although Kings Town was the nominal capital of the Protectorate and as such was the seat of the Elder Council, it was not particularly populous. It was situated in the middle of the largest arable belt in the land, a mixture of crop fields and food herds, cattle, sheep and swine. As such, the smooth paved roads linking the rest of the Protectorate's main population centres weren't really necessary. *"Would have been a lot easier on the arse though,"* thought Jonoh.

Jonoh rode with his head down, chin tucked in under his hooded cloak, in a vain attempt to keep the worst of the rain from running down his chest. As they turned the corner of the valley, he heard Bergin's breath catch in his throat, so he looked up. What he saw left him dumbfounded. Kings Town itself was unremarkable sitting at the foot of Mount Blackthorn, just an average-sized community with nothing to make it stand out, until you looked up.

Standing at least one hundred feet above the town was Fortress Kingshold. It stood on the shoulder of the mountain, vast and dark, made of black granite. Its outer walls were over seventy-feet high, split only by a massive main gate made of five-feet thick oak, studded with giant iron buttresses. Its towers rose from two huge inner walls, each ninety-feet tall and twenty-feet thick, dotted with scores of murder holes and arrow slits. Menacing and brooding, it muscled its way into the sky almost daring the heavens themselves to challenge it.

"Have you ever seen anything like it?" tremored Bergin, almost too quietly to hear above the patter of the rain.

"Only Great Harbour jetty, but even that's debatable," replied Jonoh, staring up at the castle now oblivious to the water teeming down his torso. "Let's get on with it, my arse is sore, and I'm soaked to the skin. I just want to get into the dry and get out of these clothes," said Jonoh.

"You'll get no argument here," said Bergin, pulling his hood up and putting his heels to his horse.

They fairly raced the final stretch, the Rush highway finishing with a paved half mile that ran into the outskirts of Kings Town.

There were riders there to meet them.

"Jonoh Shipwright?" asked the lead rider, a tall slim, red-haired man almost consumed by a large hooded black cloak.

"That's me," replied Jonoh, not in the least bit surprised that he was known in advance, it always seemed to be the way.

"I've been sent to accompany you to Kingshold, your companion will be taken to quarters," said the rider. "My name is Barton Logistar," he added, extending his hand. Jonoh grasped it in his, shaking it in acknowledgement.

"Thank you, it will be good to get out of the cold and change into some fresh dry clothes." Jonoh turned to Bergin. "Thank you for your company, Bergin, I hope we meet again.""

It was my honour Jonoh," replied the young officer, inclining his head in a gesture of deference. Jonoh acknowledged it, but it made him uncomfortable that after three weeks Bergin still looked at him with a degree of awe.

Barton Logistar wheeled his mount and headed up the mountain road towards the gate of Kingshold, Jonoh following suit. It was only a five-minute ride but in that brief time the mighty fortress loomed up even more dark and imposing than Jonoh could have imagined. A six-feet-wide stone bridge led to the entrance into the fortress, designed specifically to make it impossible for a large force to assail the main gate. As Jonoh rode through the gate, he got a sense of what an immense defensive structure Kingshold truly was. It was at least thirty feet of stone tunnel until you emerged into the first courtyard and there were murder holes every six feet, so even if you made the gate, getting beyond it was easier said than done. They rode across the first courtyard and through another tunnel with a portcullis at its entrance, out into a second smaller yard. Barton dismounted and gestured for Jonoh to do the same.

"If you would follow me, Master Shipwright," said Barton pointing towards a door situated at the bottom of a narrow tower.

"Jonoh will do fine," replied Jonoh, a slight hint of unease entering his voice.

"As you wish Jonoh," said Barton smiling.

Jonoh followed Barton through the door and ascended the spiral stairs that wrapped around the inside of the tower, walking up three floors until Barton stopped at a door.

"This is where I shall leave you Jonoh. I hope to see you later, maybe at mealtime." Barton opened the door and turned to descend the stairs.

"Thank you," called out Jonoh at his back. He turned back to the door and walked through.

The room was unremarkable, a bay window, an ancient-looking oak table and an average-sized hearth. Jonoh was glad to see that a fire was burning, spreading a welcome warmth through the room and more importantly through Jonoh himself. He took his gloves off, throwing them on the table and walked over to the fire, rubbing his cold damp hands together. The torches were not all lit, more than half the sconces lying empty, so the room was certainly not bright.

"Hello Jonoh, welcome to Kingshold," came a voice from behind him, making Jonoh jump with a start. He swung round to see a figure sitting at the end of the table, his eyes taking a few seconds to adjust to the dim light. As things came into focus, he could make out more clearly the figure sat in a chair. It was an old man with snow-white hair, white beard and moustache and pale liver-spotted skin. He was dressed entirely in black, tunic, breeches, boots and cape, with a wide-brimmed hat, making it difficult to see his eyes.

"Where did you come from?" stammered Jonoh, "and who are you?"

"I was here when you walked in and my name is Cerwin Shadow-master," he replied smiling out from under the brim of his hat. "You simply did not see me because you were not looking. If you had seen me, I would not be much of a master of shadows now, would I?"

"What do you want with me?" asked Jonoh trying not to give away how vulnerable he felt.

"You must be aware that you stand apart from everyone else, that you are different. I would guess that you have always felt set apart, capable of greater feats, faster, more adept. I would also guess that discovering you have the Gift has been a shock, a rude awakening and that apart from the day of your snap you have never been able to return to that place. You may not like it, but this is how it is and you must learn not only how to use it but also how to turn it to the benefit of all," said Cerwin, eyeing Jonoh thoughtfully.

"I did not ask for this. I just want to do my martial service and grow into manhood the same as everyone else." The resentment in his voice bubbled to the surface making him sound like a petulant child.

"That is not your choice Jonoh, nor your destiny. You have been given something that is only conveyed once in a generation at most, and you have a duty to use what you have for the benefit of all. In this you are no different from anyone else. You are not alone however. I am here to guide you and teach you to harness the Gift, to use it when appropriate and call it at need."

Cerwin fixed Jonoh with an incredibly intense stare, rooting him to the spot as if he'd been shackled to the floor. Jonoh felt a wave of nausea, or was it euphoria? He couldn't tell, couldn't nail anything down, just felt Cerwin's eyes boring into him as if looking into his darkest most personal thoughts. CCRRRAAACCCKK! The whole room seemed to flex, squeezing in and out, pulsing and gently changing hue, a surreal subtly moving picture. Cerwin walked towards him and Jonoh instinctively tried to bolt, but instead just cowered, still fixed to the spot. *"Relax Jonoh and listen to my thoughts. I have brought you back, to the same place you experienced during the snap. Just breathe and listen to me, you can trust me, I will not harm you."*

Jonoh tried to focus and stop himself panicking, so he reached out with his own thoughts. *"I feel overwhelmed and more than a little scared of this. I've never been a mind-walker, how is this possible?"* The panic was rising, he couldn't find a way to suppress it, so he did the one thing he remembered from his initial snap. He closed his eyes and took a deep breath.

The room returned to normal, colours, sounds, smells, just as it should be. Cerwin was standing by his side, a curious smile on his face.

"I threw you in at the deep end Jonoh, wanting to see if you would sink or swim," he said putting his hand on Jonoh's shoulder and gently guiding him to a chair. "The Gift is an incredible force, called the Gift because that is what it is. As you learn more about it and become accustomed to its touch it will feel more like a comfortable pair of gloves. At first however it is more like a shirt made of thorns, not very comfortable." The old man smiled disarmingly. "Your training has begun and I am glad to say you already show promise, to reach out with your thoughts and then bring yourself out. Very promising, very promising indeed." Cerwin laughed to himself, apparently amused at his own little joke.

"There is however something you must be told before we go any further," said Cerwin getting up and gesturing to a door on the other side of the hearth. "Follow me if you would."

Cerwin opened the door and walked across the floor of the small antechamber to a sconce on the far wall. He lit a torch and placed it there. "Look at the pictures and tell me if you recognise anyone," he said pointing at the first of a line of paintings on the wall. Jonoh looked at the first portrait.

"That's Andhonar the third," said Jonoh. Cerwin pointed to the next. "Falconer," he said in a whisper. Cerwin nodded to the next and Jonoh's breath caught in his throat. "It looks exactly like me," he gasped.

"That is Curlon," said Cerwin, "and that is why you have the Gift. You are of his blood."

Chapter Five:

Dark tidings

Three days hard ride from Lhossa to the Titan Gate, three days at least. Torbin hadn't had the time to discuss or arrange anything, he'd just had to go. Jadzia was the only person in Lhossa who knew anything about his true purpose, the reason he was so far from his birthplace. It had taken over five years and a real bond of love for him to tell her and even to this day he hadn't revealed all. He had however told her enough. Enough for her to know that a day like this may come, when he would have to go, with no notice, no explanation. Just grab a travelling bundle and go.

Saying goodbye had tugged at his emotions, their parting embrace so intense that he'd actually had to push her away. "I will be back in a week, I promise," he'd said smiling, even though he knew he had no way of being certain. Apart from the brief mind-walker exchange with Candor, Torbin had no more information to go on. It was truly a blind expedition, but one he had to make. Really there was no other choice.

As hard as it was leaving Jadzia, getting Terror to stay behind was desperate. Trying to explain that he would be leaving him for the first time was nigh on impossible. Add in the fact he was a dog, and you had an almost insurmountable problem. The look on Terror's face had almost broken his heart but the bond they shared meant that they each knew what had to happen. "Look after Jadzia boy," he whispered in his ear as he gave him a hug goodbye. As he rode away, he turned to see Jadzia crying into Terror's shoulder, both arms draped around his massive neck, whilst Terror's head sagged towards the floor.

He'd taken two mounts, grassland horses both and was sticking to riding at night as much as possible to relieve the stress on them. The road between Lhossa and the Titan Gate was sparsely populated, mainly small hamlets within the first fifty miles or so and then just groups of nomads and herdsmen scattered haphazardly along the way. Also, travelling at night made it easier to remain concealed from unwelcome attention. Even though he would always reassure Jadwan that he wasn't concerned, he was always aware that vendetta still stood. And the Hired Knives never gave up on a contract.

Keeping as close as possible to the foothills so as to have some cover when he slept during the day, he drove his horses as hard as he dared. For one thing getting there ahead of schedule would afford him a little time to scout the ground, also getting out of the open couldn't happen quickly enough. There had been over half a dozen attempts on his life before, but they'd been in Lhossa and he'd had help more than once. Bedding down made him miss Terror more than he'd expected. Even an assassin thinks twice if he's worried about being torn to pieces.

The sun was beginning to crest the tops of the mountains on the second morning so Torbin changed direction and headed into the treeline at the base of the foothills. He'd been careful as always to make sure he wasn't being followed and once he'd hobbled and watered the horses, he scouted the surrounding area. Once reasonably satisfied he constructed a deliberately irregular lean-to in order to conceal the horses and sat down to eat. Water, dried strips of salted pork and dried fruit. Not the tastiest fare but more than enough for the journey with a little extra just in case. You could never be too careful. Content that the horses had more than enough grazing to keep them happy, Torbin settled down to sleep.

He drifted into an uneasy sleep, dreaming of Jadzia and Lhossa. He was with her in their home, looking out from the balcony, but the sky was full of vast black storm clouds. There were never storms over Lhossa, it never rained. The clouds started to descend and swallow the city in front of their eyes, climbing the land walls, devouring everything in their path… Suddenly awake,

Torbin lay dead still. Two people at least were close at hand, making their way towards his camp. Being a mind-walker always meant that anybody approaching you gave off trace thought patterns however slight. He couldn't read their thoughts of course but the background noise was unavoidable. These were both incredibly quiet, obviously tutored to remain unobtrusive but no one could remain silent.

His sword lay in its sheath, within reach but moving for it would let them know he was aware. Not time yet to give them an advantage, and besides they could have bows or spears, a major problem. No, let them come in close. It wasn't as if he didn't sleep with a dagger underneath him. He lightly tensed and untensed his muscles, limbering up unseen by his stalkers. He could tell that they had circled either side of him and were approaching almost silently. Not silently enough though. He slowly shifted his arm under his blanket knowing it wouldn't be seen and grasped his dagger in a backhanded grip.

The first assassin reached the horses, expertly soothing them so that they didn't whicker while his colleague crept slowly over to Torbin. Torbin had opened his eye by the tiniest fraction and waited taut as a bowstring. His would-be killer was within a foot, a viciously sharp shortsword raised above his head in a double-handed grip. He lifted his arm a fraction, ready to drive it through Torbin's chest, when Torbin rolled over in a flash bringing his dagger round in a furious arc. All Orphans had a little touch of the Gift, for Torbin it extended about three feet, allowing him to slow time for a couple of seconds. Plenty of time to deal with those foolish enough to get up close. With his backhand grip, he slammed it into the man's neck, going straight through and out the other side.

Torbin slowly drew the dagger out of the assassin's neck and turned to face their colleague. He knew he had as much time as he needed, a second in the Gift was worth minutes in the real world so he could take his time and do it right. They wouldn't even realise their fellow assassin was down before they were dealt with, all the time in the world. He threw his knife as they turned hitting them square in the back.

The assassin dropped with a shriek. "*A woman!*" Torbin

reached her and cradling her gently, laid her softly on the grass. She was young, far too young for Torbin's liking.

Torbin held her head and leaned over, looking directly into her eyes. "Who contracted you?" She stared up at him, wide-eyed, gasping for breath, looking like a terrified child. "WHO CONTRACTED YOU?" he screamed at her.

Her nostrils flared wildly, pink spittle bubbling from her mouth "F-f-fuck you," she sputtered back at him, a look of rabid hatred in her eyes.

"Good girl," thought Torbin, *"play the game to the end."*

Torbin took his dagger and slid the point in behind her breast, a whimpering little scream escaping her bloodstained mouth. "We can do this the easy way, where you tell me what I want to know, and I finish you quick and clean. Or we can do it the hard way. Long, drawn out and full of agony," he whispered tenderly in her ear, like a lover with promises of pleasure yet to come.

"F-f-fuck you dead man, you haven't got hard in you," she gasped as he gently twisted the knife. Leaning further forward, Torbin gently kissed her on the cheek then went to work.

Torbin did her the honour of burying her, digging the shallow grave with his bare hands, the least he could do for someone so brave. It had taken twenty minutes to get the information from her. He was amazed she'd lasted so long, especially as she'd passed out twice. But in the end, she'd talked, they always did.

He was at least gratified to know that they had been contracted by Blood-spear, the same Murgan warlord who'd given him his scar. Blood-spear had counted coup on over a hundred enemies personally and was the leader of the largest Murgan tribe in the grasslands, a fierce and intractable enemy. The crossed knife tattoos on the assassin's wrists also confirmed what he'd suspected. The Hired Knives never gave up on a contract, especially vendetta.

There were still hours of daylight left so Torbin settled back down to sleep, glad of the girl's grave. Always nice to have a decent pillow.

He reached the gate by the middle of the third night, roughly three hours before dawn, enough time to thoroughly scout the area. He didn't want a repeat of the other day. Tying the horses to long ropes to give them room to graze he walked the length of the gate. The gate ran across the width of the only pass through the Titan mountains, over a mile in length at the mouth of a valley.

When he was happy that no unwelcome visitors were likely to pay him a visit, Torbin settled down to rest and waited for morning. Sleep wouldn't come but that was no surprise, killing always had a delayed effect on Torbin, as if his conscience took a while to activate. It wasn't guilt he felt, they were assassins, and it was him or them. What always bothered him was how clinical he was, as if it was just a task to be completed, no different than skinning a deer. The fact that he was waiting to meet another Orphan for only the second time since setting out from the Protectorate also had something to do with it. The sooner they got here the better, waiting was slow torture.

The sun rose in the eastern sky, slowly lighting the great gate. He'd seen the Titan Gate before of course but it never failed to take his breath away. Five hundred feet high and extending for a mile from one side of the valley mouth to the other it was at least as impressive as Great Harbour or Kingshold. What set it apart was that it wasn't known who'd built it or how old it was, an ancient relic, older even than the Hardite Empire. On this side it was almost an open structure, full of switchback stone staircases linking over forty levels and arrow slits and scorpion emplacements. There were storerooms, barracks, dining rooms and numerous other spaces dotted along the full length of the structure, creating the illusion of a deserted city in the sky. In all the recorded histories of the free territories there was no mention of its construction or of it ever having been manned.

Sitting on the furthest eastern edge of the free territories, it stood blocking the only route to the twin cities of Turan and Minari to the east. So few expeditions had ever been successfully undertaken in either direction, that the need for a giant defensive wall simply could not be explained. The Known World was vast, including the free territories, Protectorate and all the independent states. Turan and Minari were so far away, more than three hundred miles at the other end of the Titan Pass that trade was sporadic at best. So why was it there?

The sun had breached the top of the wall and was bathing the ground in heat. Torbin got up and walked over to his mounts.

They were happily grazing showing no signs of three days' hard riding. He took a brush from his pack and started grooming them, smiling as they whickered contentedly.

"Hello brother." Torbin whipped round, pulling his sword from its sheath. In front of him stood a tall slim man, a hooded black cloak covering his face and concealing the frame within.

"Candor Blackheart. Sneaking up on someone could get you killed," said Torbin inclining his head whilst lowering his sword to his side.

Candor Blackheart removed his hood, a broad smile beaming out. His hair was black, receding at the temples, face weather-beaten, and sun-browned. He looked every inch his age, late forties, although it was always difficult to tell with someone who'd obviously spent a lifetime in the open.

Torbin extended his hand in greeting. Candor beamed a huge smile and eagerly grasped it, pulling Torbin into a hug. Torbin pulled slowly back holding him by the arms.

"I'm sorry brother," sputtered Candor, "but it has been over ten years since I've seen someone from this side of the Titans. To have the first one be you is more than I could have hoped for." Candor smiled, a strange look of peace softening his features.

"No apology necessary brother, I'm greatly relieved to see you. Although I must admit to being more than a little nervous about your purpose," Torbin replied, "Why did you summon me, brother, and what is this darkness you spoke of?"

"As you know I have been living in Turan for over twenty years, Torbin. There has always been rumour and legend regarding the unknown world beyond the great storm curtain, but no expedition has ever returned and only a few incoherent individuals have ever washed up on our shores." Candor took a breath. "You know there is an archipelago of islands, the Bountiful Isles, curving out into the Grey ocean, right up to the edge of the curtain?" Torbin nodded.

"Both Turan and Minari have fishing outposts there and over the centuries sizeable communities have grown up and flourished. Seven days ago, a great force appeared through the curtain and overwhelmed the remotest outposts, landing at Storms Break and sweeping across the rest of the islands in hours. All but six of our attack boats and fishing fleet escaped and less than two hundred of our forces based there. Out of a population of nearly six thousand including our military strength, less than five hundred people escaped to the mainland and made it back to the twin cities." Candor bowed his head, the pain still pulling at him.

"They have found a way to traverse the storm barrier, how is no longer of any consequence. They are here and they have mind-walkers, how many I could not say but they are powerful. I felt them in my thoughts, they know who I am, and they know I am here. They are landing their forces, taking their time, waiting until they have numbers enough to overwhelm. It can only be a matter of days until they reach our cities and subsequently gain access to the Titan Pass."

What followed was barely believable. The story Candor related sounded inconceivable, a vast, sophisticated army had utterly conquered a vast, unknown southern continent and was now essentially encamped on the other side of the Titan Pass. Its only intention seemed conquest. From what knowledge Candor had gathered each and every land, community or individual who refused to submit were exterminated. The two cities, Turan and Minari, sat at the eastern end of the Titan Pass and had joined forces forming a defensive line between them and the Pass, but Candor seemed certain they would fail.

"They call themselves the H'Daree and from what I witnessed first-hand they overwhelm by sheer numbers as well as skill at arms and sophisticated weaponry. Death in battle appears to be a great honour and they just come on regardless of the risks. They know no fear and their numbers seemed impossible, but I know what I saw. They will come and I fear for the future of the world. I believe only the Protectorate has a chance of holding them but even that seems doubtful." Candor stared at his feet as he finished his words, a single tear dropping to the floor.

"How long do you believe the twin cities can hold?" asked Torbin.

"No more than a week, maybe two." Candor shrugged his shoulders resignedly.

"Then that gives us some time to marshal a defence, all is not yet lost Candor, do not lose heart." Torbin reached across to touch his companion on the shoulder.

"I do not believe they can be stopped Torbin. Even if you could marshal a force of tens of thousands and make a stand here at the Titan Gate it would be overwhelmed. Their numbers are unimaginable and their resolve unquenchable, you won't be able to do any more than delay them. They will conquer all or die in the attempt, and they have far greater numbers. From what little information I've been able to gather they move as a whole nation, tens of millions strong at least, probably more." Torbin stared at Candor a look of utter disbelief and confusion on his face.

"The great cities and nations of the free territories will not lay down and surrender, neither will the Murgan. We must move now Candor and rouse those that we can, to combat this threat. Time is not on our side. I'll need you to tell all you know and…"

"No Torbin, I will not be coming with you," said Candor cutting Torbin off mid-sentence.

"You cannot mean to return east, Candor. What purpose would it serve for you to give up your life?" Torbin's voice had an edge of agitation to it.

"Twenty years I have lived in Turan, Torbin. I have a family, a wife and children, friends and colleagues and I will not abandon them. I have held true to the Protectorate my whole life and have honoured my vow by meeting you and telling you all I know. Now you must carry this burden and take action on your own. I return to my city to stand with my own, no matter the outcome. What man would do less?" Candor stood bolt upright and extended his hand in farewell to Torbin.

Torbin grasped it, pulling Candor close to hug him. Tears ran down Candor's face as he embraced his fellow Orphan. Then he pulled away and turned back towards the gate. "Goodbye brother," whispered Torbin as Candor walked away.

Chapter Six:

Loss

Marisa found herself thinking about Garic as her squad scouted ahead of the night border patrol. She'd never met anyone who had managed to hold her interest in the bedroom for more than a couple of days, but this man-boy was different. He'd fumbled about the first time they had sex, much as you'd expect from a sixteen-year-old, but with a little coercion and advice he'd become more and more skilled. It had only been a couple of weeks, but she found herself becoming attached to him, missing his company and his touch on the nights they didn't sleep together.

She put those thoughts aside and brought herself to the job at hand. Her squad were on point, about fifteen minutes ahead of the main body, three centuries of infantry on patrol to the most remote settlement in the Protectorate, Seal-breaker Bay. It was a sealing station at the northeast tip of Partia, bordering the Northern wastes with a population of around five hundred. Partia had only become a part of the Protectorate a couple of centuries ago but as with all communities it was totally integrated, based on equality and vocation.

"Tommec, have you had any contact yet?" Marisa had to half shout to be heard over the wind whistling through the cold night air.

"Nothing at all, squad leader, their mind-walkers must be asleep or out at sea," Tommec called back.

"It seems a little odd that you haven't had anything at all

though. Aren't there half a dozen mind-walkers in Seal-breaker Bay?" The edge in Marisa's voice made the whole squad turn to pay attention.

"Yes squad leader, six in total." Tommec's voice had picked up an edge of its own.

"I don't like the feel of this, to have no contact at all is more than just unusual. Alright listen up, we're only five miles away. If we triple-time we can be there in thirty or forty minutes. Tommec, send back to the main body and take point, everyone else fall into two lines, weapons drawn and quiet as possible. Let's go." Marisa barked out her order, turning to start running as she spoke.

The squad broke into a fast run, shields slung at their backs, spears in hand. Even though it was summer, this far north there was always snow on the ground, albeit only a thin layer. The whole squad was fitted out in winter uniforms, full-length thermal underwear with woollen breeches and tunics covering them. The armour was tailored to each individual, moulded to fit their body shapes and was one of the wonders of military technology. Made from alternating layers of different materials, linens, metals and lacquered pulp, it was as resistant as steel to piercing weapons and only a fraction of the weight. It was also designed to circulate air around the body helping to regulate body temperature and reduce the effort needed to bear it. Along with a winter cape, as often as not used to bivouac overnight and a full-face helmet with neck guard, Protectorate soldiers were as well protected as was humanly possible and were always garbed in black for night combat.

They kept up a punishing pace, forcing themselves on, a certain nervousness washing over them. Around two miles out Tommec suddenly pulled up taking a deep rasping breath. "I can sense agitation, a feeling of unease. I can't explain it, but it feels as if there is mass distress." The squad all drew in big gulps of air, nervously looking to Marisa for direction.

"Something's obviously wrong, we have to be ready for any possibility. We're only two miles out and for those of you that haven't been here before Seal-breaker Bay lies in a small cove at the foot of a hogsback ridge. If we have contact, we'll have the advantage of coming from the high ground, so keep your discipline and remember we fight as a team." Marisa looked around at the faces of her squad members and knew they were ready and focused. It filled her with confidence and pride.

They took off at a sprint, speeding along the road that led to Seal-breaker Bay, holding in formation, moving like a single entity. About a mile out they heard the first sounds of conflict, there could be no doubt now, the community was under attack.

They reached the ridge and stopped, crouching down to stay out of sight and give themselves a moment to catch their breaths and assess the situation. What they saw was shocking, a huge press of Wasteland mountain warriors viciously attacking the inhabitants of Seal-breaker Bay. The defenders were drawn up in a defensive formation around the sleeping hall, forming a shield-wall, shoulder to shoulder, two rows deep, defenders at the rear filling the gap when someone in the front rank fell. Everybody capable of holding a weapon stood in defence, young and old, male and female, years of martial training and the inherent sense of community holding them together in the face of such ferocious violence.

"Okay listen up, the main patrol body is at least half an hour away so for the moment we are on our own. We're going to form up in arrowhead, me at point, ten to my left and two to my right. We'll hit the far right of their attack and punch a hole, the rest of the squad rolling out from the sides to turn their flank. There are not enough of us to make them break so we'll fall back in line and reinforce the far-left flank. Once we're attached to the line we'll split into pairs and take up positions across the front, understood?" Marisa quickly looked across her squad.

"Yes squad leader," came the massed reply.

"Right, on me at the sprint, no noise until we contact them, then scream to your heart's delight. Good luck." Smiling, Marisa sprung forward, sprinting downhill, Garic a foot or two behind and to her left, Tommec similarly to her right. The rest of her squad sprinted behind, holding tight formation, as quiet as the grave, silent death descending on the unsuspecting attackers. Marisa, Garic and Tommec smashed into the backs of the Wasteland warriors, each killing two men before the rest even realised that they were under attack from behind. The rest of the squad fanned out shield to shield, forming an impenetrable wall, spears darting high and low, skewering bowels and stabbing through faces and legs alike. They slowly swung around in line attaching themselves to the left-hand end of the defensive shield-wall, using the confusion they had created in the enemy ranks to achieve the task. After the shock of their impact, the Wasteland warriors had quickly regrouped and seemed to intensify their attacks, driven on by an unseen force as if an invisible whip were at their backs.

"Two and three to the far right of the line, four and five, six and seven and eight and nine at equal distance between there and here. Ten with me, bolster the line and hold. For the Protectorate!" screamed Marisa.

The squad members spread out as ordered, standing to the front where the action was fiercest, bolstering the line and giving renewed hope to the beleaguered defenders. Their presence alone lifted the defenders' spirits, their line edging forward, seeking contact and driving the Wastelanders back. Marisa began to realise the size of this assault. The Wasteland tribes had been raiding for centuries but she could not remember ever hearing of a coordinated attack on this scale. There were at least five hundred warriors assembled here, big men armed with axes, battle hammers and great broadswords, far too large a number for a single tribe to muster. That was troubling, if the tribes were organising and starting to unite it would mean great bloodshed, great bloodshed indeed.

She put all thoughts aside and let the joy of battle wash over her. She stepped to the front of the line, skewering a monstrous Wastelander through the throat with a spear thrust and using her shield to lever him off making him tumble backwards into his fellows. She stepped into the gap, stabbing left and right, high and low, hamstringing, gutting and killing anything that moved in front of her. It was like throwing an acorn in a barrel, difficult to miss. The certainty of the kill infused her, making her smile contentedly, with every deadly spear thrust. She withdrew to the shield-wall to allow herself a breath, looking down the line to her right. The shield-wall was holding, and she knew with a certainty that it would hold until the full patrol force arrived.

Then she saw Garic step forward, shield tilted forward, spear thrust in perfect form going in through the mouth of a huge warrior and jutting out the back of his skull. The man's body sagged as Garic withdrew his spear in one smooth motion, turning his torso behind his shield to skewer another foe backhanded, again sliding his spear expertly out of the man's chest. Marisa couldn't help but smile watching this young giant silently killing one foe after another, gracefully avoiding or deflecting all attacks, moving like a dancer.

A great shout went up from the rear of the Wastelanders line. Marisa looked towards the noise and saw a wolf-skin banner raised high, marching forward through the press of warriors. It was carried by a vast bear of a man, seven feet tall and clad in skins, furs and an assortment of mismatched armour. He roared as he came on surrounded by a dozen similarly huge warriors. He cast aside the banner and pulled a massive battle hammer from a strap on his back, barrelling forwards towards Garic's section of the wall, his entourage in close attendance. To her horror, Marisa saw that Garic didn't withdraw to the relative safety of the shield-wall but stood his ground, spear held high, defying the monster charging towards him.

"Ten, get back in formation!" screamed Marisa at the top of her voice, but Garic either didn't hear her or chose to ignore her. The giant Wastelander was almost on him when Garic dipped his knees, gently tilting his shield back at the top whilst holding his spear slightly behind him. He took a half step forward the bottom of his shield clipping the giant's ankles, making him stumble a fraction. A fraction was all Garic needed. He thrust his spear forwards and upwards, showing perfect form, shearing straight through the giant's jaw and out the back of his neck, spraying blood from his severed carotid artery in all directions. His momentum however made him career into Garic's shield, knocking it sideways and exposing his torso. In an instant, another of the vast Wastelanders sprang forward wielding a battle hammer of his own and bringing it down in a vicious blow. It hit Garic flush in the centre of his chest knocking him half a dozen feet backwards and out cold.

The Wastelander stepped forward to stand over Garic, yelling something incomprehensible at his prone body. He raised his hammer above his head ready to smash Garic's skull when a spear flew through the air, hitting him straight in the neck, knocking him sideways. Marisa leapt forward drawing her shortsword, her spear still embedded in the Wastelander's neck. As she ran to defend Garic she was shocked to see the shield-wall surge forward to engulf him, fiercely resisting the frenzied attacks of the Wastelanders.

Marisa didn't notice at first but suddenly she heard the sound of horns drifting across from the hogsback ridge, the main body of the patrol had arrived. The Wastelanders started to waver, uncertain of what the noise represented. Then the front ranks of the first century crested the hill and poured down the slope, spears forward, a deadly tight hedgehog of gleaming metal rushing to the fray. The Wastelanders broke and ran, fleeing as fast as they could back into the dark northern expanse.

A great cheer went up from the shield-wall, a mixture of pride at their efforts and joy at the sight of their relief. Marisa reached Garic and went to one knee, gently cradling his head in her hands. He was breathing, the relief almost making her cry. He slowly opened his eyes, a look of sharp pain written large across his face. "Fuck me that hurts," Garic wheezed out through his clenched teeth.

"I'm not surprised, you daft bastard, you tried to tackle a dozen giants on your own. Next time I tell you to get back in line you do what I say, alright?" Marisa smiled as she spoke, relieved he was alive rather than angry at him.

"Marisa Longspear." Marisa turned her head to see commander Breda Fencer standing just behind her.

"Yes sir," replied Marisa, standing to acknowledge her commanding officer.

"Are you alright Marisa? And what about your squad?" he asked, concern etched onto his face.

"I'm fine sir but I haven't yet had a chance to make a full head count. Was a little busy," she said, a little grin creasing her mouth.

Marisa stepped aside allowing the field medics to tend to the wounded, relieved to know Garic was in good hands. She looked around taking in the full picture of the battlefield. It was a picture of carnage, at least two hundred corpses littering the ground, a mixture of hulking Wasteland warriors and Protectorate citizens. Then her breath caught in her throat. To the far right of the defensive line Tommec sat on the floor supported by a number of fellow defenders, three feet of spear shaft protruding from his chest.

Marisa ran towards him, flopping down by his side, taking his hand in hers. "Marisa, that was a fine fight. I was really proud to fight alongside these people, no one took a backwards step, amazing to witness. If you're going to go at least go doing something worthwhile, eh?" Tommec wheezed the words out through bloodstained teeth. The citizens holding him wept openly, sobs wracking their shoulders. Marisa's eyes started to cloud with tears, knowing that her friend was drifting away before her eyes. Tommec blinked as if trying to bring his eyes into focus, a distant look slowly descending across his face. He looked at Marisa, motioning with his eyes for her to come in close. She leaned forward, putting her ear to his mouth. "My honour," he breathed out, his head rolling forward, chin resting at the top of his chest.

Marisa sagged to the floor; shoulders hunched still grasping Tommec's hand. Then she started shaking uncontrollably and for the first time in years, Marisa Longspear wept like a baby.

Chapter Seven:

Revelations

The answers never caught up with the endless list of questions on Jonoh's mind and Cerwin was not inclined to reveal more or faster than he deemed necessary. It was frustrating but a frustration worth bearing. So many things now made sense, for instance the fact that he'd always felt he could pre-empt what certain people were going to say to him. Not everyone as it turned out, just fellow mind-walkers. His latent ability had only become apparent after his snap, something very rare apparently, as every mind-walker discovered that talent before their measure of the Gift was revealed. Every mind-walker had some degree of the Gift, however small. He however was very different as Cerwin had been at pains to point out.

"Your Gift is beyond anything I have ever seen, or anything ever recorded, Jonoh. I can teach you how to harness and understand it, get you to a point of comfort and control, but you will eventually surpass me." Cerwin had smiled as he spoke, but there was a hint of sadness behind his eyes. "Do you remember your history? What was it that prompted the formation of the Protectorate?" he asked.

"The story tells of the Lords Dominant experiencing Ascension, the next plane of existence. It was a state of harmony and togetherness, a place where all were equal and all moved with a common purpose, a collective consciousness," replied Jonoh. "But that's just apocryphal, a story to illustrate a moral point." The certainty in Jonoh's voice wavered as he talked.

"No Jonoh, you are mistaken. The Gift is a glimpse of Ascension, something that both Andhonar and Curlon brought back with them, something that all their descendants have a measure of. You have the most extraordinary measure of all. Somehow after more than a millennium you appear, an almost carbon copy of Curlon. And it would seem you may have as full a measure of the Gift as he did."

As much as Jonoh wanted to believe him he was finding it increasingly difficult. At first being in the Gift was like wearing a shirt of thorns, everything out of his field of vision digging at the back of his mind like a press of blunted spears. The urge to turn around to try and catch them unawares was overwhelming and constantly unsuccessful. However, the more often he practised his exercises, the less the blind spots irritated him, the blunted spears becoming softer, less invasive. He was becoming able to pull his attention away from that which he could not see and reach out and begin to explore the sensations available to him. He could feel the texture of the walls, the table, the chairs, the hearth, everything within the scope of his Gift all at the same time. It wasn't just a sense of touch, it was far more inclusive, smell, sound, sight, even the taste of things was becoming real. Still the distraction of that which he couldn't see stopped him from conquering the task he was set.

Every time the exercise ended with Cerwin appearing as if from nowhere, the point of his dagger and shortsword touching Jonoh's chest. He simply could not see the old master's approach until he was right there in front of him, forever distracted by the unseen. Six days of repeating the same process, over and over again, with no change in the outcome.

Here he was again, standing by the door, immersed in the Gift, trying to see Cerwin and disarm him before he closed the gap. The irritation of the unseen was constantly pulling his attention away from the task at hand. The faint shimmer on the edges of his vision biting at his mind, claustrophobia encroaching like a dark wave. Jonoh started to feel a sense of failure, as if this task was beyond him and Cerwin's faith hopelessly misplaced.

"I can't do this, it's just too hard, oh…"

Everything suddenly made absolute sense, the shimmer a thing of distant memory. Everything in every direction was clearly visible, not just visible but open to every sense. He could feel the door behind him, sense it in its entirety. He reached out with his senses, feeling the surface of the wood, all the ridges, knots and imperfections revealing their secrets to him. He reached further exploring the grain, further still touching every ridge, every speck of dust, floating down the miniscule gaps between the fibres like a bird flying down a valley. At the same time, he explored the black granite walls, felt the edges of the flames in the hearth, followed the helix of the screws holding the lattice work of the sconces together. Everything revealed all its secrets to him at once, a sense of peace and serenity flowing through him, time suspended, floating in space.

Almost casually he saw a grey shadowed figure, practically invisible, moving with a feline grace, silent and stealthy. It was Cerwin and Jonoh could not help but be impressed by the old man's skill. He was less than a foot away, dagger and shortsword drawn, points inches from his chest. Jonoh smiled to himself, the knowledge that he had all the time in the world setting him free from his doubt. He stepped back a fraction and took the weapons from Cerwin's static hands, walking round behind him and laying the point of the dagger between the old master's shoulders. Then he snapped them both out of the Gift.

"Master Cerwin."

The shadow-master dropped to his knees, spinning to face his unseen assailant. There was a look of shocked awe on his face, the first time Jonoh had seen anything other than complete calm from him. He drew himself up, instantly composed, an impish grin creasing his lined features.

"Amazing, simply amazing. In less than a week you have surpassed me. I did not see you move even though I was only inches away. There is nothing more I can teach you about exploring the Gift my boy. The only lessons you will receive now will be philosophical and political." The grin remained on Cerwin's face, and from Jonoh's point of view he was positively beaming.

"It suddenly made sense Master, everything just slipped into place like putting on a comfortable glove." Jonoh smiled, still feeling a sense of euphoria.

"Tell me Jonoh, leave out no detail."

Jonoh proceeded to tell Cerwin every detail of his experience, leaving nothing out. When he couldn't articulate something verbally, he reverted to mindwalking, sending senses and feelings as easily as breathing. Cerwin sat silently, absorbing every word, sense and feeling given to him, smiling at every new piece of information like a hungry young student.

"Time seems to stop Master while I'm immersed in the Gift as if the world around me stands static. Is that real or just an illusion?" Jonoh looked at the old master's inscrutable features, never able to read any change in his mood.

"It is true to a point, Jonoh. Any normal person would be unaware of any difference, for them time passes as it always has. For the gifted, however, time stretches, making it appear as if they can move with impossible speed. To any normal person you would seem to disappear before their eyes. With your measure of the Gift though it is not just time you can manipulate. As you grow more accomplished, I believe you will be able to manipulate matter as well. From what you told me your ability to reach inside solid objects is unique, beyond my understanding. You stand apart and you are beginning to grasp the scope of your powers." Cerwin took a long slow breath, almost as if he was debating with himself, unsure if he should tell Jonoh something.

"What is it, Master?" asked Jonoh sensing the old man's hesitation.

"I am the most gifted of my generation Jonoh, possibly with as full a measure of the Gift as anyone in history. Let me ask you, how old would you say I am?" The old man's eyes fixed firmly on Jonoh.

"I would guess from your appearance that you are somewhere around sixty to seventy years old Master, though I'm not sure how good a judge I am in these matters."

"I am one hundred and eighty-seven years of age Jonoh." Cerwin smiled, a little chuckle escaping his lips as he gauged Jonoh's reaction.

Jonoh gasped, completely stunned by the revelation. "How is that possible?"

"The Gift Jonoh, it is not just time that slows. Somehow it slows the ageing process, extends life in line with one's measure of the Gift. It does not make us indestructible though. We can still be killed, still succumb to disease or old age. It is just that old age takes a little longer." Cerwin chuckled again, apparently pleased with his little jape.

"There is an inherent risk though. When immersed in the Gift you run the risk of losing contact with anything else and while no ungifted person would be able to harm you, trained gifted individuals could possibly catch you unawares. I believe it would be incredibly hard to surprise you but not impossible."

There was a knock at the door and Barton Logistar slid quietly into the room.

"Master Cerwin, Jonoh, apologies for disturbing you but your presence is requested by the Elder Council." Logistar inclined his head apologetically.

"No need to apologise Barton, I shall be along shortly," smiled the old master.

"Thank you Master but you are both required." Logistar kept his head inclined. Jonoh found him unnerving, he couldn't say why exactly but the man's need to defer didn't sit comfortably with him.

"We will be along shortly," repeated the old man.

"As you say Master," said Logistar, backing out of the room almost bowing as he exited.

"Why would the Elder Council want to see me?" asked Jonoh, genuinely surprised.

"I cannot speak on their behalf but what I can tell you is that it will have to do with what is happening on the edges of the Free Territories." Cerwin walked over to the hearth and poked aimlessly at the embers. Jonoh knew something of what he was talking about. Reports of an invasion force landing on the shores east of the Titan Pass had reached the Protectorate. "Have you ever heard of Andhonar's Orphans, Jonoh?" Cerwin continued to poke at the fire.

"Andhonar's Orphans?" Jonoh replied quizzically.

"Yes Jonoh. At first when word reached us of your snap it was thought you may be a perfect candidate. Andhonar's Orphans are a secret group of volunteers who live in the lands outside of the Protectorate, mind-walkers all, who spend their lives learning about other cultures and reporting back to the Protectorate. They give up their identity, their names and all proof of their heritage. It is a great responsibility and a great sacrifice on their part. It is through them that we are kept informed of any developments or threats that may arise." Cerwin sat at the table motioning for Jonoh to join him.

"Are you talking about spies, Master?" Jonoh pulled out a chair and sat opposite Cerwin.

"After a fashion, Jonoh. As you know the Protectorate has never fought a war of aggression or conquest, only expanding when a neighbouring state has petitioned to join. That does not mean that we do not take measures to protect our way of life. Without the Orphans we would be unprepared for any surprise attacks that may occur. It is no coincidence that we have always been able to marshal our forces ahead of any military incursions. It would be impossible to defend a border the size of the Protectorate without some assistance, even bearing in mind the number of permanent forces we keep in the field." Cerwin peered under the brim of his hat, eyebrows raised as if inviting Jonoh to ask a question.

"Why would I have been considered as an Orphan?" Jonoh's curiosity was piqued.

"A certain psychological profile is needed and a skill in the martial arts. You were the most gifted combatant in your age group, Jonoh. In fairness you were more gifted than those much older than you. It is also a fundamental necessity that all Orphans are mind-walkers, able to share information with their fellow Orphans and so create an open and immediate line of communication back to the Protectorate. To be an Orphan requires a certain moral ambiguity, a willingness to do whatever is necessary to defend the Protectorate. It was thought you displayed some of those traits, but your extraordinary measure of the Gift means that your talents would be wasted in secret." Cerwin looked a little uncomfortable, almost as if he'd said too much.

"My talents would be wasted?" There was a slight edge to Jonoh's voice. He had the sense he was about to hear something uncomfortable or unpleasant. He braced himself mentally, not wanting to show any fear. He failed.

"Jonoh, the Elder Council has summoned us both. The threat

that has arisen in the east is far greater than we could ever imagine. I do not know much more than you, but I do know that the news has disturbed all who have heard it and that you will have a role to play, a major role. The Orphans are about to reveal themselves, the time for covert action is at an end. If the reports are accurate – and I have no reason to believe otherwise – then the very future of our way of life may come under threat. Every citizen of the Protectorate knows that sacrifice is the greatest honour. Each individual gives of themselves for the betterment of all, it is the basic tenet of our society. Each of us must give all we can for our society, and you have something to give that nobody else does. It may seem like a great deal to ask of you, but it is no more than anyone else will give. That is why your training has been so intense, so repetitive. Let us talk no more of this until after you have met the Elder Council. Then things will be a lot clearer." Cerwin stood up and gently placed his hand on Jonoh's shoulder. "Come, let us go."

Jonoh followed the old master from the room, one thought playing over and over in his mind. *"You have something to give that nobody else does."*

Chapter Eight:

Honesty

Torbin had raced back to Lhossa, neglecting the need for secrecy, no longer concerned about the risks of discovery. He and Candor had stayed in constant touch, both being exceptionally strong mind-walkers with a range of hundreds of miles. If this new enemy could hear them, what of it? They were coming anyway so all that mattered now was preparing a strategy to stop them. The problem with that was that he would be forced to reveal the truth about himself and that could be fatal. In the Free Territories mind-walkers were generally considered to be freaks of nature or possessed by demons. Execution was the common solution and Lhossa was particularly harsh in its treatment of any who revealed this trait. If caught and condemned by the Sun Priests of Sardis, death by public vivisection was the common punishment, not an edifying prospect.

He and Candor had both sent out in every direction, sending all the information they had to every Orphan within their range. By now he knew that this had reached the Protectorate and that every Orphan would be rallying support, doing everything within their power to make preparations. However, the fractious politics and endless conflicts of the free territories meant that nothing was certain. For the moment he was on his own and Lhossa was the only available power strong enough to marshal a response to the looming threat. There was also the Murgan of course but to say that was an uncertain path was an understatement of monstrous proportions.

Two days hard riding and Lhossa appeared in the distance, a great red jewel shining in the glow of the morning sun. With its back to the Titan mountains, it rose from the desert like a great leviathan, three levels each protected by vast circular walls, broken only by the huge metal gates.

Torbin felt a warm familiar feeling, that sense of being home, a comfort unsurpassed. He was exhausted, dehydrated and windblown, his face scarred red by the sun and sandstorms. His grassland horses as hardy and resilient as they were, were lathered and blowing heavily. He slowed to a trot turning to the great main gate. The lower doors were open, allowing the usual stream of traders to slowly pass through, making their way to Market Square.

Jadran Greycloud was the commander on duty, a big well-muscled man, over six feet tall with long straight black hair, held back in a bronze loop. Nobody would ever mistake him for anything other than a native Lhossan and he was a reliable and resolute soldier who'd fought at Torbin's side on more than one occasion. Torbin was glad to see him.

"Hale Jadran," called Torbin, riding to the front of the queuing wagons. A few traders started to mouth complaints but soon stopped when they realised who it was jumping the queue.

"Torbin old friend. How are you?" Jadran beamed a smile as he strode forward to grasp Torbin by the arms.

"Tired and aching if I'm honest but glad to be home." He walked through the gate, passing the reins to one of the gate guards. "Look after the horses for me, son. They are exhausted and in need of a good rub down and a nosebag."

The young guard beamed a smile as if he had been granted the greatest honour of his life. Torbin had that effect.

"Come Torbin, take some refreshment and a little rest with me. Jadson, you have the gate," said Jadran to his subordinate, turning to lead Torbin into the guardhouse.

Torbin walked through the door, stamping his feet on the floor sending up plumes of dust and sand into the air. As sparse as the guardhouse was it had a table and benches, luxury compared to the last few days and to top it all, ale, bread and cheese.

Jadran poured them both a tankard and broke off a heel of

bread with some cheese, passing it on a plate to Torbin.

"Thank you, my friend, after nothing but warm water, dried fruit and salted meat this is a rare treat." Torbin dropped lazily onto one of the benches, leaning contentedly against the wall.

"I'd wait until you've tasted it before you show your gratitude," smiled Jadran, taking a healthy slurp of his ale, gently sliding onto the bench opposite. "I spoke with Jadzia a couple of days ago and she said you'd had to slip off quietly, but she was a little reticent. Is everything okay Torbin? You know you can trust me. If there's any trouble, I want to help." Jadran's earnest demeanour helped Torbin relax.

"I can't tell you much at the moment old friend. Suffice it to say that there are events of great import taking place and that I may call on your support very soon. Sides will be drawn, and much will need to be risked but until I've addressed the Senate I cannot say much more." Torbin knew there was risk in everything he said and did from this moment forward, but he trusted Jadran, as far as he could trust anyone.

"You mean to call an assembly of the Senate, Torbin?" Jadran looked genuinely shocked. "I mean no offence, but you are not Lhossan. There is no guarantee they will grant you an audience, even bearing in mind who you are. I will sponsor you if that would be of assistance." The commander sat upright, adopting a formal pose, a mark of respect.

"Relax Jadran, I'm the partner of Jadzia Sun-blessed, daughter of Jadwar Sun-blessed, the leader of the ruling Senate. I'm fairly sure I can arrange an audience, although as ever, I am honoured by your loyalty and friendship." Torbin smiled and sank his ale in one long gulp. He stood up and turned to the door. "I must get about my business Jadran, but I thank you for your concern. Be assured I will talk to you soon and may be asking much."

"I'll be here Torbin," replied Jadran as Torbin strode out of the room.

Torbin left the guardhouse and turned left heading for the gate to the second level. It was situated at the far-left hand end of the second encircling wall with the gate to the third level positioned at the far-right hand end of the third wall. Make any invading force take the longest route possible, another clever ploy designed to sap the energies of any attackers. If nothing else, the Lhossan's were a resourceful and inventive people.

The first level of the city was home to the great unwashed, the lowest members of Lhossan society, those with no lineage, servants all. Alongside them were the slaves and horses all relegated to a meaningless existence, horses aside perhaps. The buildings were all one-storey high ramshackle structures, in places not much more than lean-tos, just basic roofs to offer some small protection from the elements. There was little in the way of sanitation or running water, just a few deep-water wells used by everyone, horses as well of course.

To be valued no more than a beast of burden, one of the many things that rankled with Torbin about Lhossan society, but as always 'When in Lhossa…'

As Torbin walked along a group of street urchins, the oldest of them no more than ten years old shadowed his steps, hands out begging for scraps. He stopped and took his shoulder bag off, emptying the remains of his dried fruit and salted meat onto the floor. Even though he'd seen it on more than one occasion, the ferocity of the scramble for these meagre pickings still shook Torbin to the core. One little girl no more than five years old was mercilessly punched to the floor for a tiny strip of salted pork, left bloodied and weeping in the dirt. Torbin knew better than to interfere, that was just the way it was, survival of the strongest.

Torbin was waved through the second gate by the city militia guards without any delay. Everybody knew Torbin and deep down he had to admit he liked the notoriety. The great defender as he was often called, a moniker earned during the great Murgan assault a decade previously. It had earned him not only great reverence from the Lhossan natives but also a domicile on the third level and a lifelong stipend from the senate. More than enough to see him through to his dotage. There was much and more he owed the Lhossans and visa versa. He was going to have to rely on the goodwill his glowing reputation had earned him, he hoped it would be enough.

The walk through the second level of the city was a far more pleasant experience, especially on the nose. The second level was home to the traders and artisans of Lhossan society, allowed to trade freely in Market Square but not allowed to live in the third level. That was reserved for those of the line of Jadvar the Great only.

Jadvar the Great, founder of Lhossa, descendant of the Sun God Sardis himself. All his descendants had the prefix Jad attached to their name, proof of their nobility, their divine right to rule the masses. The whole of Lhossan society was predicated on this fictional nonsense, yet another ludicrous religious sect that had been used to benefit a minority of the population. As much as these issues grated at Torbin's conscience he had to suppress his distaste. There was much that needed to be risked and he had to work with what was available.

As he passed through the third gate the ground inclined far less steeply, rising gently compared to the first two levels. The difference compared to the first two levels was palpable, the buildings finished to a far higher level, streets clean and tended, palm trees lining the pavements and squares. In fact, it was the only place outside of the Protectorate that Torbin knew of that actually had raised pavements, more an affectation than a necessity bearing in mind the lack of horses or carriages used there. Nearly all the goods sold in Market Square were borne by slaves or servants, with the exception of slaves themselves of course.

He turned a corner, walking slowly, engrossed in thought when the Sun Temple came into view. He knew he'd have to cross Market Square but didn't want to bump into Jadwan, not yet, he just didn't have the time. As he walked out into the square, he stayed tight to the right, walking briskly head down, attempting to avoid eye contact with anyone.

"Hoi, Torb!" Jadwan's voice was unmistakeable, booming out from his stall on the north side of the square. Torbin kept his head down and upped his pace almost breaking into a jog, covering the length of the square without looking up once. "Moody prick..." was the last thing he heard as he nipped around a corner at the top of the square. *"I'll see him later, he'll understand,"* he thought to himself as he headed up the hill towards his apartment.

His heart began to beat faster as his home came into view. He had missed it but had missed Jadzia more. He put two fingers in his mouth and let out a shrill two-toned whistle, answered almost instantaneously by a deep-throated bark. As deep as it was it still had the timbre of an excited puppy and was quickly followed by Terror bounding out of the doorway, bowling down the street towards him. He braced himself, but it made no difference, Terror leaping through the air, knocking him off his feet and covering him in affectionate licks. He wrapped his arms around his old friend almost overwhelmed at how emotional a reunion it was.

It took a few minutes, but he managed to push Terror off and stood up, all the while the dog running around his legs, playfully nipping at him. He looked round and saw Jadzia standing in front of him looking more beautiful than ever he remembered, reminding him of just how much he loved her. She ran to him and he swept her up in his arms, both losing themselves in a long passionate kiss. She clung to him so tightly that it almost felt like a bearhug, designed to crush rather than embrace. She buried her head in his shoulder, weeping softly, gently shuddering under his hold.

"I'm home now darling and I'm unhurt. Let's go inside, there is much I need to tell you and much less time than I'd like." The tone of Torbin's voice made Jadzia's features drop, a look of concern etched instantly onto her face.

They walked into the apartment, Terror settling down on the step, setting about a massive bone.

"I see Jadwan's been keeping an eye on you both then." Torbin walked across the room shedding his soiled clothing, picking out some fresh linen garments to change into.

"You know Jadwan insisted that me and Terror went to his for dinner, wouldn't take no for an answer. Terror loved it, fresh cuts of steak and then playing with the children for a good few hours. We're lucky to have such a friend, Zeena as well for that matter." Jadzia poured fresh water from a ewer into the copper basin in the door alcove.

Torbin slid up behind Jadzia, wrapping his arms around her waist and kissing the nape of her neck. "I have missed you more than you could ever know my darling. I would never have thought a few days apart would sting so badly." Torbin turned her gently round to face him, taking in her features. "By the Sun God Sardis, you are beautiful," he said smiling, looking deeply into her eyes.

"You shouldn't take his name in vain," she replied, craning her neck up to plant a gentle almost whispered kiss onto his lips.

Torbin picked her up in his arms and carried her into the bedchamber, laying her down on the bed and tenderly removing her clothes. He stood over her, drinking in the stunning beauty of her body, already stiffening beneath his linen trousers, *"The darkness can wait for a while,"* he thought as he slid next to her.

When they'd finished, Torbin rolled onto his back, his whole body sheened in sweat, his chest rising and falling a little more quickly than usual.

"Jadzia, I know this may not seem like the most opportune moment, but I have a favour to ask and a confession to make." Torbin had propped himself up on one elbow.

"What is it my love?" Jadzia had almost forgotten her earlier trepidation, caught up in the passion of their reunion.

"I have to seek an audience with the Senate. A great threat has arisen in the east and if we do not move quickly much, maybe all will be lost." Torbin instantly regretted blurting it out, but what was the point of treading gently?

"What do you mean?" Jadzia's voice quavered, fear washing over her face.

Now was the moment of greatest risk but no other choice remained. "Remember I told you that I'm a citizen of the Protectorate? Well, I serve them still. I am a member of a secret society called Andhonar's Orphans, our purpose is to learn about all societies in the Free Territories and warn of any threats. I went to meet a fellow Orphan called Candor at the Titan Gate. He is from Turan on the eastern shores and a vast invasion force has landed, piercing the Great Storm Curtain. It appears intent on nothing other than conquest and if we do not organise resistance, they will destroy us all piecemeal. They are consolidating, building their forces until they have overwhelming numbers, and they are almost ready. I must talk to the Senate, only Lhossa and the Murgan have power enough to resist them."

"How can you know all this? Turan is leagues away, how did you know to meet this man?" Jadzia squirmed backwards, putting a little distance between them.

"I knew because I am a mind-walker, as all Orphans are."

Chapter Nine:

Goodbyes

Her sleeping cell felt smaller and more austere than before. Why that came to mind she couldn't really say and in the long run it mattered even less. She swung her legs over the edge of her cot, her back stiff from lying in bed sobbing for an entire day. The loss of Tommec had devastated the whole squad, but Marisa in particular. He had been her oldest and best friend, both joining up at the same time, never apart, always in the same squad at least. When she had been promoted ahead of him, he'd been the first to congratulate her, not a hint of envy in his voice. Even during sparring he accepted any instruction she gave out, as willing as a green recruit.

She couldn't remember the last time she'd cried, at least not since she was a young child. Even now thinking about him she had to force the tears back down. Time to get on with things, say the words, honour the dead and as if that weren't enough, the debrief.

The fact that she'd been ordered to attend the debrief was in itself unusual. Squad leaders would usually get the abridged version from a junior officer, a lieutenant at least but to be in attendance. *"You're mixing in exalted company now girl. Don't open your mouth and fuck it up!"*

She stood up and stretched like a cat, yawning in harmony with her movements. Looking in the mirror she was shocked to see what a mess she looked. Her hair was dishevelled, tufts pointing in all directions like a half-felled forest. Her eyes were red raw, endless rubbing making them appear swollen and sleep encrusted. She poured water from her ewer into the wash basin, splashing it over her hair and onto her face, puffing her cheeks and exhaling loudly, lips wobbling, making a reverberating sound. Straightening her hair, she looked over at her dress uniform. At least it was fresh and in pristine condition, she'd never forgive herself if she didn't look her best for Tommec.

She walked out of the sleeping barracks and stepped out into the crisp morning sunshine that was bathing the parade ground. For a moment the brightness stung her eyes and she shaded them with her hand, looking at the usual daily activity going on. Drilling, sparring, forms, all as if nothing had happened, business as usual. As it should be, she supposed.

"First things first. Let's see how the daft young bastard's getting on."

She strode out across the parade ground, acknowledging the odd greeting, a nod here, a hand gesture there. Everybody smiling, but breaking eye contact as soon as was reasonable. Still a little too near the mark for most, people struggling to find the right words. She upped her pace, striding purposefully to the hospital block at the northeast corner of the square.

The hospital block was a long low single-storey building, whitewashed and well ventilated, large windows set every twenty feet or so. Only half the building was in use at the time, the back half used to store supplies and extra beds which would be brought out at need. Marisa nodded to the charge nurse and walked over to Garic's bed, forcing a smile onto her face. No one had told him about Tommec, wanting to make sure his injuries were manageable before they broke the news. It had been agreed Marisa would do the deed. *"Fucking thanks a lot."*

"How are you feeling?" she asked, pulling a stool up beside his bed.

"Like I've been smashed in the chest with a giant's battle hammer." Garic grinned back at her, unable to move freely as his chest was part bandaged, part cast.

"Funny that," quipped Marisa. "Can't imagine how that might have happened."

Garic started to laugh, then grimaced as the movement made his chest sting. Marisa could see the varying shades of bruise spreading out under the bandages, the outer yellow edges almost reaching his chin.

"Sorry about that, maybe save the jokes for later." Marisa shuffled her stool forward and took Garic's hand in hers, fixing his gaze so that he knew she meant business.

"Listen Garic, I have some bad news. It was felt that it would be prudent to see how severe your injuries were before you were told. As it turns out there are no broken bones, just some muscle damage and severe bruising so I've been nominated to break this news to you." Marissa cursed herself for feeling bitter about this task. Who better to tell him? It still rankled somehow though, ever decreasing circles.

"It's Tommec, he didn't make it." The last words only just crept out in a whisper; the pain still far too fresh for her.

Garic looked numbly at her, eyes glassing over. Marisa knew that he and Tommec had formed an instant friendship, full of banter and smiles. He turned his head away from her trying but failing to hide the tears welling up in his eyes.

Marisa leaned forward, reaching out to touch his gently shuddering shoulder, trying to offer some small grain of comfort. She stopped just short, pulling her hand back, suddenly feeling that any attempt at consolation was utterly pointless. She pushed the stool backwards, got up and spinning on her heels walked briskly to the door.

"Bang up job of comforting him girl, maybe crush up a little glass and put it in his food, really cheer him up."

Marisa stormed down the steps back onto the parade ground petulantly aiming a kick at the potted tree standing like a miniature sentinel by the handrail. She stopped and drew in a long breath, forcing herself to calm down and gain a little composure. Acting like a spoilt child was no way to honour Tommec and right now that was all that really mattered, honouring her friend. She glanced over her shoulder, wondering for a moment if she should go back in and hold Garic, then strode purposefully towards the house of rest.

The rest of the squad were there along with Breda Fencer and the service orator. Tommec's body was laid out in dress uniform on a bier of dried wood and straw, ewers of oil set aside ready to use when the words were finished.

As was traditional, all present gave a personal testimonial, many laced with ribald humour and in jokes that only those close to him would have understood. Tommec was a genuinely popular man, liked by all, someone who people turned to for comfort and advice. Many of the words were mixed in with sobs and gasps, everyone, Marisa included, finding it difficult to hide their grief.

When all was said and done the orator finished the service with the words that had been spoken for centuries.

"And now his service is ended. He gave all he had for his family and he will never be forgotten."

The oils were poured over Tommec's prone form and the bier was lit, the final act performed. The squad slowly broke up, each individual walking away, shoulders hunched as if bracing against a chill wind.

Marisa stood there not moving, unaware that Breda was standing just behind her. She felt his hand gently touch her shoulder and turned absentmindedly to look at who was disturbing her privacy.

"Marisa, we need to attend the debrief. Come, let's make our way there." He smiled at her, motioning in the direction of the command barracks. Marisa glanced back at the burning pyre, one last moment with her friend, and then turned after Breda.

Marisa turned her thoughts to the debrief. Why was she asked to attend? She was only a squad leader after all, debriefs were for officers, members of the command staff, not rank and file. She was not looking forward to it, her natural distrust and dislike of authority figures welling up inside her.

Even in a society where all were valued equally pomposity still reared its ugly head, more so in the armed forces than anywhere else. At least that's what she thought. Senior officers had to be aloof to some degree, chain of command and all that but some took it too far. Master General Oleb Archer however was a rare exception, he had a warmth and an empathy with the rank and file that made him well respected. Also, it seemed to breed a certain number of brown-nosing sycophants amongst the subordinate officers. Small men puffed up by position, using it to belittle others or make themselves seem more important. It really irritated Marisa and was often a source of her discipline problems. *"Let's face it, if I could keep my mouth shut, I'd be a junior officer by now."*

The command barracks were situated at the northwest corner of the army group headquarters. They accommodated the senior officer's quarters, officers mess and situation rooms. The debrief was being held in the main situation room, the planning headquarters of army group Partia.

Marisa entered behind Breda, trying to remain unobtrusive, almost shielding herself behind him. The room was large and windowless, dominated by a huge perfectly flat table with an ornate suspended lighting rig hanging above it. This meant that the walls were relatively shadowed so Marisa took full advantage and quietly took up station against the door frame, easily the dimmest place in the room.

There was a lectern at the head of the table and chairs spaced evenly around the edges. A large map of Partia was laid out on the table where General Archer was liberally waving a riding crop, occasionally tapping at particular points. He wasn't exactly fat but he could do with dropping a few pounds, even though he was getting on in years. He wasn't known as the 'Old man' for nothing. His elaborately embroidered dress uniform was looking more than a little snug, top button undone so that his neck fat didn't flow over the edges. At least that's what Marisa thought. She had to admit that he did have the bearing though, tightly cropped pepper-coloured hair, long waxed moustache, rigid upright posture and a confidence that seemed to flow out of him like a beam of light.

His first and second officers, Major Stevan Dragoon and Captain Rander Potter flanked the general to either side. Marisa had always liked Potter, a non-vocational career officer who'd excelled during his martial service and decided to transfer vocations. He was tough and uncompromising but at the same time fair, always having words of encouragement for the ranks when needed and always to the front when contact was made. He was only if average height with mousey brown hair and although smartly turned out, nothing exceptional to look at but the ranks loved him. Major Dragoon however was another matter.

Marisa disliked him intensely. The perfect example of a pompous fool, a career officer more interested in appearances than ability, the first to snap at a common foot soldier for any minor dress violation, even when off duty. If you were looking for an example of unwarranted arrogance then this was it. Puffed up and proud, without ever having earned it. Couldn't fault him on appearance though, everything pristine and crisp, top button always done up, uniform always pressed. Still a prick though.

Marisa stayed at the back of the room at the opposite end of the table from the officers, wishing she could just quietly slip away. Or at least stay unnoticed until it was all over and done with. "Squad leader Longspear." Fat chance of that then.

"Yes sir." Marisa snapped to attention.

"Come forward Marisa." General Archer motioned Marisa to the head of the table. "Well Longspear, Commander Fencer speaks very highly of you and your squad's actions at Seal-breaker Bay, very highly indeed. But tell me, what did you make of the attack? What was the contact like? Please leave out no detail as there is a great deal resting on what has happened and the consequences of our decisions here could be far reaching indeed." The old man seemed a little over-anxious for something as mundane as a debrief, regardless of how unusual the circumstances were. However, Marisa knew better than to question, just get on with it.

"Well sir, if I'm honest I've never seen or heard of an attack on that scale. They didn't seem to have a strategy as such, but their attacks were ferocious, almost frenzied and they did seem to be pressing more at specific points. Not coordinated exactly but more organised than I've ever seen from Wastelanders. There seemed to be a sense of desperation about it, almost as if the cost of failure was unacceptable. It's difficult to be completely clear about it sir, you know how it can be when you're in it."

"I understand Marissa, I really do but did there seem to be any pattern to their attacks that you could see? Any specific targeting?" The old man seemed mildly agitated as if the need for a specific answer was more important than the truth. Maybe not that exactly, but a need for confirmation, of what she couldn't be sure.

"Well as I said sir, it was difficult to get a real overview when I was in contact myself, but they did seem to press a little harder at Tommec's section of the line." Marisa's voice tapered off a little when she mentioned her friend, a little acid reflux causing her to swallow hard.

"Sir with all due respect you cannot expect to get a concise tactical analysis from a non-commissioned soldier from the ranks, however experienced they may or may not be." Major Dragoon, it seemed, could not resist a little snipe, however well disguised.

"I am certain that it would be easier to report from the rear Stevan but sometimes it's necessary to get one's hands bloodied, though I understand your reticence when it comes to dirtying your lovely uniform." The old man arched an eyebrow at him while Marissa, Breda and Rander all stifled snickers. *"Fucking idiot."*

The colour flushed up Dragoon's neck, infusing his cheeks with an almost purple glow. "Of course sir, my apologies." He shot a baleful look at Marisa. *"I'll pay for that later, spiteful little prick."*

"What you're probably unaware of, Marisa, is that out of the six mind-walkers living at Seal-breaker Bay, five were killed in the contact. The only one to survive was a young child not yet of vocational age. We think she survived because her Gift was not yet fully developed or at least that's our best guess. The fact that Tommec was the only member of your squad to be lost in the line is unfortunate but seems to bear out the pattern. It's difficult to draw any other conclusion but it seems that the mind-walkers present were deliberately targeted." The old man seemed almost morose as he said it, as if the words themselves weighed him down.

Only Marisa and Breda seemed shocked at the revelation but even though the others obviously knew they still seemed to reel a little at the words.

"Deliberately targeted? But how?" Marisa's mind swam with the implications. For this to be plausible pointed at one horrifying possibility. They had mind-walkers. If not their own then at the least working with them, traitors to the family, killing their own. The thought made Marisa shudder, goosebumps forming on her skin.

"I'm afraid that's just the frosting on the cake. Stevan, if you would be so kind."

"Of course sir."

Stevan picked up a long wooden casket from the floor and placed it gingerly on the table, looking as if he would catch something just by holding it. The casket was made from heavy wood, cornered with iron, two clasps fixed with solid padlocks hung from its sides.

"Prepare yourselves, you will not find this a pleasant experience." The old man wrinkled his nose as if assailed by a fetid odour while Dragoon and Potter visibly edged backwards.

General Archer took a large brass key from his pocket and proceeded to unlock the padlocks. He flipped the catches up and Marisa could have sworn his hands were trembling. As he started to lift the lid a wave of mild nausea grasped Marisa, slowly twisting her insides. She steadied herself trying to fight the urge to dry heave, little pinpricks of pain stabbing at her temples. The old man turned the lid over and stood back, all the colour draining from his features.

The waves of discomfort pulsed slowly through Marisa, her heartbeat thumping at her temples. The urge to turn and get as far away as possible was overridden by the need to see what was in the box. She edged closer, Breda at her side, sneaking up on it afraid if she moved too quickly it would see her and lash out. She stepped forward, forcing herself on, beads of sweat forming on her lip, throat dry and tight. She grasped the edge of the table and leaned forward, craning her neck and then there they were.

Beautiful, perfect works of art, wrought in blue steel, edges so sharp that just looking at them felt like being cut. Two long sleek swords and a leaf spearhead, intricate patterning subtly worked into the blades, whole friezes adorning the pommels, almost moving, telling long-forgotten stories. Power and malevolence oozed from them, flowing out through the room, swirling around everybody there, infusing the very air with their presence. Marisa could feel their strength, sense the lives they had cut short, unconsciously feel the blades at the moment of their birth, tempered in the torsos of their first victims. She could almost see through the victims' eyes, watching as the mountain lord slowly pushed the blade in through the groin, feeling its cold kiss pierce their insides, the exquisite agony drowning out all other senses…

"Marisa, are you alright?" Breda cradled her in his arms, concern washed over his face.

"What happened? I was seeing, uh, I'm not certain, I…" Her head was foggy, as if she had lost contact with reality for a moment.

"You said something about 'the cold' and then you just slid down to the floor." Breda seemed a little shaken, a little pale but then no one's cheeks looked exactly flushed.

Marisa smiled at Commander Fencer. "Thank you sir, but I'm fine." She grabbed the edge of the table as she rose and looked warily at where the blades had been. The lid was once again locked.

"Are they what I think they are?" It was only half a question really, everyone knew the answer, but she needed to hear it from someone else's lips, needed that confirmation.

"Yes, Squad Leader Longspear." The old man had regained his composure and his voice had its usual command. "They are soul-forged blades."

Chapter Ten Part One:

Ardend Labourer

"If history has taught us anything it is that repeating the same actions and expecting a different outcome is akin to lunacy. Every piece of recorded history shows the same cycle. Dynasties rising to prominence by conquest, militarily superior to those they subdue, blooming in their pomp until the next conquerors appear and wipe their names from history. So many civilisations lost in the mists of time, all their achievements, art, literature, architecture, turned to ashes at the point of a blade.

What was lost can never be regained, the beauty and knowledge allowed to leak out of existence, eons of wisdom frittered away so that the victors can write their own histories. Even those that survive in some shape or form, the Hardite Empire for example, eventually diminish, lessened by ambition, each generation trying to outdo their forefathers until they overreach and shrink back. The poison that festers, jealously yearning for the days of splendour and glory, eventually sees them implode, becoming ever more reduced, evermore petty and small.

And yet the cycle continues like a great turning wheel as if all the lessons laid out before them can be ignored because they of course are different, they can do it right this time.

However, what if there were another way? What if people decided to build a new society where personal acquisition, power, tribalism, religious intolerance and status were not the driving forces? What if a society arose that placed everyone as equals, where people followed their vocation, where all contributed to the greater good, all defended each other and where the wisest and most capable offered the guidance that those less experienced needed to flourish?

Well five hundred years on here we are. While there have been mistakes and miss steps along the way, the Protectorate stands as a beacon of freedom, an example of what can be if we all strive to be the best we can. And that is worth the ultimate sacrifice, because if you would not give your life for right then what are you?"

From the collected works of Madran Scholar PP (Post Protectorate) 512

Jonoh sat at the head of the ancient oak table, back to where he'd met Cerwin, where the Gift had first revealed itself to him. In the two weeks since he had realised some profound truths, first and foremost that no other person in existence could go where he could go, see what he could see or possibly understand the breadth of his ability. Cerwin for all the remarkable skill and wisdom he possessed already knew this to be true and had ceded the task to him. So there he sat, the door bolted and locked from the inside so that nobody could enter. Not that they'd be able to anyway, once he was immersed, he was beyond anyone's reach.

He could feel the malevolent power pulsing from the heavy wooden casket lying on the table. Even though it was padlocked, and the casket was lined with lead it could not entirely escape Jonoh's reach but he knew that making contact with its contents would reveal more than anyone else could ever hope to see.

He couldn't stop thinking about the meeting with the Elder Council, especially Master Ardend Labourer. He and Cerwin had been summoned to the meeting, Barton Logistar bringing the request. He still couldn't shake off his feeling of discomfort around Barton, the man had always been unfailingly polite and friendly but there was something subconsciously pulling at him. He shook off the feeling for the moment and recalled the day's events, retracing them, needing to clear his thoughts of any clutter and be certain of his path.

He had crossed the inner courtyard on the heels of Cerwin, quickening his pace to keep up with the little shadow-master, astounded as always by his energy and vigour. They entered the great dining hall, the huge oak doors over twenty feet tall pivoting lightly on their hinges as if they weighed as little as a feather. It wasn't as big as some dining halls back in Great Harbour but it was stunning, great carved column tops, flying buttresses and intricately carved animals and friezes, all adorned the high ceiling. Nowhere could the naked eye discern any fault in the construction, the masonry perfectly aligned and fitted, a glowing tribute to the skill of the builders, raised more than 1,500 years ago.

The Elder Council members were all in attendance spread around the room in little groups or pairs, avidly discussing whatever issues were current. Nobody seemed to notice Cerwin and Jonoh's entrance with the exception of one man, only of average height but Jonoh could see straight away that there was nothing ordinary about him.

"Cerwin, good to see you and Jonoh Shipwright, it's a genuine pleasure to finally make your acquaintance." The Elder Council's leader smiled broadly taking Cerwin's then Jonoh's hand in his.

"Master Ardend," Jonoh replied courteously, amazed by the strength of the man's grip. Not that he was trying to dominate or crush his hand, just the opposite, but the power was unmistakable. Master Ardend Labourer was a remarkable physical specimen, not tall but hewed out of granite. He had a solid barrel chest, and his physical fitness was clearly visible even through his clothes, knots of muscles on his upper body standing out through his tightly tailored shirt. Not in itself all that remarkable perhaps but then you had to take into account that he was at least sixty years old, his spotted balding pate and grey receding hair unable to mask the passage of time.

"Jonoh, I apologise that we have not met sooner but Master Cerwin leads me to believe that you have been occupied with other more pressing matters." Master Ardend ushered them towards a corner of the hall where a table had a large map of the Known World unfurled and weighted down at the corners.

As they approached the table Jonoh could not help but look around at the assembled members of the Elder Council, so many great masters in one room. Master Evaleen Farmer a native of Kings Town itself, tall, fair-haired and full-figured, in her fifties and extremely attractive. Master Domen Fletcher, tall, dark-haired and physically imposing, a man filled with the quiet confidence of years of accumulated knowledge. It was a little intimidating being surrounded by a collection of such worthies, only nobody paid attention to anything other than the task at hand, Jonoh's notoriety carrying no weight at all.

The map itself was a perfect work of art, the whole of the Known World drawn in relief but with such skill that the mountains, vales, rivers and all the features seemed to stand proud as if it were a sculpture. From the great Whitecap mountains of Snowbard to the very northwest, across the Protectorate and out across the Mid Ocean to Sarjinn on the west coast of the free territories. The great grassland prairies of the Murgan to the south, the Red Desert sitting between the Murgan Lands and the great breadbasket of the world; The Kingdom of Darmat; the Golden Empire and on to Lhossa, the ruby of the east. The Titan Gate and Pass out to the far reaches of the Known World, the twin white cities of Turan and Minari, the Green-lands edged by the Grey ocean, all encompassed by the Great Storm Curtain.

Every feature, city, river, mountain range, in fact every tiny detail was represented. The Hardite Empire, the Northern Wastelands, the lands of the Robber Barons, the Confederation of Mercenary Armies, the Great Silver Sea, even the lawless lands regardless of how little was really known of them. Jonoh had never seen its like and was completely mesmerised by its beauty.

"Jonoh."

"Huh, I am sorry Master Ardend." Jonoh pulled his attention back to his companions, a little red-faced at how easily he'd been distracted.

"Hypnotic, isn't it?" Master Ardend smiled across at Jonoh a knowing grin creasing the corners of his mouth.

Jonoh nodded a little self-consciously. "Yes, it is that."

"Beautiful piece, over a hundred years old but looks as if it could have been made yesterday. I've personally spent hours staring at it and I'm certain I see a new detail every time I gaze upon it. Really remarkable." Master Ardend smiled and looked to Master Cerwin. "Do you not agree Cerwin?"

"Absolutely, a truly staggering work of art and very much fit for purpose."

Jonoh could see the map had the same effect on all three of them, even taking into account that they'd obviously both seen it before, on numerous occasions in all likelihood. He could sense another purpose underlying this little mutual appreciation society however.

"Jonoh, let me pose you a little hypothetical. Imagine for a moment that an unknown invasion force had developed the ability to traverse the Great Storm Curtain. Where would be the most advantageous place to launch an incursion?"

The answer was glaringly obvious and did not require any conscious effort whatsoever. Jonoh just knew, had always known. "Storms Break." Jonoh's reply was immediate and deadpan.

Master Ardend did well to hide his surprise, though not completely. Master Cerwin just arched an eyebrow, for him quite an admission.

"Would you mind elaborating Jonoh? Just humour an old man if you'd be so kind." Jonoh could not help but smile at Master Ardend who for all his physical presence had a very disarming, gentle seeming nature.

"Well, firstly their southern flank would be secured by the shifting sandbanks. No one has ever managed to successfully invade by sea from the south as the Brotherhood of the Golden Hand found out to their great cost. Secondly, they would instantly secure their western flank with the Titan mountains being impenetrable, the only access being through the Titan Pass, which has never even been attempted because the Green-lands are so remote. Thirdly they would secure deep anchorage on the northern side of the Bountiful Isles ensuring their supply lines. This in turn would allow them pretty much unlimited time to build their forces as any kind of counter-attack would be highly unlikely because the twin cities' only full-time armed forces are stationed there to defend against any potential incursion."

"That is a remarkably astute assessment, Jonoh. Are there any more pertinent observations you would like to make?" Master Ardend stared open-eyed as if daring Jonoh to respond.

"For a start, the ships that the twin cities have are small attack boats, shallow-bottomed and designed to manoeuvre through the shifting sands. If a force of large warships could gain access on the north side of the Isles, it would be impossible to resist them. Plus, once the archipelago was captured, they would be able to secure the far southern end of the Grey Ocean by placing a force at the

Cape of Lost Hope. They would also have unfettered control of the Grey Ocean itself, providing an almost inexhaustible supply of fish and that's not even taking into account the great fir forests and farmlands that would be within their grasp. The ability to feed their army and build ships and siege engines would just fall into their laps."

Even as he said the words Jonoh realised the implications. Whoever it was that had planned this invasion must have known all this information beforehand. It was just too precise, too perfectly thought out. It didn't seem possible, but the facts were undeniable, they knew because they had been here before, knew the precise point at which to attack, the one place where they couldn't be countered, a perfect defensible stronghold. This could have been planned for years, decades, who knew how long?

Jonoh didn't hear at first.

"Jonoh. Jonoh are you still with us?"

"Yes, sorry Master Ardend I was just a little distracted by the questions this all raises."

"Understandably so Jonoh, understandably so." The master's head was bowed, a look of weary resignation flickering across his features for the briefest moment.

"Jonoh, I would like to ask you a question."

"Yes of course Master Cerwin." Jonoh had almost forgotten about the diminutive master of shadows, sitting there silently observing all that had passed.

"Whilst I realise that you attended Red Pier Academy where the standard of instruction is unequalled in the whole of the Protectorate, it was my understanding that history and geography were not necessarily your favourite subjects."

"I did quite enjoy some of the lessons Master, but the academic side of school life was not my main focus." Jonoh almost blanched at the level of understatement but managed to avoid giggling.

"How is it then that you have just managed to furnish us with such an accurate historical and geographical account of the situation in the Green-lands?" Master Cerwin's wrinkles bunched tightly together on his forehead as he quizzically raised his eyebrows.

Jonoh mentally stopped in his tracks. He hadn't given any

thought to that question. In fact, he hadn't needed to think about it at all.

"I cannot explain it Master, for some reason I just knew. I didn't have to think about it, the knowledge is just there." Even as he said the words, he realised how inadequate an explanation it must sound.

"I am not interrogating you Jonoh, I just wanted to know if it was in any way conscious or if you had a personal interest in these matters. It is as I thought, your measure of the Gift is beyond my ability to understand but it seems that you have the facility to absorb information just by the briefest contact with any reference material. It is almost as if you can pluck any information from the ether, no matter how detailed just by seeing a small part of what is available. Remarkable."

Jonoh, not for the first time, felt penned in, disconnected from his own ability and yet almost serenely at ease with it all. The contradictions were the hardest thing to come to terms with.

Cerwin could see it in his face, read the discomfort and uncertainty it was creating.

"Jonoh, do not overly trouble yourself, understanding will come in time, but some things are maybe not meant to be fully understood. Everyone experiences this in one form or another. The sense that a certain someone is going to knock on your door seconds before they do. Thinking of a certain person you have not spoken to for a time and then there they are right in front of you. I do not believe this is necessarily any different just that in your case it is more heightened." The old man's soothing voice and empathetic look always helped to smooth Jonoh's mood.

"Jonoh, how much information have you been given regarding this incursion? Are you aware of the reports we've had back from the Orphan network?" Part question but part probe, Master Ardend wanted to see if Jonoh could garner information without being told. Subtle but admirable. A clever and nonconfrontational way of asking the hard question. Jonoh was quickly growing to like this man.

"Probably less than I actually know but that's no great mystery. Since I first learned I could mindwalk I have picked up information being passed backwards and forwards. I know what everyone else knows, that they are called the H'Daree, that they have conquered everything outside of the Known World and that they are coming here with one purpose. Conquest."

"This as you say is common knowledge, but what else do you know?" Master Ardend was forcing a crucible hoping it might draw something from Jonoh, something he may not yet have realised himself. Such a measured thoughtful man. Surprising.

"I know that they have been sending out constantly to all the mind-walkers within their range and that what could be interpreted as propaganda or rhetoric are merely statements of truth, from their point of view. It is not an attempt to confuse or mislead, more a demonstration of power and their own unwavering belief in the righteousness of their cause. They are in their own way trying to avoid what they see as unnecessary conflict and loss of life, offering an olive branch if you will. There is no attempt at subterfuge on their part, they believe their cause is just and are genuinely confused that anyone would choose to oppose them."

"It seems you have a deeper understanding of what is happening than I would have expected, Jonoh. Your assessment is remarkably insightful, but do you see what this means, what it will inevitably lead to?" Master Ardend left the question hanging in the air as if the answer itself carried an unspoken threat.

"It means they will not relent until they have achieved their goal. Unless someone can stop them. At some point we will have to confront them and win or perish."

"Win or perish." The thought sat uncomfortably in Jonoh's mind. An unknown enemy who was coming and would not stop until they had won or lost everything. What could be done to defeat such a power? He had no doubt of the incredible strength and skill of the Protectorate's forces, nearly a million soldiers permanently stationed at their borders with a whole nation of people trained their whole lives to fight in defence of their way of life. But against an enemy of seemingly inexhaustible numbers who moved as a nation?

"The blades." The blades held some secret, maybe something that could provide some answers or offer some hope. Everyone that had seen them or been close to them had felt the aura that lay within them, even those with no measure of the Gift.

Even Master Cerwin had struggled in their presence, unable to mask the discomfort they caused him while many others had fainted or thrown up, unmanned by the experience.

Jonoh pulled the casket towards himself and flicked the latches up. Waves of energy pulsed in his direction as he lifted the lid, the hairs on his forearms bristling as if in anticipation of a climactic event. The blades were mesmerising, so beautiful that Jonoh's breath caught in his throat. He just stared at them for what seemed an age, swallowed up by their shimmering allure.

He steeled himself reaching out so tentatively that everything seemed to go into slow motion. Then he touched one…

Chapter Ten Part Two:

Sliding back

Colours. Waves of colours, flushing from red to blue to green, pulsing in great shimmering, coruscating, undulating sheets of energy. Screams and whispers, pleading, boasting, begging forgiveness. Terrible malevolence, preening arrogance, great swathes of empathy all crashing in on top of each other. Birth and deaths of invisible, miniscule lifeforms, stars bursting into life and dying in cataclysmic eruptions. Everything at every moment, all that had ever been and would ever be pouring in from every direction, immersing all with an impossible burden… *"Control, must find some focus."*

Great clouds of gas, swirling in space forming giant nebulas. A single grain of sand on a beach holding an entire civilisation's secrets, washed out to sea, forever lost. Life bursting into being, cells coming together, dividing, multiplying, seeking a place to exist. *"Control Jonoh. Find a point, something to focus on."*

A whole nation, millions strong, lifting their voices to their god at the moment of their destruction. A predator choking the life out of prey, clamping down on its throat, luxuriating in its moment of triumph. A hugely dense star, spinning at impossible speeds throwing out great gouts of radiation, eviscerating everything in its path… *"Control, find one thing to focus on."*

Jonoh's conscious mind swam to the surface trying to process the overwhelming waves of knowledge and information that seemed to be trying to drown his reasoning. His vision started to make out what looked like little grey boxes as if his mind were trying to order what he could perceive. He felt as if he was floating in a vacuum, weightless, surrounded completely by all that existed, history, matter, even the indefinable subconscious.

Jonoh stared at one of the grey shapes forming all around him and concentrated, focusing on the images that were starting to gather. He felt pulled towards the scene encapsulated in the box and found himself observing the tableau as if he were floating in space above it.

It wasn't just a case of observation, for some reason he had context, an understanding of what was playing out before his eyes. It was the final battle, the end of one civilisation or another.

Drawn up in front of a great walled city was an army, arrayed in perfect formations and clad in beautiful, burnished armour. It was at least fifty thousand strong, great phalanxes of spearmen to the front arranged four rows deep all with shoulder-high embossed shields. Swordsmen with round shields formed in smaller squares behind them, two to each phalanx with mounted lancers on great destriers occupying the flanks. Great artillery pieces sat behind the formations, catapults and enormous scorpions manned by teams up to a score in number. Their lines extended across the whole of the city's width, bristling with intent, determined to throw back their adversaries.

The city itself was breathtaking, Jonoh could not quite believe its majesty. The outer wall was about fifty feet high with a main gate set in the middle and a couple of sally ports at intervals along the length of the wall. The construction was flawless, the walls seemingly smooth with no discernible joins or anything that could pass as a handhold. What really astonished were the buildings within the fortification. Giant towers and minarets some with spiralling cones, others with ornate crenulations, all embellished with gold or silver, some with precious metals he had never seen before. Great temples and manses, beautiful gardens and parks, stunning bridges, some slender with beautifully intricate ironwork, others big and bold with great gatehouses at either end. Whatever civilisation had created this wonderful vista must have been great indeed.

Jonoh looked across the valley floor facing the great city and his heart almost stopped. A vast force, hundreds of thousands strong was moving forwards like a great inexorable ocean of living flesh, all clad in black except for the blades of their swords and spears. They sparkled like an endless field of silver corn, the light shining back off them like a great moving mirror. They were all moving at a trot, building up momentum, ratcheting up their speed and closing the gap ready for maximum impact.

They stayed in formation as their pace upped, not as rigidly well formed as the golden army outside the walls but tight and resolute. As they closed on their enemy, the front rank lowered its spears, a long line of steel teeth ready to bite the flesh of those in its path.

Jonoh realised that he didn't need to be close to observe detail, in fact he wasn't actually there at all but what he saw shook him to his foundations. The great black-clothed swathe of bodies was not human. They were of a similar physicality and a little shorter and broader, but their faces were where the difference showed. Their skin was sallow with over-cropping brows and reduced lower jaws. Their upper teeth were sharp at the front, overlapping their lower mandibles like chopping saws. Hands and forearms were covered by what at first looked like a kind of harsh cloth but was really a slender covering of hard skin, like built-in sheets of thin armour.

The golden phalanxes levelled their great spears, each at least sixteen feet long so that the tips of all four rows extended beyond the front line, a bristling hedgehog of death. The great black wave of creatures crashed into the golden army's front line, hundreds instantly impaled, their compatriots leaping over their fallen corpses to get into contact. The phalanx bowed but held, the spearmen planting their feet and pushing from behind their shields, spears darting out hardly able to miss the endless stream of targets.

Behind the formations the artillery began to loose barrage after barrage. The catapults firing great stone balls, four feet in diameter crashing down into the massed ranks of black-clad warriors, wiping out dozens at a time. The giant scorpions, each loaded with three gigantic thick-shafted spears, broad-headed barbed tips at their heads, loosed beside them, firing a volley every minute. They crashed through flesh and armour, smashing and decapitating everything in their path, leaving great trails of bodies in their wake. Small gaps started to appear in the phalanxes' front line, thin channels through which the swordsmen poured, cutting their way into the front lines of the creature's army.

Jonoh could start to see the strategy, pin the enemy on the phalanxes' spears and then use the swordsmen to break them down into sections. Create an envelope cutting them off from each other, negating their numbers by only allowing the front lines to engage, making their huge numbers count against them. The artillery barrage was forcing a large part of their forces to hold back, some even withdrawing to a far safer distance. Then the cavalry started to move, swinging around their exposed flanks and trapping them in pockets.

It was so well timed and executed, perfect double envelopments, half a dozen times across the front lines. Being outnumbered proving no disadvantage whatsoever, if anything playing right into the Golden army's hands.

But something did not feel right, a sense of foreboding that Jonoh could not quantify but was sitting there in his subconscious.

Then he heard it, a deep rumbling like an earth tremor, its bass note reverberating across the valley, all action stopping for a second. It was as if a great collective intake of breath was being taken before plunging into the depths of the unknown.

The great swarm of black parted, leaving three huge channels where massive leviathans arose, vast creatures, like two-hundred-foot worms rearing into the sky. They were dank grey with huge open maws ringed with hundreds of foot-long teeth. Platforms were mounted on top of them attached by rope and hooks to their reticulated bodies. Dozens of black-clad soldiers were mounted on the platforms, riding and steering the monsters towards the city. The noise of their roars was deafening, thundering across the valley so loudly that Jonoh almost expected lightning and tumultuous rain to accompany them.

Heroism is a noble concept, one that everyone would like to believe resides in their hearts but what Jonoh witnessed barely seemed credible. The Golden army did not falter or quiver but set itself to fight the monsters. The cavalry turned on mass and charged across the valley floor, lances couched, swords drawn, a huge throaty, defiant roar thrown at the faces of their enemies. The artillery crews worked like demons to reload at double the pace, firing volley after volley at the approaching giants. The phalanxes set their spears and marched purposely forward in lockstep, trampling over the massed corpses of the fallen creatures.

The middle worm was brought down under a fierce volley of darts, rearing up in its death throes, pitching sideways killing hundreds of its own forces. But it was all to no avail, the Golden army being slain in huge numbers, the remaining worms cutting devastating swathes of destruction through its ranks, the dark tidal wave of enemies pouring through the gaps.

Jonoh witnessed the final devastation of this wonderful civilisation, the defenders overwhelmed and the great city put to the torch.

He withdrew his gaze and looked around him, all the grey boxes coalescing into little individual scenes, moments in time and space.

He focused on another and found himself looking down on a settlement snugly placed at the bottom of a great cliff face. Thousands of people stood on a beach, hand in hand raising their voices to the sky. A great collective entreaty to the deity they worshiped, begging for deliverance. At first Jonoh did not understand what he was seeing, there was no sense of context here, no explanation, then far out to sea he saw.

The whole horizon seemed to lift, and a low rumbling noise spread out across the water. The noise grew, getting louder and louder, like a vast herd of beasts thundering across a prairie. The water's edge receded twenty, thirty, forty feet, further and further back. The sea behind it arose, like a mighty tower, dark turquoise, beautiful and terrifying. The peak of the front wave was taller than the top of the cliff, as high as two hundred feet. The people on the beach clung to each other, some sobbing, some on their knees, others turning their backs, but all transfixed with horror.

Then the wave broke, smashing down from its great height, engulfing everything in view, a series of waves following on behind. Then the waters receded, settling back to their normal levels and everything was gone, washed away. Only the remnants of a small chapel remained, its corner posts sticking out of the ground at strangely jaunty angles.

Jonoh withdrew from the scene. He had gained a measure of control and could now look in all directions picking out each individual act. It was the Gift but a narrow, trammelled version of it. All the pictures were of negative or destructive events influenced by the blades' hidden powers. Something resided in them but as yet he could not discern what it was that radiated out from their cores.

Also, he realised that they acted as an anchor, tying him to his reality, keeping him connected to his point of origin. All the scenes spreading out in a myriad of directions were interconnected, appearing as grey boxes linked together by a kind of string, radiating as far as his eyes could perceive. The strings glowed red with certain ones glowing more brightly than the others. Jonoh realised that those that glowed brightest were the ones leading backwards through the timelines of the blades. He could see the line clearly, follow the direction of their history, the glow receding beyond the scope of his vision.

He started to follow the strings, going back to the source, their moment of creation. He caught glimpses of their past, the lives they had cut short and the hands they had passed through. Further and further back in time, centuries flowing by in the space of minutes.

Then his journey slowed, the box where they came into existence opening in front of him. He wasn't a hundred per cent certain, but he knew he had travelled back at least thirteen centuries.

He was looking down on a room with a stone altar at its centre, a stone staircase leading upwards. Torches sat in sconces around the walls and an open blacksmith's forge stood in front of the altar. There were heavily armoured guards stationed at the four corners of the room with metal face shields drawn down covering their eyes.

At the forge, a huge-bellied smith stood hammering away on a long steel sword, turning and folding time and time again, sparks showering the floor around him. Jonoh could see the man was blind, both eyes having been put out. Sweat cascaded down his body, dripping into the forge and spitting like angry snakes as his hammer found its mark again and again.

Disturbingly there was a young man manacled to the altar, wrist and ankle. He was naked and gagged, a look of terror stamped on his face, his head flicking from side to side, eyes frantic with fear and panic.

The only sound was the faint whimpering of the manacled figure and the repetitive clang of hammer on steel. Although the room was hot it made Jonoh shiver as if he were sitting in a snow drift.

Jonoh turned as he heard voices coming down the stairs, a strange sense of fear gripping him, gnawing at the back of his mind. Two figures descended the last half dozen steps. The first was a giant of a man, nearly seven feet tall, barrel-chested and densely muscular. He wore brown leather breeches with knee-high boots, beautifully made and of a kind few could have afforded back then. He had a white linen shirt with a short-sleeved ring-mail top covering it. His face was angular and hard, nicked with scars and sporting a badly broken nose. His long shaggy mane was a deep red and his trimmed and shaped beard sprouted its share of grey hairs. To top it all he had a small iron circlet atop his head, the crown of a mountain king.

With a sense of awe and near complete astonishment Jonoh realised who he was looking at. Erik Hardrager, Erik the Dread, founder of the first royal dynasty of Snowbard. The king who finally ended the tradition of bloodletting that had existed for millennia, the wars of accession. The pointless slaughter of the heads of all the great families by the victor, in the battle for the crown. Ensuring a never-ending vendetta, carried on ad infinitum by each subsequent generation. It was considered a measure of their national strength, enmity forging evermore powerful armies, ready to snatch power the moment a king died. But Erik the Dread finished that practice, the first man to place his son on the throne.

The man beside him wore a black hooded cloak pulled up and completely covering his face. Although shorter and far less broad than the King he emanated power, a quiet assuredness that seemed to flow from him. Jonoh could not quite put his finger on it but there was a dreadful familiarity about him that made him feel weak and slightly nauseated. To add to his discomfort, the King seemed to defer to him as they whispered to each other, too quiet for Jonoh to hear.

Jonoh strained with all his will to listen to their exchange and began to pick out snippets.

"…no going back…"

"…will pay the price…"

"…power will be yours…"

He could not make out complete sentences. It was almost as if someone was actively blocking his ability to observe and listen. A will set against his.

The hooded figure went to stand beside the smith who seemed to nod his assent and bowing handed him the finished blade. Jonoh had been so engrossed in the King and his shadowy companion that he hadn't noticed the blade being completed but now he saw it he knew it was the one he was touching, the same piece of forged metal, still beautiful and mesmerising.

The cowled figure held the blade and started to incant a kind of spell into the room. It seemed to physically coalesce around the metal, making it shimmer beyond the heat haze that had already engulfed it. He turned to the King holding the blade out in front of him and Jonoh heard his voice clearly for the first time.

"The time is now. Do what must be done."

Jonoh froze, his heart raging at an unbelievable pace, cold sweat forming on his forehead. *"That voice!"*

Transfixed he watched in horror as the King took up the blade, still glowing faintly with the heat of the forge and laid the point at the groin of the victim on the slab. The blade had to be tempered and Jonoh could see no water bath. The man screamed silently, his gag muffling nearly all noise as the King slid the blade home, entering at the crotch and pushing all the way to the hilt. The blade sizzled, the smell of cooking meat infusing the air as he slid it out slowly, lifting it and admiring the way it looked, crimson and silver in the torchlight. Then he spun around, incredibly fast and agile for a man of his size, cutting down the guards in four swift strokes, the blade seeming to slow, pushing an invisible wave of air ahead of it, almost as if the metal never touched the flesh. With a final violent slash, he hewed the smith almost in half, slicing him from shoulder to waist, his innards slopping out onto the stone floor.

It was a horrifying sight. Jonoh was shaking, desperately trying to regain control of his body and mind. The King and the cowled figure huddled close together and then Erik the Dread, the most revered and feared warrior in history went to one knee, pledging fealty to the figure in black.

Jonoh knew who the cowled figure was but at the same time had no idea, a visceral fear gripping his whole being. He went to withdraw, almost exhausted by how overpowering it had all been.

"What the…" His back hit stone, solid and immovable stone, but how? How could this be? Panic began to overtake him as he scrambled back into a corner of the room. *"I'm here, by Andhonar's ghost, I'm here."* The horror of the moment started to engulf him, the sheer terror loosening his bladder, but he simply did not care. He just wanted out. *"Just let me out, please,"* he whimpered to no one in particular, just hoping somehow he could wake from this nightmare.

The King arose, a smile of absolute joy spreading across his fearsome features and turned to look at Jonoh. The hooded figure laughed, as self-satisfied a laugh as Jonoh had ever heard, full of complete and utter self-belief.

"The voice, for pity's sake the voice." Jonoh shivered, fixed in place, utterly incapable of moving.

"So, the trap worked and I have you before you can even begin to oppose me. So very easy, I must admit to being a little disappointed." The words came out in a mocking sneer, dismissive and full of loathing.

Jonoh's mind had slowed to a stupor, unable to comprehend anything, drowning in a black ocean, endlessly deep. *"The strings."* He focused every ounce of emotion he had, all his fear, all his doubt, every yearning and then he was flying, hurtling at impossible speed back to the source, back to the blades, a screaming voice ringing in his ears. "NOOOOOOOOOO…"

Chapter Eleven:

Pay the price

The manacles chaffed Torbin, ankles and wrists both turning red raw. He'd always thought of the Lhossans as innovative and resourceful people, but this felt like a step too far. His manacles were joined wrist to ankle by heavy iron chains passed through two metal loops pinned to the wall of the cell. He couldn't stand up and he couldn't lay down. Lack of sleep and an inability to stretch out left him feeling drained and exhausted. Such a subtle way to weaken someone's resolve. It would certainly make them more susceptible to torture, more willing to give up their secrets or confess to their crime.

Part of him hoped that Jadzia wouldn't give him up but what choice did she have? She was after all the daughter of the most eminent family in Lhossa. Jadzia Sun-blessed, child of his Eminence Jadwar Sun-blessed, Primary of Lhossa and leader of the Senate. He was going to have to come forward with the truth regardless, but it stung that it had come from her.

Fitting that they had thrown him in the heretic cells, given that he had freely admitted his crime, the unforgivable sin of being a mind-walker. Abominations all by the text of the Book of Sardis and he was sure that the First Acolyte Sardon the Meek would prosecute to the letter of the law. Torbin had always despised him, a petty, vindictive little man. Always looking to advance himself even to the point of engineering a seat on the Senate's leading council. When elevated to First Acolyte he had chosen his own title as was the custom. A less meek, more full of his own self-importance man Torbin was yet to meet.

Torbin knew the risks but this was the only way. He had to address the Senate openly, he had much to ask, and it had to be now. Time was slipping away and in truth he did not know how much time they had left but someone would have to make a stand. Someone would have to try and stop the H'Daree. The only way to hope to get the support he knew he'd desperately need, was to tell the Senate everything, including how he'd come to know. A high-risk strategy admittedly but risking all was the only option left. Being stuck in a heretic cell for more than five days however was not helping his cause.

He'd only had one brief visitor, Jadwan sneaking him in some bread and cold cuts, hiding the food in the top of his breeches, his enormous stomach providing enough of an overlap to cover the misdeed. A risk on his part that could have been severely punished if caught. But he was Jad so even thinking of accusing him came with great risks. He had tried his best to be upbeat but even he seemed a little unsettled at Torbin's admission. Years of indoctrination and dogma had ingrained a subliminal fear and distrust of mind-walkers which in a way made it all the more admirable that he'd still openly showed his friendship and support by the visit. Even that spiteful little shit Sardon would think twice about going after a Jad.

They had at least left him a small water pail, but it was stale and slightly sour. Give with one hand, take with the other, age-old tricks to grind someone down, but if they worked?

He'd asked Jadwan one favour, to pass a message to Jadwar, begging an audience. It was his only real hope. If he could convince him that this invasion was a real and present danger, then he had a chance. Jadwar was the single most powerful man in Lhossa, direct descendant of Jadvar the Great, capable of tracing his lineage back to the founding of the city. It was no guarantee of success, there was still the Senate to convince but you could not hope for a more articulate or forceful ally.

Still, that had been two days ago, and he had not seen or heard anything since. He looked forlornly around his cell, the walls damp with condensation, the musty air surprisingly cool given that it was raging sunshine on the surface. But he supposed three levels down underneath the great temple of Sardis the heat would struggle to penetrate. For some unknown reason a small shaft had been built into the temple, only an inch or so wide, a tiny beam of light spearing down to hit the floor of the cell. Maybe it was meant to be another form of torture, reminding the condemned of what they were missing.

He kept going over every scenario in his mind, trying to think of what counterarguments he would be able to use, trying to stave off despair. But as time passed his hope began to dwindle. If he were brought to trial without an advocate, he would be summarily found guilty and put to death by public vivisection. He was no coward, but this scared him to the bone.

For a moment he thought he heard a noise from behind his cell door, a shuffling of feet or a kind of scraping. It was difficult to tell, a certain light-headedness affected him at all times, a lack of food no doubt to blame. His shoulders slumped, as far as they could, given his chains, an air of resignation hovering around him.

There it was again, more distinct now, feet moving towards the door. Then his spirits lifted for a second as the key began to turn in the lock. But what if they were coming to drag him in chains to his death? He steeled himself, ready to sell his life here and now. They would have to release the chains from the loops at the very least in order to move him, possibly undo the manacles relying on his weakened state to avoid any conflict. They would soon learn to their everlasting regret that Torbin Pale-skin was no animal to be butchered for the mass's entertainment.

As the door scraped open on rusty hinges, Torbin tensed, a little vicious snarl escaping his gritted teeth. Then as quickly as he had tensed, he relaxed, the sight before his eyes possibly the finest he had ever seen.

Standing in the doorway in all his finery was his Eminence Jadwar Sun-blessed. Torbin's distaste for royalty and aristocracy was a part of who he was and where he came from. However, if anyone was ever born to rule it was Jadwar. The way he carried himself was pure self-assurance, imbued with an absolute faith that his place was at the head of the table. His dress was impeccable, gold silk trousers cinched at the waist with an ornate belt, the clasp a great golden sun. His boots were made of soft calves' leather, wooden-heeled with golden buckles fixing them in place. Under flowing multicoloured robes, threaded with gold, he wore a white cotton shirt embroidered with an outline of Lhossa itself. His jet-black hair was worn loose, passing his shoulders, oiled and straight. His jewellery was all gold, rings on both hands, a pendanted necklace and hooped earrings completing the ensemble.

"So, you seem to be in a bit of a quandary Torbin." Jadwar smiled as he crossed the floor, carrying a stool in one hand and a small wicker basket in the other. He placed the stool next to Torbin and sat down. Both the movement and the sitting were graceful and elegant. Everything Jadwar did was graceful and elegant. Absolutely everything.

"Hungry?" Jadwar quizzically raised an eyebrow at Torbin as if the question needed to be posed twice. He shook out a kerchief and laid it on the floor within Torbin's reach and carefully placed a platter down on the cloth.

Torbin's mouth began to salivate; vinegary water and dried bread had not really cut it for him. Jadwar put out cold cuts of meat, olives, cheeses, sourdough bread and two small pots of sauce, little silver spoons leaning artfully to the sides.

Even in his ravenous state Torbin observed the courtesies, not willing to let Jadwar see his reduced condition.

"Please Torbin, I realise that they have hardly fed you. No need to stand on ceremony with me."

He did not need a second invitation, eschewing all decorum and cramming handfuls of food into his mouth at a time. Jadwar just sat silently, patiently letting Torbin eat his fill.

After a few minutes of gorging himself Torbin leaned back, still held uncomfortably by his chains and breathed a satisfied sigh. Jadwar produced a lidded flagon from his basket and held it out to Torbin.

"Ale as well? How did you get all this past the guards?"

"I am Jadwar Sun-blessed, Primary of Lhossa, not a purveyor of meats. I do not need permission." Jadwar wrinkled his nose as if offended by the question. Torbin's ripe aroma may have had something to do with it as well.

Torbin gulped down the ale, finishing it in three swigs, wiping the foam from his mouth with the back of his hand.

"I am sorry Jadwar, I meant no offence but as you can probably imagine I'm not at my best."

"Indeed. The only time I've seen you worse for wear was after Blood-spear gave you a red kiss." Jadwar began packing up the used cloths and flagon, neatly folding the kerchief and placing everything back in the basket.

"Ah, another happy memory," said Torbin, an ironic smirk crossing his features.

"I think we need to talk about the reasons you are in here and if and why I should come to your aid." Jadwar had finished his tidying and obviously meant to address the matter at hand.

"I'm not sure how much you know but I should imagine that you're as well informed as anyone in Lhossa." Stating the obvious didn't seem as trite as it may have done in different circumstances and acknowledging Jadwar's position of strength was a small but clever concession. Torbin could not help but notice the tiny self-satisfied twitch of his lips, not quite a smile but a good start.

"The H'daree are real Jadwar, and they are coming. If they breach the Titan Gate or Sardis forbid, gain control of it unopposed then there may be no force strong enough to stop them. Possibly the Protectorate could hold them but by then the Free Territories will have fallen, Lhossa included, and they would have unfettered access to all the resources available. My understanding is they move as a nation, millions strong and are patient, happy to bide their time, reinforce and build up their numbers so that they can overwhelm." Torbin glanced across at Jadwar and knew he had his full attention.

"But if we can hold them at the Gate, we could pen them in the Green-lands, deny them access to the Territories. They would be hard pressed to force a naval incursion to the south with the Brotherhood of the Golden Hand owning the southern seas beyond the Cape of Lost Hope. If they did then their only landfall would be the southern shores of the Murgan grasslands. You know the Hoard would easily be raised for something of that magnitude and not the part hoard that we repelled but the entire mass. Hundreds of thousands of Murgan warriors bearing down on you? I doubt anyone could land a sufficiently large force quickly enough to resist that."

"You make excellent points Torbin but there are holes in your argument. What proof do you provide? A heretic relying on the words of another heretic. You have no evidence, have not witnessed anything yourself, cannot even bring forward anyone who has witnessed any of the events you are talking about." Jadwar gently shrugged his shoulders. "And let us face it, you are basing this on an incursion into the Bountiful Isles, an insignificant archipelago of islands at the far reaches of the Green-lands. Your other proof being propaganda communications from enemy mind-walkers to a mind-walker associate of yours, all of whom espouse heresy. I think you would have to agree from the Senate's point of view you are pulling on a very thin thread. Practically non-existent." Jadwar was not attempting to belittle Torbin, it was something different. More playing the role of opposition advocate, stating the obvious arguments that would be slung like mud at Torbin should he ever come to trial. Clever, make him think more carefully, devise a stratagem, an argument that would have some genuine merit. But where to start?

"Why would the Great Defender have cause to lie? A man, not of Lhossa, that fought to defend the city almost laying down his life in that cause. A man who only survived because of the care and attention of Jadzia Sun-blessed, daughter of His Eminence Jadwar Sun-blessed. A man granted domicile in the third tier of the city, despite not being Jad. A man granted favour by the leading Senate, who has never attempted to leave and has nothing to gain from telling anyone what he believes to be happening?"

"Yes Torbin, that is much better. You must play to the gallery, use your popularity, the high esteem in which you are held by commoners and Jad alike. Cold hard facts will not avail you in this, sentiment however could help you win the day." Jadwar smiled, elegant and graceful as always and more than a little knowing.

"Wait a moment. Cold hard facts? Are you saying that you believe me, that you don't see me as a heretic?" Torbin felt a sudden rush of hope, a drowning man thrown a rope.

"Torbin there is much about me that you know. How could you not when you are my daughter's chosen? But there is also much you do not know." A small, wistful smile crossed Jadwar's face.

"My Father, Jadsur Sun-blessed, Sardis rest his soul was Primary before me. It's a title half earned, half inherited, and he held it until his passing. For over fifteen years from the age of only eighteen I travelled to all corners of the Known World and witnessed many strange and wonderful things. I have stood on the bow of a Snowbard war galley as it skimmed the edge of the Great Storm Curtain and seen the towering black swirl climbing beyond sight directly above me. I have seen slave gladiators in the Hardite arenas battle vast snow tigers and white bears with just daggers and spiked gauntlets, only to be put to death if victorious. Hardly an equitable outcome but such are their customs." Jadwar casually turned his gaze on Torbin. "I have ridden a grassland stallion into battle as part of a Murgan charge, the wind whipping the tall grass into your face as a neighbouring tribe's warriors hurtle towards you. I have watched the Golden Companies of the Kingdom of Darmat stand and face a heavy cavalry charge from the Robber Barons, thousands of armoured horse thundering across the battlefield. I have visited the pleasure palaces of Sarjinn, Minari and Turan and experienced things that would make most grown men dizzy. And I lived in Summerstown for two full turns of the moon and after travelled widely in Protectorate lands." There was no boasting here, more of a fond recollection, a nod to youthful exuberance.

"You lived in the Protectorate?" Not so much a question as a request for confirmation.

"I did indeed and met many mind-walkers, most of whom were fine people, although I've always found the Protectorate people's certainty a little distasteful. The less polite would call it arrogance but I never felt it was any kind of deliberation." Graceful and elegant even in his speech, if a little self-satisfied. Torbin couldn't help but admire him though.

Despite his admiration, the distasteful comment still rankled but Torbin knew when to hold his tongue.

"I am a child of Sardis, make no mistake, but I am not tied down by superstition. I believe in evidence, that gathered by others and observed by my own eyes. I know mind-walkers cannot invade people's thoughts, that it is just a form of communication between two similarly talented people. I know there is no direct threat posed by the practice, but I have also seen the Gift in action. That is what you call it is it not?" Torbin felt a stab of discomfort. This was dangerous territory and what he said could put him in harm's way. Well, more harm than he was already facing.

"We do call it the Gift, although many would view it as a curse."

"That I can believe. I have witnessed what should be impossible. People moving at incredible speeds and some seemingly disappearing from sight altogether. A useful tool to put it mildly. Assassins for instance would have a decided advantage. Would you not agree?" Jadwar had touched on the obvious truth, treading carefully was vital.

"It is true Jadwar, used for personal gain the Gift would be a dangerous tool in anyone's armoury, but the Protectorate does not believe in aggressive behaviour. All of our armed encounters take place to defend our borders and our way of life, we do not seek to conquer or expand our reach. Unless petitioned of course but we will not instigate the process." Torbin's words were carefully considered and measured but he couldn't help but feel a twinge of nerves.

"Is it we now Torbin? Do you not live in Lhossa and reside at the grace of its people? Are your only considerations for the land of your birth, where you haven't lived for more than twenty years? Please do not take me for a fool or some uneducated and ill-informed commoner. The assimilation of northern Partia was hardly by petition, was it? Although presented as such we both know the truth." Jadwar had a point and would not be diverted from it.

"History speaks to itself and the Protectorate does not shy away from the fact that mistakes were made along the way. They are however ones that we try to learn from to ensure we never make them again, but you are correct and it's a shame we all still feel." Even as he said the words Torbin knew that Jadwar was right. He felt as if his chances were diminishing, the balance shifting away from hope and drifting back down to despair.

"Torbin I am not judging your home or your society and the folding of northern Partia into the whole happened two centuries ago. From what I have observed and from histories I have read the Protectorate is probably the most moral and decent society in the

Known World. Every nation has its dark history, its own shameful past. Lhossa most certainly does and to this day has certain practices that grate with some but that was not the reason for my probing." Jadwar's tone was conciliatory, not at all confrontational.

"I don't understand Jadwar." Torbin looked at him with a weary frown, tiredness starting to affect every action he took. He could feel the fog of exhaustion descending like a dark curtain in his mind.

"It is not your society I needed to measure Torbin, it is you. If you had tried to deceive or misdirect, I would not have been prepared to take the risk. A dishonest or duplicitous man is a terrible bet to place." Jadwar gave Torbin a knowing smile. Something he knew at least because Torbin's mind was all at sea. Torbin just looked blankly back at him, a confused shake of his head the best he could muster.

"Torbin, I have welcomed you into my house, never attempting to stand in the way of you and Jadzia but what you are accused of is heresy, punishable by death. I had to be sure, had to be certain that it was worth the cost." Jadwar smiled, much more warmly this time.

"Torbin, I hold you as a son and I will be your advocate."

Torbin heard the words, absorbed them into his soul and collapsed into sleep.

Chapter Twelve:

Into the waste

"How is it a Longspear can be such a short-arse?" Bodger guffawed at his own joke. It was as if he could not remember telling it a thousand times before.

Rat swung her spear, butt end first, catching him a good whack on the back of his head.

Cralie Longspear may have been short, but she was a thousand times quicker than Bodger and she didn't consider her nickname an insult. Rat because she was short certainly but also because she was quick, adaptable and could sneak through most undergrowth unnoticed. Bodger was much more aptly named with a facility for fucking up few could match.

"How is it a Shortsword could a have cock to match?"

Rat whipped her spear back, taking up a half-crouch defensive pose waiting for Bodger to take the few seconds to absorb both the barb and the blow.

"Why you little…!" Bodger almost jumped up, kicking his stool out from under his feet, a nasty snarl fixed to his face. "I'll…"

"Knock it off you two! Always the bloody same, leave you alone for a minute and you're at each other's throats. I am not in the mood for it!" Marisa Longspear stalked into the squad dormitory, serious business written all over her face.

"Sorry Squad, only playing." Bodger or Barri Swortsword, all six and a half feet of scruffy haired charmer leaned over and gave Rat a playful nudge on the arm, Rat replying with a head down smirk.

"Yeah, sorry Squad, just mucking about." Rat stood, arms behind her back, looking for something of interest on the dorm floor.

"Right everyone, gather round. I need to have a word with all of you." Marisa was curt and to the point, wanting to keep this strictly business for now.

The rest of the squad stopped whatever they were doing and gathered round, Mortan Longspear, Lummox as he was affectionately known, almost having to lean down to avoid banging his head on the roof beams. Carlin Longspear or Whisper was tall, slim and apparently aloof, unless you knew him because it was just a quiet shyness. Marta Swortsword, way too attractive to be a full-time vocational soldier, at least that is what Marisa thought. Everyone in the squad called her Fugly, shorthand for fucking ugly, probably the funniest joke they had ever come up with. Jevon Hand-axe or Skin, though nobody had ever found out the origin of that little gem and lastly Cenna Archer, dark skinned, dark eyed and deadly as it came with the bow, always known as Shadow to the squad.

"What's up Squad? Are we in trouble again?" Lummox put on his best innocent little boy face and everyone started to laugh, even Marisa.

"No more than usual Lummox." Marisa smiled back at him

"Remember the debrief a few weeks ago?" Marisa looked around them, as if anyone could forget Tommec but it was still far too fresh for anyone to talk about. Everyone's head went down, nobody prepared to be the first to break the silence.

"Listen I know it still stings but I'm not talking about Tommec. I'm talking about the blades, remember?"

Heads started to lift, the relief of not having to mention Tommec lifting the mood somewhat.

"What about them Squad?" Bodger started the ball rolling.

"Well, I can only remind you what happened to me and how I felt but there is obviously something to them, possibly something important. The thing is, no soul-forged blade has ever been left on the field and the few that have ever fallen into our hands have had to be torn from the cold dead grip of a Snowbard warrior." Marisa looked around them hoping one would pick up the thread.

"So why would three be left on the field and by Wastelanders? Soul-forged blades are only ever wielded by Snowbard warriors. They are well beyond heirlooms, they are the very heart of Snowbard warrior culture, and they would die before they surrendered them." Shadow as always was as sharp as the edge of a knife, always the first to see.

"That is the question and I've been asked to find an answer. I've been given authority to pick a squad to go on a mission into the Wastelands. We don't have any formal lines of contact as well you all know, but you were all there, so you saw as well as me. Something was way off about that contact, it was far too organised, almost military and who's ever seen that? Wastelanders organised and with a battle plan? They are tough as fuck as we all know only too well. But organised? Really?" Marisa looked around them and decided to plunge in, no point dicking about.

"Listen, this is purely voluntary so if you don't want to go nobody will think less…"

"Oh shut the fuck up Squad. As if any of us would let you bugger off without us. You must be going soft in the head." Didn't say much Carlin, but when he did, he made it count.

Everyone stood there and started to bang their spears on the floor, slapping each other on the back, whooping and shouting, "Yeah!" "C'mon!" "Squad Seven!"

"Thank you, I didn't want to put you any further in harm's way, but I'd hate to take a squad out I didn't know." Marisa was beaming. She just couldn't help herself. As much of a pain in the arse as they were, she loved and trusted every one of these reprobates.

"I hate to be the one to bring it up but what about Garic?" Jevon asked.

"What about me?" Garic stood in the doorway smiling, a mischievous look on his dark stubbled face.

"Why you little bastard!" said Lummox, picking him up and spinning him round, the whole squad cheering and taking it in turns to hug him.

"When did you get out?" said Rat, beaming from ear to ear.

"They passed me fit about an hour ago, ready and willing." The smile was glued to his face, so happy to be back with his comrades.

"We're still one down though." Bodger said what they were all thinking, the mood darkening instantly at the thought of going without Tommec.

"And it'll have to be a mind-walker," said Jevon, stating the obvious but it needed to be said.

"Breda Fencer will be coming, but for this mission he will cede field command to me. For the duration he'll be number two, the rest of you the same as always." Marisa waited for the response, uncertain of what the reaction would be.

"Class act that Commander Fencer, stepping aside for this as well, classy. He'll do for me." Shadow voiced what they were all thinking, confirmed by a round of spear butts banging on the floor.

"That's it then. We're setting off at first light and the plan is to try to contact some of the Wasteland tribes to see if we can establish some kind of friendly communication. At the very least, see if we can establish a dialogue. Not all the Wastelanders attack us, or we wouldn't have any trade with them, but we are completely blind going into this. It's vital that we try to find out who was behind the attack or even if it was orchestrated by some other faction." Marisa stepped into the middle of her squad making it feel like a conspiracy.

"The Wolfs-head clan have always had reasonable relations with us, at least as reasonable as Wastelanders get. I know their banners were flying but something didn't feel right about that so we're going to seek them out." Marisa looked around their faces, reassured that no one seemed to baulk at the idea.

"That's all well and good, but where do we start? They don't exactly leave signposts. 'This way to Wolfs-head town'." Marta had a point but that was the task.

"Well, we have Skin with us and let's face it if he can't sniff them out nobody can." Marisa slapped Jevon on the back while everyone else grunted their assent. Skin was born in the frozen north after all, even though he was small for a Wastlander.

"I've got some ideas," he said thoughtfully.

"First I ever heard of it." Rat shuffled away from Skin, giggling and avoiding a clump. Everyone else smiled and laughed while Skin just flipped her the finger.

"Alright, let's start prepping. Full winter gear, full rations and weapons sharp and ready." Marisa looked at each of them in turn, confident and proud at the same time.

"Squad!" was shouted back at her in unison.

Marisa left the dorm, and everyone set about their gear, Skin and Rat heading off to the armoury to get a head start on weapon sharpening.

Lummox and Shadow went to Garic, sitting perched on the end of his cot.

"How's the chest, Newbie?" Lummox patted him on the back nearly knocking him to the floor, heavy handed would be something of an understatement.

"Not too bad all things considered." Garic gave him a friendly punch on the arm in return. Like hitting a tree.

"Let's have a look then." Shadow nodded at his shirt just to make sure he understood.

Garic lifted his shirt over his head, his muscles gently tensing as he pulled his sleeves over his hands. The bruising had turned a dull yellowy brown and covered almost his whole torso, waist to neck. On his sternum the outline of the war-hammer was visible in a thin almost healed scab.

"Nice imprint, you should get that tattooed permanently as a reminder not to behave like a total prick." Shadow smiled as she said it but Garic still felt like a naughty schoolboy. She had a way about her that was for sure.

She leant forward and cradled his face in her hands. "We've grown quite fond of you Newbie and we're not ready to lose you just yet." She planted a gentle kiss on his forehead, got up and walked away. Garic could have sworn there was a little moistness around her eyes.

Garic shot Lummox a look but he just shrugged. Bodger flopped down on the cot next to Garic and gave him a little nudge.

"So, what's that then? You building up a harem or something?" Lummox nearly fell on the floor laughing and despite himself Garic joined in.

"I'm not sure Bodge. I think everyone's just a bit tender after what happened and just happy it didn't turn out worse." That brought the laughter quickly to a stop, the thought of Tommec hanging in the air even without mentioning his name.

"For what it's worth, Newbie, we're all pretty glad you made it." Strange coming from Bodger but welcome none the less.

"Here, here." Lummox nodded in agreement.

"Who else would we have to take the piss out of?" Bodger grabbed hold of Garic, bundling him to the floor, playfully digging him in the ribs, Lummox unable to stop himself joining in.

"Will you children stop messing about and give a hand getting the kit ready?" Marta stood there, hands on her hips looking like a disapproving teacher.

"Sorry Fugs, right away." Bodger smirked knowing full well that Marta wasn't keen on her nickname, let alone the abbreviated version.

"Grow up, you fucking idiot," she shot back, placing a hefty kick to his backside. Bodger just laughed all the more, Lummox and Garic unable to stop themselves joining in until even Marta added to the chorus.

"C'mon, seriously though. We've got to get the sleds ready and pack the rations."

They got up and followed her out to the winter stores.

The next morning, they were prepared and ready to depart. They had two sleds, hand drawn as horses simply couldn't operate in the far north, too cold, with snowdrifts far too deep. They'd packed one of the sleds with rations, dried and salted meats and fish, dried cheyro powder to make hot drinks and plenty of tubers. On the other they had utensils, five three-man tents, spare weapons, snowshoes, a grinding whetstone and furs to trade with.

Autumn was starting to settle in, the weather turning a little colder, but it wouldn't matter once you'd really entered the northern Wastelands. It was always winter there.

The squad were drawn up in line, weapons slung on the sleds, warm weather gear on except for one. Skin would go shirtless if permitted, a consequence of having grown up a Wastelander but for proprieties sake he had at least worn one today. Also, Marisa was fairly sure the old man would frown upon it and Major Dragoon would cite him for some kind of uniform infraction.

Master General Oleb Archer had come out to see them off, flanked as usual by Major Dragoon and Captain Potter.

"Squad leader Longspear, all prepared and ready for the off?" The old man was looking as good as ever, that natural way of leading never deserting him.

"Yes sir, I think we're about as ready as we're ever likely to be." Marisa smiled back, always feeling lifted just by being in the old man's presence.

"Well, if you're not sure perhaps you should cede command to Commander Fencer, Longspear?" Major Dragoon's snipe was not unexpected, but why couldn't he just shut the fuck up for once.

"I'm a volunteer foot soldier for this mission, Major sir. I would not presume to step on Squad Leader Longspear's toes or pretend that she was not the best person for the job." Marisa could've kissed Breda at that moment, jumping in before she said something she'd truly regret.

"Well, the suitability remains to be seen." He just could not resist, a real last word hogger.

"Does that mean you're questioning my command decision Stevan?" The old man turned to face Major Dragoon; eyebrows raised for full effect.

"Not at all sir, just suggesting the possibility that a non-commissioned officer may lack the range of experience required for a mission of this magnitude." Trying to wriggle off the hook, using long words as usual, thought Marisa.

"Well, I intend to resolve that Stevan before we go any further." The old man turned deliberately away from Major Dragoon, leaving him standing open mouthed.

"Squad leader Longspear, I am conferring the rank of First Centurion on you." He reached inside his jacket and pulled out a rolled paper tied with a ribbon and wax sealed with the stamp of Army Group Partia.

Marisa's mouth hung gaping open, a look of genuine bewilderment covering her face. "Sir I don't know what to say." Her eyes started to well up and she had to force the tears back down.

The old man stepped forward putting his hands on her shoulders "Marisa you have earned this a hundred times over and would have received it years ago if you could just stop getting into fixes. You are ready or I would never have given you this command.

Just make me proud and don't make me regret it."

"Congratulations Marisa." Breda took Marisa's hand warmly, a genuinely pleased smile on his face.

"Well done Marisa." Captain Rander Potter patted Marisa on the shoulder smiling warmly.

"Longspear." Major Dragoon gave a curt nod, turned on his heels and marched briskly back towards barracks.

Marisa turned back to the old man, stood bolt upright and gave a salute.

"Squad attention!" she bellowed out, all of them falling into ranks, snapping out perfect salutes, Breda joining in as if he were a mere foot soldier.

"Good hunting Centurion Longspear. Good hunting to you all." The old man flourished his own impeccable salute, turned on his heels with Captain Potter at his back and marched back to barracks.

Marisa visibly relaxed for about a second then was engulfed by the whole squad, beaming, laughing, hugging and backslapping, buoyed by the turn of events.

"Okay, thanks you lot but let us remember what we're here for. First sled teams harness up, change out on the hour. Let's get to it then." Marisa barked out the order to move just wanting to get underway, return to a bit of normality.

"Yes sir!" They all called back at her and then it started to sink in.

"Fuck! This'll take some getting used to."

Chapter Thirteen:

The long wait

It was the tenth day in a row that it had rained. Not just rain, it was teeming down, vertical, relentless oceans of water pouring down like the tears of great titans, engulfing everything. It was making the digging of fire pits extremely difficult, keeping the tinder dry almost impossible but if they were to stand any chance they couldn't ease up.

They had built wooden redoubts every two hundred yards, miniature forts, one on either side of the valley leading up to the earthwork. Between the earthworks and the mouth of the Pass behind them they had built a maze of pits, filled with spikes and effluence, making the way impassable. If the enemy breached the defences, they would have to fight their way through the city streets to reach the Pass. Forward of the rampart, fire pits had been dug and filled with wooden spikes and caltrops, covered with wood, straw and tinder, vats of oil standing ready to pour. Harass and fall back, abandoning one redoubt at a time, then lighting the pits funnelling the enemy narrower and narrower into a kill zone. Hopefully negate their numbers or at least cause enough loss to make them reconsider.

It was the only plan they had, and it was paper thin at that, what with so many of their finest already lost but what else could they do? Only two hundred of the Water Spears had returned, two hundred out of fifteen hundred? It still didn't seem possible, the sheer overwhelming speed and force of the attack brushing them aside. He had only witnessed the final fall of the Isle of Grace, but it was enough to make him despair. And then instead of pushing on they just stopped as if satisfied for now, as if it were time to rest and recuperate.

That was more than three full turns of the moon ago.

"Candor. Candor are you alright?" Willet looked at him as if he was scared he had passed away.

"I'm fine Will, just thinking." Candor pulled his hood up a little more, shaking off some of the excess water. He'd forgotten how young Willet looked but he was still a big lad and it had been difficult finding armour to fit. "What seems to be the problem Will?"

"Brownleaf's back."

"How is he?"

"A little worse for wear. Apparently, he struggled getting away and had to go to ground. But considering what he's been through he's holding up well." Willet nodded towards the Turan end of the rampart. "He's in the end fort being checked out by the medics and getting some food inside him."

"Okay Will, I need to speak to him. You've got command, keep your eyes open." Candor clapped him on the back and set off along the top of the rampart. They'd done a remarkable job throwing it up, twenty feet high and ten feet deep with a good solid wooden palisade to the front. If you took into account the murder pit dug along its front another twenty feet wide and ten feet deep, it made a formidable defensive wall. But Candor knew it was still only made of soil and he'd seen what they were going to face so his hope was only a hair's breadth thick.

Everything was against them, the fact that Willet was now an officer spoke to the sheer volume of the Water Spears that had been lost. Only two hundred got out alive! Most of those that were lost were officers and veterans, brave souls who'd tried to stand to buy time for others to escape. However on open ground against the H'Daree's sheer numbers and not inconsiderable skill they stood no chance. Willet had less than two years' service and was only twenty-one, but he now counted as a senior trooper.

Candor stopped and leaned on the parapet. He looked along the length of the rampart, running from Minari's wall to the south crossing in front of the mouth of the Pass to Turan's wall in the north. It looked solid and strong, a formidable line of defence but they only had two hundred trained soldiers to man it and the twin cities walls. Retired soldiers and every male citizen capable of wielding a weapon had been pressed into service but they only had enough metal for three thousand as it stood. The forges were working as hard as they could to put steel in every defender's hands, but even with that in mind he doubted they could stand for long.

He had split the remaining Water Spears up, fifty to each city wall and a hundred to man the rampart, spreading them across the line to bolster the untrained. He'd posted archers on the three palisade forts, one at either end and one in the middle of the earthworks, plus some on the city walls and a few of the hardiest in the furthest redoubts. Loose two volleys, light the fire pit and withdraw to the next redoubt. Strangely the one thing they didn't lack for were arrows, unfortunately the same couldn't be said for archers. There was little else he could think of to do apart from wait.

It was such a slim hope however well planned and prepared for. He took in a long slow breath and gazed at the twin cities knowing he may not get that many more chances. They were beautiful to look at, both enclosed by circular walls, originally growing in opposition to each other but ending up being almost mirror images. The stonework was nearly all white granite, the slated roofs a rich earthy red. In the summer with the sun high in the sky the buildings appeared to shine, glistening in the warmth of the heat, but now in this incessant rain they looked sad and forlorn, more grey than white.

In his heart he knew they stood no chance but convincing the Grandees and rulers of the need for evacuation had been an almighty struggle. In the end a compromise had been reached and all women, children and the elderly had been moved far behind the lines, close to the mouth of the Pass and ready to move at a moment's notice. It offered him some small comfort to know Marye and the children were at least out of immediate danger.

He hunched his shoulders against the wind and upped his pace along the rampart, eager to talk to Brownleaf, hoping against hope for some shred of encouraging news.

As he approached the fort, he thought about the last time he'd seen him, sending him and five other scouts to reconnoitre the enemy. He was the first and only to return. Candor liked him enormously probably because he was a bit of a rogue, a real poacher turned gamekeeper. But he was the best woodsman Candor had ever seen and could disappear in the blink of an eye. Just what was needed, especially as there was not much in terms of intelligence on the H'Daree. He'd witnessed them himself but hadn't exactly had the time to study them closely

Candor ducked into the fort through the rampart gate and walked across its small inner yard to the only rooms inside it. He couldn't help but smile as he crossed, looking up at the elevated walkways, manned by three Water Spears. He gave them a cursory wave before entering the small wooden keep tucked under Turan's wall.

Brownleaf was sat at a table, the medic having finished his ministrations. Candor was a little shocked at the state of him, head wrapped in a thick bandage, blood already slowly seeping through. His clothes were dishevelled, and he seemed to be almost completely covered in nicks and bruises, his black hair pointing in all directions but he still beamed his toothy smile as he saw his commander stride towards him.

"How are you Brownie?" Candor clasped his arms giving him a warm shake, happy to see that to all intents and purposes he seemed little the worse for wear.

"I'm fair to middling Candor. Glad to be back amongst my own and away from them." He almost spat 'them' out as if the word was poison.

"Tell me everything you can and take it slow and easy. It looks like you've been through hell." Candor took up a more relaxed pose hoping to put Brownleaf at ease or at least relieve his tension.

"Well, all six of us set off together and then we split into pairs just past Hookers Lake. Skeeve and Roughneck were going to hug the shoreline, try to get as close to their Palisade as possible and see if they could get a read on their naval strength. Motley and Crander were going to skirt the eastern shore of Hookers and creep up through the Red Wood, climb the trees see if they could get a good look over the wall. That palisade stretches from the shore to the edge of Bolders Forest, but it's not built that tall, only thirty feet or so. Me and Quinlan were going to make our way round the outside of Bolders, hug the edge of the Titans and try to get around the side of them, catch a good look at what they were up to. It took us about two days, travelling at night and laying low during the day but we managed to get around the end of their wall unseen. Or so we thought." Brownleaf's shoulders sagged his chin dropping to his chest.

"What is it Brownie, what happened?" Candor reached out and gave his arm a squeeze.

"Well, the Beckoner had his fill of us that day I can tell you." Brownleaf's eyes began to mist up.

"Take your time son, take your time." Candor moved to sit next to Brownleaf, putting a friendly arm around his shoulder.

"We'd crept up to the treeline, nice, slow and careful. No one would have seen us unless they were staring at one spot for ages. We put about two hundred yards between us so that we could get a more complete view. I've got to say what they've done already is amazing. They've already started to build communities, houses, barns, jetties where fishing boats were tied up. We could see a bridge on the far side of the Isle of Grace, and one connected to the shoreline both joined by a paved road. There were dry docks where ships were being constructed and I'm not certain but what looked like siege engines and these strange giant yolks. I probably saw them wrong but that's what they looked like at least. Struck me as pretty odd though." Brownleaf took a deep breath as if steeling himself against some unseen horror. Or in this case one seen.

"That's when it began. A troupe of soldiers led by what could only be described as a priest of some kind began to walk towards the treeline. There was something right odd about him, like he had a dark aura. You couldn't see his face at all, full-length black hooded robe he was wearing, covered everything. I couldn't even see his feet. The soldiers were formed in a kind of circle or so I thought until they stopped about fifty feet from us. It goes without saying we were well camouflaged; we were woodsmen after all and neither of us was moving a muscle." Brownleaf seemed to be tensing up, his voice getting tighter as if he was afraid to carry on.

"Do you want to take a minute Brownie?" Candor was

concerned for his condition now, almost certain he could see him starting to shake slightly.

"No, no I'm okay, I just want to get it out and be done with it." He breathed in deeply and ploughed on.

"Well, the hooded man, priest, whatever you want to call him, he called out 'Is this what you're looking for?' and they opened up and on their knees in the midst of them were Motley, Crander, Skeeve and Roughneck." Brownleaf's shoulders began to jump as a breathless sob escaped his lips.

Candor pulled him in tight. "Alright son, it's okay."

"The bastards, they just sawed through their necks, big, serrated knives, no warning." He gasped out the words, tears rolling down his cheeks. "The screams, all gurgling, trying to catch a breath…" Sobs racked his body as Candor tried forlornly to comfort him

"What happened after that Brownie?"

"Standard innit? Two of you either in or close to contact, split and run. I lost sight of Quinlan and belted back through Bolders. I only just managed to evade them, but it took four days and a lot of eating dirt and hiding in places you simply wouldn't want to know." Brownleaf sagged so far, that he nearly slid to the floor, Candor catching him and helping him to a cot in the corner. The release of telling someone took the last ounce of energy out him and he was asleep before his head hit the pillow.

"Fucking savages!" Candor spat the words out, rage coursing through his veins.

"Savages you say? Candor Blackheart you of all people should understand the benefits of a savage act. Surely the most humane thing to do in any conflict is to bring it to a conclusion as quickly as possible and with the minimum loss of life?"

It had started when they landed but Candor still couldn't get used to the invasiveness of the voices, especially their ability to tune in to his despair or anger. He could block them when he needed to, if he had to sleep or just if he felt like silent contemplation but only if he was concentrating. Otherwise it would always catch him by surprise.

On the plus side, however, it had given him an insight into their culture and torrents of information about their history. There was no boasting or propaganda going on here, not in a deceptive sense at least. It was more a case of laying their cards on the table, telling him facts of their past conquests, letting him know what was to come. It was all still littered with their own dogmatic idealism, however they dressed it up as some great deliverance. "How can humanity attain the H'Dar unless we come together as one?" Nonsense, just another mad religious sect espousing their version of an idyllic afterlife, their picture of paradise. He had seen fanaticism many times before and this was just as bigoted, just as hateful. We promise you heaven but will send you to hell unless you agree with us, ridiculous.

"Your version of humane does not sit well with me. Where's the humanity in summary executions, especially ones fomented with such vicious intent. Putting brave souls to such a terrifying violent death is as inhumane as it gets." Candor still couldn't quite get used to these mind-walker exchanges, never seeing the face he was conversing with and knowing that it was rarely the same person. What was truly unsettling is that whoever he exchanged with carried on as if it were the same conversation he'd been having from the start, just picking up the thread as if nothing had changed.

"Really Candor? Do you suppose we are unaware of how you earned the name Blackheart? Would not the firing of just one Brotherhood galley have been sufficient? Was the burning to death of thousands of the Golden Hands men really needed when all they were doing was trying to withdraw? Could you not have captured those that abandoned ship to escape the flames? Did you have to kill them all? You see we understand, a message had to be sent that the consequences were so dire that it would be folly to ever try again." Candor could feel a self-satisfaction behind the words, a condescending 'I told you so' aimed at his very soul. *"We believe it would be a mercy if the loss of four brave souls saved tens of thousands. You felt it reasonable to kill thousands to save tens of thousands, is our solution not far more equitable? Strange that you only mention four when you know that five of your scouts never returned. Are you not concerned for young Quinlan? A brave young lad indeed, he did not give up any information without a great deal of encouragement."* In his mind Candor could see a smirk on the face of his enemy, like a cat toying with a mouse, having fun before going in for the kill.

"Is he still alive?"

"For now."

Anger welled up in Candor but he knew it would be a pointless exercise to vent it.

"Drawing comparisons is all well and good but there is a world of difference between defending your way of life and invading someone's sovereign soil." He needed to change the subject, put them on the backfoot.

"Sovereign soil, that is such a quaint expression. We believe the whole world is the sovereign soil of the H'Daree and that everybody else are merely squatters. You know our purpose and we will fulfil it. I'm afraid to say that your pitiful attempt to resist us will not avail you. Earthworks, sharpened sticks and any man capable of holding a blade? Why do you resist? We only wish to unite the world, bring all of mankind together so that we can ascend to a higher plane. We do not demand that you change your customs or your way of living, just that you accede and follow us."

Candor could sense the same thing as always, an almost religious fervour, a sense of undeniable righteousness. He put up his blocks. He'd heard enough from the H'Daree for now.

He walked out of the fort and back up onto the rampart, looking out across the valley floor. It was the waiting and the incessant rain dragging at his last reserves of endurance. Nobody alive could ever remember weather like this enduring for so long, not a hint of clear skies. It was almost as if the H'Daree had brought the rains with them, but he knew how ridiculous that sounded.

Still, it somehow felt like more than a coincidence, as if some unknown power were willing it, putting up as many obstacles as possible.

Whatever was happening one thing was certain. At some point they would have to face an onslaught and from what he'd witnessed, defeat seemed inevitable. The only hope was that the fire pit strategy would work, funnel them into a narrow enough gap that manoeuvre would become almost impossible. Trap them using their huge numbers against them. His nerves were starting to fray, the endless rain, the endless waiting.

He knew they were coming but when?

Chapter Fourteen:

The way back

Blackness was all he could remember as far back as his memory stretched. A deep all-consuming blackness, empty and devoid of anything but himself, floating alone in a sea of nothingness. So quiet and peaceful, no cares or concerns, just himself and the void, the endless blackness.

Through the blackness he could see a tiny dot of white, another world? A sense of familiarity gripped him. *"There was something else, what was it?"* The thought felt fuzzy, as if something were affecting his balance. *"What's balance? What am I forgetting?"*

Something stirred in the back of his mind, something locked away and hidden somewhere safe. *"Did I not put it there on purpose? Was it supposed to remind me?"*

The dot grew bigger. Not by much but enough to draw his attention. He swam through the void towards the light, a mild yearning tugging at him, pulling him closer.

He could make out something new, a sound. At least that's what he thought it was, not being certain what the word meant. In the void words were meaningless.

"Jonoh."

There it was again, the word. It felt familiar but what did it mean? He swam towards the word, the strange elation of something new, something different. He felt something, an emotion, a feeling, pulling him upwards towards the light. It was loss.

"Jonoh."

The voice was more insistent, an urgency lay behind it, a plea. He swam towards it, intrigued, wanting to see for himself, experience this new sensation.

"Jonoh."

The voice was stronger now, more like a lifeline than an appeal for help. It felt like a soul reaching out as if someone were trying to rescue him.

"But why would I need to be rescued from the void? It surrounds me and comforts me. It holds me up and keeps me free from harm." The thought pleased him, and he started to float serenely back down into the warm embrace of the void, safe and happy, free of responsibility.

"JONOH!" The voice was urgent now, begging for help, depending on him, needing him. A sense of belonging swept through him, spearing him upwards towards the light. A shape appeared in the middle of the light, it looked familiar, he'd seen this before in another time, another place. It was a hand.

He knew there was something he needed to do but he couldn't remember what it was. It was so much easier to float away on the nothingness, be carried along in all-consuming peace and quiet.

"JONOH!" Louder, more insistent, more needy than before *"PLEASE JONOH!"* The hand, grasp the hand. Then he reached out.

"Jonoh, are you alright? Can you hear me?"

Jonoh slowly opened his eyes. The light was so bright, almost blinding. He shaded his eyes with his hand, taking a couple of seconds to adapt and focus. A familiar face, wrinkled and smiling slowly came into focus.

"Master Cerwin." Jonoh's voice piped out like a little boy's, unable to hold down his excitement.

"Yes Jonoh, welcome back." The old shadow-master smiled down at his pupil, a look of pure relief washing over his exhausted features.

Jonoh tried to lift himself up on his elbows but pain lanced through his body making him shudder and collapse back on the mattress.

"Take it slowly Jonoh. You have been beyond our reach for ten days. I was beginning to think we would never get you back."

Cerwin sat perched on the bed and Jonoh realised he was shattered, his features grey and drawn.

"Jonoh, we have all been so very concerned and Master Cerwin has not left your side since we found you passed out with the blades." Master Ardend stepped into view, Jonoh still struggling to acclimatise to normality.

"I don't understand," said Jonoh, the tiredness he felt almost overwhelming him. "What happened?"

"Well, we broke down the door when we could not get an answer from you. We had left things for a few hours, thinking you would come out when you were ready, but I could not get a sense of you or of the Gift, so we had to take matters into our own hands. When we finally managed to put the door through, we found you lying on your side on the floor with your arms stretched out over your head, as if you were clinging onto something. Since then, I have been reaching through the Gift trying to find you, or at the very least trying to contact your conscious self." Cerwin looked relieved as well as shattered and he nearly slipped off the bed, Master Ardend catching his fall.

"I feel exhausted and drained, like I've been fighting or running. I can't think clearly, everything seems so muddled." Jonoh felt useless, as if he'd let everyone down, especially Master Cerwin.

"I cannot imagine what you have been through Jonoh but the only food you have had is soup we have been able to spoon-feed you and that does not amount to much. We both need rest and sustenance then we will talk. For now, rest my boy." Cerwin patted the side of his head and Jonoh felt safe for what seemed like the first time in ages and sleep took him.

It was two days later before Jonoh had recovered enough to get out of bed. The soreness that he felt still lingered but he was glad to be up and about again. He had made his way back to the great dining hall and was waiting in an antechamber off to the side. It was small with a table and chairs, a small hearth in which someone had already kindled a fire and a neat little bay window. Jonoh had sat down straight away as even the walk across the yard felt tiring, his body taking time to properly regain its strength.

Master Cerwin entered, still looking a little wan but far

healthier than the last time they saw each other. Master Ardend was with him and someone Jonoh had not met before. He was a big man, around six foot tall and a little on the rotund side of things but well-built with forearms like ham hocks.

"Jonoh, good to see you looking so much better." Master Ardend grasped his hand in greeting. "This is Master Erik Armourer, here to offer his insight in all matters metallurgical."

Master Erik stepped forward grasping Jonoh's hand in both of his.

"Having experienced those blades first-hand Jonoh I'm mightily impressed you survived your ordeal. I threw up three times examining them." He chuckled to himself at the memory as if it were fondly held and smiled warmly at Jonoh. He liked him instantly.

"As Master Erik said he spent some time examining the blades over the last couple of days, so I thought we may as well learn what he discovered together." Master Ardend beckoned them all to sit down around the table.

"Well, I can tell you this straight away, they are like no other blades I have ever seen. I can't even be sure how they were made or exactly how old they are."

"At least thirteen hundred years," Jonoh cut in.

"Well, I'll defer to you on that one, but I would agree that they are ancient and created using methods that even today with all our accumulated knowledge are still superior to anything we can manage. The edges are razor sharp but will not take a whetstone and I couldn't blunt them with hammer and anvil. What is truly amazing is that I could not melt them down even in our hottest forges." He absentmindedly shook his head, as if saying the words held little sense. "I am not without skill in these matters so there are some things I can tell you. I have never seen a blade that has been folded as many times as these, if I had to guess I'd say thousands of times, even though that doesn't seem possible. If you folded metal that many times it would lose its integrity and you wouldn't be able to forge it but not so with these. Also, there's something beyond my understanding and beyond all scientific logic but I know it's there. There's something other than metal in them, something almost spiritual and I feel ridiculous saying it." He sat open-mouthed as if disappointed in himself for having uttered such drivel.

"I understand your misgivings Erik, I truly do. We are all men of science, all trust in what we can see, measure and gather sustainable evidence but at the same time we must accept that there are some things we may never be able to explain. The mysteries of the Gift and mindwalking may be forever beyond us and appear almost magical. But exist they do. No need to berate yourself for using language that we would normally ridicule; these are unchartered waters in which we swim." Master Cerwin looked around the room and found no dissenting voices.

"Jonoh, if you think you can manage to recall your experience, we are ready to listen." As always with Master Ardend even the difficult requests landed gently. So Jonoh relayed his encounter in all its fantastical glory, not editing or reducing it in any way. When he'd finished, even Master Cerwin seemed taken aback, a condition Jonoh didn't expect to ever see again.

"I consider myself fairly open-minded but that's beyond me. What you witnessed; did it happen already? Is it yet to happen? Did it happen on another world?" The last question hung in the air, everyone almost too afraid to face the implications. "Was any of it real or was it all real?" Master Erik was a master armourer but even he hadn't hit that many nails on the head all at once.

"I can't answer many of those questions with any real certainty but one thing I do know is that the altar room was real, and it happened over thirteen hundred years ago." The memory of it made Jonoh feel woozy and claustrophobic, sweat breaking out on his forehead.

"I believe it was all real, all events that have or will occur. Where is irrelevant, what matters is the fact that it was a trap. Set thirteen hundred years ago specifically for the purpose of capturing Jonoh. It points to a level of power being wielded that is beyond anything anyone has ever heard of. The ability to set a trap in time and lure someone backwards is mind-boggling, but it points to a far more worrying and immediate issue." Master Cerwin was up and pacing across the small room's floor, spinning around every four or five paces.

"It is not just that the blades were there at that particular moment, it was the fact that it was coordinated so precisely. For this to work, the knowledge must have been passed along for over thirteen centuries until the right person, Jonoh, came along. For it to work there must be agents alive now, working towards this purpose. A coincidence that this all happens at the very moment that the H'Daree invade the Known World? I think not." The shadow-master was talking almost as fast as he was pacing, almost thinking out loud, a pure stream of consciousness.

"Someone close knew that by leaving the blades to be captured they would end up back here and they knew the moment when Jonoh would be here because they saw him."

The silence in the room was more powerful than any collective gasp would have been.

"This is all conjecture, Cerwin. We need more than theories; however plausible they sound. We need some form of proof or at least a way of narrowing down the possibilities." Master Ardend was on his feet now as if Cerwin's restlessness was becoming infectious.

"It is not theory, Ardend, it is pure logic. Follow the pattern and the timelines and there cannot be any other explanation. However, I believe we have learnt some very valuable lessons here. As powerful as this force is – and I use a loose term because we do not know if it is a person or persons – I believe that they are limited in using certain aspects of their ability. Otherwise, why not come backwards or forwards in time at their leisure and capture Jonoh themselves? I think we have seen the answer already. Look at what it cost Jonoh to do it once, we very nearly lost him in oblivion forever and the physical toll has been harsh. I believe it is only because of his youthful vigour and extraordinary measure of the Gift that he made it back at all. There is a price to pay for this ability and one that cannot be ignored or overcome."

"If what you are saying is true Cerwin, then the traitor is here, in Fortress Kingshold." Master Erik at least stayed seated, Jonoh didn't think he could cope with following three of them pacing about in such a confined space.

"Traitor is a strong term do you not think? Should we not first discover the causes that led to these actions or if they ever took place at all?" Master Ardend had stopped pacing and stood by the door, hands behind his back. He reminded Jonoh of Philos Scholar.

"No, no Ardend. The word fits because treachery it is, to sell the most powerful asset we have for the coming fight. And believe me that fight is coming, and sooner than any of us want. No Ardend, this is the basest treachery and done deliberately to cause the most confusion and sow the seeds of division. They know distrust will lead quickly to inaction." Cerwin was in full flow now, Jonoh could picture him at a lectern giving a lesson to a room full of willing students.

All these thoughts of school and teachers made Jonoh realise just how far out of depth he felt. He'd only just finished school himself and now he was in the middle of events so momentous that they could shape the future of his world.

"Masters please excuse me but 'the most powerful asset'? I feel like I'm being spoken about as if I am some kind of weapon to be used. It was only a short while ago that I was a schoolboy. I am sixteen years old, not a great general or a master of my vocation. You'll forgive me, but this is all a bit much for me to cope with, especially after my narrow escape. I mean no disrespect, but from now on if you are going to talk about me then include me in the conversation." Jonoh had just enough anger to get the words out but as soon as he had he instantly felt guilty, snapping at three great masters.

"I apologise unreservedly Jonoh, my behaviour is intolerable, please forgive me." Cerwin bowed his head much to Jonoh's amazement, followed instantly by Masters Ardend and Erik.

"Apologies Jonoh, I meant no disrespect." Master Ardend's words were so genuine and heartfelt that Jonoh's sense of guilt ratcheted up a notch or two.

"Forgive me Jonoh." Master Erik almost flourished a full bow before him.

"Masters, you humble me." Jonoh looked at his boots feeling too ashamed to look these grand old men in the eye.

"Jonoh, while my apologies were necessary the fact remains that you are our most powerful weapon. Your measure of the Gift is unprecedented, and I believe it was that combined with your youth that may have saved you." Master Cerwin sat next to Jonoh apparently having paced enough for the moment.

"How so?" Jonoh's interest was piqued as was that of the other two masters, who sat close forming a little circle of intrigue.

"I believe that it was your youthful inexperience that protected you. An older, so-called wiser man, a master for instance would probably have tried to figure his way out of the situation. With you, however, your inexperience aided you because your reaction was based on pure emotion. It was that terrified reaction that released a wave of pure and powerful emotion, your instincts taking over and finding a path of escape. I also believe our enemy underestimated you, giving little credence to your abilities, as raw as they are. Your power is so intrinsically linked to your emotions and your youthful vigour that it bursts in waves, whereas once you learn a greater measure of control some of that ability may be lost. Perhaps we should work on retaining a measure of it and maybe us 'so-called' masters are not quite as wise as we think." Cerwin smiled that wrinkled smile of his while Ardend and Erik nodded their assent.

"One thing we must do, at least for now, is keep what we have discussed between ourselves and the Council. It is an alien feeling to distrust any Protectorate citizen, but if the traitor is here, we must tread carefully. The fact that the plan failed will be a body blow to them and they may be forced to act to create a favourable outcome. What that is and who they are in league with is the great unknown. Admittedly we do not have a great deal to go on, but this is where we stand. Agreed?" Cerwin looked at the others, all of whom nodded their assent.

"There is one other thing we need to address Jonoh."

"What is that Master Cerwin?" Jonoh was feeling drained talking about what happened but knew he had to see it through.

"You spoke of a sense of familiarity with regard to the hooded man's voice." Cerwin sat forward, elbows on his knees, drawing the conspirators closer.

"Yes Master. I don't really know how to explain it. It was such a sense of familiarity, almost as if I were hearing someone else speak with my voice, like a reflection. I just thought it was my own subconscious somehow interpreting what I was hearing, although now I think about it that doesn't feel quite right." Jonoh tried to maintain a calm façade, but he could feel the tension seeping through his pores, unable to shake off the discomfort.

Cerwin reached across and gently laid his hand on Jonoh's shoulder. As always it helped him focus and get control of his fears.

"What do you think it means, Master Cerwin?"

"I do not know Jonoh, but I do have some theories. Let me think about it some more before we talk about it again. For now, let us see what information comes back to us. We have a squad going to investigate how the blades came to be at Seal-breaker Bay and we are waiting for reports from the far east. Until the H'Daree move we do not know what we will be facing."

The masters all acknowledged each other with knowing looks and made their way to the door.

"Trust only those closest to you Jonoh and take the greatest of care," Master Cerwin whispered in his ear as they went to leave the room.

As Master Ardend opened the door there was Barton Logistar, apparently about to knock.

"Masters, Jonoh, we have reports from the far east." He gave an imperceptible bow and smiled at Jonoh.

Chapter Fifteen:

Tried and tested

At least they'd allowed him to bathe and change into fresh clothes, after all they wouldn't want their spectacle ruined by a dishevelled prisoner. The manacles stayed in place though, a shuffling walk creating the appearance of a penitent. They did enjoy a bit of theatre in Lhossa, and the Sun Priests of Sardis were only too happy to oblige.

The trial was to be held in the Golden Amphitheatre, nestled behind the Great Temple of Sardis, easily able to accommodate a thousand people. It was as appropriate a place as any to hold this drama and the conductor of the show would be the one and only Sardon the Meek, First Acolyte of Sardis.

The First Acolyte stood on the steps into the Golden Amphitheatre, resplendent in his orange and red robes, shaven head covered with a red mitred hat. In one hand he held an incense burner, its sickly sweet fragrance inescapable even in the open air. In the other, the Book of Sardis, the holy text from which he derived all his power.

Sardon watched with a self-satisfied smirk as the warrior monks tasked with guarding him guided his shambling steps through the crowd. Torbin knew this would be a vital moment. How the crowd reacted could sway the judgement passed down by the jury of Jads, the need to appease the commoners as always important.

He was shocked at the size of the crowd; many having been

let in from the second level just to witness the trial. There were so many that more than two hundred militia were on duty to hold them back. As he shuffled along, he saw many faces that he knew, especially among the soldiers but plenty in the crowd as well. He couldn't sense any open hostility although few were prepared to keep eye contact with him, most looking at their feet or turning to talk to a neighbour when their eyes met.

As he approached the steps leading up to his place of trial there was Jadran Greycloud, in command of the detachment of militia on crowd duty. Torbin's breath rasped in his throat, his heart picking up its pace in anticipation of his friend's reaction.

Jadran made eye contact, staring straight at Torbin, not looking away for a moment.

"Hail Torbin Pale-skin, The Great Defender of Lhossa!" Jadran bellowed out his greeting, standing rigidly tall, right hand touching his chest in salute. Torbin could have kissed him right there and then. And then it started.

"Hail Torbin Pale-skin!" someone shouted from the crowd. "Bless the Great Defender!" came another. "Torbin the brave!" followed behind it. "Blessed of Sardis!" And then the whole crowd burst into a cacophony of raucous cheers and whistles, all praising and supporting the man they loved. Torbin could feel the tears welling in his eyes but didn't care. He wrenched his arm away from one of the monks and turned to face the crowd, mouthing thank you.

He didn't see it coming, caught up as he was in the moment but the warrior monk he'd slipped away from, punched him viciously in the stomach, doubling him over. Torbin fell to his knees, all the wind sucked out of him but as he looked up through watery eyes, he saw Jadran leap at the monk, lifting him bodily from the floor by the throat. The other monk drew his steel, a long evil-looking blade while several of his fellows descended the stairs from behind Sardon to join the fray.

Jadran's militia ran to his side, all levelling their spears at the approaching monks, the whole situation teetering on the edge of blood.

"Stand down Jadran." Torbin stood holding out his arms, palms out in a gesture of peace. "Stand down my friend please.

Now is not the time." Torbin placed his hands on Jadran's arms willing him to let the monk go. Jadran released his grip on the man's throat, turning around and signalling his men to lower their weapons.

"If you lay hands on my friend again monk, I will fillet you where you stand." Angry cords stood out on Jadran's neck as he spat out his challenge.

"Temper your actions young Jad, do not come between Sardis and his justice." Sardon had descended halfway down the stairs, a look of mild amusement on his face.

"What justice is there in hitting a shackled prisoner? Only a coward's justice." Jadran sneered at Sardon, apparently as fond of him as Torbin was.

"It is not for you to question the will of Sardis, young Jad, for you are not The Chosen. You do not interpret his will or see it carried out and you are not beyond his reach." Sardon raised his voice high enough to be heard above the hubbub. It grated on Torbin's ears, a reedy, scratchy voice, like that of a young man flirting with adulthood. Everything about Sardon was slightly off, his voice, his spindly physique and his fanaticism.

Torbin laid his hand on Jadran's arm, feeling the tension on the cusp of snapping.

"Peace Jadran, peace."

He felt the young soldier's muscles relax a little, enough to know that the worst was over.

Sardon nodded to his warrior monks, flicking his head up the stairs and they grabbed Torbin by the elbows and led him into the Amphitheatre.

"Mind your duties Jadran Greycloud and keep the rabble back." Sardon looked down on Jadran with disdain and a look that said, 'this is not over.'

Torbin crested the top of the stairs and looked down upon the crowd gathered inside the auditorium. It was made up exclusively of Jads, not quite full but at least eight hundred of them. Quite the accolade to have so many in attendance but then he was only too well aware of his own notoriety. He had good relations with most of them but there were a few who still didn't accept an outsider being granted such elevated status. He was still *kulfoldi*, foreigner.

In the centre of the stage there were two lecterns raised up from the floor and off to the side two rows of benches with twelve Jads sat on them. First Acolyte's podium, one for his advocate and of course seats for the jury, as fair and impartial a system as he'd ever witnessed outside of the Protectorate.

"Still based on superstitious shit though, but we have to work with what we have. When in Lhossa…" He smiled to himself in spite of things.

The amphitheatres benches were nearly full spanning out one hundred and eighty degrees around the stage. At the front to the advocate's side, he saw Jadzia sat next to Jadwan. What was surprising was to see Zeena there, probably the only other non-Jad in the place.

The monks walked him down the steps onto the stage floor, all heads turning to see the accused. He was placed in front of the lecterns, manacles hanging down from his hands.

Sardon took his place, standing on his podium scanning the crowd, a look of righteous satisfaction on his face knowing his moment had come.

"Citizens of Lhossa, descendants of Jadvar the Great. We are gathered here today in the light of Sardis, blessed be his name, to determine the guilt or innocence of Torbin Pale-skin." A cruel little smile twisted his lips making him look ever more rat-like."He stands accused of heresy, of being an abomination to the Sun God, a mind-walker." Gasps and tuts whispered around the amphitheatre while Sardon paused for effect.

"As is our custom, laid down through the ages, he has the right of advocacy. Does anyone stand forward on his behalf?" He swept the room with an extravagant flourish of his hands.

"I will stand as his advocate." Jadwar's voice boomed out across the open space as he walked to the other podium. He was resplendent in white and gold robes billowing out behind him as he mounted the lectern. "I am Jadwar Sun-blessed, Primary of Lhossa, descendant of Jadvar the Great and I tell you now there will be no trial!"

There was a stunned silence as if all the assembled voices had been snuffed out. Torbin stood rooted to the spot, confused and staggered. Had he really just heard that?

Shouts went up from the assembled throng and great cheers could be heard from the crowd outside.

Sardon rounded on Jadwar, a rabid look on his face, spittle bubbling from the corners of his mouth. "By what right do you interfere with the righteous application of the will of Sardis Jadwar Sun-blessed?" Sardon's reedy voice spat out of his mouth with a raging venom. "I am the vessel of Sardis and the wielder of justice, chosen to light the path for all Jad to tread!" His voice rose to a pitch almost unnatural, a painful, scratchy sound. "I am the hand of Sardis and I say justice will be served."

"I will not bend to the likes of you, Sardon the Meek!" Jadwar roared back at the priest, powerful and implacable. "I can trace my lineage back to Jadvar himself. My family has helped rule Lhossa for more than a millennium and has sacrificed its lifeblood in defence of its people. Tell me Sardon, what great deeds did your forefathers do? What have you done, other than climb over the backs of others to further your own ambitions? The representative of Sardis you may be, but you will never rise high enough to look down upon me." The weight of his words carried around the amphitheatre, whispered words of assent, nods of approval spreading across the seats like a tide lapping at the shore.

Torbin could sense a groundswell of accord, the assembled Jads warming to Jadwar's words. Something else was going on here, another purpose being fulfilled.

"Brothers, harken to me!" Sardon's childish squeal shot into the air and the warrior monks flooded to the front of the stage. They drew their steel as one and advanced towards Sardon and Jadwar, more than forty of them emerging from the crowd. Gasps and outraged shouts went up from the Jads, a few of the men trying to get across the stage to aid Jadwar but they were beaten back and of course none of them were armed. Why would they be?

Torbin was amazed to find himself left unattended so he turned and screamed up the stairs. "Jadran! Jadwar Sun-blessed is under attack!"

Within a couple of seconds Jadran mounted the stairs with more than twenty of his militia at his side and sprinted down to the stage. Jadwar had left his lectern and was backing away towards the rear wall of the amphitheatre when Torbin noticed something odd. He wasn't at all afraid.

Soldiers began to stream onto the stage from behind Jadwar, his personal guard, fully armoured and ready for action. The captain of the guards, Guido Tivosi, six and a half feet tall and built like a raging bull, stood to the front. With his red-plumed helmet and polished, gilded armour he looked like a titan from the age of myths. He wielded a double-headed axe, the blade twinkling in the sunlight, a predator's set making him seem ever more deadly.

The warrior monks stopped in their tracks forming a defensive circle around Sardon, slowly edging backwards.

"Jadson, leave a hundred men to hold the entrance and bring everyone else now." Jadran ordered his subordinate up the stairs. "Hold the line!" he bellowed out to his men, who moved forward, spears lowered towards the retreating monks.

Torbin took a moment to adjust to the situation. It had all been a set-up, a ruse to lure Sardon away from the temple and the rest of his acolytes. Jadwar had relied on Sardon's arrogance and the fact that he'd want to keep all the glory for himself. Spilling blood in the temple of Sardis would be a step too far even for someone as powerful as Jadwar but out here in the open? A clever trap and it was about to snap shut around Sardon.

Torbin felt used, Jadwar's advocacy just a tasty morsel to bait the trap but given the circumstances he wasn't going to complain.

Around a hundred more of Jadran's men poured down the stairs, fanning out to encircle the warrior monks. In the middle of their defensive circle stood Sardon, drained of what little colour his already pallid skin carried. His eyes nervously flickered in all directions, the realisation that he was surrounded and trapped sinking deeper and deeper into his fevered mind.

"You would desecrate this place with the blood of the holy, Jadwar?" Sardon screeched out his words, his fear raising his voice another almost impossible octave.

"This is not holy ground Sardon, and you are far from holy, false priest." Jadwar's response was smooth and level, borne from a certainty of success. He smiled, almost but not quite benignly at Sardon, holding out his hands in a conciliatory gesture. "Sardon, you are surrounded and outnumbered at least five to one. There will be no escape here, only unnecessary bloodshed, do not sacrifice your followers for a lost cause. Have your monks lay down their arms and surrender yourself and none shall be harmed."

Sardon began to sway, eyes closed, head tilted back, and arms spread wide. He started to spout what could only be described as gibberish to Torbin's mind, an incantation to Sardis. His warrior monks lifted up their arms in praise, inebriated smiles crossing their faces as if they had just turned out of the Cleaver after a night's revelry.

Sardon flung his arms out wide and screamed out his words, cursing all who offered him opposition. "Let Sardis's hand guide you, my children. Be not afraid, strike down the infidels and if you fall you shall rest in the embrace of Sardis himself this night!"

The lead monk, Brother Saul, Torbin thought he'd heard him called, shouldered past his fellows and stood forward in front of Guido Tivosi. Tivosi accepted his challenge with a shrug and leapt forward swinging his great axe with incredible speed, swiping hard at waist level. Saul caught his axe on the edge of his blade, sliding sideways like molasses, smooth and sweet. He counter swung, Tivosi ducking under his slice and countering with an overhand right. Torbin watched fascinated, thinking how well matched they were but feeling certain who would triumph. And as quick as a thought it happened.

Tivosi dropped his hands and waited for Saul to strike, swivelling around and deliberately taking the sword stoke on his vambrace. He reversed his axe in his hands shoving the spiked tip into Saul's stomach and wrenched the point upwards, opening him from naval to throat. As he slumped forward open-mouthed his guts sliding out to the floor, Tivosi just shouldered him off and ploughed into the rest of the monks. The rest of Jadwar's household guard closed from the front while Jadran's militia lowered their spears and closed from behind. It was over in minutes, the unarmoured monks a pitiful match for such heavily protected opponents. All were killed apart from Sardon who knelt quivering in the middle of his dead followers, wild-eyed and covered in their gore.

"Sardis will strike you down for this blasphemy Jadwar Sun-blessed, you have forever tainted your family's name." Sardon spat the words out, the last defiant rant of a man about to die.

"That's as maybe Sardon but it will be Sardis and Sardis alone who decides my fate not some snivelling little social climber who has people executed on a whim. Your sadism couldn't be obscured by any amount of piety no matter how hard you tried. The days of people living in fear of voicing opposition to you are done with. Your fanaticism and brutality are over and the cost is already too high." Jadwar cast his face around the corpses strewn across the stage. "These men died because you poisoned their minds with your dogmatic rhetoric, your narrow interpretation of the holy text. Well, no more shall follow you or follow them to a pointless death."

"You talk about the text, Jadwar, but choose to ignore it. The Book of Sardis is the word of Sardis and cannot be gainsaid by you or anyone else. Do with me as you will but your punishment will come, and it will be brutal and just. It is written that mind-walkers are abominations and should be removed from existence." Torbin watched as this pitiful, vile little man knelt there still espousing his beliefs, full of hateful conviction.

"You should study the text a little closer Sardon. It says 'The unwelcomed invasion of someone's mind by another is a crime punishable by death.' Unwelcomed invasion. If you knew anything about the true nature of mind-walkers, you would know that they cannot read the minds of anyone but other mind-walkers. They cannot read the minds of those without this talent so cannot launch an unwelcome invasion of anyone other than another mind-walker. Your charge is baseless and unsubstantiated and for this false trial and false imprisonment of Torbin Pale-skin you shall face the consequences. The deaths of your monks are on your hands and your hands alone."

Torbin looked around not quite able to believe what he'd just witnessed. "Torbin let me help you." Jadran had taken the keys from the dead monk and undid Torbin's manacles, hand and feet. He suddenly felt so much lighter that he almost lost his balance, readjustment to the reduced load taking a second or two.

"Thank you Jadran. Your loyalty leaves me humbled and speechless." Torbin took his friend's hands in his and bowed touching his forehead to Jadran's fingers.

"Torbin please, there is no need." Jadran withdrew his hand, his face flushed red with embarrassment.

"I told you at the Gate that I would be asking much more of you Jadran. Well, I'm asking you now if you will come with me to defend the Titan Pass from what is coming?"

Jadran clasped Torbin's forearm with his outstretched hand. "I have followed you whenever you have called Torbin, and I will not stop now."

Torbin couldn't help but beam a grateful smile at his friend. *"That's a good start."*

Chapter Sixteen:

Looking for clues

Sometimes compasses could get twitchy when you ventured far enough north, something to do with the magnetic poles or so Marisa had heard. Some may have said that it didn't really make a whole lot of difference seeing as how they didn't know where they were going anyway. Either way, making contact was going to be difficult. The Wolfs-head clan had been the most approachable Wastelanders Marisa had ever known but that was only if they approached you first. She'd spoken with them a few times when they'd come down to trade and even had an evening drinking round the fire with a couple of their warriors once. That was some kind of hangover, it made her head sore just thinking about it.

As always Lummox did sled duty on his own, pulling the two-man harness over his shoulders, complaining that sharing the load was a "pain in my arse!" because his pulling partner kept getting under his feet. Rat and Bodger had the other sled, inseparable as always and as always bickering like children.

"Why I have to be paired with a big ox like you is beyond me, constantly stumbling about, treading on my feet and farting like you're getting paid for each one." Rat hawked a gob of spit off to the side, grumbling away, firing acidic glares at Bodger.

"Will you stop fucking moaning? It's not like anyone can smell anything in this cold anyway, and it helps keep my arse warm. As for standing on your feet, it's difficult not to when I'm the one doing most of the work." He smiled that smile at her, the one he knew always got under her skin. She aimed a kick at his shin but caught her snowshoes together and stumbled face first into the snow. Bodger guffawed, holding his sides as if scared something important may slip out so Rat aimed a sly punch at his cock, bedlam.

"Will you two just leave it alone for two fucking minutes!" Marisa had had enough.

"Sorry sir, only playing," Bodger said whilst cupping his balls. "Sorry sir, just breaking up the monotony." Rat brushed off her breeches whilst getting upright.

"Sir? This is going to take more getting used to than I thought."

"Okay, let's take a rest and get some food into us. We must have been at it for five or six hours by now." Although how would you know trudging through this endless white was a thought that came to mind, but Marisa suppressed the urge to voice it.

The Wastelands were well named, great swathes of ground with hardly any vegetation or even out-croppings of rock. You could travel for over a hundred miles before encountering any trees or animal life although Shadow had managed to bag a couple of small deer. It amazed Marisa that anyone could see these white deer let alone bag them but Cenna was uniquely gifted, seemingly with the eyesight of a hawk.

They unpacked the cooking gear, tripod, pots and put up a windbreak, something to get half comfortable behind and settled to the task.

"So how much longer do you think we should stay on this course, Marisa? Apologies, sir. I forget my place sometimes." Breda Fencer looked across at Marisa sheepishly, still finding it hard to adjust to life as a foot soldier.

"Don't apologise please Breda. I need a little reminder of normality after eight days straight of white nothingness." They had held to a northeasterly course, hoping at some point to pick up some hunting tracks or sign of encampment, but as of yet, nothing.

"I think we'll have to consider cutting back south and east at some point soon bnd hope we can pick up a trace, but it's like looking for one leaf in a forest." Marisa was losing confidence in their strategy. At first it made sense, follow what they thought would be the traditional migration routes of the snow buffalo herds, but no one from the Protectorate knew for sure where they were so at best it was guess work.

"As far as anyone knows for sure we think we're on the right track. At least there's mountains and forests to the east. A bit of shelter from the elements won't hurt that's for sure." Marisa tried to stay upbeat, but everyone was starting to feel it. They all knew they couldn't hack it out in the open for much longer, plus they had to think about how long they should persevere. If they couldn't get a lead after three or four weeks, then they would have to face the inevitable and start for home.

Whisper was boiling up a pot of water while Fugly was cutting the shanks from one of the deer carcases, Rat chopping up some potatoes and onions to add to the pot.

"Have you thought any more about how we'll approach the Wolfs-head if we eventually pick up their trail? They ain't likely to welcome us in with kisses and hugs." Bodger had sat down next to Marisa and was warming his hands over the flames.

"Nice bit of understatement as always, fat head." Rat nailed Bodger on the head with a chip of potato just to help make her point.

"It's a fair question though and not one I have a definite answer for. I'm thinking we need to be very wary and show some humility. We are after all on their ground." Marisa made a point of looking pointedly at Bodger.

"What?" Bodger's voice squeaked out far higher than he'd intended, making everybody chortle, Rat rolling onto her back holding her ribs for effect.

"Hahaha. One time I got the wrong end of the stick and gave that Partian the back of my hand and I'm never allowed to forget it." Bodger sulkily flicked the chip back at Rat who'd only just got back upright. "People seem to forget that there are still some strange traditions in certain parts and I just thought he was trying it on with me." Everyone just fell about laughing at the memory while Bodger just sank down to the floor deflated. "Never let me bloody forget either."

"C'mon Bodge. Who else could barge into a wedding and start a mass brawl?" Fugly gave Bodger a mock hurt look and then blew him a kiss.

"Fair enough I suppose but how was I to know that he was the father of the bride and custom said he kissed all strangers in welcome?" Once again everyone fell about laughing while Bodger thought better of trying to defend himself further.

"Seriously though, we're going to have to be careful and respectful. Show that we are here on peaceful business and be prepared to give some ground, but at the same time be on our guard and not allow them to dominate us." Marisa shrugged. "To tell you the truth I'm no more certain than any of you, but I know who's lead we'll all be following when it comes to it and that's Skin."

A chorus of 'here heres' came back from around the fire. Lummox came crunching through the snow and plonked himself down across the fire from Marisa.

"What's on the menu today then Squad, sorry sir?" Lummox had already got his bowl and spoon out and even though it was twice the size of anyone else's it still looked tiny in his hands.

"Venison stew Lummox, unless you've managed to catch some fish." Rat shot him a cheeky grin and Lummox gave his version of a giggle which sounded more like a small earthquake.

The pot was bubbling away nicely by now, Fugly adding some herbs and spices that she'd packed on one of the sleds, the smell making everyone feel ravenous.

"Should we wait for Skin, Newbie and Shadow?" Fugly looked over to Marisa whilst stirring the pot and having a little taste to see if the seasoning was right.

"No point, we don't know how far out they are or when they'll be back. We'll just save them some." The fact was in all this endless, bleak white it would be impossible to know which way was up without a compass. Skin however was a different matter. There were some things you couldn't teach an adult, skills that you were brought up with from the moment you could walk, and he had them. Marisa had never known anyone like it, someone who could disappear in plain sight, sneak up on an enemy unseen and track anything that drew breath.

And then there was Shadow. Lithe and agile, slipping in and out of sight at will and as far as bowmanship was concerned? Well Marisa had never seen better, her aim unerring which was extremely unfortunate for those she was shooting at. She couldn't help but notice that Shadow had taken a shine to Garic, treating him like a little brother and he'd fallen under her spell. She could twist him round her little finger which had become a useful tool whenever he got ahead of himself. He'd insisted on going with them to scout and in truth was the only other person they'd allow to go. He really had become a well-loved part of their little family very quickly indeed, not hindered by the fact that he was an absolute animal in a fight.

Fugly started to hand out bowls of stew for everyone, steam pluming into the air. Lastly, she filled hers and Breda's bowls and sat down next to him. "There you go handsome, enjoy." She shot him her most alluring smile which from Fugly was pretty bloody alluring.

"Hadn't noticed that before." Breda at least had the good grace to blush a little although his return smile had more than a hint of happiness about it.

Considering they were in the middle of nowhere in freezing conditions, hunting for dangerous tribesman with no plan what to do once they'd found them, Marisa had to admit to being fairly contented.

Rat came around the windbreaker from being on watch. "I think we may have some contact sir. Coming in from the east."

"Could it be ours?" In a second Marisa was on her feet, spear to hand, scanning the horizon.

"Difficult to say sir, I only caught the glimpse of an outline. The way they were moving though I'd put money on it being Skin and company." Rat gave a little smile, not completely certain, but obviously not feeling too on edge.

Marisa peered out looking for any sign, the snow whipping across the horizon making it difficult to pick anything out. Then she spotted them, but something wasn't quite right. She could only make out two figures walking towards them and then she saw, Garic was carrying Shadow.

"Bodger get the medical kit out and Fugly get some fresh water on the boil." Marisa hoped against hope that it wasn't too bad, but it was always best to expect the worst.

Lummox was already up and running towards them. He

reached them and took Shadow from Garic, Marisa noticing him stumble a little as if being relieved of his burden happened just in time.

Lummox was back in camp in a matter of minutes, closely followed by Skin, Garic wearily bringing up the rear. Shadow's leg was badly mauled, what looked like bite and claw marks raked from thigh to ankle.

"What happened?" Marisa looked to Skin for an answer.

"We found the buffalo herd's trail and picked up on the Wolfs-head camp. They've herded a whole load of them into a valley about twenty miles east, so we crept up to get a closer look. Trouble was we weren't the only ones following them. Three snow tigers were tracking the herd looking for stragglers and then they saw us. How I didn't spot them is beyond me, I took my eye off the job cos I was so set on my task. They stalked around behind us and tried to pick off Shadow. She took a pretty bad hit from two of them before me and Newbie got them." Skin kept his eyes on the floor as if the shame weighed so much, he couldn't lift his head. He threw a sack on the floor. Bodger picked it up.

"Nice pelts, lovely markings." He said it casually without thinking but he was right, they were lovely pelts.

"Sorry sir, force of habit and it only took a couple of minutes to skin them." Skin looked so downcast that Marisa couldn't help herself and reached over to give him a squeeze.

Breda, Fugly and Whisper were tending to Shadow, cutting away her breeches and starting to clean the wounds.

"How are you feeling, Cenna?" Marisa dropped to her knees and clasped Shadow's hand.

"Not too bad considering a fucking huge cat tried to swallow me." Shadow winced as Whisper cleaned out some grit from her wounds.

"It's not too bad, no broken bones and it seems pretty clean. I'll just double check to make sure there's nothing in there to cause infection then I'll stitch and bandage. She'll have to take it easy for a while, but I think she'll be fine." Whisper got to work, his practised hand working away at Shadow's leg.

Marisa laid her hand on Shadow's face "Don't worry girl, you're still beautiful. Just have a good story to tell your next lover is all."

Marisa left Whisper to his ministrations and walked back over to Garic and Skin.

"So, what's their disposition then?" She looked at Skin for a report.

"Well, I'd say there are around three hundred in their village and they've been tracking the buffalo for about fourteen or fifteen days. They've corralled enough of them in the valley that they'll stay in place now until they've built up their meat larder and pelts for trade. If we're going to attempt an approach, any time in the next four or five days would do the job."

Bodger, Lummox and Rat had come over to join the others, leaving Whisper and Fugly to tend to Shadow.

"Shadow will need a couple of days to get back on her feet so maybe we should go and take a careful look, make sure there's no nasty surprises waiting for us." Breda pretty much voiced what they were all thinking.

"Agreed. You, Skin and Bodger go and have a good look and try to skirt around to the north. Hopefully, they won't expect anything to come in from above them. Skin, get some food down you first." Skin nodded and grabbed a bowl of stew from the pot.

Garic had sat down next to Shadow and was holding her hand as Whisper began stitching up her wounds. Marisa felt a little pang of jealousy at how gentle he was with her and had to remind herself how ridiculous that was. Shadow looked at him like a little brother after all.

"Right, we're going to set up camp here until Breda, Skin and Bodger have gone to take another close look. Get the tents up and let's get Shadow inside in the warm, maybe wrap up in those pelts, teach them to try eating you." Marisa smiled down at Shadow who chuckled back at her. The rest of the squad got to work pitching the tents, all low roofed and white, perfectly hidden from prying eyes. Marisa wasn't taking any chances though, not now they were so close to finally making contact.

She posted Rat and Fugly to first watch and made sure that Shadow was warm and comfortable. Whisper got in with Shadow to offer some body warmth and to keep an eye on her. Lummox as always got his own tent, no one else could fit in at the same time and Marisa slipped into Garic's and crawled under the furs with him.

She nudged up close, spooning from behind as he lay on his side, curled up like a child in a cot.

"Are you all right Garic?" she gave him a little squeeze and couldn't help but feel him tense up a bit.

"First Tommec and then five minutes after I'm back with the squad Cenna nearly gets it. I'm a fucking jinx, that's for sure." He sounded like a spoilt child but then Marisa had to remind herself that he was only just seventeen even if he was built like a monster.

She turned him around so that they rested head to head, and took his face in her hands. "Firstly, you're no jinx. Tommec was targeted because he was a mind-walker which is why we're out here in this forsaken shit hole. There was nothing that we would ever have done differently, we performed our duties and so did he. You dishonour him if you think otherwise. As for Shadow, that was just the luck of the draw, if either you or Skin had been guarding the back door, you'd be half inside a snow tiger's guts right now. If you hadn't been there and taken care of business, then maybe Shadow wouldn't get to see the light of a new day. So much of what happens in life is chance Garic, you just have to grab the joy when it's right in front of you." She leaned in and kissed him tenderly on the lips, sliding her hand down his back to gently squeeze his buttock.

He pulled her close, his kisses growing more urgent. Marisa could feel his power, feel the growing strength of his body. In less than a year she was looking up to meet him eye to eye. He pulled her closer still, slipping his hand between her legs, teasing the inside of her thighs.

She shuddered and started to pull down his breeches.

"CONTACT!" Rat screamed at the top of her voice, the sound of clashing weapons and gruff voices suddenly filling the air.

Marisa and Garic jumped up gathering their gear and clothes as they went. Marisa darted from their tent, grabbing her spear and shield, Garic hot on her heels. Lummox was up and charging towards Rat's position but in the snow, Marisa couldn't make things out clearly. She quickly looked around, saw Whisper armed and crouched in front of his tent, determined to defend Shadow no matter what. He looked at her and pointed in two directions, holding up ten fingers twice. So, twenty coming in from two directions, but where the hell was Fugly?

Off to her right she saw a shape emerging from the white. It was Fugly, but her feet were off the ground and then she realised she was being carried, arms pinned behind her back, a cruel, grey piece of steel held to her throat. A great bear of a Wastelander had her tightly wrapped up, no chance of fighting her way out of it. To her left, another group appeared pushing Bodger, Breda and Skin in front of them, all of them roughed up and bleeding.

"Put up your steel!" barked the Wastelander holding Fugly.

Marisa looked about the campsite. They were surrounded, but if they wanted them dead, they'd be gone already. This was not a fight they could win.

"Weapons down." The remaining squad members reluctantly laid down their weapons, especially Whisper.

"Fuck, I hope this isn't a mistake."

Chapter Seventeen:

They come

"Fucking rain!" It hadn't stopped raining for thirty days straight now and it was more than four turns of the moon since the H'Daree had arrived and still they waited. It was so bad they'd had to dig drainage ditches to run the water away from the fire pits and cover the tinder with oil skins.

At least they'd been able to make enough steel to arm over four thousand men and enough arrows to ensure a steady stream would rain down on their enemy. It still didn't calm his fears. At times it felt like he was the only person prepared to face reality. The truth was only a miracle would save them, even if everything went perfectly to plan. What they were facing was just too overwhelming.

As far as Candor was concerned the prudent course would have been to evacuate and retreat through the Titan Pass. If a stand was going to be made, make it behind a five-hundred-foot-high, purpose built, defensive wall. Out here behind their earth palisade Candor felt horribly exposed almost as if they were doing exactly what the H'Daree wanted.

He'd argued the case long and hard. A joint council had been formed with the leading families from the twin cities as representatives. Turan's spokesperson was Jarod Conglan, the Conglans being the wealthiest and most influential family in the city and likewise Abel Quinlan stood for Minari.

If it had been anyone but Quinlan, he may have swayed the argument, but with his son missing and his condition unknown

Abel was never going to bend.

"These bastards invade our land and kill our people without cause or provocation and you're saying we should abandon our homes and flee? The Quinlans have lived in the Green-lands for more than a thousand years and our ancestors built Minari. The same is true of the Conglans and Turan. These are our lands Candor, our ancestral homes and the bones of our fathers lay beneath our feet. We will not give them up without a fight or at the very least an attempt at some sort of negotiation." Abel was not a big or impressive specimen, not much over five feet tall and with the frame of a teenage boy, but he looked bigger when fired up.

"I understand how you feel Abel, really I do, but what if they enslave or kill everybody? Whose ancestors will weep if we're all gone and every trace of our existence and history wiped out?" Candor did not enjoy spreading terror, but he had to try to make them see reality.

"But nobody has even spoken to them. We don't even know what they want. Maybe it's a ransom they seek, and this is just a show of strength to demonstrate their intent. Maybe the cost they will have to endure to take our cities will be too high? How do we know anything until we talk to them? Minari will not simply surrender without even asking a question." Candor almost told them there and then that he was a mind-walker, that he knew their purpose, but the danger was too great. Not to him necessarily but to Marye, the children and her family. Plus, there was no guarantee that they would believe a word he said anyway. Mind-walkers were no more understood or tolerated in the Green-lands than anywhere else in the Free Territories.

"We stand with our kinsfolk in this, Candor. Will you still lead the fight?" Jarod Conglan was a big man and although slightly gone to pot still carried weight behind his swords.

Candor knew it was pointless to continue the argument. "I will."

Now standing on the earthworks looking out across the valley floor he was at least grateful for the H'daree's seeming tardiness. It had given them time not just to arm but to train the men they had. There were enough old veterans and ex militia to at least form some sort of structure with experienced men leading the training and taking command of squads. Brownleaf had insisted on going back out and getting as close to the enemy as he dared. It gave Candor comfort to know they'd at least have some warning when the attack came. Lot of good he thought it would do them.

He was worried about Brownleaf. Normally he was the very life and soul of any situation, always with a quip or a smile, constantly upbeat and engaging. However, since escaping the clutches of the H'Daree he had become withdrawn, his moods much darker. He had insisted on going back out to scout, ignoring all advice to stay a while longer to recover his strength. "I'll not stay here while Quinlan's still out there. If there's a chance he's still alive I have to try to find him and help him." Those were the last words he'd spoken to Candor and he knew that he'd brook no argument.

Candor hunched his shoulders, pulling his hood forward and wrapping his cloak tight. He started heading back towards the end fort at Turan when he noticed a cowled figure, bent and leaning into the rain walking along the palisade. Then he realised what was out of place, it was a woman.

As he approached, she threw back her hood, Marye!

"What are you doing here Marye? It's far too dangerous up here and who's looking after Tanny and Jenna?" Candor's voice carried a little more edge than he'd intended but still.

"Don't you take that tone with me Candor, I am not a child, and I will go where I please. The children are with my ma and pa along with all the other women, children and elders, cowering under canvas as far away from here as you could send them." Marye stood defiant in front of him hands on hips, defying him to test her. He looked at Marye and remembered why he fell in love with her in the first place, her blaze of red hair marking her out as a native of Turan. She'd broadened a little with age and children but was still a fine-looking woman and as always, she was right. Or at least that is what he'd learned to concede down the years, regardless of whether her argument was factual or correct, she was always right.

Candor swept her up in his arms and gave her a quick swirl. "I'm sorry my darling, what is it you need?"

She aimed a quick cuff at the back of his head. "I should think so too. The conditions back there are getting ridiculous, Candor, foot deep mud and overflowing cesspits. We can't remain there and some of us want to go back to our houses, get in the warm and dry, cook proper meals. It's hardest on the children and especially the elders. They're finding it difficult to cope with the constant rain, it's playing havoc with their aches and pains and some are starting to come down with fevers. If we stay out there much longer, we may end up with some of them dying." She'd calmed down a little, but was deadly earnest. Candor knew she was speaking for everyone, so convincing her this was the right path was crucial.

"Come Marye, please." He gently took her by the elbow and led her along the rampart back to the Turan end fort.

They ducked down through the rampart gate, Candor acknowledging the nods from the guards manning the walkways whilst hurrying Marye along and went into one of the rooms used as sleeping quarters.

They pulled off their cloaks and hung them on the coat pegs on the back of the door. Candor sat on one of the cots and pulled Marye down next to him. He gently brushed back some loose hair from her face and kept his hand there touching her cheek.

"Marye, I have some things I have to tell you, but I cannot tell you how I know. You will have to trust me and know that I am telling you the truth. I swear on our children's lives." He placed his other hand on her face so that he held her looking straight at him.

Tears began to well in her eyes, that knowing look, completely trusting Candor, but scared of what he was about to say. It almost broke Candor's heart, but he steeled himself and ploughed on.

"What's coming is beyond anything ever seen in the Known World, an army vast and implacable with only one goal in mind. They will conquer every people, every country and every land until all fall under their sway. They have already conquered every land on our world beyond the Storm Curtain and they are here to complete their task. Their numbers are beyond comprehension and I do not believe there is a force in existence that can resist them, not even the Protectorate." Candor could see Marye's eyes widening in terror as his words began to sink in.

"Why have you not said this to me before? Why would you keep this from me?" Her lips began to tremble as the tears started to swell in her eyes.

"Because I could not risk having you tell anybody else. If the leading families had heard this, they'd want to know how I came by this information. They have all of our reports about the size and disposition of the forces that have landed, but they don't know their intent, their history or the sheer size of the forces they can bring to bear. We are talking millions of troops Marye, millions. Do you understand what I am telling you?"

Marye began to gently sob, tears cascading down her face. "But how do you know all this Candor? How is it that you are the only person who knows this? Nobody has even spoken to them, or at the very least no one that has have ever been able to tell anyone else."

"Marye darling." Candor's shoulders sagged. He could not think of any other way than the truth, he'd just have to trust to their love.

"You know I was born in the Protectorate?" He breathed in trying to steady his nerve.

"Yes, you told me. You were born in Kings Town." Her reddened eyes narrowed a fraction.

"I belong to a secret society of sorts known as Andhonar's Orphans. There are hundreds of us spread across the Free Territories and our task is to watch for any potential threats and report back to the Protectorate in order to give them advance warning of possible danger. We still live normal lives out here and nothing we do causes harm to the societies we live in. You know how much of my life I have given to Turan; this is my home and you are my family. I chose to come back and face this, not turn tail and run back to the Protectorate. This is where I belong and this is where I stand." Now it was out there, it just remained to see how she reacted.

"This must have hurt you, keeping it a secret all these years." She reached across and cradled his face in her hands. Her smile melted his heart, the relief of unburdening causing him to physically dip. "Just answer me one thing."

"Of course, my darling, anything."

"How have you managed to report back? The Protectorate is thousands of miles away and apart from one ride to the Titan Gate you've never left the Green-lands in twenty years."

Now came the truly hard part. Even now Candor wavered,

trying to think of how he could spin this, what story would sound most plausible. But no, this was the time, trust her, she will be there.

"I went to meet another Orphan, an old friend named Torbin who lives in Lhossa. I contacted him and arranged to meet so that word could be passed along."

"Still holding back from the final truth. Just tell her."

"Never trusted those sun-worshipping savages. Why would anyone choose to live there?" She couldn't help her prejudice slipping out, Lhossa and the Murgan were not well liked in the Green-lands. "How did you arrange to meet your friend? Lhossa is over five hundred miles away." Marye looked at him as if he was talking nonsense.

"Because like all other Orphans I am a mind-walker, Marye."

She edged back along the cot a look of confused shock on her face, her brow crinkling while she tried to take it in.

"All these years and you kept it a secret. So, you've always known what I've thought, manipulated me by reading my mind. How could you?" She shuffled backwards along the mattress and went to bolt. Candor caught her arm and pulled her wriggling towards him.

"That's not how it works, Marye. Mind-walkers can only read other mind-walkers. If it ever appeared that I was reading your mind it's because I love you and know you better than anyone else alive. You must believe me; I would never lie to you and I never have. I just kept this from you, but it wasn't a lie." He stared into her eyes and felt her relax, enough at least to know that she believed him.

"You understand I didn't tell you because I didn't want to put you, Jenna and Tanny at risk. They are not particularly fond of mind-walkers in the Green-lands." He shrugged his shoulders and grinned, hoping that this would be enough. Much to his relief, Marye hugged him and planted a kiss on his cheek.

"So, what now?" Marye looked up at him with a slight little girl lost lilt to her expression.

"Now I need you to go back and be ready. I don't know why, but I can feel it in my bones. They are coming soon and you need to be ready to move at a second's notice. Can you do that for me my love?"

She leaned in and gave him a passionate kiss, clinging to him like a drowning man to a piece of flotsam.

"Yes my love." She took his face in her two hands and fixed him with an intense look. "Just make sure you come back to us."

She smiled at him, nodded and turned on her heels, making a beeline for the door.

Candor slumped back into the cot, the whole situation having drained him of much of his composure. Someone knocked at the door.

"Candor." It was Willet.

"Yes Will, come in." Candor got up and moved towards the door. "What is it?"

"I think you should come, Candor. Brownleaf's been spotted heading back here and he's moving like the wind."

Candor grabbed his cloak from the door, pulled his hood up and strode for the rampart. He crossed the fort yard in seconds, jumped up onto the earthworks and headed straight for the centre fort, Willet hot on his heels. A real sense of urgency gripped him, an unseen feeling tugging at his subconscious. He couldn't see Brownleaf yet, his view obscured by the incessant rain, so he made a decision.

"Will, get me a horse, I'm going to ride out and meet him."

"Yes Candor." Willet ran off to find a mount, scurrying down the rear bank of the rampart, stumbling and nearly losing his footing. He returned in a couple of minutes with a brown gelding, saddled and ready to go.

Candor trotted through the gate built into the middle of the earthworks and carefully made his way between the fire pits. The rain had made the footing uncertain, the sides of some of the pits collapsing inwards only to be dug out again. It was a solid defensive strategy, no two pits in a straight line so that they would have to be carefully negotiated, slowing the attacking force down and funnelling them closer and closer together. Pack them in so as to kill them in greater numbers, even clog the ground with their dead, but Candor didn't believe it would make any real difference. The fire might hurt them though, if only they could keep the tinder dry enough to light.

He'd posted spotters every few miles out from the redoubts,

putting them on high ground with beacons to light, an early warning system but he knew Brownleaf would've gone as far out as possible. It worried him a little that he may take a risk too many given his anguish about Quinlan, but he knew there was little point trying to hold him back.

It took about twenty minutes at a gingerly trot, but he finally cleared the last redoubt and put his heels to his steed. He'd only ridden a few hundred yards when he saw Brownleaf galloping towards him at breakneck speed, churning up mud behind him. He pulled up hard alongside Candor, breath rasping in and out, clouds of mist spraying out on each exhale.

"Brownie, take a breath lad. What's the situation?" As Candor asked the question a beacon burst into flame on a nearby hilltop, the one he'd stationed closest to the redoubts. He knew Brownleaf's answer before he gave it.

"They're on the move Candor, heading straight for us." He gulped in a breath as if the effort of talking was suffocating him. "If I hadn't seen it myself, I wouldn't believe it, but from what I could safely observe they are at least fifty thousand strong and that's just foot. I couldn't get close enough to get a really clear view plus this bloody rain, but it looked like they had big double-axled wagons. They looked huge as if they were carrying parts to be assembled. I don't know Candor, like I said I couldn't get close enough and once they saw me, they sent riders in pursuit. I only just managed to stay ahead of them at one point, but they ended up dropping back." Brownleaf leaned forward, hands on his pommel, chest rising up and down like bellows.

"How far out Brownie?" Candor didn't really want to hear the answer but the question had to be asked.

"Hours at best, but at the rate they move, who knows? It doesn't seem possible that large a force could move that quickly and if I hadn't seen it with my own eyes, I would dismiss it as rubbish. But Candor they move together like a river flows, smooth and quick and they won't stop until they're done." Brownleaf looked at him like a condemned man resigned to his fate.

"What about the beacon lighters? Did they get out?" Candor was fishing for some small crumb of comfort, a tiny piece of good news.

"I don't know Candor, they'd have seen what I saw, but whether they could have made it down to the floor of the valley in time…" Brownleaf just shrugged.

Candor reached across and put his hand on Brownleaf's shoulder. "Alright Brownie, you've done all you could. Only one thing to do now." Candor turned his horse and started back towards the twin cities, Brownleaf on his tail and the rain kept falling.

Chapter Eighteen Part One:

Conspiracy theories

Jonoh had neglected his forms for too long, more than three turns of the moon since he'd picked up a staff. He twirled it across his hands, letting his fingers remember the feel, texture and smell of the wood. He spun it left and right, alternating one hand to two hands then back to one, moving his feet in half stance, full stance, defensive and attacking forms. A small crowd had gathered to watch, everyone knew who Jonoh was and word spread quickly, especially in Fortress Kingshold.

He'd asked around the household guard for sparring partners, but had encountered some reticence, most crying off with excuses like duties to perform or niggling injuries that would prevent them from fully competing. In their shoes he supposed he'd feel the same, but it didn't stop his frustration. Then someone stepped forward and volunteered. Barton Logistar.

They stood opposite each other in the middle courtyard's training square, slowly circling each other. Jonoh couldn't help but admire the poise and focus that emanated from Barton, attired in a brown leather sparring jacket and padded brown breeches. He had a slim, honed physique, lithe and obviously strong and with his shock of red hair cut quite the dashing figure. His movement mirrored Jonoh's, even down to hand adjustments on the staff, and then Jonoh realised something that struck him as quite profound. This is what he used to do to Garic, mirror his movements, knowing that would irritate him as if he was being mocked. It had always given Jonoh the edge he needed, always goaded Garic to strike first, give away his intent. It itched inside Jonoh's mind. *"Is he doing this on purpose to try and get under my skin? Could he know this is what I did to Garic?"*

More and more Barton Logistar put Jonoh at unease. It was almost as if Barton knew things about him and was aware that he knew it also. It was so uncomfortable, always leaving him feeling a little unbalanced, just a little off key. He tried to put it to the back of his mind, focus on his forms, on his breathing, just let his body flow with the staff.

It felt good to hold the ash in his hands again, the staff feeling like an extension of his arms, the forms flowing from the pairing. He breathed as he moved, centring his mind and body, merging them into one fluid being, then he moved.

Jonoh whipped forward on the balls of his feet, moving and feinting, constant motion, fixing his opponents stare. Looking for that opening, that imperceptible moment of doubt or hesitation before pouncing. He saw Barton double take as if confused by his movement, the tiny slip of concentration that let him know he had him. He swung under Barton's guard, the staff light as a feather in his hand, the effort to swing nothing at all, perfect motion and rhythm, all too easy.

Thwack!

Barton's staff swung to meet him, catching his blow and turning the momentum, almost making Jonoh lose his balance, then swung up and over at his head. Jonoh gasped just interposing his own staff at the last second, ducking and sliding to the side in order to regain his footing.

This was not what he expected at all. For all his mild-mannered deference, Barton Logistar was as good as he had ever seen and troublingly maybe better than him.

Jonoh slid round the outside of the square still spinning his ash from hand to hand, perpetual motion at all times. He attacked again, this time varying his attacks, high, low, sweeping arcs, urgent jabs, as much variety and speed as he could muster. Barton just parried everything, flowing in and out of range like liquid, never quite where Jonoh expected him to be.

It wasn't just his skill, which was exceptional, it was his ability to read situations. He was always in the right place at the right time and when he counter-attacked it took all Jonoh had to stave him off.

Jonoh slid sideways and backwards, pulling out of range for a moment. He needed a little space, a little time to gather himself. Try to formulate a new strategy because this one simply wasn't working.

The crowd had grown a little, but more concerning from Jonoh's point of view was the fact that Masters Ardend and Cerwin had joined the throng. Cerwin stood there thoughtfully stroking his beard, a knowing little grin turning the ends of his moustache slightly up. Obviously Cerwin knew all about Barton, but had failed to divulge the information, a test maybe?

Jonoh kept moving around the outside of the square, Barton mirroring his every move, never quite instigating contact. Jonoh breathed deeply, in through the mouth out through the nose, repeating the process, centring himself, calming his mind.

They came together in the middle of the square almost moving like they were under water, smooth and rhythmical, their staffs ringing the air, a melody of ash and brawn. They punched and countered, every blow beautifully arced and then caught and turned, creating dizzying shapes and forms that seemed to phase in and out of reality.

It became a dance, a duet of grace and violence, always on the edge of pain yet so smooth and light it almost floated like silk. Jonoh rejoiced in the music, the sounds reverberating in his mind like a great symphony, the notes flowing over him like a warm embrace. In his heart he wanted to add a discordant note, bring the whole thing crashing down, tearing it away from Barton. This was for him alone, not to be shared with anyone.

He knew he shouldn't, but for the tiniest fraction of a second, imperceptible to anybody's eyes he slipped into the Gift, plenty of time to outmanoeuvre Barton and end his display. As he did, he could have sworn he saw a flash of anger cross Barton's face as if he was aware of what Jonoh had done. Then he was stood over Barton's prone figure, having swept his ankles, the whole crowd clapping and whistling. "Bravo" and "Fine show" was interspersed with "I've never seen a better match" and "Unbelievable." Jonoh felt a wave of guilt wash over him, his need to win having overridden any attempt at fair play.

Barton rose to his elbows, eyes fixed on Jonoh and reached out his hand. "Would you be so kind Jonoh?" Jonoh grasped Barton's hand in his own, pulling him to his feet as the crowd closed in, patting both of them warmly on their backs.

"Bravo Jonoh and you Barton. That was one of the finest spars I have ever seen, beautiful to watch." Master Ardend's smooth tone washed over Jonoh but Master Cerwin was no longer by his side.

"Thank you Master Ardend and thank you Barton. You really do have exceptional skill and poise. Where did you learn your forms?" Jonoh was starting to feel a little guilty that he'd in essence cheated, but his slight unease around Barton just would not go away.

"I was stationed with army group Snowbard for my martial service and had the good fortune to be taken under the wing of Master General Jacoh Fencer. I had always had a certain natural aptitude for the martial arts, so he very generously agreed to tutor me." Deferential and humble as ever, but something just would not stop tugging at Jonoh's mind.

"It was an honour to spar with you Barton, truly." Jonoh gave a small bow of respect.

"Thank you Jonoh. If ever you need a partner, I would be only too pleased to oblige." Nobody else seemed to notice but Jonoh caught an edge to Barton's voice. He didn't see how, but it was as if he knew what Jonoh had done.

Jonoh looked around the yard searching out Master Cerwin whilst happily acknowledging all the congratulatory praise. He saw him stood by the bottom of the staircase of the same narrow tower where this little adventure had started. He wore the look of someone who'd just found out his true love had betrayed him, shock and disappointment. He stared straight at Jonoh shaking his head and then nodded for him to follow. Jonoh made his excuses and extricated himself from the backslapping throng.

He ran up the stairs after the diminutive shadow-master and followed him into the same anteroom they always ended up in, ancient oak table and all.

Master Cerwin rounded on him as soon as he'd pulled the door shut.

"What in the name of all that is good were you thinking?" Jonoh had never seen Master Cerwin this angry and despite his modest frame in that moment he appeared a giant. Jonoh nearly stumbled backwards, shocked and shaken by the little master's reaction.

"Master, I don't understand." Jonoh bleated out the words weakly.

"Do not try to play me for a fool Jonoh! You used the Gift so that you could win a sparring contest? Why? Because you are too immature to accept that there may be someone better than you. Are you so weak-willed that your fragile ego would shatter in defeat? The Gift is not a toy, it should only be used when needed and if I saw it who is to say that a spy in our midst could not have spotted your ploy? Did it not occur to you that downplaying your abilities would serve us better wherever an enemy agent was concerned?" Master Cerwin turned away as if needing a moment or two to calm himself, afraid of what he might do otherwise.

Jonoh thought he'd felt a sense of shame in the yard, but it paled miserably to how he felt now. He stood rooted to the spot, shoulders slumped, eyes staring at the floor.

"I'm sorry Master Cerwin, it was selfish and thoughtless, but there's something about Barton. I can't quite put my finger on it, but something is constantly nagging at me in his presence." Jonoh had the good grace to keep his head down, at least appearing contrite.

"That is not all of it, is it though Jonoh? You simply do not ever want to lose, so rather than fighting honourably or fairly you used the Gift to satisfy your own selfish need. With what is coming you cannot afford to act like a child anymore, you must throw off these foolish things." Master Cerwin had turned back around and evidently calmed his temper.

"I know you have been through a terrible ordeal and much has been placed on your shoulders at such a young age, but things are as they are. It is not I or Barton or anybody else who has your ability, it is you and you must hold yourself to a higher standard." Cerwin's brow creased. "As for Barton, I believe I understand what you mean. I have never seen anything other than complete dedication to duty from the man, as unswerving a servant of the

Protectorate as there is. However, there is something I cannot quite put my finger on, something that feels just a fraction out of step, but to this day he has yet to put a foot wrong. Suspicions will only ever be that until some evidence is produced so do not let it occupy your thoughts Jonoh."

"But Master, if you sense something too would he not be top of the list of suspects?" Jonoh had picked his chin up and was looking at Cerwin rather than the floor.

"We do not have anything concrete to go on Jonoh. Our suspicions are just that, a feeling we share, but that could be any number of things manifesting themselves. I think you share my discomfort at his constant deference as if it is a calculated ruse. But what if that is just his natural manner? What if he is just a humble man happiest in service and we are reading something into his actions that do not exist? Barton Logistar is the foremost member of the Guild of Logistics currently alive, that is why he is here at the centre of all the great decision making of our time." Cerwin began to pace, head down and arms behind his back. "You do not become a member of the Elder Council unless it is earned and his record of service is beyond criticism, his expertise invaluable. We can be wary because of our own intuition, but unless he takes action that demonstrates some sign of betrayal, we must give the man the respect he has earned." Master Cerwin stopped pacing and began to build a fresh fire in the hearth, brushing the excess ash from the grate and putting in tinder.

"Master, why does Barton not take the title Master? Surely he would be considered to have earned it?" Jonoh started to pile logs on top of the tinder.

"Because the Guild of Logistics believe that the title of Master can never be obtained within their vocation, that the very nature of what they do is constantly evolving and moving forwards. From their point of view the title Master implies that one had reached a level of perfection that can never be attained, so relinquishing the title keeps them grounded and focused on progression." Cerwin poked the fire as the flames started to flicker into life.

"How do you feel about the title?" Jonoh pulled up a chair next to the fire and warmed his hands.

"Well there is no reward in our society other than personal

growth and achievement, but I see no problem with an honorific. It is merely an acknowledgment of accumulated learning and an attainment of excellence. It is also a reasonable thing to accord a certain level of respect to those that have earned it, beyond that it is fairly meaningless and does not personally benefit the one upon whom it is bestowed." Cerwin gave Jonoh his 'would you not agree' look. Jonoh just nodded.

"Jonoh, have you given any more thought to what happened to you with the blades?" The fire had taken hold, the warmth spreading out enough for them to both relax a little.

"I've thought of little else Master. The things I saw seemed fantastical, like a live viewing of legends and myths. I still don't fully understand the breadth of my abilities, but was what I saw real or just an illusion? If so, was it created deliberately or was it just a by-product of the contact with the blades? If it was real was it events on our world and was it in the past or the future? I can't say with any certainty that I know one way or the other." Jonoh looked at the old man hoping that he may shed some light on the subject or at least help him understand.

"I wish I could answer some of those questions Jonoh, but you have already gone far beyond anything I am capable of experiencing. I am certain though that the physical experience in the chamber was real. How that is possible is beyond my understanding but the stress it caused you was undeniably powerful. It was undoubtedly a deliberate trap although the power and skill required to set it is terrifying. I am certain of one thing, although I have no proof." Cerwin stroked the end of his beard, looking as though he was trying to decide whether he should say what was on his mind.

"What is it, Master?" Jonoh could sense the uncertainty and it made him anxious.

"As I said, I have no proof, but I know it to be true. This is all linked to the H'Daree. It is no coincidence that this all occurred since they invaded, the timings are just too close, too interlinked. What the connection is I do not yet know but I do know it is real. The reports we have had back suggest they are on the verge of moving but until they do, we are blind to their intentions. From the information we have received, only one individual has survived an encounter with them and been able to pass on any intelligence. For such a seemingly huge force they seem incredibly adept at hiding their movements and disposition. As it stands, we will not know what we are facing until they attack Minari and Turan and little good that knowledge will do us when we are thousands of miles away." Cerwin had picked a thread from his sleeve and flicked it irritably into the fire.

"Master, you said before that you had some ideas as to who the cowled figure was?" Jonoh let the question hang in the air, almost too frightened to ask it.

"I had what can only be described as a foolish notion Jonoh, one born out of an old man's fascination with history. I do not think it is worth even talking about it to be honest." Jonoh thought he saw a hint of embarrassment on the old man's face.

"Did you think it was Curlon?" Cerwin's eyes flicked up in a flash, surprise etched on his wrinkled face.

"Yes, I did have that thought Jonoh. What made you think so?" The old man had leant forward on his chair, intent on his young apprentice.

"Partly timelines, thirteen hundred years ago so in the right time frame at least. But it was something else, something more. When you showed me his portrait it was like looking in a mirror, and the voice I heard felt the same. My voice but not my voice, if that makes any sense?" Jonoh felt slightly foolish saying it as nonsensical as it sounded.

"Jonoh, I cannot emphasise this enough. Are you certain?" Cerwin had leaned so far forward he was almost out of his seat, his gripped knuckles whitening on the arms of the chair.

"I know it must sound baseless but now I think about it I am certain, as senseless as that sounds." Jonoh picked up on Cerwin's mood and mirrored his actions.

"It makes perfect sense Jonoh, perfect sense. The implications if this is true however are beyond conception. It is not just the power required to achieve such a thing, but the will to see it through. And the possibilities are mind-numbing. Are the H'Daree Curlon's descendants, is this a long planned for revenge thirteen hundred years in the making? If as they claim the H'Daree have conquered and subdued the rest of the planet outside of the Known World, are they here to complete the task? If Curlon did in fact escape is this what he set in motion all those years ago? It fits so many scenarios that have played out, the fact that they knew the optimal place to land their invasion force, their seeming knowledge of the terrain. That Curlon would target you at such a specific moment having put that plan in motion over a millennium ago." For the first time ever, Jonoh saw a look of bewildered resignation on the old master's face. For about five seconds then he was lucid and focused again.

"This is the worst-case scenario imaginable. We cannot wait for them to reach us; we must try to counter them at the first possible opportunity. Jonoh we must convince the Elder Council to mobilise and do what has never been done in the history of the Protectorate. We must launch a counter strike of our own. We must launch an incursion into the Free Territories."

Jonoh's jaw dropped, unable to process the sudden switch in conversation. Even he knew the Elder Council would never sanction such a move.

Chapter Eighteen Part Two:

The great debate

Jonoh sat at the round table in the Elder Council chamber, a huge polished wooden circle, open in the middle with room for at least thirty chairs. The chamber was smaller than the great dining hall but none the less impressive, circular with ornate columns around its edge and a huge stone fireplace on the back wall. He could almost feel the history, the great debates and decisions that had been reached there.

All the members of the Elder Council were in attendance, including Masters Evaleen Farmer, Erik Armourer and Domen Fletcher. Jonoh could not help but feel a little intimidated by this gathering of elders, so much accumulated knowledge and experience in one place left him feeling a little inadequate.

Despite not claiming the honorific Master, Barton Logistar was still counted as a member of the Council and was accorded his place at the table. Jonoh sat in Master Cerwin's seat, his mentor stationing himself in the open centre of the table.

"Friends, fellow masters, we have convened the Council today to hear a proposal submitted by Cerwin Shadow-master. My old friend you have the floor." Master Ardend brought the meeting to order, gesturing for Cerwin to present his case.

"My friends and fellow Council members, as you know we are facing the greatest threat in the history of the Protectorate. The force that has invaded the Green-lands, the H'daree as they are called, are now moving towards Turan and Minari. The network of

Andhonar's Orphans are doing all they can to muster some kind of counter force at great risk to themselves. All reports indicate that the response is somewhat laboured to put it mildly, with many of the Free Territories' sovereign nations being bitterly opposed to the existence of mind-walkers. I realise none of this is exactly news to you but allow me this small indulgence." Cerwin was slowly pacing the three steps available in the open centre of the table. "The dangers to the Orphans will undoubtedly include the possibility of summary execution and at best banishment. The fractured nature of politics in the Free Territories means a coordinated response will be almost certainly impossible. If the H'Daree are not met with an organised response before they make the Titan Gate however, they will be free to sweep across the Free Territories all the way to Sarjinn. If we wait for this to happen, we may not be able to resist them, so I am asking for the Elder Council to consider sending an expeditionary force to meet them in the field and stop them before they can get a foothold."

"So, you are suggesting we launch an incursion into the Free Territories?" Master Domen Fletcher could not keep an edge of incredulity out of his voice.

"I realise it is much to ask…"

"Much to ask?" Master Evaleen Farmer cut in. "You are asking that we go against one of the central tenets of our society, Cerwin. We do not and cannot launch an invasion of other nations' sovereign territories, not unless a request for aid or a petition to join us is sent. What you are asking is out of the question, regardless of the arguments put forward." A murmur of accord rumbled around the chamber, nods of assent and whispered asides filling the air.

"But do you not see that if we do nothing, our way of life, our very existence may be in jeopardy. No, I correct myself, not may be but will be in more than just jeopardy. From what I have garnered in terms of information I genuinely believe that we will be hard-pressed to survive what is coming." Cerwin's voice had the hardest edge Jonoh had ever heard from him, falling like a hammer blow, making all present pay the very closest attention.

"It is my understanding that our intelligence is limited Cerwin, much of it based on mind-walker exchanges between your Orphans and their forces. Did it not occur that these exchanges are merely propaganda? I have seen nothing in these reports to suggest any of the intelligence gathered so far is anything more than misdirection." Master Benfer Scribe was an average-looking man, grey-haired, thin-faced with reading glasses perched on the end of his pointed nose but as the foremost recorder in the Protectorate well respected. And his words carried weight.

"I trust the instincts of my Orphans, Benfer, and they are convinced that is not the case, that it is not propaganda or boasting but more an exchange of factual information. There is no deliberate subterfuge on their part, although I believe they are well aware that it can be an effective terror tactic." Jonoh could tell that Cerwin was doing everything he could to be non-combative, to avoid upsetting anyone, not to risk putting them offside.

"But as you say, this is the interpretation of a few individuals, an opinion. Hardly quantifiable facts upon which we can make a decision." Master Benfer peered up through his glasses making his eyes seemingly double in size.

"The Orphans are in the field, risking everything, even their lives. They have been doing so for centuries and because of their selfless efforts many disasters have been averted or countered. Everyone around this table, in fact the whole of the Protectorate owes them much and we should accord them the respect they deserve." Cerwin's voice had turned flat and cold and more worryingly Jonoh could sense him projecting, a shimmer of the Gift rising unseen by anyone else.

"No one is suggesting otherwise my friend, please let's not allow our tempers to fray. We are all servants, Cerwin, consensus will always be our way." Master Ardend was not a mind-walker but Jonoh could see his intuition at work, his honed senses helping him realise Cerwin needed to hear a calming voice. More and more Jonoh admired this gentle man.

"My apologies Masters, I mean no disrespect, but I hope my passion conveys how urgent I believe our current situation to be." The shimmer disappeared and Jonoh relaxed a little but the tension in the room was still palpable.

"You have all read the report I prepared, including young Master Shipwright's experience with the blades. Well, there is something that is not in the report, something that has only just come to light, which puts an even more disturbing twist on our situation." Master Cerwin had the undivided attention of all the Council members, some of whom shuffled their chairs forward or leaned closer. Jonoh felt extremely self-conscious and more than a little uncomfortable knowing exactly what information Master Cerwin was about to impart.

"I realise that for the ungifted this will all seem fantastical, but after discussing his experience with him, myself and Jonoh could only come to one conclusion. The cowled figure who laid the trap was none other than Curlon himself."

A round of spluttering, coughing and intakes of breath burst from the table's occupants.

"And what may I ask do you base this on? I am, as you say, ungifted. Please do not misunderstand me Master Cerwin, I have nothing but respect for you and I know that the Gift and mind-walking are real and as of yet, inexplicable talents. However even those with the Gift explain it as if being in a dream or alternate reality, so you cannot expect us to act on a supposition. This is yours and Jonoh's interpretation of events that he experienced, and I would point out that no one knows exactly what Curlon looked like, so even if Jonoh had seen a face, how would he know it was him?" Master Kristof Sculptor had stood up, spreading his arms as if to encompass the breadth of his scepticism. He made a point of looking at all the assembled masters before continuing.

"Are you in some way suggesting that Curlon instigated this chain of events and that he was lying in wait for Jonoh over a thousand years ago? He is long since dead, 'beckoned' to use the common slang. Even if this were true it still couldn't justify sending an armed force into another sovereign land uninvited." Master Kristof's unremarkable frame, average in every way, from his mousey hair to his nondescript facial features, belied his oratory. He held the floor with a good degree of comfort and command.

"I am not suggesting, I am stating it as fact. Look at the events that have happened. Firstly, a previously unknown force invades the Known World at the one point where they will be secure from counter-attack, at the exact point mind, within a matter of feet. They have mind-walkers never recorded anywhere else apart from the Protectorate, in the written histories of the Known World. At the same time three soul-forged blades are left on a battlefield for our forces to recover. No soul-forged blade has ever been left behind; they have only ever been recovered from the corpses of dead Snowbard warriors. How could this happen unless someone knew the ground, knew the land they were invading? You cannot possibly believe that this is all coincidence, you must see the pattern. Curlon may be dead but that does not mean his descendants are or that they have forgotten his history, his legacy, his revenge!" Cerwin almost spat out the last few words, his anger at their refusal to see the obvious causing a shimmer that looked like a heat haze to Jonoh. "This is too orchestrated, too organised and too coincidental to just be a matter of chance. If we do not act now and allow the H'daree to get a real foothold in the Free Territories, we may never dislodge them. We are so sure of our own invulnerability that we forget the fact that the whole of the Known World covers less than a third of the planet. What do we know about the power and resources they could bring to bear? As it is, they possess a knowledge that is far beyond us, the ability to traverse the Great Storm Curtain. Not just traverse it but to do so in vast numbers and so far, they have swept all before them. You must open your eyes."

"That is as maybe Cerwin but what you're suggesting not only goes against everything we espouse as a society, but it is also impractical. How do you suggest we send a force large enough to counter this threat across thousands of miles of hostile territory without suffering huge losses?" Domen Fletcher stood up catching the attention of all in the room. Jonoh could feel the tension rising, a sense of exasperation beginning to spread amongst the assembled masters.

"What you're asking is impractical at best and downright reckless at worst." Domen Fletcher shook his head, sitting back down with a weary shrug.

"Then what would the Council suggest? That we sit on our hands and wait for the enemy to land on our doorsteps? If it comes to that we will not have the resources to withstand the kind of attack they will be able to mount. Also, we seem to be disregarding Snowbard's part in this. Do you suppose that they will stand idle while we attempt to repel an invasion, or do you think they may invade and open a second front? I know what outcome I believe will happen." It was starting to turn into a lecture, Cerwin talking down to the rest of the Council as if they were naive children. Jonoh knew for certain at that moment that the argument was lost.

"Masters, if I may." Barton Logistar stood to address his fellow Council members.

"Please Barton, you have the floor."

"Thank you Master Ardend. While I agree that this is a thorny subject, I find that I cannot completely disagree with Master Cerwin." Jonoh was taken aback, Barton being the last person he'd expected to lend support to their cause.

"From a logistical point of view, it would be difficult but not impossible to get a counter force to the Titan Gate. If we landed our forces north of Sarjinn we could march across the Lawless Lands, head south of the Kingdom of Darmat skirting their border and cross the Red Desert thereby avoiding any sovereign territory. There would of course be risks but we could provision our forces adequately for the desert crossing and could get a vanguard there in a moons-turn if we pressed hard. I know forty-five days doesn't sound like enough time, but a large cavalry detachment could make it with the main body following on. I have studied the Titan Gate in some detail and am fairly certain that a force of twenty thousand well-equipped and determined soldiers could hold it indefinitely against a force of any size." Barton scanned the Council members. "I am not saying it would be easy, but from a logistical point of view it would be possible." He looked to Cerwin and nodded, ceding the floor back to him.

"Thank you, Barton. My friends I can tell you that the Orphans closest to the Gate are doing all they can to try to raise a force of some kind to defend it, but there are no guarantees that they will succeed. If we do not act our best chance to stem this invasion force may be lost. I beg you to consider this carefully before we come to any decision here." Cerwin had calmed himself, the shimmer not visible to Jonoh at all.

"I am sorry, but nothing I have heard here convinces me of the true nature of the threat we are supposedly facing or the need for us to put our citizens at unnecessary risk. As far as I'm concerned the H'Daree are self-aggrandising opportunists at best, using mind games to spread fear through propaganda. As you say, the Known World covers only a third of the planet so why would mind-walkers not exist outside of it already, independent of the Protectorate? I believe we are giving far too much credence to a threat that so far has amounted to little more than conquering the weakest military nation in existence. Two battalions of our own forces could walk through the Green-lands in a matter of days without a great deal of exertion." Master Kristof waved his hand as if dismissing the whole argument. A small burst of 'here heres' went around the room, the Council seemingly in accord with the Master Sculptor.

Jonoh could sense Master Cerwin beginning to bristle again, angry that the rest of the Council seemed almost wilfully oblivious to what he considered the blinding truth.

"You cannot be so blasé about this Kristof. Have you not read the reports we have received? Are you not listening to what I am telling you, what Jonoh has experienced first-hand?" Cerwin's voice was creeping up, the shimmer rising from his body in waves. Jonoh could feel a slight change in the atmosphere, like the air after a lightning strike.

"May I ask, how many enemy troops have actually been observed?" Master Kristoff's point was well made and from Jonoh's point of view was the final nail in the coffin of their argument. The silence that met his question was deafening.

"While I respect the Gifted Master Cerwin, I will not base my decisions on a seventeen-year-old boy's interpretation of a dream. Apologies Jonoh, but you are not yet a master." Master Kristof sounded genuinely sorry to use Jonoh in this manner. He didn't believe him to be malicious, just trying to state his case as forcefully as possible.

Jonoh felt it before it happened, sensed the change in the visible spectrum. Gasps went up around the table as Master Cerwin disappeared in plain sight, the papers in front of Master Kristof fluttering as if disturbed by a breeze. He reappeared less than a second later behind Kristof, his dagger drawn and settled between the Master Sculptor's shoulders.

"Cerwin this is outrageous, what do you think you are doing!" Master Ardend shouted across at Cerwin, at the same time getting up from his seat and striding round the table to confront him.

The rest of the assembled masters broke into uproar, all apart from Barton. Cerwin instantly lowered the dagger, backing away palms raised in peace.

"Apologies my friends. I beg your forgiveness Master Kristof, but I felt the need to make a serious point, and this was the only way I knew how." Kristof had turned to face him, his face flushed red and his breathing quickly snatching in and out. Cerwin bowed low before his fellow master, almost prostrating himself. Kristof quickly regained his composure and although obviously flustered nodded magnanimously to the little shadow-master.

"My sincerest apologies my fellow masters. I merely seek to make a point. I am as you say gifted and that is what I can do in a room full of people without any of you being able to thwart me. I am a true master both of my vocation and the Gift, few if any before me can match my abilities. However my measure of the Gift is but a drop in the ocean compared to Jonoh's and the reach of his ability is beyond my comprehension. What he saw was not a dream, but an actual physical manifestation of events, somehow seen first-hand. We may not understand this ability, but we must recognise it and honour its truth. To do otherwise would be folly." As demonstrations went, Jonoh felt that that was fairly powerful. Then he realised that everyone's attention had turned to him, and his sense of discomfort went up a notch or two.

"We all have the very highest respect for you Master Cerwin, probably even more so now. We do not question the validity of your arguments or young Jonoh's experiences. If as you say this whole situation was instigated by Curlon himself more than a millennium ago that is indeed a worrying turn of events. However I do not believe that can change our decision here. We must of course endeavour to do all we can to prepare ourselves for what is to come, starting with sending envoys out to all corners of the Known World to tell everyone what we know and to offer support. If called upon to aid any other nation we will respond as we always have but as to launching an independent incursion? I for one will be voting no." Master Benfer gave a shallow bow, happy to have made his point.

"My fellow masters, I believe it is time to call a vote. Should we grant Master Cerwin's request to launch a military incursion into the Free Territories, yay or nay?" Master Ardend went around the table, every master in turn giving nay as their answer except for Barton Logistar and Master Cerwin himself.

"I am sorry Cerwin, but the nays have it." Master Ardend did indeed look a little crestfallen as if he had somehow let his friend down.

"My friends, as always, I bow to your wisdom. However I will be taking ship for the Free Territories as soon as I can book passage. I will not do less than I ask of my Orphans and their need is greater than any of ours. I resign my seat on the Elder Council."

A collection of gasps and mumbled asides swept around the table as the little shadow-master turned quickly on his heels, pausing only to put his hand on Barton Logistar's shoulder. "Thank you my friend." he whispered in his ear as he strode from the room.

Jonoh stood rooted to the spot, the events seeming to rush by him as he watched Cerwin exit the chamber, Master Ardend hot on his heels calling for him to wait. In the chaos of the moment, the shocked faces of the Council members imprinted into his mind, he made his decision.

"I'm going with him."

Chapter Nineteen Part One:

Preparing for the fight

Jadwar Sun-blessed's guest quarters were sumptuous to put it mildly. The living room looked out onto a beautiful, sculpted garden, date palms, cherry blossoms, fountains and manicured lawns laid out in perfect geometric patterns. Silk drapes hung fluttering from the back of the room, screening the servants and slaves going about their daily tasks.

Torbin stretched out on the low padded benches, velvet scatter cushions spread out to aid in the guests' comfort. The chafe marks from his incarceration still showed on his wrists and ankles, but they were slowly fading. The whole ordeal had left a mark on him, being used as bait in what was in essence, a political coup. The speed with which events took place almost took his breath away. He had despised Sardon, his overtly zealous interpretation of Lhossa's religion regularly spilling over into bloody retribution. However, the way he was played, and his subsequent show trial and execution, smacked of political expediency, not any moral imperative. Even now Torbin felt a pang of grief that someone lost their life because of him, even though his complicity was involuntary.

The sun was high in the afternoon sky, bathing the city in its warm embrace. Torbin got up and walked out onto the balcony, breathing in the fragrant smells from the garden. As always, slaves and servants were going about their daily tasks, making sure that Jadwar Sun-blessed's palace was pristine and beautiful, as would befit a man of his station. As much as slavery appalled Torbin he had to concede that those owned by Jadwar were treated with much more care than most and their faces were left unbranded. It was also true that Jadwar freed them at the end of their working lives and continued to feed and clothe them until they were beckoned. Most other slave owners either worked them to death or cast them out of the city, whereas there was a small corner of the first level that was seen as an oasis of comfort in the blighted lives of the great unwashed. Jadwar had built a complex there to house his slaves and provide a home for those that had been freed of their chains.

It undoubtedly had something to do with his elevated position and education, but there was also something higher, more moral about Jadwar. To many he appeared cautious, but Torbin saw it for what it was, a careful almost painstaking attention to detail. No decision he ever made was done without examining all the facts, all the information. Torbin admired him greatly and was acutely aware of how far he was in his debt, although that was not a subject Jadwar ever raised.

His reasons for removing Sardon the Meek had nothing to do with personal gain and everything to do with moving his society forward. Jadwar knew that it was impossible to force a society into a more enlightened way of living, it had to be done incrementally, one step at a time.

Torbin was also painfully aware that time was running out to marshal a defence of the Titan Gate, having just heard from Candor that the H'Daree were finally on the move. He doubted Turan and Minari would be able to hold out for long, an opinion shared by Candor, so it may only be a matter of days until they marched on the Gate itself. He could only hope that Jadwar's appeal on his behalf to the Senate would meet a favourable response.

He heard servants behind him bringing in trays of food and drink, laying them out on the low table stationed in the centre of the beautifully woven rug on the floor of the living room. Torbin ambled back out of the sun just as Jadran Greycloud entered the room.

"Hail Jadran my friend. What news?" said Torbin, grasping his friend's forearms in greeting.

"Hail Torbin, not all you hoped for but probably better than you expected."

"Please Jadran, not so cryptic eh." Torbin's eyebrows jumped in response.

"Apologies Torbin. The Senate would not grant you the force you requested as they were not prepared to deplete the militia to that extent. They have however granted you permission to select a volunteer force of three hundred men from the City Guard and I have been given leave to command if you'll have me as your second." Jadran bowed his head in respect, keeping his eyes fixed to the floor.

"Of course Jadran I would be honoured to have you by my side. In Sardis' name man, pick your head up please." Torbin was very fond of his young counterpart but he wished he could drop some of the formalities.

"Sorry Torbin, force of habit." The young Jad flushed a little red at the rebuke but still managed a grin.

"No need to apologise Jadran. Three hundred is a start but it will never be enough to hold the Titan Gate. For a start it's over a mile wide and the enemy will be at least fifty thousand strong and that is a conservative estimate at best." Torbin scratched at his chin, going over the possible scenarios in his head.

"I've seen the Gate Torbin. There is only one main entrance through which to pass in either direction, and on the defensive side it runs through a tunnel as deep as the Gate itself. There are murder holes all along the tunnel ceiling and room for how many men? Six or seven abreast? A small, determined, well-armed force could block that access against a far greater foe and the only other access doesn't start until you reach the first artillery emplacements, at what? One hundred feet straight up at least. One hundred bowmen spread across the Gate could rain down bloody murder on any attacking force with little or no fear of retaliation." Jadran seemed to be warming to the task, almost excited at the prospect.

"Jadran, these people, the H'Daree, were able to cross the Great Storm Curtain with tens of thousands of troops, more pouring in every day for all we know. If they can traverse that then I think they may have a few ideas about how to scale the walls. No, we need more men and we are running out of time. I need you to select the three hundred and be ready to depart in two days. Can you do that for me my friend?" Torbin knew the answer before he asked the question.

"Leave it with me Torbin, we will be ready." Jadran turned in a hurry, nearly knocking over a servant in his haste.

Almost at the moment he left, Jadwar Sun-blessed sauntered into the living room in what for him would be considered modest attire. He wore only white linen trousers and an open-necked shirt, his robes of office discarded whilst inside his own home.

"Your Eminence." Torbin gave a small bow, a little formal but appropriate.

"Please Torbin, Jadwar will do just fine for now." Jadwar smiled and swept his hand in an invitation to sit and talk.

"Jadran tells me the Senate have granted me leave to recruit three hundred men from the City Guard, if that many will volunteer." Torbin absentmindedly picked at the dates laid out and dipped one in honey.

"I believe every militia man in Lhossa would follow you given the choice Torbin, but the Senate believes that the H'Daree is a real threat and that they are coming." Jadwar rested on one elbow and selected a sweet pastry to nibble on.

"But if they know, why would they only grant me three hundred? Surely, they must realise that this would simply not be enough men to hold the Titan Gate? The enemy we face will bring vast numbers to bear and who knows what kind of weaponry?" Torbin poured himself a glass of wine from the decanter, holding up the bottle to offer it to Jadwar.

Jadwar shook his head, instead reaching for a glass of water. "They believe it would be folly to deplete the city's defences any further and that we should rely on the fact that Lhossa's inner walls have never been breached. I have to say in large part I agree with them. However there may be a way to bolster your forces." Jadwar paused, waiting for Torbin to pick up the thread.

"Any help would be most welcome, but I think my opportunities for recruitment are a little limited. I hardly think the Murgan will oblige and Darmat's a little too distant." Torbin instantly wished he hadn't laced his comments with sarcasm but what was done was done.

"Well, that wasn't going to be my first suggestion, but if you are confident that you can resolve your problems, I would be only too happy to leave it in your capable hands." Jadwar sat upright as if getting ready to rise. It had the desired effect.

"I'm sorry Jadwar that was crass and uncalled for. I am of course both grateful and happy to receive any help you can offer." Torbin bent his head in both embarrassment and apology.

"Very well then. Whilst the Senate will not grant you anymore than three hundred soldiers they will grant you leave to recruit five hundred men from the first level. I will recompense any slave owners for their losses and any servants who volunteer will be free to go." Jadwar paused for a moment as if expecting some kind of rebuke. Torbin just sat there and gently nodded. "I have also arranged for one hundred horses, a dozen oxcarts and enough provisions to last you for two months. I have my armouries forging as much steel as we can make in the time you have before you depart. I assume you plan to move as quickly as possible?"

"Two days was my thinking. The H'Daree are on the move and if they crush the twin cities' resistance as swiftly as I fear they could be at the Titan Gate within seven days. We must be there and entrenched before they arrive if we're to stand any chance." Torbin tried to hide his sense of hopelessness with a grim smile, but it felt like a weak ruse.

"I know this sounds like a desperately poor joke Torbin, but a freed slave with a purpose has more resolve than you can imagine. To give a man an identity and a reason to live is a powerful tool and remember there are captured soldiers amongst them, fighting men from all kinds of backgrounds. There are also smiths and healers within the servants and I believe your great popularity amongst the common people will vastly improve your chances of gathering capable men around you. As it is, I believe that the three hundred who will follow you will be among the best we have, and I have one other gift to bestow. Guido Tivosi the captain of my household guard has asked to accompany you and I have granted him permission along with ten of his men, selected by him. They will be your personal guard and will stand beside you whatever end you may face." Jadwar looked sad, almost crestfallen at the prospect of losing Torbin, one he considered a son.

"I would ask you to reconsider Torbin, but I know that you will not. I do not wish to lose my son." Jadwar held Torbin's gaze, sadness written all over his face.

Torbin could feel the tears welling in his eyes, but he did not care. He reached out and took Jadwar's hands in his as he felt the tears drip from his cheeks.

"I intend to return and make this their end and not mine, but please understand I do not wish to leave, it is my duty to myself and both of my homes. You honour me Jadwar, and I am lost for words that could express how proud I am that you see me in this way." Torbin dropped his head and gently wept while Jadwar took him in his arms and cradled his son as any father would.

They sat on the rug not saying anything for a good while until Jadwar gently pulled back and lifted Torbin's chin.

"You have some visitors who I know have missed you greatly, if you will see them?" Jadwar smiled and Torbin could feel his pride and love. It was all he could do to hold down his tears even though he felt cried out. "I will take my leave." Jadwar cupped Torbin's face and then turned to leave.

As he pushed past the drapes Jadwar nodded a greeting to Torbin's as yet unseen guests. The drapes parted and there stood Jadzia with Terror at her side. She looked beautiful in a long low-cut blue dress, her hair falling across her shoulders, curled and shining jet black. Her head was hung low, a look of shame and fear crossing her face, the guilt of what she had done overwhelming her.

Try as he might, Terror simply could not contain himself, bounding the few steps to Torbin, wiggling like an over-excited puppy, little high-pitched whelps escaping his throat. Torbin went to his knee and wrapped his arms around Terror's neck, the bear-hound burying his face in his torso.

Jadzia hadn't moved, standing rooted to the spot, her shame biting too deep for her to talk. Torbin went to her, enveloping her in his arms. She broke down and wept uncontrollably, her shoulders heaving with each sob, while her tears soaked Torbin's shirt.

They sat on one of the benches, Terror laying his chin on Torbin's lap while Jadzia scratched his head, a little contented rumble escaping his throat. Torbin and Jadzia just sat looking at each other for what seemed an age, neither of them able to find the words until Torbin broke the deadlock.

He brushed a stray hair from her face and gently let his fingers stroke her cheek. "I can see that guilt is weighing you down my darling. Don't let it. I don't hold you responsible for anything. Given the circumstances, what else could you do?" The warmth of his smile acted like a dagger to her heart, tears coursing down her already damp cheeks.

"I could and should have been loyal to you. I betrayed you out of fear and it nearly cost you your life." Try as she might, Jadzia could not hold her head up, looking into Torbin's eyes seeming to break her spirit.

"It's not your fault my darling. You cannot break centuries of social indoctrination in a day, no matter how strongly you may feel about someone. Your whole life you have been told that mind-walkers were abominations, an offence against your god. These beliefs become ingrained through centuries of browbeating, so called 'holy men' telling you what you should or should not believe. If everyone you know and have ever known believes the same what else could you do? I do not deny anybody their right to worship in their own way or to believe in whichever deity they choose, I am not the arbiter of such philosophical questions. However I believe that if there is truth in any of the stories and fables they use to teach then that truth is in the intent. They are only meant as morality tales not some literal retelling of actual events. The message always gets twisted, corrupted and used to elevate individuals or subjugate people. I'm all for celebrating what brings us together not that which pulls us apart." Torbin lifted Jadzia's chin and gently kissed her. He suddenly felt a keen sense of embarrassment with the realisation that he'd just preached to her as assuredly as any sun priest ever did. The irony was not lost on him.

Jadzia pulled back a fraction, a slightly harder expression in her eyes. "I love you Torbin and will never forgive myself for what I did, but please do not misunderstand me. I am a child of Sardis, of the line of Jadvar the Great and I will never relinquish my heritage or lose my belief in my god."

Torbin knew he had gone too far, his own distaste for the

nonsensical deity-based religions overpowering his tact and respect for others. *"Stop being such a fucking preachy idiot!"*

"I would never expect or ask that of you, my love. I am sorry, please forgive me. It's just that I feel a little testy given everything that's happened. I shouldn't take it out on you." He took her hand in his and gently kissed her fingers, doing his best chastened little boy impression.

Terror nudged his nose between their clasped hands, puppy-dog eyes as big as saucers, not happy with being left out of the tender reunion. They both relaxed, Jadzia laughing and planting kisses on his snout, terror slobbering licks all over her face.

"Will you come home with me?" Jadzia looked up, a nervy timbre to her voice, expecting rejection.

"Only for a short while my darling. I will be leaving for the Titan Gate in two days and taking as large a force with me as I can muster. You knew this was going to happen if the trial went my way. It has to be done Jadzia and not just for the Protectorate, but for the future of Lhossa. If we cannot stop the H'Daree, everything we know will end and not even Sardis will be able to save us."

"I know Torbin, and I will not try to talk you out of it. Just come with me for now so that we can be together, however short our time may be." She leaned forward and kissed him; her urgency conveyed by her lips.

He pulled her close, her passion burning hotter than he could ever remember and that was really saying something. He leaned back a tiny bit and held her face in his hands. "For a short while." He kissed her again and got up, leading her and Terror out across the garden and towards the rear gate, heading for their apartment. They both knew this may be their last time together, so they walked slowly, hand in hand, almost as if they were walking to the gallows.

Chapter Nineteen Part Two:

The muster

They had done all they could. The tent was raised alongside the main gate, pitched back against the wall to keep it in the shade. An open canteen area had been set up beside it to prepare meals for all that would sign up. Torbin sat behind the table, nervously fiddling with the recruitment forms, shuffling them over and over as if he could not quite find a way of stacking them that made him happy.

A herald had been sent out the night before to the first level to proclaim the terms on offer for slaves and servants alike. Freedom for the slaves if they signed up for a period of one year and the cancelling of bonds of servitude for those servants bound to a Jad household. Torbin had also made sure they were aware of the risks, no point telling them half-truths.

All things considered, he did not feel positive about the outcome. Who would want to volunteer for almost certain death? Five hundred seemed a stretch at best. At worst he doubted five hundred would even turn up. Jadran and some of the men he'd selected were on duty outside the tent to act as marshals, but Torbin doubted that would be necessary.

It was a sweltering day as well so at least he was glad to be in the shade, but he could see no point in dragging this out any longer.

"Jadran."

The young Jad poked his head through the tent flap. "Yes Torbin?"

"We may as well get this over and done with although I doubt it will take that long." He knew he must sound surly, but right now he really did not care.

"You might want to come and take a look first." Jadran almost smirked as he held the flap open.

"What the…?" Torbin could hardly believe his eyes. Jadran's guards were struggling to hold back the throng crowding in at the front of the line with thousands more stretching out along the great land wall. It was as if every slave and servant in Lhossa had turned out, a sea of humanity apparently eager to sign on.

"Torbin!" The shout went up and every single one of the great unwashed assembled picked it up. "Torbin, Torbin!" The sound echoed back and forth, a great cacophony of voices filling the air. It grew so loud that it reminded Torbin of the trumpets of the armies of the Kingdom of Darmat, a noise to challenge the heavens. He stood there dumbstruck, his jaw hanging low as if it was no longer attached.

The size of the task suddenly dawned on Torbin. Instead of hoping that maybe five hundred would turn up he now had to sift through what looked like the entire slave population of Lhossa. He raised his hands, waving for the huge mass of people to calm and quieten down.

"Right Jadran we need to rethink this and quickly because we're still setting off tomorrow. Set up another three tables inside the tent and start to break this throng down into manageable sections. I want three lines, military experience, tradesmen, and cooks, medics and orderlies. Send them in ten at a time to the appropriate tables, fighters to me, you organise tradesmen and Jadson can take the cooks, medics and orderlies. We have a vast number to choose from so be particular, grade them according to skill and experience and don't be afraid to discard people. I know it sounds harsh, but this isn't a popularity contest and we only have today to get it done. You'll need to send up the hill to check the carts and see what we have in the way of clothing and footwear before we even look at the weapons and armour." Torbin looked at the assembled City Guards that Jadran had brought down to manage the selection, all standing there as if stuck in mud.

"Jadran, let's get moving." He leaned in and quietly whispered to the young commander, not wanting to undermine him.

"Jump to it you idle dogs! MOVE!" Jadran screamed at his troops who all jumped up, each man frightened to be seen doing nothing. There were a few comical stumblings and coming togethers that Torbin would have laughed at given different circumstances. He could not help but admire Jadran though, his men immediately springing into action at his commands, corralling the mass of bodies into organised lines while a dozen of their colleagues set off up to level two to inventory their supplies.

"Ten minutes and then start sending them in. Ten at a time and no disturbances. We want to make this as smooth and quiet as possible, and we have to get it done quickly." Torbin looked at Jadran who just nodded his assent. *"Good enough for me."*

Torbin was about to turn back to the tent when a nervous murmur went up in the crowd. A channel slowly started to open, bodies nervously edging back as if in fear of their wellbeing. At first Torbin did not realise who it was that split the throng, then he saw. It was Guido Tivosi. Torbin could not remember ever seeing the captain of Jadwar's household guard out of his armoured uniform, but he somehow seemed even bigger. He was dressed in brown leather breeches and an open-necked cotton shirt with black leather-soled boots. His jet-black hair was tied back in a ponytail leaving his face visible for the first time Torbin could recall. He was a huge man, densely muscled, his shoulders so broad that he almost appeared neckless. His face was hard-edged and scarred, the most prominent one almost cutting his nose in half. *"Thank Sardis he's on our side."*

"Captain Tivosi, I'm honoured to have you with us." Torbin extended his hand, Tivosi grasping it in his almost making it disappear.

"The honour is mine Torbin Pale-skin." Tivosi's voice was almost as big as he was, his deep bass tone booming out like a thunderclap. "I have brought my ten best and we are yours to command." Tivosi's men were lined up behind him, teak tough-looking warriors, all of them big men. Not as big as their captain however, Torbin doubted there were many that were.

"Could your men help with controlling the crowd and ensuring things run smoothly out here?"

"Of course, sir." Tivosi barked orders at one of his lieutenants and his men went straight to work, backing the throng up and quickly sorting them out into a more organised shamble.

"I would appreciate your counsel with the selection process. We only have today, and your expert eye would be of great help."

"Any task you require of me will be done sir." Tivosi bowed to Torbin making him feel more than a little uncomfortable.

"Guido, may I call you Guido?"

"Of course sir."

"Guido, this is completely voluntary, no one is under orders here. Whilst chain of command is obviously important, please let's keep it informal for now. Just call me Torbin." Torbin flashed him his best friendly smile.

"As you wish." Tivosi's expression did not alter a jot.

Torbin smiled and extended his arm towards the tent, ushering Tivosi inside. He'd never really heard him talk before and on the few occasions he did it was muffled by his helm. Now that he had heard him clearly his accent sounded west coast of the Free Territories, maybe even Santatoria. He was almost as far away from home as Torbin himself. *"I bet that's an interesting backstory."*

They settled behind their respective tables, Tivosi looking like an adult sat with the children. Torbin signalled the guard at the tent flap to start ushering them in.

It was as sorry a collection of undernourished souls as Torbin could ever remember seeing, all of them scabrous, ribcages clearly showing and distended bellies bloating out like fleshy balloons. A few had a smattering of military experience, a couple of Darmat infantrymen, some former mercenaries but most were just hopeful of an opportunity to escape their bonds. Of the first fifty to pass their table, Torbin and Tivosi only pulled aside three to sign up as foot soldiers. Torbin's mood began to darken, the thought of sifting through this heaving mass of humanity for such meagre scraps had little appeal.

Then a group came in together, obviously used to each other's company, pushing one man forward as if he was their spokesman. He was tall and fair-haired, broad but thin, underfed like all slaves. He had a rat brand on his left cheek, a sewer rat, as low a station as any slave could have, usually doled out as a final punishment, one stop short of execution. There was something different about him, something stronger, more confident despite his condition. He approached the table head held high, not looking away but looking directly at Torbin.

"What is your name friend?" Torbin had determined that he would treat everyone with respect regardless of their standing.

"Jek." He was not exactly surly, but he wouldn't win any prizes for effusiveness.

"Well Jek, what is your background? We need experienced fighting men but only those that wish to go and those that understand the consequences of that choice." Torbin leaned back in his chair. He had to hold his tongue, wait for this man to show him something worthwhile, if there was indeed anything worth having.

Jek took half a step back and pulled up his tattered shirt showing a crossed-cutlass tattoo, blood dripping from the point of the blades. The Brotherhood of the Golden Hand and a senior deckhand to boot. The criss-cross of scars covering his torso pointed to his independent nature. Torbin sat forward, encouraged that he finally had some genuine talent to work with.

"I was senior deck 'and on *The Wavecrest*, when we was taken by a squad o' Snowbard galleys jus' off the coast o' Santatoria." Jek's expression told Torbin much, his distaste for Snowbard glaringly obvious.

"So, you were on a raid of Santatoria then? Ironic you should be captured while committing a crime against my homeland, do you not think?" Torbin no longer had to keep the secret, knowledge of his roots having spread far and wide in Lhossa.

"That's as maybe methinks. One man's crime's another man's opportunity. Those bastards made me pay the price though, so if you're looking for an apology, you'll 'ave to wait a twhile." Jek stood his ground and was not cowed by Torbin or surprisingly by Tivosi.

"How is it a man of your size and obvious experience ended up a sewer rat?" Tivosi looked Jek up and down like a horse trader weighing the value of flesh.

"Bit too much to say for myself I 'spose. I don't like being told what to do by those that ain't earned the right." Jek held Tivosi's stare, quite a feat for anyone let alone a slave. Torbin had to admit it, he was definitely warming to this man.

"A man that won't take orders is of no use where we are going. So, do you think we have earned the right corsair?" Tivosi had pushed back his chair and stood up just to accentuate his point.

"'E has." Jek nodded at Torbin. "I guess we'll 'ave to wait and see where you're concerned."

Tivosi walked round the table and stood face to face with Jek, everybody else backing away a little, the threat of violence hovering in the air.

"What about now?" Tivosi was inches from Jek's face and although they were of a similar height Tivosi was much the bigger man. For that matter he was much the bigger man in just about every situation.

To everyone's amazement Jek nudged forward, literally going nose to nose with the hulking captain of the guards.

"Like I said, we'll 'ave to wait and see." He didn't back down an inch while the tension in the room started to become unbearable.

"Guido." Torbin had stood up, both arms out in front of him, gesturing for calm.

"Oh, he'll do." Tivosi laughed, a noise so deep and threatening that it felt more hazardous than funny. Tivosi smiled and clapped Jek on the back, the sewer rat breathing out a sigh of relief, the first outward sign that he'd felt in any danger.

"These other men, are they with you?" Torbin gestured at the other nine who'd entered the tent with Jek.

"Yes sir, they are. We're all Brotherhood, the only ones still alive in Lhossa that is." Jek's respectful response was rooted in his background Torbin did not doubt, but the little scene played out with Tivosi had certainly lifted the man's spirit.

"Okay sign up over there and get a meal inside you. We'll talk soon Jek, and I may have important tasks for you." Torbin ushered them to a table set off to the side where one of Jadwar's scribes was registering all of the new recruits.

From that point onwards, the selection process seemed to go far smoother, the mood of the whole endeavour seeming to lift. By the end of the day, they had selected five hundred men from the slaves and servants that had volunteered, many more being sent away disappointed.

Torbin had delegated most of the organisational tasks to Jadran who in turn had set his subordinates to work. All of those selected were fed and where possible and at times necessary, given fresh clothes and more importantly footwear. They would be setting off in the morning so Torbin had gathered his command staff in the tent to go over the final preparations, Terror of course in tow. Now that they were definitely going into action Torbin would not leave him behind. Jadran was there as his first officer with Jadson as his second and Guido Tivosi was there, even though he refused any official title and insisted he was acting only as Torbin's personal guard. Much to everyone's surprise and especially his, Torbin had included Jek in the meeting.

"Jek, I assume as senior deckhand you must have been responsible for recruitment and training where your ships sailors were concerned." Torbin and everyone else was sat down while Jek stood rigidly to attention. He appeared far better than the sorry-looking figure who'd entered the tent that morning. A fresh set of clothes and sandals, a haircut and a good wash revealed a far more vigorous individual, the brand being the only obvious reminder of his former condition.

"Not much in terms of recruitment sir, as you know most are born t' the life in the Brotherhood. I was in charge o' training, what you would refer to as martial training I 'spose. I trained 'em up and disciplined 'em I 'spose you could say." Jek held his posture, chin upright, clearly addressing whoever he was speaking to.

"Good, good. Jek this is a volunteer mission so while we are in conference first names are fine, the less formality the better. Let's keep our sirs for in the field. Please sit." Tivosi pulled out a chair for Jek and nodded for him to sit. "We had a far more productive selection process than I could have ever hoped for. We even found a construction engineer from Darmat who'd been working as a porter for a Jad family. Unbelievable waste of talent but there it is. We will be setting off tomorrow with a hundred of us on horseback forming an advance force with the sole purpose of securing the Gate. Myself, Tivosi and Jadran will be in the advanced force with all foot and supplies following under Jadson's command." Torbin nodded to the young officer who beamed with pride. "Jek, I am appointing you a sergeant and Master of Arms." Everyone looked at Jek who sat there slack jawed as if someone had just asked him to solve the world's most impossible riddle.

"We need someone with organisational experience and someone with a bearing others will respect. We'll be organising the volunteers into the squad system, ten to a squad, ten squads to a century, with me in command, Jadran and Jadson as my first and second officers. Everyone else will report to you, with the exception of Guido and his guards of course, so I will need you to choose centurions and squad leaders and coordinate any training needed. Do you think you could do that?" All eyes remained on Jek and it took him a moment to close his mouth and realise Torbin was speaking to him.

"Yes sir, sorry Torbin, I'd be honoured." Jek looked shell-shocked until Tivosi slapped him on the back, nearly knocking him off his chair. Torbin, Jadran and Jadson all got up smiling to congratulate their new confederate, Jek grasping each of their hands in grateful acknowledgment.

"All of you know what we will be facing. It seems an impossible task, but it is one that we have to attempt or else all we know may be lost forever. The Titan Gate, for those of you that have never seen it, is the most astonishing construction I have ever witnessed, possibly the greatest anywhere in the Known World. It's a five hundred-foot tall, mile-long fortress and offers us the best chance of turning back the H'Daree but make no mistake we will be outnumbered by more than fifty to one. That's why this is voluntary." Torbin looked around at his companions needing to know they understood what they were facing.

"I will always follow you Torbin, you are after all the great defender." Jadran beamed a smile at his friend. "As will I." Jadson looked proud beyond measure to be included.

"I am a warrior, Torbin. To fight in one of the great battles of our time is a privilege for me and my men." Guido Tivosi seemed genuinely enthusiastic about the business at hand.

"You have given me back my life Torbin and I will gladly follow you into the fire." Jek's eyes sparkled proudly.

Torbin looked down at Terror. "What do you think boy?" The mighty bear-hound barked his assent.

"Right then, we go."

Chapter Twenty Part One:

Parley

This was not what Marisa expected at all. The inside of the cave system had been carved out to form several rooms, with sconces holding torches and furs covering the chiselled-out platforms. There were tables and chairs with rushes covering the floors, all of it warm and comfortable with the entrance sealed with a well-fashioned wooden gate. All their preconceived ideas about how savage and backward the Wasteland tribes were, were obviously way off the mark. There was real skill and finesse at work here, the construction wrought by accomplished builders.

Marisa had feared the worst when they were taken by the Wastelanders, but in truth their treatment had been fairly gentle. At least by normal standards. They had not been roughed up too badly and everything had been loaded onto the sleds, cooking equipment and tents included. They had even laid Shadow on one of the sleds and made her comfortable, which seemed scarcely believable. They had all been bound, gagged and their weapons taken from them, but they were alive and well. Now it was just a matter of waiting to see what the Wastelanders wanted or what they were going to do.

A reed curtain hung down across the entrance to the room in which they were being held. Marisa could hear voices and see shadows flickering in the light on the other side of the screen. The Wastelanders' language sounded guttural and harsh, but she thought she could pick out the odd word or phrase. One thing was for sure, there was an argument going on and they were the subject.

She looked around at her squad, all looking miserable, but in pretty good condition. They had taken Shadow somewhere else, and Whisper had taken a heavy hit to the head when he tried to break his bonds to defend her. Apart from that they had all gotten away pretty lightly.

The voices outside suddenly became much more intense, as if an argument were about to spill over into violence. There was what sounded like a short scuffle and some barked words, then it fell quiet. The curtain was pulled back and a great hulking Wastelander ducked through the entrance. He was about the same size as Lummox with a thick black beard and a shaggy mane of hair. He was dressed in untanned skin breeches and a rough-spun shirt with laces instead of buttons. He crossed to Marisa, pulled her up by the elbows and led her out of the room, muffled threats from her squad slowly receding behind her.

He pulled her along deeper into the cave and ducked into a smaller side chamber. It was carved out of the rock in a circular shape like the inside of a dome and there was a small tunnel that ran from the ceiling upwards until it hit daylight. In the middle of the floor was a fire pit, a smouldering blaze pouring smoke into the room, some but not all of it venting through the shaft. Marisa's eyes watered, stung by the acrid fume, a mixture of wood and flowery scents. It was difficult to adjust her eyes properly, the smoke and heat clouding everything. The great Wastelander sat her on the floor and removed her gag causing her to cough, breathing in the smoke making her feel a little light-headed. As her eyes adjusted, she saw another figure sat on the opposite side of the fire. They were small and sitting on their haunches, a mismatched collection of skins covering their skinny frame and a mask fashioned out of reeds and wood obscuring their features.

The great Wastelander passed his hand over his face and breathed in the smoke before turning to face Marisa.

"I am Urdhoa, chief of the Wolfs-head Clan and this is our spirit-raiser Chetta. I bring you here to talk by the sacred fire, where only the truth can be spoken, and that truth will set you free." Urdhoa held Marisa's gaze waiting for her response. Her head swam, a strange warm feeling, akin to being drunk enveloped her. She knew this was a safe place, a place of truth and light, there was no need to burden herself with deception. The truth would set them free.

"I am Marisa Longspear, First Centurion of army group Partia and servant of the Protectorate. I come on a mission of peace to our neighbours from the Wastelands." Marisa felt warm and content, so nice to sit and talk to good friends.

"Huh, Wastelands you call it. This is The Wilderness Marisa Longspear, the Great White, home of the ancients and realm of the Great Maker, provider of all." Urdhoa spoke as if correcting a small child's mistake, an offence forgiven because they know no better.

"I meant no offence great chief; it is just the common word for the lands north of the Protectorate. We come in peace seeking only information and to try if we can, to discover the reasons for the attack on Seal-breaker Bay." Marisa swayed slightly, a faint wooziness making the room tilt from side to side. A warm pulse flowed gently up and down her body, keeping perfect time with her movements.

"We did not launch the attack. It was not our doing." Urdhoa swept smoke up to his mouth passing his hands over his face, breathing deeply and holding his breath in. He blew it out in a great gout of fume, a cloud rolling out in front of him. Marisa watched as it twisted and turned, throbbing in time with the rushes of warmth that pulsated through her body.

"But I was there and I saw the Wolfs-head banners held aloft, saw your warriors charge our lines." Marisa smiled as the words came out of her mouth, fully aware of what she was saying but unwilling to allow the colours to pass by unnoticed.

"Chetta, pull back a little. Our guest is not used to this much truth." Urdhoa laughed, a deep belly rumble that filled the room bouncing backwards and forwards off the walls. Marisa had the urge to get up and try to catch it, but her hands were still tied, and she was far too comfortable.

Chetta threw a handful of green powder on the fire, little flashes and explosions sparkling into life, the smell turning ever so slightly towards that of vegetables.

Marisa's head started to clear a little, her eyes able to focus and her mind capable of staying in the moment, however temporarily.

"Some of our young warriors were tempted away with promises of wealth and power. It has always been so with those that seek to use others to fulfil their own desires." Urdhoa spoke without relish, the words almost held back, a reluctant admission.

"Who tempted them away and why?" The haziness was still there, the pulsing less intense but no less enjoyable.

Urdhoa paused, words seeming to hang on the edge of his mouth, uncertain if they should stand forth.

"A party of mountain men came to our Kaimas…"

"Common tongue." Chetta spoke for the first time, a strange slightly dreamy voice.

"Sorry village, asking permission to address the clan. They came on dog-drawn sleds, laden with supplies and weapons and although they did not tell us where they hailed from, I had my suspicions. They addressed the clan fully armoured, as some sort of show of strength and the heads of some of our younger more restless warriors were turned. They convinced more than twenty to go with them, promises of wealth and glory turning them from their homes and families." Urdhoa drew in a deep breath. "There were those of us that wanted to stop them, kill them or at least cast them out, but then they drew their steel. It is not possible to fully explain, but they wielded some sort of magic beyond the power of even Chetta to overcome. It flooded most with a sense of terror, many overmanned by sickness and cramps, even the hardiest among us felt dizzy and sick. As soon as they had left with our young blood, we removed to Wolfs Hearth and here we stay. This is an ancient stronghold, deep in old magic and they will not find it so easy to seek us out here or take any more of our youth." Urdhoa breathed out a sigh, the memory still too fresh for him.

"I am sorry for your loss Urdhoa, but this is why we have sought you out. These mountain men organised an attack on our community at Seal-breaker Bay using young clansmen to lead it. Many were sacrificed for their cause, but we are no wiser as to who they were or what their objective was. They did however leave three of their blades behind on the field for us to capture and while we have captured suchlike before it has only been from the corpses of our enemies." Marisa paused, that warm light-headedness making her nearly lose her thread. "They are Snowbard soul-forged blades, holy to the warrior caste of Snowbard, never to be surrendered while alive. I have been in contact with the blades myself and I felt their power, some malevolence resides within them I think, something dark. We seek alliance with our Wastelander neighbours, apologies Wilderness, to guard against these aggressors. We don't as yet have any proof, but I believe they are agents of Snowbard and this is just a feint, a small test to see what if any countermeasures may be put in place." Marisa stopped talking, a strange, detached feeling of having been listening to someone else's words washing over her.

"We know of Snowbard. They have long haunted the steps of our brother clans to the east, but they are far from their home. Why would they travel so far, crossing all of our homelands to reach us just to take a score of our young warriors?" Urdhoa took his time asking his questions, his patience and thoughtfulness surprising Marisa. She felt more present, still warm and content but able to stay in the moment, hold enough focus to talk.

"Do you honestly believe we would send out a scouting party to seek you out if twenty or so men attacked one of our communities? There were more than five-hundred Wilderness warriors attacking Seal-breaker Bay Urdhoa. I know because I saw with my own eyes." Marisa felt another rush seep through her being making her take a little gasping inhale.

"Five hundred?" Urdhoa seemed shocked by this revelation. "Were they all children of the Wilderness?"

"As far as I could tell, they all looked like clan members." Marisa sighed and shook herself like a dog loosing water from its fur.

"They must have gathered young warriors all the way across the Wilderness to have put out a force of that size." Urdhoa looked as if he was talking to himself, trying to puzzle out how this came to pass. "We have withdrawn to our haven and haven't spoken to the other clans for what feels like an age. Chetta, I seek the counsel of the Great Maker, can you call him?"

"I will try." The little spirit-raiser's voice sounded full of colour and music to Marisa, little rivulets of warm pleasure running up and down her body in concert with it.

Chetta scattered handfuls of different powders onto the fire, each giving off little bursts of sparks and aromas. It reminded Marisa of fireworks on feast nights, the memory helping the rushes running up and down her body, tickling her skin.

The spirit-raiser sat cross-legged on the floor and began to sway back and forth, little musical incantations loosing themselves from her being. Marisa could see waves of colours rising from Chetta's skin, forming into shapes, a tree, a deer running, water pouring over a rock. Breathing in deeply she closed her eyes and was floating in the sky, speeding towards the stars, feeling colours and emotions rushing by her, tugging at her heart, making her yearn for something but she couldn't say what.

She opened her eyes, and the room was full of colours and shapes, all swirling around each other, joining and pulling apart, sweeping around in great arcs, musical chords pulsing out in great blooms. Chetta's swaying had become maniacal, tearing from side to side, her shoulders shuddering in time with her motions. Urdhoa was laying on his back his eyes wide open, a look of ecstasy enveloping his face, his back arching upwards towards the ceiling.

Marisa tumbled backwards, feeling as if she was floating off a cliff. Laying on her back she saw what looked like a face coalescing in the smoke gathered at the top of the dome. Then she heard the voice, gentle and caring but malevolent and terrifying, ancient words far too wise for her to understand. So much thought, so many words, answers she did not understand or want to know. Then the blackness took her.

She woke up laying on a bed of furs in a warm well-lit antechamber. Her head pulsed, little pin pricks of pain stabbing at her temples. Something felt a little strange, then she realised. Her bonds had been cut and her hands were free.

"How are you feeling Marisa?" Her eyes slowly adjusted, Breda coming into view leaning over her, a look of concern on his face.

Marisa pushed herself up on her elbows. "Not too bad, just a bit of a headache. How long have I been out?"

"About eight hours. You were brought in here by a couple of the Wastelanders and you had a beaming smile on your face. I assume you had a good time?" Fugly was sat on a step across the room, a wicked little smile lighting up her features.

"Well, it was different I can tell you that. Is everyone okay and are we all present and correct?"

"We're all good, they have fed and watered us and removed our restraints. They let Whisper go and tend to Shadow but she has been well looked after. What's going on here Marisa?" Breda asked the one question they all wanted an answer to.

"I think they were being cautious where we were concerned because if it had been otherwise I don't believe any of us would still be here."

"That's a fact. If they had wanted us dead, we wouldn't have even seen them coming." Skin sat at a table whittling away at a piece of wood, carving what was starting to look like a snow tiger. "For Shadow when she comes back. A little reminder." Grinning he carried on his work.

"Nobody's arguing with that but why the soft treatment?" Bodger held up his free hands as if to accentuate the point.

"I think they are as concerned by what happened as we are Bodger. They were not aware of the scale of things. All they knew is that a score of their young warriors was taken by these so-called mountain men. I think they are as worried as we are by the turn of events and are open to some sort of cooperation, but how far that might go is anyone's guess. This is all speculation anyway. Until they talk to us, we are no more certain of the outcome than when we got here." Marisa sat upright, swinging her legs over the edge of her sleeping platform.

"So, these mountain men were from Snowbard then?" Garic had been sat in a shaded corner out of view but the sight of him warmed Marisa's heart.

"I don't know for certain, but it looks that way. The mountain men were carrying soul-forged blades and they could not stop them from taking their young warriors. Just so you know they do not refer to themselves as Wastelanders but as Children of the Wilderness. Let us respect that." Marisa stood up, a little dizziness still affecting her.

"How come you never told us that Skin?" Lummox propped himself up on his elbows, his sleeping platform not quite big enough to accommodate his whole body, feet dangling over the end.

"It never came up." Skin shrugged his shoulders as if the

question was a waste of everyone's time.

"So, what now?" Rat sounded more than a little surly, a deep-purple black eye standing out like a ripe plum, making her face seem lopsided.

"Now we wait and see what our hosts have to say on the matter." Marisa knew how inadequate an answer that sounded but what else was there to do?

As they were standing there mulling over their prospects Whisper walked into the room, flanked by two Wastelanders who waited at the door. Everyone went to greet him, smiles and backslapping all round, delighted to see their comrade.

"That's quite a lump you've got there." Marisa gently stroked Whisper's hair, running her fingers over the egg-shaped bump on his head. "Maybe next time you should duck." Everyone chuckled at that, Whisper having the good grace to blush a little.

"How's Shadow doing?" Marisa ushered Whisper further into the room.

"The leg's healing well. These people are skilled healers. They used a kind of poultice on the wound. There's no infection and I think the scarring will be minimal which is amazing considering how deep some of those cuts were. They are not what I expected at all."

"I think we are all a little surprised Whisper." Marisa gave his shoulder a little squeeze.

"So, Marisa, you still haven't told us what happened in there." Fugly had wandered over to join the rest of the group.

"Well, I don't believe in magic, spirits or any kind of god but if you asked me to explain the Gift or mindwalking I couldn't. Even though I could not explain it I still don't believe it's magic, just something we don't yet have the answers for. We may never be able to explain it fully, but I would still believe that some rational explanation would exist. However, what I witnessed in that chamber has definitely given me pause. I know I was intoxicated, and my vision was undoubtedly impaired but I saw a face and I clearly heard a voice that did not come from any of the three of us. If I didn't know better, I'd say that I saw the face and heard the voice of god."

Chapter Twenty Part Two:

Take my hand

"Will you take my hand on it, Marisa Longspear?"

"It would be my honour Urdhoa."

Nothing about the Children of the Wilderness was as expected. They were a resourceful and sophisticated people with a literal and visceral connection to their land. Marisa and Breda had sat with Urdhoa, Chetta and the senior warriors in his tribe or gentis and talked long and hard about events that were shaping their future.

Marisa was still troubled by what she had experienced but Urdhoa would not speak about what he saw by the sacred fire, not in specifics anyway. However, he did say he'd communed with the Great Maker and had heeded warnings of the great battles to come. He spoke of a great black wave that would engulf the world and that the only chance they had was to stand with those that would oppose it. A little florid from Marisa's point of view but better than no information at all she supposed. Then with a simple handshake the deal was sealed, the Protectorate and the Children of the Wilderness were allies. This wasn't a negotiated deal between neighbouring states with points of contention and treaties that needed ratifying but an understanding that they would come to each other's aid when needed.

Marisa had sent Shadow back with Whisper and Lummox to allow her to convalesce and to report back to the old man. There was still work to be done and the sooner they got to it the better.

Urdhoa had to contact the other Kaimas and most importantly

find and stop the mountain men that were stripping their youth. Urdhoa had dispatched messengers to the other gentis urging their leaders to come to a gathering, hoping to forge a workable alliance between the tribes. Marisa and the remainder of her squad had set off to track them down and Urdhoa had sent three of his best with her to see the task done.

All of their gear had been returned and they had been given extra coats and breeches, fur-lined and incredibly cold-resistant for which Marisa was most grateful.

"I will see you upon our return, Urdhoa, and I give you my word that if any of your youth are still alive, we will bring them back to you." Marisa had held Urdhoa's shoulders as she said her goodbyes.

"May the Great Maker watch your steps, Marisa Longspear." Urdhoa had embraced her as a friend.

They had started west, crossing the Great White bearing slightly south in the hope that they may fall upon their targets skirting the border with the Protectorate. Marisa figured that the mountain men had been tasked with harassing settlements close to the Wilderness, for what purpose exactly she couldn't be sure, but it felt like the most likely ploy.

On the second night they made camp in the lee of a rock formation, the shelter offered being minimal but better than nothing. The wind was stirring up spin drifts, the snow whistling around forming little dancing sprites that swirled across the ground. You hadn't experienced winter until you'd seen winter in the Wilderness.

Rat and Bodger took guard while the rest of them set about pitching the tents and getting a cooking fire going, Skin lighting the tinder, Fugly and Garic preparing the food. Garic's continued dark mood was starting to fray Marisa's nerves, more akin to sulking than depression but they had to press on regardless. Marisa sat down by the fire with Breda and started to sharpen their blades on the whetstone they had hauled with them.

Ungforth wandered over to sit with them. As far as Marisa could work out, he seemed to be the senior man of the three Children of the Wilderness so she would speak to him first of any plans that came to mind.

"Can I sharpen my steel, Marisa Longspear?" He was a big man, as most Children of the Wilderness were, although not quite Urdhoa's size and he was a child of winter, made even more so by the myriad of icicles hanging from his beard.

"Of course Ungforth, please help yourself." The big man smiled his gap-toothed smile and set to work sharpening his gigantic sword. It was the biggest Marisa had ever seen, at least in actual use, nearly five feet long and six or seven inches wide at the hilt. How he managed to wield it, even given his size was beyond her.

"Where are Urdoon and Andmar?" Marisa started to re-strap the leather grip on her sword.

"Scouting ahead." Ungforth was about as forthcoming as most Children of the Wilderness that Marisa had met.

"What can they expect to see in this light?" Marisa looked up quizzically.

"If you put your faith in the Great Maker, he will grant you sight, even in the dark Marisa Longspear."

"Marisa is enough, Ungforth." Marisa smiled at the young warrior.

"Is your name not Marisa Longspear?" Ungforth's brow creased as if confusion reigned in on him.

"My name is Marisa, Longspear is my vocation, my calling if you will."

"Then you are a warrior by choice? We have heard of the women warriors from the lands to the south, but I didn't think to meet one. I am honoured to do so now." Ungforth smiled and dipped his head in what Marisa assumed was meant to be some kind of bow. This was by far the longest conversation she'd had with Ungforth since they set off and she felt none the wiser, but she supposed it was a start at least.

"We are happy you are with us Ungforth. Your people are not what we expected, we have much to learn from each other I think."

Ungforth nodded his agreement and stood up sweeping his blade in great circular arcs, the edge gleaming deadly sharp in the firelight.

"I thank you for the use of your whetstone." He bowed and went to leave the fireside.

"Ungforth, will you not stay and eat with us?" Marisa wanted to keep him there for a while and try to wheedle out some information from him.

"I must search out my brothers and see what they have found but I will return and share your food, Marisa." He beamed out his gapped-tooth smile once again and disappeared into the night.

"Not exactly chatty, are they?" Breda had picked up his sword and started to sharpen it on the stone.

"No, but I must admit I'm starting to like them."

"Me too." Breda chuckled as he worked, and Marisa nodded her assent.

"Have you thought about what we're going to do if we manage to track them down?" It was a question Marisa had avoided addressing until now, but it had to be faced.

Garic, Fugly and Skin came and sat down with bowls of venison stew for everyone, the smell making some stomachs rumble. Marisa took her bowl from Fugly, a little smile of gratitude acknowledged.

"I'm not sure yet Breda. We will have to try and isolate the mountain men somehow, that and hope the presence of Ungforth and his brothers will help sway his compatriots to our cause."

"That's a lot of ifs." Skin sat cross-legged on the snow in just his shirt and breeches, apparently oblivious to the cold.

"Yeah, far more than I'm comfortable with Skin but we're not exactly working from a manual here." Marisa spooned a mouthful of stew and chewed away. *"Fugly sure can cook."*

"We could try a stealthy one, creep into their camp in the dead of night and give them each a red grin." Skin gave his deadpan smile which always made Marisa feel uneasy as if he was the only one who got the joke.

"We could have picked them off if Shadow was here. She could shoot the wings off a fly at a hundred paces." Fugly chirped in, little grunts of agreement passing round the fire.

"Even if she was, that armour they wear is Snowbard-forged steel. It can turn a broadsword or a battleaxe with ease, so I doubt arrows would do us much good. No, I think we'll have to work out a way to separate the three of them and bring them down the old-fashioned way, steel on steel."

"Do you think our Wastelanders will be able to convince their young blood to return to the fold? Because if not I don't fancy our chances ten against hundreds." *"For fucks sake!"* Garic sat elbows on knees, that familiar sullen look on his face.

"Firstly, I've already told you we respect them by calling them by their proper name, Children of the Wilderness. And in answer to your question, I certainly hope so but that's as far as it goes because like everyone else here I don't know. We all miss Shadow and feel bad about what happened but that doesn't excuse your tetchiness because now it's bordering on insubordination. Get your gear together and go and relieve Rat, NOW!" Marisa felt a small pang of guilt balling him out in front of everyone, but it had to be done.

Garic got up without saying a word and snatched his gear up on the walk, thundering off in Rat's direction. Marisa turned to Fugly.

"When you've finished can you go and relieve Bodger so that he can get some food?"

"Of course sir." Fugly smiled and gave Marisa's shoulder a little sympathetic squeeze. They were all really close and everyone knew each other's business, which wasn't always a good thing.

Fugly finished up and grabbed her gear, setting off in the opposite direction to Garic.

"That was a little brutal." Breda looked sideways at Marisa, eyebrows arched as if asking a question.

"Not you too Breda, I've got enough problems without adding to them. It had to be done, he's been getting worse ever since we got caught out by Urdhoa's boys."

"I don't disagree Marisa, just thought it was maybe a little bit of an overreaction is all. I am not second guessing you because so far you've coped far better than I would have." Marisa felt some of the tension leave her, Breda had a way of smoothing off the rough edges.

"Maybe, but a bit of time alone on watch might help him calm down a bit. I'll go and talk to him in a while but for now we have more important things to deal with."

"I have an idea, but that's all it is at the moment, a working theory at best." Breda had lowered his voice making it feel like a conspiracy to Marisa. "Come, walk with me Marisa and I'll try to explain."

They got up and started to amble away from the fire, Marisa throwing a nod in Skin's direction. If he saw he didn't bother to acknowledge it, just got up and started to clear the cooking utensils away.

"So, what's this working theory then?" They had wandered out of earshot so the lowered voices no longer mattered.

"It's something I noticed when we experienced the soul-forged blades. Everyone else seemed unmanned by the experience, as was I at first but I slipped into the Gift for a moment and the nausea and fear almost disappeared. No one knows if there are any mind-walkers in Snowbard but if there is one among these three mountain men, I should still be able to go undetected. My measure of the Gift is limited, maybe fifteen seconds at best but that would allow me to cover a comparatively long distance. If we can get within a mile or so undetected, I could get close, hide and wait for you to make your move. We'd need to time it because it would take an hour or so before I was able to immerse again but if we timed it right, I could attack from behind unseen and possibly take them out. If not all three I could certainly shorten the odds." Breda had stopped walking and looked at Marisa, warm breath blasting out of his mouth in the bitter night air.

"Why did you not mention this earlier?" Marisa's voice was hard, a subtle edge to it.

"I don't know, it just hadn't occurred to me. If I'm honest Marisa it's not something I'm overly keen on doing but think it may be our only real advantage. We are obviously at a huge disadvantage in terms of numbers, and we know how soul-forged blades can affect combat." Breda shrugged, a little embarrassed that he'd neglected to tell anyone until now.

"As Skin said, that's a lot of ifs Breda. But as you say this may be our one real advantage. I don't like the thought of you being isolated though and what if they do have a mind-walker? That was a major implication as a result of the contact at Seal-breaker Bay or how else did they manage to target our mind-walkers? It's fraught with risk." Marisa was just voicing what they were both thinking.

"Keep it to yourself for now and we'll revisit this when and if we need to." Marisa nodded and Breda mirrored her.

"CONTACT!" Fugly's shout echoed across the ground and Marisa and Breda sprinted the short distance to the campfire, weapons and armour neatly stacked ready for a quick change, the lessons of their first contact with Urdhoa's people well remembered.

Fugly came into view, backing up towards the fire, Bodger already having made it to her side. The pair slowly retreated spears lowered, shields held in front, both of them sideways on. Rat and Skin stationed themselves on either side of the fire waiting for their comrades to make it back to them. They would all form up in a circle and fight with their backs to each other, leaving no gaps and no way for an enemy to come at them from behind. If they were going to die, they would exact a terrible cost.

"TEN! TEN!" Marisa screamed at the top of her lungs, hardly able to see more than a few yards in the darkness. A great cloud of snow-dust plumed into the air off to Marisa's right, closely followed by Garic sprinting towards the circle. He charged up and took his place alongside his friends, a look of grim determination on his face. Marisa pitied the first few enemies who came within reach of his spear.

"Okay we're all here, stick together and hold the circle. No one gets through alive!" Marisa spat out the words, adrenaline coursing through her body, every muscle tensed and ready to explode.

"Marisa Longspear!" Ungforth's voice bellowed across the darkness, coming from the direction Fugly had been patrolling. "Peace Marisa, I bring friends and good tidings." The great warrior loped out of the darkness, Urdoon and Andmar flanking him. Then out of the night a whole crowd of Children of the Wilderness rose up and followed their fellow tribesmen.

"Stand down." Marisa breathed out her order with an audible sigh of relief. The squad all lowered their spears, the tension receding as quickly as it had built.

Ungforth strode out in front of the gathering, a single young warrior by his side, palms out in peace.

"Marisa, these men fought at Seal-breaker Bay but they were misled. They have slipped away in the night and were making their way home when we came across them. This is Urdlin, son of Urdhoa."

The big young warrior stepped forward head slightly bowed in what Marisa assumed was some sort of mark of contrition. He was as expected a great bear of a man, of a height with his father if not quite as full in body. He was handsome in a slightly brutish way, with a shaggy mane of red hair tumbling across his shoulders.

Marisa extended her hand to the young giant, a warm smile fixed to her face. He beamed a broad grin and gratefully clasped her hand in his, a slightly embarrassed look marring his features.

"Welcome Urdlin, your father will be greatly relieved to know you are well." Marisa led him by the arm back to the fireside and ushered him to sit down. "Can you tell us what happened to you Urdlin?" Ungforth and Breda had joined them while the rest of the squad packed up the gear warily eyeing the remainder of the Children.

"I am ashamed to admit that the mountain men bewitched us, Marisa Longspear. It is difficult to explain but we felt compelled to go with them. They told us that the southerners were planning to invade the Great White and kill our people and that we had to stop them. They said that the southerners used mages with the power to control minds and if we were to survive, we had to kill them all. We are all young men, and our heads were turned with promises of wealth and glory. We believed we were defending our families and our way of life. It was as if everything they said rang true and our cause was righteous. That is until after the battle at Balta-uostas where so many of my friends and my brother Urdhon fell. They handed out punishments…" Urdlin trailed off, still too close to whatever happened to be able to talk about it.

Marisa put her hand on Urdlin's arm and the young giant's shoulders rose and fell with sad little sobs.

"We lost family at Seal-breaker Bay as well Urdlin and it broke my heart. I am so sorry for your loss but I need you to tell me as much as you can. How many of you escaped and where are the mountain men headed? Do you know their names? Anything you can remember would help."

The young warrior composed himself and sat bolt upright, looking Marisa square in the face. "I feel a sense of shame that we attacked your settlement Marisa Longspear and killed your people and for this I ask your forgiveness. They all fought with great courage and strength."

"We do not blame you Urdlin and your people also fought with great courage but I need to know all that you can tell me. Please."

"Over a hundred of us slipped away two nights ago but there are still over two-hundred warriors that they have bound to their sides. They would not tell us their plans and anyone who questioned them were punished, some even killed as examples. I think they intend to raid along the border and continue to gather more Children to their cause. Their leader was called Haftor Thorsen. He wielded a great war axe that overwhelmed anyone who came near it. Myself included. A sickness and fear crept into one's very soul when he hefted it and it almost seemed to shimmer as if it had a life of its own." Urdlin gave a little shiver as if he still felt the blade's presence.

"We know of these weapons Urdlin, they are called soul-forged blades. We will hunt them down, stop them and free your people. You have my word."

Chapter Twenty-One Part One:

They come

And just like that the rain stopped. Small patches of blue sky began to poke through the clouds, little rays of sunlight spearing down to the valley floor. The last beacon still alight flared into life, the wind shifting the flame back and forth.

Candor stood in the centre of the rampart looking forward towards the mouth of the valley. It was yesterday that Brownleaf had come galloping back towards the twin cities and the H'Daree had still not come into view, but they were there, just out of sight. It felt as if it were a ploy, designed to shred the nerves of the defenders, eat away at their resolve. He'd despatched two-hundred archers to the furthest redoubts, one hundred on each side of the valley mouth with instructions to loose a few volleys and then withdraw, lighting the fire pits as they pulled back.

As they withdrew, they would hand off to another force of archers placed at the next redoubt heading back towards the rampart. They would fire volleys and withdraw in the same manner, hopefully drawing the H'Daree further and further towards the centre, bunching them up so as to concentrate their firepower. That was the hope at least.

The blacksmiths had worked miracles, over four thousand men shod in good armour with enough steel for swords and spears, but it still felt woefully inadequate. Willett had insisted on leading a company stationed forward, protecting the retreating archers and he'd held two thousand to man the earthworks and the walls. He'd tried and tried again to convince the city leaders to evacuate the population into the Pass but had met with flat refusals.

So here they stood waiting, the anticipation spreading an aura of fear throughout their ranks.

"Just bloody get on with it you bastards."

"Patience Candor Blackheart, you will get your wish soon enough." He'd dropped his blocks without realising it, letting them slip through as smug and self-satisfied as always.

"Why do you wait? Not so eager to walk into the face of danger?" He didn't suppose goading them would do any good, but he just couldn't help himself.

"There is little to fear from your pitiful efforts Candor, you will be swept aside like ash from a grate. We are not unmerciful however. Surrender now, accept your lot and no one will be harmed. Upon that you have our word." It was more than just confidence they exuded. It was an absolute certainty.

"The word of murderers and invaders holds no meaning. We will make you pay dearly for every inch of land, mark my words." Candor was drained from these exchanges but if he could glean any tiny piece of information that may give him an edge it was worth the discomfort.

"We are coming Candor and none who remain to defy us will be left alive. This is your last chance. Consider carefully less you condemn all of your people to the darkness."

"I can only hope I meet you on the field, where it will be your end and not mine." Candor put his blocks back up but could have sworn he heard a mocking laugh before he'd done so.

The sounds of subdued chatter were all that broke the silence, men trying to give each other courage before the battle. A distant sound began to fill the air, a low rumbling noise, like a great wave or flash flood pouring towards them. The valley veered to the right about a mile away from the first redoubts which was as far as anyone could see when he spotted it.

A great wall of black, like a river running down a dry bed rounded the corner. At first it was difficult to make out anything specific, the whole mass moving as one like a great flat-bodied snake. The vast host all moving in time with each other made it difficult to single anything or anyone out but as his eyes adjusted Candor's heart nearly stopped. The massed ranks spread across the whole width of the valley floor, thousands of men all attired in black armour, spears and shields locked together forming a wall of dark steel. As they rounded the corner and marched in perfect lockstep towards the first redoubts, Candor saw a thin line of men standing to the front, long back cloaks with their hoods pulled up covering their faces. They had someone tied at the wrist and stripped to the waist forced out in front of them, their footsteps unsteady and stumbling, red marks covering their torso.

"Bastards!" Brownleaf hissed out the insult, gripping the palisade, knuckles turning white.

"Easy Brownie." Candor placed his hand on Brownleaf's forearm, feeling the dreadful tension. It was young Quinlan.

The H'Daree moved relentlessly forwards and finally came to a stop a hundred yards or so before the last redoubts, just out of bowshot range. The cowled figure at the centre of their lines strode forward twenty feet, dragging young Quinlan behind him.

He threw back his hood, his long fair hair standing out like a beacon. Then he spoke.

"Citizens of Turan and Minari." It shouldn't have been possible to hear his voice from this distance, but it rang clear and true so that everyone could listen.

"We are the H'Daree, and we have come to clear the way. The All Father follows behind and shows us the path to the H'Dar. All will follow or perish in their resistance, for we will scour the face of the planet until all are united. You have been offered freedom and the chance to join us in Ascension but have chosen to turn your backs to the light. So, shall it be for all unbelievers."

He forced young Quinlan to his knees and drew a long curved sword, the sunlight flashing off its razor-sharp edge. In one swift stroke he lopped off Quinlan's head, his headless corpse flopping forwards, blood gushing from the wound.

"BASTARDS!" Brownleaf screamed his challenge at the H'Daree and darted forward, intent on engaging them single-handed. Candor managed to grab his arm, stopping him in his tracks.

"No Brownie, you would be giving your life up for no good

reason." He enveloped Brownleaf and clung onto him for dear life, desperately trying to stop his friend from charging off into battle.

"Let go of me Candor!" Brownleaf spat the words out, spittle bubbling from the corners of his mouth.

As they wrestled atop the rampart a couple of guards helped Candor try to subdue Brownleaf, the four of them staggering around like drunkards. Then they heard the battle cry go up from their forward ranks. Candor had forgotten for a brief moment that Abel Quinlan had posted forward with Willet and about a hundred of his household, mainly made up of extended family. He watched in horror as they poured out of the forward redoubts and charged the H'Daree. They were all well armoured, Abel Quinlan at the front wielding a broadsword, shield out in front. It amazed Candor that a man as diminutive as him could lift, let alone swing a sword of that size but the rage of grief seemed to lend him strength.

It was one of the most heroic things Candor had ever seen, brave men charging into the face of certain death. But it was a terrible waste and threw what flimsy plans they had laid into chaos. They all stood transfixed as the small band of men closed on the front ranks of the H'Daree's vast force, when the rest of the cowled figures stepped forward and threw back their hoods. From a distance they all looked the same, long straight fair hair flowing past their shoulders. They lifted their arms to the sky and began to incant some unknown song, their voices forming a haunting choir.

The charging band were within yards of the cowled figures, howling their battle cries when all of a sudden, they disappeared. A great haze that spread across the valley floor and high into the sky obscured all beyond the redoubts, everything disappearing behind a great shimmering barrier.

Candor's breath caught in his throat, the realisation of what he was witnessing proving hard to process. He'd never seen or heard of anything on this scale but somehow they were using the Gift, combining their powers to create a wall of altered reality, engulfing the attacking band. Candor knew that there was no way to fight this, and their only hope was to flee.

"Stannard, Rory!" He barked out to two of his subordinates, the pair of young soldiers hurrying to his side.

"Stannard, get a horse and ride to the front now as fast as you can and order everyone to retreat and light the pits. For all their sakes, ride like the wind." The young soldier nodded his assent without question and took off down the back of the rampart. Candor knew he may be sending him to his death but what choice did he have? A few moments later Stannard tore past on his mount paying little attention to the perils of the rutted ground and staggered trenches. As bad as he felt, there was no time to dither.

"Rory, get messengers back to the cities and start the evacuation, everyone into the Pass, now!" Rory set off, passing the message down the line and lighting the signal pyres, letting the watchers know to start evacuating. The lack of military structure was now heading them towards disaster. Candor had no command staff to speak of, just a few old, retired veterans who'd overseen the training of the enlisted. He looked about him and saw the looks of panic and terror in the men's eyes, many of them abandoning the rampart and fleeing back to the cities and the Titan Pass itself.

Candor mounted the rampart, standing atop the palisade wall.

"Men of the twin cities. Will you abandon your posts and leave your loved ones defenceless? If you run then we will all be cut down but if you stand your wives and children may have the chance to escape. There will be no deliverance unless we earn it ourselves. We must stand and hold for as long as we can, for Turan! For Minari!" Candor bellowed out as loud as he was able, banging his spear on the palisade wall.

Many faces turned to him, looks of hopelessness and despair washing across them.

"We must flee!"

"Run for your lives!"

"Save yourselves!"

"If you run your families will perish. You all heard what they said, there will be no mercy. There is nowhere to run to anyway so I say stand and die on your feet like men rather than dying on your knees begging for a mercy you will never receive. Be proud of your heritage and honour your ancestors. Match the courage of Abel Quinlan and his men or die like cowardly dogs, running away and hiding until you are hunted down and put out of your misery!" The anger Candor felt in his heart boiled to the surface, spitting out venomously at all those who stared hopelessly up at him.

"How can we fight that?" Ardel Murtagh was a baker from Turan. Candor knew him well and regularly visited his shop.

"With courage Ardel. Would you run and leave Connie and your children to their fate? The only chance they have is if we can buy them enough time to get out. We have to try at least." Candor knew how unconvincing and weak his argument sounded but he had to try.

"What is that? If your enemy can disappear, how can you fight it?" Candor didn't know this man, probably from Minari but his question was valid none the less.

"I don't know, I don't have the answers but one thing we all know for sure is no one will be spared. Do you understand me? No one!" Candor looked at the faces of the men looking back at him. They were all lost, all on the point of despair.

"Stay and man the wall at least until I have tried to give us a chance. Will you grant me that at least?" Candor was desperate but he had an idea. The last desperate stroke of a drowning man maybe but it was all he had.

A chorus of ayes rang out, the men returning to the rampart despite their obvious terror. Candor had to admit that he wasn't sure he'd do the same in their shoes.

He turned just at the moment the shimmering wall came down. All of those that charged the lines were laying in pools of blood, just Abel Quinlan was still alive, stripped of his armour and on his knees. The same cowled figure that had beheaded his son grasped him by a handful of his hair.

"So, shall it be for all unbelievers!" Abel Quinlan's headless corpse tumbled to the ground; his head still held in his executioner's hand.

Instead of turning to flight as Candor feared, it seemed to give a new resolve to the defenders, roars of anguish and anger going up from the rampart.

Candor could see Stannard almost up to the last redoubts, furiously waving everyone else back to the palisade as he passed them. All the archers at the front loosed as one, the front ranks of the H'Daree now well in range. As the arrows arced into the sky and began their murderous descent the line of cowled figures incanted their song, moving inexorably forward. The great shimmering wall went up once again, engulfing the furthest redoubts just as Stannard drew alongside. Candor cursed under his breath, all the renewed resolve seeming to leak out of the men on the rampart.

He looked down the line to see Rory sprinting back to his position.

"The evacuation is underway Candor, all the elderly, women and children are moving toward the mouth of the Pass." He gasped out his message, still trying to catch his breath.

Looking back towards the Titan Pass, Candor could see lines of people streaming out from the traders' gates. At least he'd been allowed to station provisions wagons, some horse and cattle there but it would be less than enough to feed everyone on the journey through the Pass. *"Let's not get ahead of ourselves, we've got to stay alive first."* Candor's head was swimming, the chances of surviving let alone escaping alive seeming to diminish by the moment.

"Rory, Brownie, I need you now more than ever." Rory nodded and Brownleaf shook off the two guards and stared hard, straight into Candor's eyes.

"I'm sorry Brownie but I couldn't let you charge off to die, I need you, my friend." He placed his hand on Brownleaf's shoulder hoping for a conciliatory sign. Brownleaf's muscles relaxed a hint and Candor breathed an inner sigh of relief.

"I have an idea that may buy us some time, maybe give a chance of mounting an effective fighting retreat but I will need your help." Both Rory and Brownleaf nodded their agreement.

"Rory, you have the command. If I don't return do everything you can to buy our people some time." Candor clasped the young soldier's hand in his and no words needed to pass between them.

"Brownie, if you're willing I need you to come with me." Candor waited for a moment, nervous that Brownleaf would be too overwhelmed by grief and anger to maintain a clear head.

"Of course my friend, but give me your word that you won't try to hold me back again."

"I promise you Brownie, when the time comes, I will not hold you back. As I said I have an idea but that's all it is and it's fraught with danger." Candor could hardly believe he was thinking of trying something so insane, but he had to make the attempt.

Brownleaf nodded and they both slipped down the rampart and began picking their way between the fire pits, keeping low and urging all those they passed to hurry back to the palisade.

"Brownie I need to tell you something and I need you to trust me." Candor paused for a moment, ducking down behind a redoubt, less than a few hundred yards from the front of the shimmering wall.

"Of course Candor, what is it my friend?" There was a slight nervous timbre to Brownleaf's voice as if he was afraid of what Candor was going to tell him.

"You know of mind-walkers, but have you heard of the Gift?" Everything he did was fraught with risk now, but he had no choice.

"Yes of course I have. It's a common trait in the Protectorate, a strange ability to move out of time. Is this what you think they have, the H'Daree?"

"Yes Brownie, but more than that, they are somehow merging their abilities to create this great barrier. If we can't bring it down, then we are lost. I have an idea that it's dependent upon their leader, that it is all funnelled through him. If we can bring him down, they may not be able to maintain it but it's only a working theory."

"Even if that's true Candor, what hope do we have of stopping him?"

"I am a mind-walker Brownie and I have the Gift."

Chapter Twenty-One Part Two:

Flight

Brownleaf pulled back suddenly, his hand dropping to the hilt of his sword. A look of distrust and revulsion flowed across his features, his body setting for violence. Years of indoctrination had taught him that mind-walkers were an abhorration, akin to a disease that must be eradicated.

"Brownie, you have known me for years. You know what I have sacrificed for my home and I have never played you or anyone else false. You have to trust me; this is the only chance we have."

"How can I trust a man who knows everyone's secrets, a man who's probably been inside my mind whenever the fancy took him?" Brownleaf let his words out through gritted teeth, hostility rising in him like a noon tide.

"Brownie you must listen to me. It doesn't work like that I swear to you on Marye and my children's lives. Being a mind-walker doesn't mean you can read minds only that you can talk to other mind-walkers by thought. I can no more read your mind than I could that of a horse." Candor had rolled back onto his heels, his back hand slipping down to the pommel of his shortsword. He didn't want to but time was of the essence and if he had to, he'd take Brownleaf out. "We don't have time for this Brownie, not now. Please you have to put aside your distrust or we will both die where we stand."

Brownleaf took his hand from his sword hilt and Candor blew out a sigh of relief.

"I want to trust you Candor but let's put this aside for a moment. Tell me your plan."

"It's not much of a plan Brownie, more of a hunch. I hope that I'm right because if I'm wrong you won't have to worry about killing me, I'll be dead before I get ten feet." Candor smiled and Brownleaf chuckled in response. It was a start at least.

"I hope that the ability to use their combined Gift centres on their leader. Think of him as the centre of a wheel to which all the spokes are connected. If I can kill him the wheel will collapse as the spokes will have nothing to connect to." Candor looked at Brownleaf as he absorbed the information, working out the obvious flaws in the plan.

"Sounds great in theory Candor but how do you plan to get close enough to kill him?"

"If I'm right, I believe that they will require all of their combined efforts to hold this barrier in place. I'm hoping that this leaves them blind to anything else inside the barrier. You're going to witness something that will disturb you Brownie, but I will have to slip into the Gift in order to penetrate their creation. Once inside I hope I can approach their leader undetected. That's the plan or should I say a wing and a prayer?" Candor arched his eyebrows in an earnest appeal to his friend. "Please, trust me."

"What do you need me to do?" Brownleaf leaned in towards Candor, ready to help. It made him smile that this man could put aside his prejudice and focus on what needed to be done.

"The moment the barrier comes down, light every fire pit you can and run like the wind back to the rampart."

"What about you?"

"Worry not, I'll be hot on your heels."

Brownleaf put out his hand and Candor gratefully grasped it. "Good look Candor."

"Good luck to us both Brownie."

Candor turned and started to creep towards the great shimmering barrier, keeping low, trying to stay out of sight. As he approached, he could feel the power emanating from it, the hairs on his arms standing out straight, the smell akin to the air after a lightning strike.

Candor took a deep breath to calm himself and turned to look at Brownleaf staring after him. Then he slipped into the Gift and stepped forward into the barrier. As soon as he stepped forward, he felt the current flowing between the fair-haired figures, could see it manifested in wavy lines of energy pulsing out from the lead figure, connecting them all together. All of them had their heads turned to the sky, all seemingly oblivious to anything around them, confident in their invulnerability. Candor focused on the lead figure, the executioner and used his hatred to drive himself forward. He'd never experienced anything like this in the Gift, the air seeming to thicken, making moving that much harder. It was like swimming but as he focused, he started to move a little quicker, closing the gap on his target.

He could see the faces of all the fair-haired figures, and it made him feel queasy, his head starting to spin a little. He stood still for a moment and composed himself, looking again just to make sure he wasn't mistaken. They all looked identical. Not similar but as if they were twins, six sets of identical twins. They all had long straight golden hair, not just fair as Candor first thought, long thin noses and handsome features which gave them a slightly haughty bearing.

They reminded him of something, a picture maybe? He shook his head, mildly annoyed that he'd let anything distract him.

Inside the barrier was an extraordinary experience, not just the shimmering of vision but the subtle shifts in colour, the flexing of sound and the sense of being connected to something else, something more ethereal. A glance at Ascension indeed, certainly a higher plain.

As he forced himself forward, he began to perceive the barrier in more detail. It only extended twenty or thirty yards in depth, like a rolling screen of energy, shutting off both sides from each other. Candor could loosely make out massed ranks of people on the other side but couldn't focus enough to make out any detail. However he knew enough to know that if he couldn't bring the barrier down everyone trapped on the inside would perish.

He pushed forward, drawing his sword in readiness, all his focus concentrated on the lead figure, from whom everything seemed to emanate. It was like wading through treacle, each step a slow painstaking effort.

The golden-haired figures simply did not seem to perceive him, completely entranced, caught up in a kind of religious fervour. He crept forward, staying crouched low to the ground, as if that would make him less obtrusive. Still, it gave him an illusion of stealth and right now any comfort was worth clinging onto.

He edged closer and closer until he could clearly see the cords on the neck of his target standing proud, the strain of holding the barrier in place obviously taking its toll. He raised himself up, standing only a foot or two away and pulled back his sword, the effort to move his arm taking every ounce of his strength.

He focused, using all of his knowledge and power, all of his years of martial training and drove the point of his blade straight into the heart of the leader. At the moment of contact the golden-haired figure snapped his head forward, eyes ablaze and screamed. The sound tore through Candor's very being, ripping at his soul, tearing at his mind, draining every last reserve of his strength. The other golden-haired figures took up the terrifying wail as if desperately trying to block the pain, like drowning men gasping for that last breath of air.

The shimmering wall disappeared and Candor wrenched his sword from his victim. All the other golden-haired figures collapsed to the ground and lay prone on the floor, no hint of movement from any of them. The front ranks of the H'Daree were yards away from the archers in the redoubts, advancing in unison, spears lowered with deadly intent.

The archers having been freed from the barrier suddenly realised their peril, some scrambling back and running towards the rampart. Astonishingly however some stood their ground, drawing their swords in defiance. Stannard took control, standing forward to face down the enemy. He turned to the remaining archers and screamed out his orders.

"Nock, draw, loose!"

The massed groups loosed a volley, over one hundred arrows at almost point-blank range thundering into the front ranks of the advancing H'Daree.

"Nock, draw, loose!" Stannard shouted out again and again, over a dozen point blank volleys smashing into the H'Daree, dropping them in great clumps until something astonishing happened. They staggered and then pulled back, confusion seeming to take hold, almost as if they were leaderless.

Candor grasped the opportunity.

"Stannard, get your men out of there. Retreat to the rampart!" He had to shout over the yelps and war cries of his own men to get their attention. They piled out from the redoubts, sprinting past him back towards the palisade wall.

Brownleaf stood where he had left him, mouth agape, a burning torch in each hand.

"C'mon Brownie, let's get out of here." He grabbed one of the torches and the pair of them began to light the fire pits behind them as they hurried back to the rampart.

They paused for a moment, the last to retreat and through the flames and the heat haze they could see the corpses of Abel Quinlan's company littering the ground. However they could also see a swathe of H'Daree dead spread out across the line, proof that they bled and died.

"Candor, I still can't quite believe what I saw, I mean that was incredible, probably the bravest thing I've ever witnessed. I'm sorry I turned on you, I know who and what you are. Ashamed I am." Brownleaf bowed his head as he spoke, looking at his feet rather than Candor's face.

"Let's leave that till another time Brownie, I think we've got other things to worry about right now. Back to the wall." Candor clapped him on the back, taking one last look behind him and then he ran for the palisade.

Stannard was already there when they arrived, ushering the last of the surviving archers through. The H'Daree may have faltered momentarily but it didn't stop them loosing a barrage of their own. A lot of men had fallen on the retreat, feathered in the back trying to escape.

As they passed through the palisade gate Candor was astonished to see Willet standing there, bruised and bloodied but still in one piece. He grabbed him by the shoulders and pulled him in for a hug, the young officer looking mildly stunned by the attention.

"But it's good to see you Willet, I thought you'd joined Abel Quinlan's charge and were laying up there with the rest of them."

"I tried to stop them Candor, but the rage of grief was on them and there was nothing I could do." Willet's shoulders slumped, the reality of the situation finally hitting home.

"We'll have time to grieve later but for now we have to look to our defences. We may have bloodied their noses, but they will regroup and come again. Rory what's the state of the evacuation?"

"Most of the women and children have made the mouth of the Pass, Candor and we've got a couple of squads sweeping the cities to ensure everyone gets out. The problem is there are so many that getting them moving is going to take time and we don't have the means to transport them all, just not enough pack animals and carts. The journey to the Gate is a long one Candor and I don't know if everyone will be able to make it." Rory looked like a little boy lost, Candor forgot at times just how young he was.

"Rory, I want you to take a hundred men and start to get them moving. Use the carts to ferry the wounded, most infirm and the youngest, those that can ride get on horseback. Start to get the rest moving as quickly as possible. We have to try to get some distance between them and the H'Daree because trust me they will be coming soon, and I don't know how long we can hold them. Will I need you to take Turan's wall and Stannard you take Minari. Two hundred men each, the rest will man the rampart with me and Brownleaf. When they breach the rampart, we'll fall back to the cities and fight a rear-guard action through the streets, keep them occupied for as long as possible." Candor nodded to his lieutenants, their quiet acknowledgment giving him a swell of pride.

"Good luck everybody."

They all took off to their posts apart from Brownleaf who mounted the rampart with Candor. They stood there nervously looking for any signs of movement. The fire pits were blazing, sending up great gusts of flame, the heat haze so intense that it made it seem as if the sky itself was dancing.

"That should buy us some time Brownie, but those pits won't burn forever, and I don't think we'll hold them for long. They seemed to freeze when their leaders passed out, almost as if they couldn't move without their say so. It looks like they use a kind of caste system with those that were using the Gift operating as their command structure. I don't know if the others were just knocked unconscious when I killed their leader or if it's something more serious, but I doubt we'll get another opportunity like that. We need to hurry the evacuation and get as many of our forces as possible into the Pass to form a rear-guard. We have to defend the people Brownie, at any cost."

Candor felt a sense of unease. It was if he'd prophesised the moment when he'd killed the golden-haired leader. *"I can only hope I meet you on the field, where it will be your end and not mine."* Was it him or one of his compatriots? It shouldn't have mattered, but he couldn't shake the feeling.

"We'll make them pay for every inch of ground, Candor. It'll be them beckoned today, not us." Brownleaf ground his jaw, growling under his breath, anger barely suppressed. Candor squeezed his shoulder, a vain reassuring gesture at best.

In the distance, beyond the furthest pits Candor could make out the faintest hints of movement. Great shadows seemed to loom over the flames, almost as tall as the walls of the twin cities themselves. He could hear the noises of men straining to a physical task, like a chorus of grunts and the sound of some kind of machinery, metal on metal reaching out from beyond the flames. The shadows reached their peaks and a great whooshing sound echoed out, followed by the noise of something heavy hitting the ground. The flames fanned towards the rampart as if a great bellows were blowing on them. Great plumes of smoke rose in the distance, like the dying embers of a great fire, doused and sizzling in its death throes. Then the shadows rose again, the noise of physical exertion and mechanical movement lifting in unison, closely followed by the whoosh and thump. The fanning flames and great plumes of smoke seemed to creep ever closer as if the fire was a living creature, inexorably crawling towards them.

The next time the cycle started, Candor could finally make out what was happening and nearly all of his resolve leaked away. Great platforms, long and broad, wooden and banded with iron were being lifted vertically by a series of chains and pulleys end over end, covering the pits and extinguishing the fires within. Teams of black-clad soldiers were hauling them into the air, pulling on great chains so that they tilted end over end, covering one pit after the other.

"That explains the great double-axled wagons I saw." Brownleaf almost said it to himself.

"Damn! At this rate they'll be under the walls in less than an hour." Candor gripped the top of the palisade wall, the veins on his arms standing proud under the strain.

Candor turned to look at the mouth of the Pass. The entire populations of the twin cities had flooded into the entrance, more and more joining them, bolstering their ranks and slowing the evacuation to a crawl. There must have been close to thirty thousand people, all terrified and on the brink of total panic. At the furthest point he could see movement, Rory finally getting the exodus under way, but he was hours away from getting the rear of the crowd moving. They had to hold for as long as they could, put as much space between the H'Daree and the escaping population as possible.

Once again, he climbed onto the palisade wall and this time, he didn't need to gain their attention, every head was turned towards him.

"Men of the twin cities, stand with me! All of our loved ones are depending on us to give them a chance to live. Will you give all you have to give them life? We must stand and break this army against our walls. For Turan! For Minari!" Candor bellowed out his plea and a great throaty roar went up all along the walls, the men of the twin cities calling out their defiance.

He turned to face the enemy, great clouds of smoke and ash obscuring his view.

"Let them come."

Chapter Twenty-Two:

The sun rises

"Beautiful."

The sunset never failed to take his breath away, layers of orange, pink and purple, all mirrored by the Great Silver Sea. A perfect picture, the faraway hills reflected in the water, so it appeared to almost float, two horizons, one on top of the other.

The palm trees swayed in the light warm breeze, the fronds all waving in a gentle motion. Aromatic smells wafted up to the balcony, rich fruits and sweet-smelling flowers filling the air with fragrant odours. The gardens were stunning, beautifully tended lawns, flower beds bursting with colour, fountains and statues adorning the grounds in every direction. He breathed deeply, trying to capture the moment, commit it to memory by somehow burning it into his brain.

He loved it here so much, he couldn't imagine being any happier, any more fulfilled. To be an advisor to the Royal Court would be the greatest privilege imaginable for a true born subject of the Golden Empire but for a foreigner to have climbed so high? He'd worked tirelessly and honestly for more than fifteen years, his list of achievements enviable but he'd made enemies along the way. Not deliberately of course but in order to stand his ground it had been unavoidable. Now it came to it he could feel himself faltering, unwilling to give it all up but in truth what choice did he have?

"Advocate Sorkin."

He turned from the balcony to see his hand servant Matoc standing in the middle of his office, head bowed as was appropriate for someone of his station. He was dressed in the traditional slave attire, toga open at the left breast, cinched at the waist with a gold-braided sash, a symbol of his seniority. Although his head was clean shaven, he had a single braid, tied with gold thread, an indication of complete trust, the highest rank any slave could ever attain. He was an old man by slave standards, his skin wrinkled and dark brown from a lifetime under the harsh sun. It was still slavery however and would never fail to rankle.

"Yes Matoc." He stepped forward and lifted Matoc's head by the chin. "Please." He smiled at his faithful servant indicating for him to lift his head, the same dance they played out every day.

"His Highness, Prince Lor has requested your attendance. A delegation from the Protectorate has sent word that they are travelling cross country from Sarjinn and should be with us in a matter of weeks." The old retainer bowed after delivering his message, the traditional sign of obedience.

Sorkin sighed. "One day you'll drop the formalities when we are alone."

"As you command Master." The old man looked up with a grin and a twinkle in his eyes.

Sorkin patted him on the shoulder and made his way out of the door. The walk to the great reception hall would take a little while, time to think at least. He knew this day was coming but part of him had secretly hoped that the events playing out would somehow pass Darmat by.

The Royal Ziggurat had never lost its splendour in his eyes. He always felt he could notice some new ornate detail in its construction no matter how often he walked its halls. The corridors were all supported by vast decorated columns, great carvings of stories from history adorning each one. The Kingdom of Darmat was commonly referred to as the Golden Empire with good cause, gold inlay covering nearly every inch of the hallways, golden statues standing on golden plinths, the ziggurat itself rendered in gold so that on a bright day the sun would reflect off it for miles in all directions.

He was eternally grateful for the masterful construction, the whole palace designed to draw cool air through the corridors. Even after all these years he still could never get comfortable wearing the high stiff-collared, full-length dress coats. It always felt like he was wearing a tailored carpet, the traditional wool versions weighing far more than was comfortable. He still wore breeches underneath his robe of office, much to the amusement of his contemporaries but it stopped the chaffing on his legs.

Eventually he came to the anteroom that led to the great reception hall, although anteroom was a woefully inadequate description. The corridor opened out into a vast high-vaulted ceiling room, giant thirty-foot high columns, posted like vast sentinels every fifteen feet, all standing guard around the outer walls. Two guards from the Golden Legions stood either side of the entrance doors, resplendent in their polished, gilded armour. They stared straight ahead, never moving unless required to do so in order to open the doors or defend their master. And of course, they were mute, having had their tongues removed in order to earn the great honour bestowed upon them.

He knew he shouldn't judge but these arcane traditions would always prick at his conscience. But of course, he never voiced his distaste.

He stepped forward and stood in front of the huge doors, the guards breaking their stillness to pull them open. He stepped across the threshold and flourished a bow, eyes fixed to the floor.

"Ah, Sorkin. Good, good, come in." Prince Lor was sat behind a great polished table, his seat a grand carved throne, as one would expect generously upholstered and finished in gold. The Prince was dressed all in white, a great high-collared long coat with golden embroidery running down the arms and front. He had white breeches similarly embroidered with white leather boots and a small gold circlet atop his head. He also wore white cotton gloves as was tradition with all members of the royal household, no one but royalty being permitted to touch their flesh.

As big as the table was it was dwarfed by the sheer immensity of the great reception hall. It made the anteroom feel like a small cupboard, its great domed ceiling reaching for the heavens, at least one hundred and fifty feet high. The ceiling itself was adorned with breathtaking scenes from antiquity, great battles and legends of the gods. It was enough to silence the most verbose of people.

It struck Sorkin as almost implausible that a structure of this enormity simply did not collapse under its own weight. Just as well the construction was not reliant on his belief.

"Your Highness, I live to serve." Sorkin had stopped short of the dais the table was situated on and flourished another florid bow.

"Come old friend and have a seat. No need to stand on ceremony." Lor smiled at Sorkin and nodded for him to sit at the table, on a smaller less extravagant chair of course.

"I have invited Captain General Mitter Wane to join us." He swept his hand to the side where the mercenary commander was seated. If you could call it seated that was. He seemed to be poured over the chair rather than sitting on it, one leg hanging over an armrest, his arms artfully slung wherever the fancy took them. He was an extraordinary sight, brown leather trousers with knee-high spurred soft-hide boots. His jacket was red and black with great ruffled collars, crossed with two bandoliers, each one holding a selection of evil-looking blades. He was undoubtedly handsome with a tumble of auburn hair falling in artful curls across his shoulders. Then of course there was his scar, a thick ugly welt running from his left eyebrow to the corner of his stubbled jaw. You could not be a soldier in The Maimed without a scar, let alone be its commander.

"Captain General Wane, an honour to make your acquaintance sir." Sorkin offered a small bow to the almost horizontal soldier. "Have you just arrived in Darmat?"

"It is a pleasure to meet you, advocate Sorkin. I have heard so much about you." The Captain General slowly unfurled himself from his seat and offered a perfunctory bow to Sorkin. "We have indeed just arrived; the cycle of secondment has just started again so we will be tendering our services for the next two years." He smiled disarmingly but as charming and instantly likeable as he was, Sorkin felt a little stab of wariness.

"Does your army come alone?" Sorkin only asked because the agreement with the Confederation of Mercenary Armies called for two forces at a time on a two-year secondment. Odd then that only one commander would be in attendance.

"We are by far the largest army in the Confederation at five thousand strong Advocate, more than sufficient to fulfil our contract."

"Of course Captain, please forgive me, just naturally curious I suppose." Sorkin offered a little bow of apology.

"Nothing to forgive, Advocate." There was that smile again. He didn't imagine the Captain General struggled too much where the ladies were concerned.

In the exchange Sorkin had hardly noticed General Kaif standing behind the throne. The old commander of the Golden Legions still cut an imposing figure in his intricately decorated gilded armour. Over six feet tall, with tightly cropped grey hair and in remarkably good shape for a man in his seventh decade, the General had stood there silent, observing the courtesies and waiting for his introduction.

Lor flicked his hand indicating for the old general to step forward.

"General Kaif, good to see you sir." Sorkin inclined his head in greeting.

"Advocate Sorkin, likewise. Wane." The old man was curt and to the point as always, his distaste for the mercenary hardly disguised.

"Gentleman, please be seated." Lor waved his hand for them to sit.

Servants carrying trays of food and drink buzzed around the table carefully placing them down, taking great pains not to spill a drop. Once they had laid out the refreshments they stepped back into the shadows, silently waiting to be called to further service.

Lor leaned forward, absentmindedly picking at an olive. "You have no doubt already been informed of our coming visitors, gentlemen. Any ideas as to what their purpose might be?" He popped the olive in his mouth and spat the stone onto the floor, a slave scurrying forward on his knees to pick it up.

"If I had to hazard a guess Highness, it would probably be in connection to the news from the east." Sorkin felt a shudder of nerves run through his body. The thing he feared the most appeared to be coming to pass. Outwardly however he maintained his usual measured impression.

"Yes, that does seem likely but to what end? Do you think it likely that they would seek some sort of alliance? I think that any step in that direction may be a little premature. Our spies inform me that it is the Green-lands that have been overrun and let's be honest that would not require much of an invading force to accomplish the task." The Prince laughed at his own jape, throwing an olive into the air but failing to catch it in his mouth.

"Indeed, it would not Highness." Wane smiled at the Prince's little joke. "But I have my own informants and they tell me that these H'Daree are indeed a formidable force. I think it would be prudent to at least keep a close eye on the situation, should they begin to move in our direction." Sorkin couldn't help himself; he liked this Captain General immediately and it would be useful indeed to have a supporter when the time came to press for action.

"I hardly think we should concern ourselves overly. Ousting those godless fishermen from their quaint little cities is hardly a great military conquest. I think it more likely that the vaunted Protectorate is looking to flex its muscles and expand its sphere of influence. They may be quite the force to be reckoned with on the other side of the Mid Ocean, but we are Darmat, the Golden Empire. Lest we forget gentlemen, the Hardite Empire at the very height of their power came badly unstuck when they presumed to challenge us. I do not think we will concern ourselves with rumours or adventurers from the west. We will receive them of course but we will show them our strength and our resolve, not any weakness."

"Of course Highness, but may I suggest that we do so with an open welcoming hand. At least until we know for certain what their intentions are?" Sorkin was having his worst fears realised, the resolve and preparation needed would be focused in the wrong direction. Instead of preparing to repel the real threat, the H'Daree, Prince Lor would rather puff his chest out to the representatives of the Protectorate. So little credence was paid to events east of the Titan Pass, that he could see everything crumbling because of lack of readiness. He could speak out now and tell them all he knew, but in all likelihood, he would be charged with heresy and executed, his concerns dismissed as the rantings of a madman.

"Sage advice, as always Sorkin. It is always your caution that tempers my rashness." The Prince nodded at the advocate.

"Highness you pay me too much honour." Sorkin looked at the floor, keeping his eyes down.

"General Kaif, what advice would you offer?" Lor looked to his side at the old man.

"I am not worthy of an opinion Highness; I merely implement whatever strategy you command." The old general averted his eyes, unwilling as was custom to look royalty directly in the eye.

"Quite right Kaif." Prince Lor gave a self-satisfied smile. "Do you have an opinion to offer Advocate?"

"A formal honour guard made up from the Golden Legion would set the right tone I believe Highness." Sorkin averted his eyes as he spoke, observing protocol as always.

"Then it is decided, two hundred of the Legion and if you would be so kind to attend with fifty of your finest Wane?"

"As you wish Highness." Wane's bow was there but far from extravagant. Sorkin thought he saw a little twitch of annoyance on Lor's face.

"Then you will have to excuse me gentlemen, I have other affairs of state to attend to." Prince Lor waved a pocket kerchief at his advisors, spun on his heels and marched out of the Great Reception Hall, servants and slaves alike scurrying in his wake.

Once out of sight the three men arose from their bows. *"I pity his poor concubines; someone will pay for his displeasure."*

"Advocate Sorkin." General Kaif politely inclined his head. "Wane." He fixed the mercenary with a withering stare before turning and marching out towards the anteroom.

Wane stood there with a broad grin on his face. "I don't think he much cares for me." He shrugged his shoulders, his indifference obvious.

"Do not take it personally Captain General. He has little regard for any mercenary. He is of the old school where honour, loyalty to a cause and obedience are everything." Sorkin started to walk towards the anteroom, hands behind his back, nodding for Wane to follow.

As they exited the hall Sorkin leaned towards Wane. "May I speak frankly with you Captain General?"

"I assume you wish this conversation to remain private

Advocate Sorkin? And please call me Mitter." The mercenary shot Sorkin a conspiratorial glance.

"I do, for the moment at least. Will you join me for refreshments in my office?"

"It would be my genuine pleasure Advocate."

"Sorkin, please." This was a hopeful turn of events, the Captain General certainly struck him as a shrewd man.

They arrived at Sorkin's office where they seated themselves on the balcony. Matoc brought out a ewer of cold honeyed milk and some glasses and then stepped back three paces with his head lowered.

"Thank you Matoc, would you give us some privacy please?"

"As you wish Master." The old slave backed away head bowed before turning and leaving the office.

"A little long in the tooth for a slave is he not?" Wane took a sip of his honeyed milk, eyeing Sorkin over the rim of his glass.

"Yes, well past what would be considered tenable, but I find him both comforting and reassuring." Sorkin sipped his own drink, a particular favourite of his. "Captain General, may I enquire as to the truth of what your sources have told you?" Sorkin arched a brow, trying to land his enquiry gently.

"Mitter please and you are very astute Sorkin, I can see you are skilled at the game." Wane smiled his disarming smile. "My information is that the H'Daree are mobilising in huge numbers with the intention of conquest. Not just the Green-lands mind but the whole of the Known World. At least that is according to their propaganda machine, a no-other-option approach as in 'join us or die'. I think we underestimate what is coming at our peril." Wane's smile was still there only a little more hard-lipped, a little more serious.

"I agree entirely, I believe we should be joining the force being marshalled to defend the Titan Gate. That is the best chance of stopping them because if they break through all may well be lost. Convincing the King or any of his royal household is fraught with difficulties however."

"Apart from the fact that Darmat will never agree to even joint command of its forces let alone serving under another's, the royal family of Darmat is deluded. It is so insulated from reality that it considers itself invulnerable, not a good situation to find oneself trapped in." Wane was a little more forthcoming than Sorkin expected, almost careless, but confidence was a necessary trait for a mercenary.

"Then I think we should work as hard as possible to provide more solid evidence, because if we cannot change their minds, everything we know and love may come to an end."

Chapter Twenty-Three Part One:

And so it begins

Silver fish sprang from the ship's bow waves, leaping in joyous unison, little twinkling flashes of sunlight on the water's surface. A gentle warm breeze ruffled Jonoh's hair and swept the crisp salty aroma across his face. He'd sailed on the Mid Ocean before but never on the prow of a navy cutter and never this far from the Protectorate.

He'd never travelled outside of the Protectorate, so he felt understandably nervous, the thought of seeing Sarjinn filling him with an edgy excitement. It made him think back to his childhood, playing by the docks with Garic and looking forward to seeing old Xanda. Part of him still yearned at times for those more innocent days but that youthful naivety and wonder had long since slipped away.

He still found it a little difficult to get his bearings, everything seemingly happening at such a pace that he'd struggled to keep up. Thinking back on events it felt almost a little surreal that he now found himself here.

After the Council meeting there had been a great deal of uproar and a great deal of argument. Master Ardend preferred to call it debate but argument it was. Much was said about Cerwin abandoning his post, reneging on his duties but in response he pointed out that he was twice as old as everyone else and had been doing it for twice as long so was due some consideration. It made Jonoh smile just thinking about it, "due some consideration."

The 'debates' had gone on long into the night, but they could not convince Cerwin to change his mind. Instead, they charged him with the task of being the Protectorate's envoy to the Kingdom of Darmat, Master Ardend's idea he suspected and a clever ploy indeed. It was difficult to turn down when he was essentially going in that direction anyway. By the time most of them realised Jonoh's intention was to go with him the heat had gone out of the argument. There were some half-hearted entreaties for him to stay but most had expended all of their energies in Cerwin's direction.

They had packed their gear and were ready for the off the very next morning, no time to stand on ceremony as Cerwin was so fond of pointing out. Jonoh had quietly observed the little shadow-master's goodbyes and had to admit to being quite moved by the genuine affection he seemed to be held in by all. Whilst everyone was genuinely warm in their goodbyes to him personally the depth of feeling they had for Cerwin was obviously greater. Much to his surprise however it was Barton who seemed most concerned that he was leaving.

"I will miss your company Jonoh." Barton had inclined his head as if he didn't want Jonoh to see his pain.

"Thank you Barton, I shall miss yours as well." Even though conflicted where Barton was concerned, he actually meant it.

"Be on your guard at all times Jonoh. The Free Territories are fraught with dangers, especially in the ungoverned areas like the Lawless Lands. Master Cerwin is not quite as young as he once was although still quite formidable, so you will have to carry your share of the burden. I wish I was coming with you but with what is coming I am needed here at the centre of things. I do not think we can afford to lose you young Master Shipwright, but I remain confident that I shall have the good fortune to be in your company again." With that Barton had proffered a small bow, turned on his heels and strode back into the bowels of Fortress Kingshold. For all the doubts that still troubled him Jonoh had been moved by Barton's words.

They had journeyed east along the Rush Highway stopping once more at Falconers Rest where he'd been pleased to see Torbut Mason once again. Master Cerwin and Torbut obviously knew each other and it was something of a joyous reunion, the pair of them locked in conversation well into the night.

It had been decided that rather than travelling as a pair, a small company would be assigned to them and they had rendezvoused at Main Harbour. As they arrived at the docks their welcoming party was waiting for them, a small company of soldiers only ten strong. Much to Jonoh's surprise Bergin Shortspear had been given the command and he had to admit it had been nice to see a familiar face.

"Bergin, it is good to see you again." Jonoh had offered his hand and Bergin had grasped it gratefully. The look on his subordinate's faces told Jonoh that Bergin's stock had risen instantly, the fact that he knew Jonoh Shipwright being quite a coup.

They'd boarded with the bare minimum of gear, just weapons, a change or two of clothes, tents and of course the silver that they would need for currency. They were heading for the Titan Gate via Sarjinn, the Lawless Lands, the Red Desert and of course the Kingdom of Darmat. Although this was officially a diplomatic mission Jonoh knew what Cerwin intended. He meant to be there with whichever of his Orphans were still alive to join the fight, stand at the Titan Gate and resist.

Still there was no denying the excitement of visiting all these fabled places, seeing first-hand what he'd only ever read about in books. First things first however. They had to secure whatever extra provisions they may need for their journey and also find an experienced guide. Crossing the Free Territories came with a fair measure of risk, although travelling in numbers would help to ease their peril.

The sea crossing would take three days and Jonoh knew they would be approaching the Free Territories' west coast relatively soon, so he'd decided to stand on the prow and see it for himself. That sense of adventure left a little tingle, the anticipation holding all of his attention.

He didn't notice Bergin coming towards him and almost jumped when he cleared his throat.

"Forgive me Jonoh, would you mind if I stood with you for a little while?" Bergin still held himself a little formally, his behaviour a little too deferential for Jonoh's taste.

"Of course Bergin and please relax a little, will you? I've spent what feels like an age in the company of old wise masters so to have someone closer to my own age is a nice change of pace. I need you to be yourself around me. I am just a teenager after all." Jonoh smiled and ushered the young soldier to stand next to him on the prow.

"Sorry Jonoh, of course you're right but you must understand that we all know who and what you are and with what may be happening in the world you do have a certain unique status." The young officer smiled sheepishly; an ironic little grin fixed to his face.

"I know there's a great deal of truth in that, but I think people forget how young I am sometimes. You're what, twenty-two?"

"I've just turned twenty-three Jonoh."

"Then you're six years older than I am Bergin. I should be looking up to you. Sometimes it feels like the world has turned upside down, I just need a little hint of normality because whatever it is I'm meant to be destined for, I simply don't feel ready." Jonoh looked away from Bergin, the emotions inside of him putting him on the edge of tears.

He composed himself, annoyed that he still let his emotions get away from him at times.

"Where are you from originally Bergin?"

"Heartfield in Westfall."

"So right on the border of the Hardite Empire?"

"Yes, do you know it Jonoh?" Bergin looked up apparently delighted that Jonoh knew of his home town.

"I haven't been there personally Bergin but everyone in the Protectorate knows of the border towns and the dangers they face on a daily basis. The people of Heartfield are known for their fortitude and courage as are all who sit across from our less than friendly neighbours." That made them both chuckle.

"The Hardite Empire are certainly interesting neighbours, that is for sure Jonoh."

"Tell me about your home Bergin. I have never visited either of the Falls, but I am told they are very beautiful."

"I've only been to Eastfall on a few occasions Jonoh but it's almost a mirror for Westfall. Heartfield's not a big town by comparison to some but it's beautiful, right at the mouth of a long, low valley where the River Tab flows. Westfall is as green as you could ever imagine, forests, rising hills, farmlands and great sweeping plains. Even though it's hot being so far south it stays green most of the year, the trees only shed their leaves for a couple of turns of the moon. And the girls Jonoh, oh my." Bergin leaned forward on the rail, a big beaming smile lighting up his face.

"Now I really want to visit." Jonoh clapped Bergin on the back and they both fell about laughing.

"Something amusing gentlemen?" Cerwin had slid up behind them unnoticed and unheard. Jonoh thought he should have been able to spot it by now but the little shadow-master had lost none of his skills.

"Just organising a trip to Heartsfield, to visit Bergin and his family." Jonoh winked at Bergin and the young officer pulled a mock bashful face.

"Bergin, would you be good enough to give us a few moments?"

"Of course Master, please excuse me. Jonoh." Bergin gave a little nod and made his way back down the deck where his company were sparring and doing forms.

Cerwin sidled up close to Jonoh and leaned forward onto the rail, taking a deep breath of the salt tanged air.

"You honour me Jonoh by choosing this path, but I have to ask why you chose to come with me?" Cerwin absentmindedly picked at the hem of his shirt sleeve, worrying a loose thread.

"I don't agree with you on everything Master but I do believe that we must take action. If as you believe I am blessed with this extraordinary measure of the Gift, then it is surely most needed where the danger is greatest. We have so little time that it feels better to act rather than to expend energy endlessly talking about what we should do. The latest reports coming through are disturbing to say the least, it seems as if they have found ways to harness the Gift that are completely unique and terrify me. We have to meet them and find a way to turn them back. If we cannot stop the H'Daree at the Titan Gate we may never hold back the tide. There's also the fact that I'm still only seventeen and a good adventure is irresistible to a boy of my age." Jonoh offered his mentor a sly grin and the old man smirked back at him.

"I agree about the reports from the twin cities. Combining their powers to create some kind of shield of energy is remarkable and frightening. However, it points to something we must investigate ourselves. We have tens of thousands of Gifted in the Protectorate and we must start to look towards developing our own skills, learn new ways to manipulate our powers. However, Jonoh that task must be ceded to those that stay behind. We have a task of our own. We must gather all the remaining Orphans between Sarjinn and the Titan Gate as well as try to muster support and we must act quickly. One of my Orphans has gathered a fighting force and is heading for the Gate as we speak. They will secure the Gate from the western side and make their stand there and we must meet them before they are overrun." The old shadow-master had a hard set to his face, a look that Jonoh had rarely seen.

"Where have they been able to raise a force from Master?"

"Believe it or not Jonoh from Lhossa. There was some kind of political power struggle and our man came out on the right side. Rather than being executed for heresy it would seem he was granted leave to raise a volunteer force and their vanguard is approaching the Gate as we speak. A remarkable turn of events without question but that is what the Orphans are trained for, to do whatever needs to be done. Having said that he has only been able to raise eight hundred men and that will not be enough. Then there is the question of the evacuees from Turan and Minari, in excess of thirty thousand by all accounts and precious few of them fighting men. We must convince either Lhossa or Darmat to accept refugees or allow them to settle within their lands and one or the other to commit some serious forces or we will not be able to hold back the tide." The little Master stood for a moment pondering his choices. "You know it is a funny thing but I had this noble notion of charging off to join the fray, sword in hand and free of responsibilities. As it turns out I end up doing exactly what I would have done at home, strategising, organising and planning for the long term. Just for once I thought I would have a little fun, huh." Cerwin wistfully shook his head, caught up for a moment in the thought.

"So, what is the plan then Master? Do we seek military support from Darmat? They would seem the obvious choice especially as only the Murgan Hoard could possibly hope to match their strength in arms." Jonoh seemed to warm to the idea.

"We must try Jonoh, but that path is full of peril. We will be afforded some protection as we travel under a diplomatic flag, but we may have to reveal how we came about such detailed information. Therein lies the risk, for in Darmat more than any other country in the Known World, mind-walkers are considered an abomination. And to make matters worse they are an absolute monarchy where members of the royal household are considered living gods. The excesses of the truly mad ones would be enough to give anyone nightmares. You need to know what we may be walking into my boy." Cerwin peeked out from under the rim of his hat and for possibly the first time Jonoh sensed genuine uncertainty.

"So, treading carefully would be the order of the day?" Jonoh raised his eyebrows and beamed out a toothy smile.

"Yes, indeed it would my boy." Cerwin patted Jonoh on the back, a proud grin creasing his wrinkled features.

A cloud bank covered the horizon, white and fluffy, seeming to sit on the water itself. Jonoh could make out a few indistinct black shapes drifting in and out of it and then he realised what they were, ships.

"We are not far now Jonoh, Sarjinn is just beyond that cloud bank." Cerwin could sense his young student's excitement, the first time seeing something he'd only ever read about. He called Bergin back from his training and left the two young men at the prow.

"Have you ever seen Sarjinn, Bergin?" Jonoh's voice quavered upwards, pitching like a young boy's, try as hard as he might he just couldn't quite contain his excitement.

"I haven't Jonoh but I have read the histories and seen the drawings. I wonder if it is as exotic as the stories make it out to be?" Both of them were leaning forward on the rail, straining to catch their first glimpse of the grand old city of legend.

The cutter still ploughed through the water, the little silver fish now being stalked and picked off by dolphins riding the bow waves and porpoising in time with their prey's leaps.

They hit the cloud bank, cut through it in less than a minute and then there it was. The fabled and ancient city of Sarjinn, spreading out across the coast from under the Mount of Light, like the pleats of a skirt fanning out below a lady's waist. It was breathtaking, a mad patchwork of buildings, all crowded in together, clinging to the base of the Mount of Light. Great temples and mansions, crowded tenements and town houses, the multicoloured renderings confusing the eye. Hundreds of ships of all shapes and sizes bobbing up and down in the harbour like corks in a water barrel. Jonoh could see people in their thousands buzzing about, pulling handcarts, selling goods from market stalls, embarking from ships and doing just about anything one could imagine.

As fascinating as this all was, it paled against the Mount of Light itself. It was a tall almost perfectly conical hill with a great road that climbed it like a helix, winding its way round and round the sides, climbing slowly up until it reached the peak. There were ever more elaborate and beautifully crafted buildings, their status determined by their height until you reached the summit. The great Magistrates Palace, rendered in white marble, shining in the sunlight, sat resplendent atop the hill. It must have been visible for miles with its wonderfully rounded towers and great golden gates. Jonoh felt certain he'd never seen anything so magnificent, so majestic in his whole life.

"Well what do you think of that Bergin?" Jonoh looked across at his companion whose mouth was so wide open he feared a silver fish may jump in to escape the dolphins.

"I've never seen anything like it. I mean I know it's big but not as big as Great Harbour but it's so full of colour and life and the Mount of Light. Well I'm a little lost for words to describe it." Bergin's wide-eyed stare made Jonoh smile and truth be known he wasn't far behind him.

"Trim the sails and extend the oars!" The deck commander bellowed out his orders, sailors scampering across deck to attend to their tasks.

"Well Bergin, now the adventure really begins."

Chapter Twenty-Three Part Two:

Smoke and mirrors

Jonoh could smell it before they'd even tied up. It wasn't just the bad smells that you would associate with the dockside, rotten food, effluence and the bodily aromas of thousands of sweaty people crammed into a small space, it was something else. Decay.

Up close, the grand old city was just that, wrinkled and fraying at the edges, everything appearing bright and vibrant from a distance but once you got in close, well shabby hardly described it. It had started at the dockside, the piers themselves were creaking and covered in algae, the smell of mildew and rot just rolling off them. The construction of the jetty walls was haphazard, random blocks of stone missing, half of it unmortared, whatever paint had been applied was rubbed away or scratched off.

The market stalls that attached themselves to the back of the jetty walls were rough and dirty looking, much like the people. Their wares hardly elevated them, cheap rough-spun clothes not much better than rags, pungent meat, fish and vegetables that looked nine parts mould, one part fresh.

Further out across the seafront the buildings although brightly painted were ramshackle, falling down in places, with broken windows and holed roofs, some being held up with poles and ropes. If you paid close attention, everything you looked at was not what it appeared, a dejected weariness seemingly infecting every aspect of life. This was a city in decay, slowly rotting away and falling in on itself, it made Jonoh shudder.

"Not quite what you expected Jonoh?"

"No Master it is not. It looked so breathtaking from the sea but up close… I am lost for words."

"It is a sad thing to witness, the slow and inevitable decline of a once great nation. Sarjinn is as old if not older than the Hardite Empire Jonoh, for thousands of years it has stood. It has seen the rise and fall of many great empires, survived conquest, famine, even the great plague but it cannot survive indifference. It has reached this sorry state because no one cares about what once was, about stories of past glories or claims of great wisdom. The world has moved forward while Sarjinn just looks back and so eventually becomes obsolete. Nothing new of any worth has been built here for centuries and instead of being what it once was, a great hotbed of trade, the trade just passes through."

Cerwin nodded at a squadron of soldiers, all in tarnished armour, their plumed helmets tatty and discoloured.

"There was a time when the great legions of Sarjinn were feared across the Known World, great battalions of fierce spearmen, mighty armoured knights on fearless steeds, their realm encompassing thousands of square miles. Now those that are left try to keep the peace and clear the dead bodies off the streets. All they have left is what lies within the boundaries of this once great city, safe only because no one is interested in conquering it."

"But there are still so many people here Master. Why do they stay?" Jonoh felt almost dizzied by the odours and the deprivation, an urge to get out almost overwhelming him.

"They do not know anything else Jonoh and if all you know is hardship and want, you will fight tooth and nail to keep your tiny piece of it. There are still some here who enjoy the trappings of wealth but you will not find them this close to the ground." The old man looked up at the Mount of Light with a resigned shrug.

Even the buildings that wrapped around the hill road seemed less impressive the more you looked. The whole city had the feel of watching someone slowly die, waiting while they gasped out their final breath.

"We need to secure provisions Master and horses for that matter." Jonoh stared out across the marketplace with a look of utter hopelessness, the best horse flesh he could see being a small enclosure of bent-backed nags and mules.

"Yes we do but we will not find them here. Come Bergin, bring our packs and follow me." Cerwin grasped his walking staff and started off in the direction of the Mount of Light without waiting to see if he was being followed. Bergin and his men scrambled to collect their belongings and hurried after him.

The road bent round either side of the base of the Mount of Light and Cerwin scurried off to the left. The road was once cobbled but only patches of stone remained, intermixed with potholes and varying puddles of mud and waste. It led into what Jonoh could only think of as slums, one- and two-storey ramshackle buildings all crammed in behind the Mount of Light. Hills ringed the city with a valley in the middle leading out onto the open plains behind it. It would take a good while to pick their way through before getting to the other side.

As they entered the great maze of roads and alleyways the whole mass seemed to close in on them. There didn't seem to be any plan, the rutted paths weaving in and out, almost as if the city itself couldn't make a decision.

"I don't like the look of this Jonoh, far too many places to ambush the unsuspecting." Bergin was walking with his hand by his sword hilt, his eyes flicking left and right as if he expected an attack at any moment.

"I'm sure we'll be alright Bergin. Let's just keep our heads down and go about our business, but just in case." Jonoh tapped the hilt of his own sword and Bergin nodded his understanding. The further they moved into the slums the less they could see ahead or behind, the buildings seeming to loom in on them just adding to the sense of danger.

They rounded a corner into a narrow street that opened out at the far end when a group of men stepped across their path. There were about twenty of them, all rough looking, wearing an assortment of mismatched armour and carrying a variety of evil-looking weapons, spears, swords and daggers.

Cerwin stopped about ten feet from their line and held his hands palm up in a gesture of peace. "We are just passing through friends. We mean no harm and are just looking to be on our way."

Jonoh saw Bergin and his squad very slowly spread out, just

enough to give themselves room to fight if needed. They were outnumbered two to one but Jonoh felt that they would be more than a match for this tatty band of thugs.

"We'd be only too 'appy t'let ya pass ol' fella. Trouble is me misses needs some new clobber so I'll 'ave t'ask ya for a little contribution." Their leader stepped forward, a big ugly-looking brute with greasy brown hair and a stubbled pockmarked face. He carried an evil-looking curved blade, serrated on one edge and gleaming sharp on the other. As dirty as they all were, their blades looked well-honed and well used.

"I must apologise sir but I am afraid we are a little short of funds." Cerwin had edged back very slightly and offered a small deferential bow. "I did not catch your name by the way my friend. Mine is Cerwin."

"Very nice t'meet you Cerwin. I'm Sunshine Bill on account o' me sunny disposition." He leered a brown-toothed smile at the old shadow-master and offered a florid bow in return. "I do so 'ate bein' rude but I'm afraid we will need some kinda payment before we can let ya pass. Can't make exceptions even for such fine gentlemen as y'selves."

"Then if you will excuse us, we will find another path." Cerwin backed up, ushering his small troupe backwards but as they turned to go another heavily armed group of ruffians blocked their exit.

Cerwin turned to face Sunshine Bill, a hard, implacable set to his features. "I would ask you to move aside and allow us to go about our business. We do not want any trouble but if you force us to defend ourselves it will be to your everlasting regret." Cerwin moved his lead hand to the top of his staff and opened up his stance. For the briefest second, Jonoh pitied Sunshine Bill and his little band of cutthroats. They had no idea that the Beckoner was calling.

Sunshine Bill hefted his sword and began to amble forwards, his gang of thugs following his lead and drawing their weapons. Jonoh stepped up beside his Master, sliding his short spear from his backpack, happier with that than a sword even if it was only four feet long. Two of Bergin's men stationed themselves to either side of them while Bergin himself turned with the rest of his company to face the men behind them.

"Try t'be nice and look what it gets ya. Ah well if it 'as to be the 'ard way." Sunshine Bill lifted his blade above his head and charged roaring at Cerwin, swinging his great sword double-handed at the shadow-master's head. In the blink of an eye Cerwin had pulled off the top of his staff revealing a long thin sparkling blade. As Sunshine Bill's blade whistled down, Cerwin slid sideways just out of reach and a moment later was pulling his rapier out of the big brute's eye.

Sunshine Bill slumped to the floor, his highwayman days behind him. For a fraction of a second his band of thugs seemed to freeze. Then all hell broke loose.

They attacked ferociously from both sides, blades and spears swinging and jabbing at the small band. In such close quarters the thugs' wild swings were easily turned aside, their numbers counting for nothing. Jonoh parried one brute's great double-headed axe, turning it so that the thug lost his balance, stumbling sideways. Jonoh slammed his spear in through his side, a gurgling grunt of surprise escaping his lips as he crumbled to the floor. As he slid his spear free another foe swung a huge spiked mace at Jonoh's head, but he simply leaned to the side, the rush of air ruffling his hair. He slid his spear in and out of the man's neck, spinning sideways and slicing the next man's neck with a backhand counter.

Then as quick as it started the remaining thugs broke and ran, fleeing for their lives as if the Beckoner himself was on their heels. Jonoh hadn't noticed, caught up in the fight as he was but over a dozen corpses lay on the ground, all of them members of Sunshine Bill's little band. The fight had lasted less than a minute.

"Is everyone alright?" Cerwin looked around at Bergin's company and breathed an audible sigh of relief that they were all intact. "Good. Gather your gear and let us make a hasty exit. We still have some way to go to clear the city boundaries and I had rather hoped to stay a little more incognito. Word of this will spread quickly in this rabbit warren and we do not need any official entanglements."

Cerwin span on his heels, doubling his pace which was quite considerable and headed for the far side of Sarjinn.

Only then did it begin to sink in. *That was my first ever kill.*

For a moment Jonoh visibly sagged, the burden of taking

a life beginning to weigh him down. It was different for Bergin and his troops, they were all vocational soldiers, it was in the job description. Master Cerwin must have had need to take lives before if for no other reason than his vocation and of course his age. But for Jonoh all he'd ever done was spar, occasionally inflicting injuries of course but never to snuff out a life.

"Jonoh." He staggered slightly, a little light-headedness affecting his steps. "Jonoh."

"Uh, sorry Master I was distracted for a moment." He looked over at Cerwin whose face was wrinkled with concern.

"It is alright Jonoh, I know this was your first time. It may not feel like much of a consolation but just hold on to the fact that you were not given a choice. You did what you had to do." Cerwin put a fatherly hand on his shoulder, giving him a little squeeze.

"I know Master but it's still a life. Three lives." Jonoh was shaken but composed enough to carry on for the moment without overly showing the effects. It would take some time.

As they pressed on, the narrow alleys and rough leaning buildings started to close in, making Jonoh feel as if the city was judging him. He hardly even noticed the smells or the degradations all around him. They found themselves having to pick a path over drunken bodies lying on the floor every time they passed an inn, some of them probably dead, drowning in two inches of muck and grime.

The smell of death and decay pitched Jonoh further into darkness. He'd never thought, not even for a split second of entering the Gift during the fight. He simply hadn't felt the need, the brief clash of arms not really providing any kind of test. Now however the Gift called to him, drawing him into its warm and comforting embrace. The trouble was that if he entered it now, feeling this distraught he may never return, never get back. The feelings of remorse and regret pressed in on him, darkening his thoughts, pushing him closer and closer to the Gift. Or was it the Void that he yearned for, the freedom of nothingness, the comfort of the quiet.

Yes, that was it. The release from regret, the detachment from remorse, the unfettered freedom, all responsibility taken away, no fault, no blame.

The pressure of the emotion was weighing so heavily that he was finding it hard to stay conscious, struggling to breath. He staggered forward, grasping Cerwin's cloak on his way to the ground. He was trapped in his own thoughts, his own emotions, all of his options compressing in his head, slowly decreasing like water running down a plughole.

"Jonoh. JONOH!" Cerwin held Jonoh by the shoulders, shaking him, trying to keep him awake. Jonoh could see Bergin and his men all crowded round, looks of concern on their faces. He could see it but he couldn't feel it, didn't have any way to reach out, any way to connect. He could feel himself drifting down to the warm safety of the Void, the black stretching out like a great blanket ready to wrap him up, safe and sound.

"Jonoh listen to me, hear my voice." Cerwin's voice came in loud and clear, like an anchor to reality.

"The pain is overwhelming, it's crushing me. I feel so alone, like I'll never find peace again." Jonoh's thoughts cried out, his desperation flowing out of him in waves. *"I can feel their loss, feel their end, just snuffed out of existence, all their hopes and dreams snatched away in an instant, no time to prepare, no time to grieve."*

"Jonoh you are not alone, never alone. Your grief is your first experience of transference, as if you are taking on the ills of others, somehow making yourself responsible for lives lost. It is not something you can ever prepare for, just something you will have to learn to endure although closing your mind will block it out. You did what you had to do Jonoh to protect yourself and your fellows. You did not choose this. The choice was forced upon you. Do not blame yourself for the poor decisions of others, it is not your fault and you are not alone, never alone. Listen."

"Jonoh you are not alone. We are with you. We will help you, let us shoulder some of the burden." Jonoh could hear them, a chorus of voices, friends, family, all reaching out, putting their arms around him and holding him up. His head started to clear, the fog of despair beginning to lift. He sat up and looked at the faces of his companions, all of them looking sick with worry.

"What was that Master? Who were those voices?" Jonoh stood up, his head clear, the overpowering sense of loss receding more and more with each passing moment.

"We are nearly there now Jonoh. Just a little further and you will see for yourself. Are you able to continue?" Cerwin looked up at him, the concern plain on his face. Jonoh nodded his assent.

They hurried on their way, the slums beginning to thin out, becoming less crowded until they could see clear sky ahead of them. They rounded a corner and then the land before them spread out into a valley sat between two rows of hills. About a hundred or so yards ahead of them there stood a large group of cloaked and hooded individuals with saddled horses, more than enough for themselves.

"Master?" Jonoh gave Cerwin a bewildered look. "Who are they?"

"They are your brothers and sisters Jonoh. Or to put it another way they are my Orphans." Cerwin strode forward, his arms outstretched in welcome. He greeted each Orphan in turn, pulling them in to a hug as if he was greeting a long-lost loved one, which of course he was.

Jonoh held back a fraction, feeling too embarrassed to interfere in the touching reunion. Bergin stepped up behind him, Jonoh having almost forgotten he was there.

"Are you all right Jonoh? We were worried for a while back there."

"Thank you Bergin, I am fine. It was just a residual effect of the Gift, just a lesson well learnt. Please do not trouble yourself." Jonoh clasped the young officer by the arm and gave him a look that let him know how grateful he was.

"Jonoh." Bergin nodded behind him with a look of slight confusion. Jonoh turned around and saw all the Orphans standing there looking directly at him, Cerwin standing off to the side. As one they bowed to him.

"Welcome Jonoh, where you lead, we will follow."

Chapter Twenty-Four Part One:

Running out of time

It was only a matter of hours now until Torbin reached the Titan Gate with his vanguard. He was starting to feel a sense of desperation though, ever since he heard Candor's thoughts. The H'Daree had attacked and breached the twin cities' defensive rampart and Candor's forces were hard pressed, fighting a close combat withdrawal through the maze of streets that made up Turan and Minari. It always hurt to be connected in times of great stress, the pain and loss your compatriot felt rushing out in waves, like an emotional slap to the face.

Torbin had wept when Willet had fallen, the fact he'd never met or known him being of little consequence. The intensity of the moment was almost overwhelming, Torbin having to pull up and dismount in order to catch his breath. They were still engaged now, fighting tooth and nail to buy time for the evacuation, give them a realistic chance to escape and survive. He knew Candor's measure, knew he would fight to his last breath to buy his loved one's time but he also felt his heart and knew that deep down he expected them all to perish. But what if they did succeed and managed to escape? What were they going to do with thirty thousand non-combatants? How would they feed them, house them or for that matter protect them?

The reality of the task ahead was starting to properly sink in, the odds were just stacked too high. As things stood there was no way he could see them winning. They were just too few.

He knew the Orphans were gathering and heading for the Gate and that gave him heart, to have his brothers and sisters with him at the end, was far more than cold comfort. There would be many happy reunions before the end and at least as many new friends to be made. He'd been in contact with an Orphan based in Darmat who'd revealed his name, Sorkin. Torbin could not think of a more hazardous place for an Orphan to operate, apart from maybe Snowbard or with the Murgan. An official delegation from the Protectorate was on its way to Darmat, which meant they would be reaching out to all the nations of the Known World, but it would be done cautiously. They would never impinge on a sovereign nation's territory and right now caution was the opposite of what was needed.

"Torbin are you alright? You seem more than a little distracted." Jadran sat a horse with ease, the mark of a born rider.

"Yes, thank you my friend, just going over a few things in my head. The fighting is still going on in Turan and Minari, my friend Candor right in the middle of it. I could put my blocks up but that would feel like a betrayal, so I have to keep my mind open. It's difficult to explain to a non mind-walker Jadran but I can feel all of his fear, his loss and his pain. Sometimes it can be quite overwhelming." Torbin offered a weak smile, the strain he was under plain for all to see.

"I knew the other day when you had to dismount for a moment that something was affecting you. You already carry a large enough burden Torbin, to saddle yourself with even more if you can avoid it seems almost masochistic. At least let me take some of the weight when we arrive at the Gate. I can see to our dispositions and organise the initial deployment, we've discussed the plans often enough. You need to rest and re-gather your strength. I know that you will not stop until your friend's ordeal is over, one way or another." Jadran reached across and squeezed Torbin's shoulder.

"Let's see when we get there Jadran but thank you my friend. I will need you more than you know with what's to come."

"I will be there Torbin, whatever our end." Jadran smiled at his friend and wheeled away, heading for the rear of their column.

"Candor, can you hear me? How do you fare old friend?"

"We're holding but they are closing in Torbin. We've withdrawn

to the furthest corner of Turan and we're trying to funnel as many men as possible through the traders' gate but we are hard pressed. I can only hope that those in Minari are doing the same. The people have been marshalled well and are out of sight into the Titan Pass now but they are not far enough. There's no way they can outrun the H'Daree, they'll be mown down like scythes cutting wheat. We're going to try to withdraw to the narrowest part of the Pass and make our last stand there. If you make it to the Titan Gate, try to save as many as you can, Marye and the children are there. Goodbye old friend." Just like that Candor cut off, his blocks going up and Torbin lost his voice.

Torbin pulled his mount up and just sat there looking at nothing, his shoulders sagging, an empty grief consuming him. The rest of the column rode past him, heads down, all too nervous to disturb him, apart from one.

"Torbin, come with me." Guido Tivosi sat on the biggest stallion Torbin had ever seen but he still looked like a grown man on a hobby horse. He leaned across and grabbed Torbin's reins and led his horse towards the treeline just as Jadran pulled up alongside them.

"Jadran, please push on to the Gate. We must get there as quickly as we can and secure it. I need a few moments to gather myself." The words came out in a strangled croak, the effort to hold onto a fraction of his composure proving as hard a task as any he'd faced.

"I will stay with him." Tivosi dismounted and went to help Torbin from the saddle. Terror barked his concern and as Torbin slumped to the ground he nuzzled straight into him, the look of sadness on his face appearing almost human.

"Of course Torbin, leave it with me. I will see you soon my friend." Jadran whipped his mount around and headed back to the column, barking out instruction, driving his men forward.

Tivosi sat next to Torbin and scratched behind Terror's ears, the great bear-hound returning the compliment by licking his hand. Torbin had his knees pulled up to his chest, his head resting forward with his hands wrapped around his shins, little shudders coming in time with wheezy breaths.

"It's almost overwhelming Guido. The sense of loss, grief and fear, the sheer despair of it just floods over you. It's called transference, bearing the weight of another's grief but all at once, in a great wave of emotion. It's not just with other mind-walkers, any death especially one you are personally responsible for can flood you with negative emotions unless you close your mind. When it's someone you're close to the intensity is that much sharper. If it's intense enough it can consume you, rob you of your faculties, leave you in a state of catatonia. I am sorry that you should see me like this, unhinged like a helpless child." Torbin didn't lift his head as he spoke, the words sputtering out. Keeping his face covered somehow offered him a crumb of comfort.

"You do not owe me any explanation Torbin Pale-skin. I know your worth. I was there, remember? When the Murgan Hoard came. I saw you rally the militia and hold the wall, saw how many men you threw back, saw you fight to the last." Tivosi reached out and put his arm across Torbin's shoulder and Torbin looked up, the strain of bearing the transference fixed on his face.

"Thank you Guido, I just need a little time to recover. Being cut off so suddenly is like having a piece of your soul ripped out." Torbin took a deep breath. "I don't remember a great deal after I passed out but I'll never forget Blood-spear. He was the best I've ever seen. The sheer power and speed of the man was beyond anything I have ever witnessed."

"Three of my men fell before him trying to defend you Torbin. He gave me these." Tivosi grinned at the memory, pointing to three parallel scars that crossed his face.

"I had no idea Guido. It would seem I owe you a debt of honour and your men."

"They died well Torbin and they knew what was asked of them. It took myself and four of my men in tight formation to force Blood-spear back. He was a magnificent warrior, easily the best I have ever seen. I hope I get the opportunity to fight him again." Tivosi beamed out a huge smile, as if the thought was the grandest thing he could think of.

Torbin sat back a little more upright, his composure returning. Terror nudged under his arm and licked his face, Torbin wrapping his arms around his friend's neck.

"I think if you'd been there, Blood-spear would not have gotten off so lightly." Tivosi smiled whilst ruffling Terror's fur, the bear-hound barking his assent.

"That I don't doubt for a moment." Torbin laughed out loud, the burden of the transference receding more and more by the moment. Tivosi was the only other person apart from Jadwan who Terror really warmed to. It was like one warrior respecting another.

"You carry a great weight on your shoulders Torbin, but I think you do not need to walk alone. Jadran is a good, capable and brave warrior, and his loyalty to you is steadfast. He has brought the best he had with him and I think young Jadson is following in his footsteps. You have many around you who will stand by your side no matter what, you just have to trust them and let them bear some of the weight."

"I know Guido, I just feel the responsibility. I am asking them to risk their lives for me and it is a burden that's hard to shake off."

"Torbin, I like you and I respect you but if you think that everyone here is doing it for you then you are a fool. They will follow you Torbin because they admire your courage and your skill at arms, but they are here for their loved ones, their futures and their country. Maybe the slaves are different but even they are doing it to gain their freedom."

That made Torbin bridle a little even though he knew in his heart that Tivosi was right. He took a moment to compose himself, painfully aware that the wrong reaction could put Tivosi offside, something he could ill afford.

"You are right of course Guido, sometimes I forget that I am not the only one taking a risk here. Please accept my apology."

"There is nothing to apologise for Torbin. Even though what I said is true it doesn't change the fact that you bear a heavier burden than any of us." Tivosi smiled and Torbin could not help but think that his smile was scarier than another man's scowl.

"Guido, may I ask a personal question?" Torbin scratched at Terror's head, the bear-hound having settled in his lap.

"Of course."

"Your accent sounds as if you are from Santatoria or maybe even east coast Protectorate. Where are you from originally?" With the connection cut, Torbin had recovered his composure if not his legs, so there was a little time to kill.

"I was born in Crotone on the east coast of Santatoria."

"I know of it Guido, by all accounts it is a beautiful town." Torbin had turned to give his full attention to the guard captain.

"It is beautiful Torbin, running from cliffs down to the edge of golden sands. On a warm summer's evening with the breeze blowing and the sun setting you could almost believe you were in paradise. 'The sea provides' is a common saying there and it does with a great bounty. It was a good place to grow up." For the first time ever Torbin thought Tivosi looked almost wistful, caught up in a warm memory.

"What happened Guido? How did you find yourself here?"

"We were raided by the Brotherhood when I was fifteen and we fought them on the beach. I cannot describe the feeling I had to anyone who hasn't experienced it Torbin, but I heard the cry of the warrior, felt it in my blood. I knew then that I had to seek battle, had to spend my life searching for the thing I crave the most."

"Searching for what Guido?"

"A glorious death." Tivosi's eyes lit up, his smile so wide it almost cut his face in two. "To find someone that is better than me, stronger than me and fight them anyway, even knowing that it will cost you everything. To test your courage when it really matters, when the peril is at its height. I knew I could never find this in the Protectorate, so I left home and set off for the Free Territories to ply my trade as a warrior for hire."

"Do you still seek it Guido? Some people would call that a death wish and someone with nothing to lose could become a liability in the heat of battle." Torbin felt nervous following this line of questioning. Poking a bear with a stick had never been a course of action he would endorse.

"It is not a death wish Torbin. I want to live to be an old man, living out my days in comfort surrounded by my loved ones, but the call to battle, the need to put yourself to the ultimate test is either in you or not. I may never find what I seek but it will not stop me searching and it will never interfere with my duty." Tivosi stiffened a little as if the question itself had stung.

"I do not question your loyalty Guido, after all you are here of your own volition, I just need to know where I stand. I do not know what will happen at the Gate, but I think our chances are slim at best and dependent on everyone doing what is required of them, holding to the plan no matter what." *"Well if you're going to poke the bear you may as well get it all done at once."*

Tivosi turned and held Torbin's stare. It was all Torbin could do not to look away, but he knew he could not, not now, not when Tivosi was judging him.

"I will carry out whatever orders you give me Torbin and I do not intend to relinquish my life cheaply but understand when and if the moment comes, I will not seek your permission."

Torbin held his look, staring into that chipped granite face being one of the hardest things he'd ever had to do and then nodded his assent.

"Thank you Guido, your loyalty honours me. I hope that you don't find what you seek for many years to come."

Tivosi clapped him on the back and laughed out loud. "Ha, I think you're ready to get underway again Torbin, the colour has definitely returned to your face." Terror barked his agreement, jumping to his feet, tail wagging like a puppy.

Torbin breathed out in silence, relieved and happy that this giant bear of a man was on his side. He was not what Torbin had expected but a much warmer more thoughtful human being, admittedly one that could crush a man with his bare hands, but still.

Torbin stood up, his legs still feeling a little shaky but well able to ride again. The main column wouldn't have got far, so catching up would be fairly easy.

They mounted up and set off towards the Titan Gate again, not pushing too hard, in part because Torbin felt sorry for Tivosi's horse having to bear that massive frame. They skirted the treeline that ran along the foothills of the mountains to take advantage of the shade and to catch the light breezes that blew there. Winter was over and spring just beginning in the Known World but this close to the Red Desert it was always hot and Terror needed some relief from the relentless sun.

"Have you ever seen the Titan Gate Guido?"

"I have not Torbin but I have heard many stories, most of them fantastical tales." Tivosi's horse looked a little less strained walking in the shade of the trees.

"It is something to behold Guido, an astonishing structure.

The first time I saw it, it took my breath away. You simply cannot comprehend its size." Torbin gently shook his head from side to side as if he still had trouble believing.

The line of the mountains turned slightly to the right and as they made the turn there it was, casting a vast shadow as they sun moved across its back. Tivosi stopped in his tracks and stared up at the monstrous structure, his mouth forming an awestruck circle.

"I have seen some things in my life Torbin but I don't think I've ever seen anything quite like this." Tivosi shook his head in exaggerated disbelief, opening and closing his eyes just to ensure it wasn't a giant illusion.

"It does tend to have that effect Guido, even when you've seen it before." Torbin sat there smiling at his companion's awed reaction. It never failed to surprise.

Tivosi beamed a huge, almost ecstatic smile at him. "What a magnificent place to make a stand Torbin. Perhaps I will find what I have been searching for after all."

Chapter Twenty-Four Part Two:

The calm before the storm

It had taken four days for the first of the rest of the eight hundred to arrive at the Gate. They had been drawn out over the journey, those on horseback arriving first and returning to the column with fresh steeds to ferry the remainder back more quickly. They were nearly all up now, Jadran organising the deployment with Jadson relaying orders along the line.

Torbin had been to the Gate on a number of occasions but had never taken the time to really study it closely. It was an incredible structure, five hundred feet tall with a level every twenty feet, each one containing every kind of facility imaginable. There were barracks, enough to house ten thousand soldiers, kitchens, medical bays, forges and dining rooms all built into the backside of the wall. The first embrasures were at one hundred and fifty feet high, each opening being twenty feet wide and ten feet high with a four-foot-high wall offering cover from return fire. Torbin had climbed to the top, inspecting all embrasures and ending with the emplacements at the very peak of the Gate. As a defensible position it was unparalleled, the field of fire was all encompassing and if forced to withdraw by retreating upwards the cost of taking the upper levels by direct assault would be devastating.

Torbin looked out from the top of the Gate, feeling better about the prospect of holding it than he'd ever thought possible. One thing was certain, the view was incredible. He could see for miles down the Pass, losing sight of the bottom as it snaked its way along, until it finally turned to be obscured by the rising peaks.

"Quite a view eh?" Guido Tivosi had sidled up next to him completely unnoticed. How a man of his immense size could do that was a mystery to Torbin.

"That it is Guido. To think it runs for hundreds of miles, carved right through the heart of the Titans is incredible. Were you aware that nobody knows who built the Gate or who carved the Pass? It's one of the Known World's great mysteries, no mention of it in any of the recorded histories, almost as if one day it just turned up." Torbin turned from the edge and walked towards the switchback steps leading down to the next level, gesturing for Tivosi to follow.

"Well Guido, what do you think?" Torbin had taken to using Tivosi as his primary advisor even though the guard captain refused any official appointment.

"It's the best defensive position I've ever seen Torbin. Two levels of embrasures at one hundred and fifty and three hundred feet, with ridged emplacements at the top of the wall. Very impressive, very impressive indeed." Tivosi eagerly nodded his approval, a little too enthusiastically for Torbin.

"With the Orphans gathering we should be well over a thousand in strength. If we station two hundred at the entry gate, with the reinforcement that we are expecting, they should be able to bottleneck that well enough to hold indefinitely. Plus, with the murder holes fully manned and fifty of our best archers added into the mix that should be plenty to cause bloody carnage. Three hundred at each embrasure level?" Torbin posed the last statement as a question, the reassurance of Tivosi's agreement being the one thing that gave him peace of mind.

"I would have thought two hundred more prudent, keep a larger mobile reserve, plug the gaps a little quicker." Tivosi's input was invaluable, always cutting straight to the point, addressing the most pressing needs.

"The forges on the first three levels are all fired up now, so we need to prioritise. Arrow heads have to take precedence, armour and spear heads next. We need to think about some old-fashioned equipment as well, billhooks would be more than useful to defend against assaults on the embrasures." Torbin was thinking out loud, going over and over the necessary preparations in his head.

"The first embrasure is one hundred and fifty feet straight up Torbin. Repelling any attack on the wall should be the least of our problems." Tivosi arched an eyebrow, as if Torbin's concerns bordered on hysteria.

"Guido, the equipment they brought to bear during the assault on the twin cities shows that they are both prepared and capable of taking any entrenched position. From what Candor told me their tactics and weaponry are advanced and we can expect them to have a few surprises up their sleeves, so we must prepare for anything." Torbin's face gave away the sense of loss he still felt about his friend and it had been over five days since his last contact.

"Torbin you should not lose heart. We do not know if your friend survived or not. Until we find out for certain you should not give him up for dead." Tivosi smiled that terrifying smile and Torbin snapped himself out of his slump.

"Quite right, thank you Guido." He slapped Tivosi on the back, as usual stinging his hand as if he'd slapped a wall.

They descended to the second level of embrasures, over three hundred feet up where Jadran was locked in conversation with a short but well-muscled, dark-haired man. The man had a heavy leather apron on with a tool belt around his waist, filled with hammers, rasps and assorted tools. If that wasn't clue enough his oversized right arm sort of gave the game away.

"Torbin, Guido, come and meet Shaloh Torm." Jadran stood up and waved Torbin and Tivosi towards him.

"Jadran, Torm." Tivosi nodded an acknowledgement to the pair and Torm flourished a low bow keeping his eyes to the floor.

"Torbin Pale-skin, Captain Tivosi, I am at your service."

"Lift your head man, there are no slaves or servants here and my name is Guido." Tivosi stepped forward, offering his massive hand in greeting.

The smith looked up gingerly and then straightened. Tivosi stayed where he was with his hand extended until Torm took him up on his offer.

"We are all equal here Shaloh. Every man has volunteered, and every man has earned his freedom by that act. You are held in high regard by us, and you honour us with your presence." Torbin stepped up with his hand out and this time the smith needed no encouragement to grasp it.

"So, what are you two doing up here?" Torbin sat himself down on a small wooden stool.

"Well, I have been getting to know our artisans and Shaloh here was originally from Darmat before he got into some difficulties and sought refuge within Lhossa. He has spent the last five years in the service of Jadwar Sun-blessed." *That explained the smith's reaction to Tivosi, and indentured servitude would be more appropriate. One rung up from slavery.* "But when in Darmat was a weapons smith and something of an inventor." Jadran gave a self-satisfied grin and a look that said, 'Go on ask me.'

"Okay Jadran, you've got us. What was it he invented?" Torbin played along just to keep his young colleague happy.

The young officer beamed out a smile, delighted to have them on the hook. "Shaloh was working on building a crossbow large enough to fire a two-pound metal bolt at the rate of six a minute."

"Ridiculous, I doubt even Guido would have the strength to ratchet back a drawstring powerful enough to do that. Two a minute, maybe five every two but no more than that." Torbin dismissed the notion as fanciful at best and ludicrous at worst.

"Shaloh if you would be so kind." Jadran offered the floor to the smith, smiling as if he and only he knew the punchline.

Shaloh pulled out some rolls of paper wedged into his tool belt and rolled them out onto the floor. On them were a number of detailed drawings showing a great crossbow supported on a triangular stand. Suspended underneath the front end was a box of some description that had lines running from trigger to string and back to the box. Technical plans had never been a strength of Torbin's, knowing how things work being of little interest.

"Fascinating I'm sure but what are we looking at?" Torbin really didn't have the time or patience to be indulging fantasists however well meaning. Shaloh looked at Jadran for permission to continue.

"Shaloh you are free to speak your mind here with no consequences." Jadran gave him a friendly tap on the shoulder, and he seemed to relax a little.

"Well, this is a cartridge box that is filled with bolts. Every time the bow is fired, the energy from the release is redirected through a system of lines and pulleys and it snaps the string back into position whilst automatically loading the next bolt into the firing slot. It can actually fire every three seconds, but the cartridge can only hold six bolts and it takes a moment to reload it and set the system back to the start."

Torbin looked at the smith, then turned to look at Tivosi, a look of utter astonishment plastered to his face.

"Have you made one before? Does it work or is this just theoretical?" Torbin fired the question at Shaloh, barely able to contain his excitement at the prospect of this being real.

"We are set up in the next embrasure along Torbin. We only came in here to triangulate our targeting but if you want a demonstration?" Jadran realised he was taking over, making it sound as if this was his achievement. "Apologies Shaloh. Do you believe we are ready to test it?"

They all looked around at the smith who seemed frozen in place and so out of his comfort zone that he might pass out. "Yes, I believe so my lord… sorry Jadran." Even having corrected himself he still didn't manage to completely stifle a bow.

Torbin grinned and slapped the smith on the back. "Don't worry Shaloh, you'll get used to things soon enough. It's a brave new world and we're all walking into it together."

They walked the thirty feet between embrasures and stepped in. Torbin was taken aback by what he saw. The great crossbow was at least five feet long and its wingspan easily exceeded six. It had been mounted on the embrasure wall, resting on a metal triangle with the box fixed to the underside of the body. The trigger was double-handed and attached to the backend of the stock and Torbin could only assume it was meant to be fired from a seated position.

"Would you care to do the honours Torbin?" Shaloh stood back and offered Torbin the firing position.

"I would be honoured, Shaloh."

The smith sat him down behind the wall and Torbin realised it was mounted there so that the wall could be used to anchor your feet. The one drawback was that he couldn't see over the wall. "I can't see a thing Shaloh, how am I meant to aim?"

"We had restrictions because of the embrasure walls Torbin

so these are two-man artillery pieces. One to aim, one to fire. We have some wicker screens set up as targets at about two hundred yards. It's about as far as we think they'll fly before they just turn into falling chunks of metal." Shaloh was warming to his task. "We have lined you up so when you are ready just pull back on the triggers. When you release it will snap back into place and as soon as you hear the click you can fire again."

Torbin put his hands on the triggers and braced himself against the wall with his feet. He pulled the trigger and the bolt flew from the stock – TWANG! A quick series of whooshing sounds purred out and a fresh bolt loaded into the stock – CLICK. He pulled the trigger again and repeated until all the bolts were spent. The whole process took less than twenty seconds but Torbin's arms buzzed with the effort and the recoil.

He realised he was still concentrating on holding the stock and hadn't even looked up. Tivosi was standing leaning over the wall, pointing and laughing into the distance.

"Torbin, come and look." Tivosi's smile was full of joy, the first time Torbin had ever seen it looking anything other than intimidating.

Torbin stood up and looked over the wall to where Tivosi was pointing. About two hundred yards out a large wicker screen was shredded, two of the bolts wedged into its wooden supports, the others not visible.

"Only two hit?" Torbin looked round at his companions, all of them looking absolutely delighted.

"All six hit Torbin, the other four just smashed through." Tivosi laughed out loud and Torbin simply could not quite believe how happy this made him.

"Shaloh, you sir, are a truly gifted man. Before this is over everyone in this fight will owe you a debt and know your name. Thank you my friend." Torbin bowed to the smith, Tivosi and Jadran mimicking his action.

Shaloh stood rooted to the spot, utterly bemused by the turn of events but with the good grace to flush red at the compliment.

"How long does it take you to manufacture one of these and could you teach others? Let us know what you need, materials, labour, whatever and we will provide it." Torbin grasped the smith's hand while Jadran and Tivosi both clapped him on the back nearly knocking the poor man over. "Jadran, please see to it that Shaloh gets whatever material he needs and assign him the main forge at ground level. He is now our master armourer."

Shaloh followed on behind Jadran as he began his descent, a look of utter bewilderment on his face.

"I would say our chances are on the up Guido. If we can get a battery of those crossbows made it could really turn the tide." Torbin grasped the top of the embrasure wall, shoulders back, chest out, looking somehow bigger and more confident.

"I am happy to admit that I have never seen anything like that. With that kind of fire power, I'd feel confident we could hold this position indefinitely, maybe even go on the attack." Tivosi was positively beaming, the prospect of levelling the playing field really did seem to warm his heart. "If they attack us here Torbin, they will be in for a terrible shock."

"From what we understand Guido, they have conquered everything outside of the Known World during the last millennia. As positive as this turn of events is, I think we should temper our enthusiasm just a little. The H'Daree are powerful and sophisticated and have achieved what no one has ever come close to in the history of the Known World. They have found a way to traverse the Great Storm Curtain, so I'm fairly sure they'll have a few surprises for us as well." Torbin stood leaning against the embrasure wall, staring out across the Titan mountains, a far more positive set to his body. "But we'll have a lot more for them to think about, that's for sure my friend."

He turned smiling towards Tivosi and suddenly stopped dead in his tracks.

"Torbin old friend, can you hear me?"

"Candor?"

"Torbin, yes it's me. You have no idea how good it is to hear your voice my friend. I don't want to stay in contact for long, you never know who's listening, but they didn't pursue us Torbin. They stopped at the mouth of the Pass and just let us go but that was six days ago. We have thirty thousand people here, all heading for the Titan Gate, but we have nearly run out of food Torbin and are in desperate need. Can you help us?"

Torbin staggered forward a couple of steps and slumped down, Tivosi catching him by the shoulders.

"I thought you were dead, I thought you were all dead. Why didn't you contact me, anything just to let me know?"

"I couldn't risk it until we had enough distance between us and them my friend. I am sorry but right now we need your help, or thousands will die. Please Torbin can you help us?"

"We are coming Candor, hold on, we are coming."

And with that their exchange ended and Torbin found himself sitting with his back to the embrasure wall, Tivosi kneeling down, looking concerned.

"They are alive Guido. The people of the twin cities are alive and in the Pass. We have got to go to their aid now, before it is too late." Torbin's head was clear, the impact of the contact easing.

"What if it is a trap Torbin? Lure a portion of our force out into the open to destroy it all the more easily." Tivosi helped Torbin back to his feet.

"It matters not Guido, we must go."

"Then we go together."

Chapter Twenty-Five Part One:

Hunt

The wind blew great gusts of snow horizontally, whiting out the sky, the field of vision reduced to feet. They had skirted the border between the Protectorate and the Wilderness for more than two hundred miles, evidence of contact intermittent but there none the less.

Skin, Ungforth and Urdoon had taken over scouting and would be gone for days at a time. It had been two since Marisa had last seen them, slipping off on a northerly angle, Ungforth confident that they had picked up a hint of a trail. Even Skin had shrugged his shoulders at that one. How can you see a trail in this endless white?

Over the last few weeks their force of Wilderness warriors had grown, so that they had over two hundred with them now, all of them choosing to stay and help oust the mountain men. The longer she spent with them the more she realised how little the Protectorate actually knew about these people. Rather than being a scattered, nomadic and sparse people, the Children were numerous and closely tied to each other, despite tribal rivalries. There were Kaimas all over the Great White, nearly all in hidden cave systems, some natural but not all of them. Some of the systems were hewn out of the rock by hand, sophisticated communities, housing thousands upon thousands of people.

They had developed ways of growing crops and raising herds in impossible conditions. It made Marisa admire them all the more and they were warm and funny, with a rich cultural heritage, stories passed on from generation to generation. Marisa was rightly proud of the Protectorate and all of its achievements but on occasion couldn't help but feel that there was an undercurrent of arrogance, as if it knew better than anyone else. Clearly that was not always the case.

Marisa stood leaning into the wind, trying to scan the horizon but as she couldn't even see it, decided that discretion was the better part of valour.

"Right, let's make camp and try to sit this out for a bit. Andmar, is there anything resembling shelter around here?" Ungforth's young subordinate had chosen to stay with the main force and act as a guide.

"Yes Marisa, there is an outcropping, a few hundred feet to the north that should provide some cover." The young warrior pointed off in the direction of the shelter, but Marisa had absolutely no idea which way was north, south, up or down.

Ungforth had told Marisa that Andmar had a bit of a soft spot for her and had sworn to defend her with his life. A little over the top from her point of view but sweet none the less, and she had found herself growing very fond of him.

They struggled through the storm until they reached the outcropping which was of a good size, about one hundred feet across by about thirty feet high. Shelter of this size was a genuine blessing out here in the Great White. They broke out the tents and windbreaks and set up under the lip of an overhang, Fugly and Rat getting the fire going while Garic and Bodger raised the canvas.

"Andmar, can you get a few of your men to post guard duty? I want to set up a picket line about fifty to a hundred feet west of our position and put some guards to the north of the outcropping."

"Of course Marisa, how many do you require?" Andmar had to lean in close to be heard, the wind whistling around the rocks making it almost impossible to hear.

"Two dozen should do it, switch them out every couple of hours to keep everyone fresh."

"I'll get to it straight away." Andmar smiled and strode off to select the men.

"They've turned out to be good company as well as resourceful allies Marisa, don't you think?" Breda smiled across at Marisa whilst setting about peeling vegetables.

"That they are Breda, but the biggest surprise is their numbers. How is it that we were so unaware? However, as resourceful as they are, I'm starting to think that the mountain men may be one step ahead of us."

"How do you mean exactly Marisa?" Breda stopped his peeling and focused his full attention on Marisa.

"I'm not sure, it's just that it feels as if they are deliberately leading us by the nose. It's as if they are laying down a trail of breadcrumbs for us to follow, keeping us moving in a certain direction, either to trap us or just wear us down." Marisa shrugged. "It's just a thought."

"I know what you mean Marisa, but we have an advantage that they cannot counter. The network of Kaimas means that eventually we'll be forewarned and have the chance to intercept them. Even if they are still gathering warriors to their cause they have generated so much enmity with the Children that they will eventually run out of options. Then they will stand or run, but either way the mountain men will seek an escape route I should think."

"That sounds reasonable Breda but we don't have any idea what it is they are doing. They've made no statement of intent or demands and there is no discernible pattern to their actions. It's as if the whole purpose is to keep us off balance. But why? What purpose does that serve?" Marisa picked up a piece of peel and flicked it at the fire.

"It's all speculation until we catch up with them and even then, there's no guarantee they'll reveal anything." Breda shrugged. "It's pointless tying ourselves in knots over it, what will be will be."

"True." Marisa gave Breda a playful punch on his arm. "When did you become such a philosopher?"

"Since we began wandering around the Great White. Lots of time to think." Breda smirked at Marisa and they both laughed.

"What's so funny?" Fugly planted herself next to Breda and gave him one of her come hither looks.

"Just debating life's loftier questions." Breda raised an eyebrow at Marisa and that set them off again.

"What? Like how does Bodger count past ten when he's run out of fingers?" Now everyone joined in the guffaws, Bodger excepted.

"Ha bloody ha!" Bodger rounded on them with a particularly indignant look on his face. "I take my fucking socks off, that's how."

Everyone roared with laughter and Marisa felt reassured that no matter what happened they'd always have each other.

Rat and Garic wandered over from the cooking pot, the aroma of stewing meat and spices seeming to follow them. Similar fires had sprung up along the shadow of the outcropping, the Children setting to their own needs.

"Andmar just signalled, three coming in. Looks like our scouting party is back." Rat sat herself next to Fugly and started to wash the starch off the peeled vegetables in the snow.

"Let's hope they've managed to catch more than a sniff of them this time." Garic had lost his surly attitude and was stating what everyone else was thinking. They all just wanted to finally find the enemy and engage them. Wandering around in endless snowstorms wasn't doing anybody any good.

The air was so white that Marisa didn't catch a glimpse of Ungforth until he was nearly on top of them.

"Ungforth my friend, it is good to see you. Please, share our fire and our meat." Marisa ushered the hulking warrior to the fireside, Skin sitting down next to him. They had obviously formed a close bond and Marisa was glad of it.

"What news my friend?" As Marisa asked the question everyone stopped talking and turned their full attention to Ungforth.

"We have found them Marisa, about ten miles northeast of here, just inside the Snow Eagle's Kaimas. Urdoon has stayed to keep watch on them, and he'll leave markers for us to follow if needed. I don't think they plan to go anywhere for a day or two, their camp is well dug in." Ungforth had taken his giant sword out of the sheath on his back and laid it across his lap. Marisa still couldn't quite believe that anyone could wield it, but she figured she'd find out soon enough.

"What about the Snow Eagles. How much danger are they in?" Marisa realised she was leaning so far forward that she was nearly in Ungforth's lap.

"The Snow Eagles will only be found if that's what they

choose Marisa. Their Kaimas is underground, and no one knows the secret entrances. They will remain hidden for as long as they wish." Ungforth glanced across at Skin, as if waiting for him to say something. Skin just sat there, tight-lipped as always.

"What is their condition?" Marisa ploughed on. *"I'll have to ask Skin about that later."*

"They are about two hundred strong and the three mountain men are still with them. They have posted watch around their campsite but haven't sent out any scouts that we could see. If we move quickly, we could get around their flanks and hem them in." Ungforth seemed more than a little keen and Marisa could hardly blame him, the Wolfs-head Clan had lost a lot of their youth to the mountain men.

"Well, no time like the present." Marisa looked around the fire and couldn't help but notice the confused look on Ungforth's face. "It means there's no point in waiting Ungforth, that now is the time to move." Ungforth still didn't look completely convinced. "It's just a turn of phrase." Ungforth nodded.

"Right let's get a meal inside us and then gear up. Ungforth, have you chosen your captains?" Marisa took a bowl of stew from Fugly who started to hand them out to all by the fire.

"I have Marisa."

"Good then this is the plan." Everyone leaned in as Marisa laid out her strategy.

Marisa was impressed with how quickly the Children had made ready. Ungforth had divided them into three groups as requested, Andmar taking his company east and wide of the enemy's camp, while Ungforth himself headed to the western side. Marisa led the third group south to cover any escape attempt, knowing that's where the hammer blow would fall hardest. Skin and Ungforth felt certain that once battle commenced some of the Children would switch sides, possibly turning the course of the battle. It was a risk, but they had to go with what they had, as they may never catch up to their quarry again.

The Children of the Wilderness were not exactly organised, mismatched bits of armour, boiled leather and lots of furs being the uniform of choice but their weapons were impressive. Most favoured great double-headed, long-handled axes or huge spiked mauls. Fewer had blades but those that did carried great two-handed broadswords, much like Ungforth. The only trouble was so did the opposition.

Urdlin had stayed with them and had stuck as close to Marisa as possible and was now with her company. It was as if he felt a personal debt was owed and until it was paid, he wouldn't let her out of his sight.

Marisa had the largest force, nearly a hundred all told with Ungforth and Andmar splitting the rest between them. The mountain men had made their camp in what amounted to a hollow of sorts, no ridges or outcroppings just a dip in the ground that offered the most meagre of protection. They had posted sentries but not too many and none very far from camp.

Marisa stopped about one hundred yards from where Urdoon had said the first sentries were. He had opted to stand with Marisa's squad in the front line and she had to admit she felt better having him there. The almost non-existent visibility meant that if they couldn't see the enemy, the enemy couldn't see them.

The squad, Urdoon and Urdlin all squatted in a circle, listening intently.

"Right, this is it. We're going to advance in line but bowed outwards in the centre, forming a convex shape." Marisa scraped a curved line in the snow with her spear butt, like an upturned bowl. "Then we will contact them and withdraw, but a fighting withdrawal staying in close contact. It's vital we do so because we want them to believe we are fighting our hardest and they are pushing us back. We must hold the line but let it bow backwards in the middle so that it becomes concave." She drew another line, bowl right way up. "With poor visibility the hope is that they will drive forwards, believing they have us on the run. As we draw them forward Ungforth and Andmar will hit them in the flanks, hemming them in and preventing their numbers from engaging, apart from their front lines of course. If they surrender, we will accept it. Is that understood?" She looked hard at Urdoon and Urdlin and they both nodded their ascent.

"Alright then let's get to it. Only carry what you will need, any packs or unnecessaries leave here." Marisa slipped her backpack off and pulled out her armour, the squad all doing the same and beginning to make ready. The Children all dropped their various odds and sods and quietly limbered up, little exchanged grunts and nods shared amongst them.

"Urdoon you go left and Urdlin right. Stretch your line as far as your numbers will allow but no gaps, remember we want to hold them and fix them in position, so shield-wall and no solo heroics." The two young warriors nodded and passed on their orders down the line, all of the assembled force raising their shields in readiness.

"Breda, are you sure?" Marisa leaned in to whisper her question, half hoping he had changed his mind.

"I am Marisa and I'll see you after." They grasped each other's forearms and exchanged a knowing glance. Then Breda slipped out of sight, skirting around the end of the line and circling behind the enemy. At least that's what Marisa assumed, as he disappeared from sight after about twenty feet.

Now all that was left were the rituals, people using whatever methods they needed to prepare for the fray. Bodger and Rat checking and double-checking each other's straps. Rat grasping Bodger's face in her two hands and saying the words she always said, words only her and Bodger ever heard.

Fugly practising her sword forms for when it got properly up close and personal, the fluid movements and grace simply highlighting just how stunning she truly was.

She turned and there was Garic, stood a couple of feet away.

"Check your straps?" He smiled casually as if this was just another drill. She'd never met anyone who remained so calm and level before a fight.

"Thanks, that'd be good." She smiled back, hoping that the recent tension between them may have lessened.

Garic dropped to one knee and started to tug on Marisa's greaves, making sure the straps were secure but not so tight as to pinch. She felt a tiny shudder, not having had his hands on her since their first contact with the Children. Garic stood up and checked her vambraces and then reached around her back to test the straps on her cuirass, keeping his eyes on the task and not on Marisa.

"Garic." He looked up and they locked eyes. They both knew

what was coming, this may be their last moment together, no time to waste. He pulled her close and kissed her passionately, Marisa responding in kind. They stayed that way for a while, clinging on as if the contact could become a permanent memory, something they could hold on to.

"About fucking time you two sorted it out." Fugly smiled across at them and the tension was broken.

Marisa pulled away and took her place at the centre of the line. *"Just how I like it."*

She stood forward and looked up and down the line, every eye now turned to her. She raised her spear and stepped forward, banging her weapon on her shield. The whole of her line followed suit and they started to march towards the enemy, shields locked, inviting the enemy to fight. If they didn't know they were coming before, they did now.

Chapter Twenty-Five Part Two:

Battlesong

Marisa looked right, Garic and Fugly shields locked tight, no room in between. To her left Rat and Bodger were exactly the same, all five of them moving as one impenetrable wall of flesh and steel. It felt a little odd to be missing so many, but Skin wanted to go with Ungforth, and Marisa had let it happen. But with Whisper, Lummox and Shadow missing as well, the balance wasn't the same. She pushed any negative thoughts aside and concentrated all her focus forward. The line was moving exactly as she wanted, bowed out with her at the apex, the rest of the wall spread out beyond her limited eyesight. They advanced in lockstep, weapons banging out a rhythm on their shields, a slow drumbeat of impending violence.

She could hear noises from up ahead, weapons and shields being hefted, orders being barked out, warriors readying themselves for battle. Still no sighting of the foe, snow billowing across the ground, whiting out everything in sight.

She could sense the tension all around, every person in every direction bracing themselves, waiting for the release that contact brought. Then the rumbling roar of massed bodies careering towards them, closing the gap, charging towards the fray.

There, only feet away, crashing towards them.

"Brace!" Marisa shouted as loud as she could and ducked her head below the rim of her shield, pushing her lead shoulder forward and stamping her back foot down.

"Take the hit. Take the hit."

She shuddered at the impact, if she had to guess a battle hammer or a great axe, her shield absorbing the hit, her rear foot nudging backwards. A spear darted over her shield rim, sliding sideways and bouncing off Garic's pauldron. He grunted as if offended by the strike and snapped out a response, his spear darting out, hitting flesh and then pulling back in. Marisa noticed the grim smile on his face, a little 'How dare you' aimed at the opposition.

Marisa double-tapped her shield, the prearranged signal to begin their withdrawal and she heard it echoed down the line, everybody slowly easing back. The contact was fierce, muffled screams and moans drifting into the air whenever someone was hit. She saw a couple of her own go down, one of the Children on Urdlin's side of the line toppling backwards with an axe buried deep in his shoulder. The gap was filled instantly, the line shuffling up to close the hole, just like they'd practised.

They had dropped a few of their own however. She'd taken down one bear of a man herself with an upwards thrust to the throat and Garic had put paid to a couple at least. However, they seemed as if they'd taken some instruction themselves, their attacks feeling more coordinated, less frenzied, almost as if they were fighting to a plan. Plus, their numbers felt greater than the two hundred they'd expected, far greater truth be told.

They continued to give ground, bowing backwards at the centre, encouraging the enemy to push forward in the belief they were winning. The numbers pitched against them were beginning to tell, the holes appearing in the line getting harder and harder to plug. They were starting to struggle to hold, and Marisa could sense that her force was on the verge of breaking when she heard the most beautiful sound imaginable.

A great roar rung through the air from both sides of the battlefield, Ungforth and Andmar's forces crashing into the flanks of the enemy. The sound of steel on steel rang out, mixed with curses and barked orders but Marisa knew from the furore that the trap had worked. They had them surrounded on three sides, hemmed in with only their front lines able to engage, the majority of their forces crammed in, waiting for the warrior in front to fall before they could swing their own blades.

She banged three times on her shield, signalling to attack. She planted her back foot and shoved forward with her shield, nudging the attackers back a fraction, just enough to open up and begin totting up the butcher's bill. The Beckoner would have his fill this day.

A great spiked maul whistled towards her head, just missing her helmet as she bent backwards, countering with a backhand slice, catching the man across the top of his arm. He leapt back, surprisingly quick for such a large specimen, switching his stance, favouring his as yet wound-free side. Marisa smiled to herself, feinting left and watching him take the bait as she switched right and skewered his unprotected neck with her spear. A double-headed axe swung towards her from the left, the snow seeming to part before it, but as she ducked forward and under, she realised her spear had pinned its victim in the ground. Letting go she drew her sword and parried the axe's return swing, turning it aside and slicing the warrior's head clean in two. As he dropped stone dead at her feet, she couldn't help but wonder whether the eye in the severed part of his skull winked at her on its way to the ground.

She could sense the pulse of battle flowing out as if it had a life of its own. She had time, as much time as she needed, all the little dramas playing out before her eyes in slow motion. Garic and Fugly to her left, dancing a deadly duet, him all power and destruction, her all grace and subtlety. To her right Bodger and Rat working in perfect tandem, all their rehearsed moves, all those hours of practice coming to fruition.

A giant broadsword swept sideways, parallel to the ground, flying towards her hip while a shining battle hammer flew towards her head from above. Inches away from oblivion she dove forwards, ducking under the sword and inside the reach of the hammer, stabbing the hammer wielder through the chest and opening the swordsman's stomach.

She rose back to her feet, her sight slightly obscured by the steam rising from the gutted man's entrails. There was a space around her, the attacking Children all pulling back slightly, looks of confusion and fear washing over their faces. She leant down, rubbed her hands in the eviscerated blood and guts and smiling, drew lines on her forehead and cheeks. Dropping her shield, she wrenched the spear from the dead corpse it had pinned to the ground and with a weapon in each hand roared at those facing her.

"The music, the beautiful music. The whistling of steel, rushing towards me, singing a song of cold, hard existence, looking for my blade to ring out a fresh note. Skin parting under my spear, the warm engulfing flow of blood pouring out to fill the void, melodic and smooth. Whisper of wood and metal, strings and trumpets, great sweeping notes full of angst, great bold strokes of immovable power. Fear letting out little whimpering sounds, tinkling high notes dancing on top of the melody. Crashing of metal on wood, the splintering of shields, the shattering of bones, percussion beats, keeping a cold malevolent rhythm, driving the chorus. Where are my dancing partners? Don't run away, come to me, embrace my sword and spear, hear the tune they play and rejoice at your end. Over the top of everything, the symphony plays, all the different chords coming together, the song of battle engulfing all true artists, showing the way..."

Marisa stood stock still, slowly opening her eyes, a strange pink hue affecting her vision. She drew in a deep breath, filling her lungs, making her feel ten feet tall, letting her drink in the silence. It took a second or two to focus and then she saw. There was a blood-soaked circle about ten feet in diameter around where she stood, the remains of what looked like seven or eight corpses. There were a lot of bits, so she couldn't be certain.

Some of the Children in front of her were on their knees, heads bowed, weapons laid on the floor in front of them. Marisa took a step forward but stopped, irritated by something in her hair, two fingers, one with a silver ring on it. *"Well that's new."* She felt light-headed, giddy almost, like a young maid in the first throes of love. She'd heard the old veterans talk about it, how some got to hear it. Not all, absolutely not, but some. *"Battlesong..."* She stood tall, stretched out her arms and roared like a great beast, the kneeling Children cowering down before her.

"Marisa."

She spun round, teeth bared, ready for the next challenge but it was only Fugly. The look on her face told a story however, and not a pretty one.

"Fuck Marisa. Are you alright?" Fugly had instinctively taken a step back and it made Marisa feel desperate. Why would one of her own pull away?

"I'm fine Marta. What's the situation?" Marisa slowed her breathing and offered Fugly a smile.

"The plan worked like a dream sir. They were caught completely by surprise and on top of that over a hundred have joined us. There were more of them than we thought though and they're pulling back, shield-wall up, well organised. What do we do sir?" Fugly had stood to attention and from what Marisa could tell, was oblivious to the wound on her thigh.

"We have to keep the pressure up Marta. We have got to break them here and try to take at least one mountain man alive. Pass the word that we will press the attack until they break."

"Yes sir." Fugly spun round and set off to the front line which had moved away to the north. *"When did that happen?"* Marisa had almost forgotten about the Children prostrate before her feet. She turned to address them only to find they were all still looking at the ground.

"In the name of the Great Maker stand up, will you?"

The Children all stood, though their overwhelming sense of shame kept their heads down.

"We don't have time to fuck about here. If you're with us, then come now and help us drive these mountain men from your lands. Or run away. However, if you raise your hands against us again it will be the last thing you ever do." Marisa spat out the final words just for effect. It worked.

"We are with you…" They stopped, uncertain how to address her.

"Marisa. My name is Marisa Longspear. Come." Marisa turned and ran towards the battle lines; the half dozen Children close on her heels.

The enemy had closed ranks, shields locked tight together, slowly pulling back in an ever-decreasing semicircle. Garic, Bodger and Rat were leading the attack at the centre of the line, the defenders falling in ones and twos but holding to their task. At the rear Marisa could hear orders being barked out in a language she was unfamiliar with, although she could catch the odd word. Snowbard.

Marisa joined the fray, stepping up next to Garic and much to their credit her band of Children threw themselves into the action. Suddenly the defenders pulled back to either side, creating a gap through to the rear of their position and three figures marched forward. They were all three big men, fully armoured in forged plate steel, the two on the flanks wearing great eagle helms, round shields and huge sleek broadswords. The one in the middle stood out though and Marisa instinctively knew who he was, Haftor Thorsen.

The line of defenders withdrew and all of Marisa's Children did likewise, nervously trying to put some distance between themselves and the mountain men. Marisa stood her ground, as did her squad, by then bolstered by Skin, Ungforth and Andmar.

The mountain men strode into the space that had been created and stopped opposite Marisa. Thorsen was a giant of a man, touching seven feet and as broad as an ox. He pulled a vast double-headed axe from straps on his back, planted his feet and stood staring at Marisa.

"Lay down your arms and no one else need die here today." Marisa spoke evenly and calmly but there was steel in her voice.

"That is a bold statement from a little girl with little friends. I may not kill you all but that depends on how well you behave." Thorsen's voice boomed out, almost as if there was something amplifying it, making it reverberate with power.

"By what right are you here, mountain man? You were not invited and you are certainly not welcome. We are here with the blessing of the Children of the Wilderness and with their warriors. We shall see you gone, dead or alive. That choice is yours so make it now." Marisa slid her feet into battle stance, slowing her breathing, calming her mind.

"We are here because this is our realm. The King of Snowbard does not recognise your Children, they are his subjects and he will have his way, as and when he sees fit. Take your pitiful band and leave little girl whilst you can. You will not get a second opportunity."

"So be it." Marisa sprang forward, shield up, spear thrusting out, Garic and Fugly on either side. Suddenly her shield was torn almost in two, the great axe shredding it like paper, a great gout of nauseating energy pulsing out of it. Marisa rolled and just slipped under the backswing, her stomach roiling. She stepped back as Thorsen swung again when suddenly Garic launched a frenzied attack from behind, Fugly darting in and out, sword thrusting and cutting, forcing Thorsen to reset himself.

She looked around quickly and saw Urdoon and Urdlin had joined the fray, attacking the two swordsmen to either side. More and more Children joined the attack, pouring in from all sides against the three mountain men. There was something that flowed from the mountain men's blades, Marisa had felt it before in the debrief back at barracks, but they weren't magic, just metal and the men wielding them were flesh and bone. Nothing more.

Marisa shook off the remains of her shattered shield, drew her sword and charged, roaring…

"The symphony rose up, great high notes piping over the top, all the players synchronising in perfect harmony. Strings full of emotion, heart wrenching, like an ocean of tears. Horns announcing their power, subtle changes of mood following the ebb and flow of blood. Woodwind notes drifting, high and low, laying in the spaces in between. The percussion of clashing steel, drumming out those familiar patterns, driving the whole movement, forcing the pace. Wild discordant sounds crashing into the arrangement, smashing towards the harmonies trying to disrupt all the beauty. The symphony rising up, again and again, only to be smashed back, instruments forever silenced, strings cut, drumskins slashed. The power of the orchestra will not be broken, all the instruments fighting to be heard, taking up the slack where their brothers and sisters had fallen silent…"

Marisa's vision slowly came back into focus. She started to scan the field around her. To her left a body lay face down, its right forearm almost severed, strings of flesh and dark armour just about holding it together. A few feet away Garic stood, his half-broken shield hanging limply from his shattered arm, dangling pointlessly at his side. There was blood everywhere, hardly a patch of white snow to be seen, corpses littering the ground like fallen leaves in autumn.

Bodies lying prone in every direction were being tended to, brothers in arms desperately trying to save their comrades. She thought she could pick out some of the bodies lying motionless on the ground, Urdlin, Andmar and… Her breath caught in her throat, Bodger and Skin kneeling over a diminutive figure… Rat.

Tears started to flood her eyes, all the joy of battle, the thrill, the rush, all seeping away. She looked further right scanning the vista of bloody horror when she noticed it. A great figure, wrapped in steel, lying flat on its back. A spear was buried in its armpit, another forced through its kneecap from behind, snapped off halfway, probably as it fell. It was Haftor Thorsen, brought down but not before taking at least a dozen warriors with him, bodies scattered all around, blood and gore littering the ground about him.

There was a figure crouched over him, kneeling on his chest, driving a dagger through his helm's visor. Breda stabbed up and down, up and down over a dozen times before he stopped. Just making sure.

There was a brief respite in the storm, a far bigger picture revealing itself. One of the other two mountain men lay dead on the ground but the third was fleeing, using the diminishing band of enemy Children as cover. *"Fucking coward, run while others die for you."*

The fight had gone out of everyone now and the remaining enemy began to lay down their arms and fall to their knees. Part exhaustion, part survival.

Breda had stood up and was making his way towards her. She could feel stinging pains in her arms and legs and a sense of disconnection. She looked down and saw the blade jutting out of her leg, blood pumping out like a red waterfall. She looked up, smiled at Breda and then the darkness took her.

Chapter Twenty-Six:

A price to pay

Endless stacks of paper piled on the desk in front of him. A necessary part of his duties, but tedious none the less. Sorkin took a deep breath and nodded for the guard to usher in the next overseer.

He loved his life inside the Royal Ziggurat but did not relish when his duties took him to the outlying districts. The counting houses were invariably one-storeyed, mean little buildings with barely any windows. Close and stuffy, making his woollen robes of office chafe, sweat running down his spine in irritating rivulets. This was his lot however and what had elevated him to the post of Advocate of the Count, so grumbling about his responsibilities seemed petulant at best, downright ungrateful at worst.

"Many Orphans will have only their wits and skill at arms to sustain them. You however, young Master Sordel have the great advantage of being a gifted Logistar. This is a talent that will avail you opportunities few other Orphans will ever see, for the wealthy and powerful will always need someone to tally their riches and keep track of their possessions. Bury your distaste deep and use your extraordinary skills to advance yourself."

Sorkin could still hear Shadow-master Cerwin's words clearly in his mind, the last piece of advice he had offered before setting him to his task. It barely seemed possible that that was over twenty years ago.

The door swung open, and the guard ushered in Overseer Lorent. He was a small, unremarkable looking man with mousy, thinning hair and a nervous, fidgety way about him. He was responsible for the Shellow Ward, a vast agricultural area bordering the Great Silver Sea, far to the north.

"Please be seated Overseer Lorent. Can I offer you a glass?" Sorkin smiled, gesturing towards the ewer of honeyed milk sitting in amongst the sheaves of paper on his desk.

"Thank you Advocate, but no." Lorent sat, his eyes darting nervously at the great piles of accounts spread before him. Sorkin could not help but note that his nervous demeanour was exaggerated by the amount of sweat that was staining his otherwise pristine, white uniform.

"How was your journey? Not too testing I trust?" Sorkin could feel the nervousness seeping out of Lorent. He knew that being summoned to meet the Advocate of the Count was unnerving but only the guilty were this jittery, at least that is what experience had taught him.

"It was pleasant enough Advocate, if a little bumpy." Lorent offered a nervous smile, desperately trying to mask just how ill at ease he truly was.

"Well, it is a long distance from Shellow to the capital, but it must still be a great honour to see the City of the Living Gods?" Sorkin wanted to try and put Lorent at ease, at least a little. It felt less like an interrogation then, even though he knew the outcome in advance. No point having the man soil himself before the end, with such little ventilation the smell would be most unpleasant.

"It is indeed a long way Advocate, but worth the hardship to be able to witness the grandeur of the Royal Ziggurat." Lorent was choosing his words carefully, ingratiating but not overly, trying to give off the air of an upstanding citizen. Not that it would save him, it was well past that point.

"Well, I should imagine you are wondering, why the summons?" Sorkin arched an eyebrow, his eyes flicking to a large pile of papers, affixed with the Shellow seal.

"It is not my place to question Advocate, only to obey." Lorent inclined his head as he spoke, meticulously following accepted protocol, but obsequience would not save him.

"So, you were not in the slightest bit curious? A little difficult to believe when summoned from the furthest corner of the Kingdom.

Surely it must have piqued your interest, if only a little?" Sorkin wanted an open, freely offered confession. At least that way he may be able to justify a degree of leniency, a quick and painless death with no consequences for the man's family. The alternative never failed to make him shudder.

Lorent looked up sheepishly, sweat beading on his forehead and running down his nose. Drip, drip, drip, a little puddle beginning to take shape on the tabletop. A wan smile crossed his lips, and he opened his mouth as if to speak, but then dropped his eyes again to look at his little lake forming on the wooden surface.

"Would it interest you to know that the Inquisitors Office has been conducting interviews in your ward?" Lorent's eyes looked up sharply, fear etched into every line on his face.

"The Inquisitors Office Advocate?" Not so much a question as a plea, desperately hoping he'd misheard or that Sorkin had confused his facts. Sadly, neither was true.

"Yes, Inquisitor Malek and a hand-selected team of questioners have spent the last week interviewing a wide range of workers, from field hands to grain supervisors. His report was quite thorough. Care to guess at its contents?" Sorkin slowly thrummed his fingers on the stack of papers, the ribbons attached to the Shellow seal dancing in time with his taps.

"I, I, I..." Lorent began to shake, little convulsive shudders making his shoulders hop up and down. Tears began to cascade down his face, the dust from the road creating dark lines, like the running make-up of a jilted woman. A sad little scene, but merely a delay to the inevitable outcome.

"Lorent, the words must come freely from you, without coercion or they will count for nothing." Sorkin reached into his pocket, pulled out a cotton square and offered it to the Overseer.

Lorent knew the law, everybody did. A confession offered after questioning or physical encouragement (call it torture for that is what it is) was meaningless. It was seen as nothing more than confirmation of the facts. Only a freely given admission and a plea for mercy could lead to clemency and that, in itself, was no guarantee. There was no adversarial system in place, no court in which you could argue your case. Once the Inquisitors Office became involved, guilt or innocence was rapidly established and all that was left was meting out the appropriate punishment. Sorkin supposed it was as fair a system as any other he had seen. To be an Inquisitor was a calling after all, almost a religion.

Lorent's choices were thin at best, non-existent really. Confess and throw himself on the mercy of the Royal Officers or deny everything and see his family thrown into slavery. No choice at all.

"Advocate, I freely confess to my crimes. I and I alone am responsible for the deception, no one else was involved." Lorent had pushed his chair back and fallen to his knees, his words mingled with desperate sobs. Sorkin had to lean across his table to see the pitiful performance. So distasteful to see a grown man weep like a chided infant, but understandable he supposed as they both knew what would follow.

"I need you to confess to at least one or two specific acts Lorent so that the Inquisitors Office will be satisfied that you are truly contrite." Sorkin tried to keep his tone gentle and understanding even though the man's behaviour was starting to aggravate him. He knew what was coming and that his best outcome was a pain-free death so face it like a man, on your feet with your head up.

"I falsified accounts and syphoned off a small measure of the harvested grain to sell privately. It was such a small measure Advocate, just a tiny amount, hardly noticeable. I was so careful, moving the monies and goods about, never letting the same vendors or supervisors have direct contact. I don't understand how I was caught. It is such a trifling amount, can we not overlook it or come to some arrangement?" The desperate pleas of a dead man walking, coughed out in a wheezy, weeping shrill tone. All to no avail, the wheels were already in motion, the outcome set in stone.

"You were betrayed of course. Isn't that always the way? Someone further down the ladder, eager to advance in any way possible. You did not cover your tracks as well as you hoped I'm afraid." Sorkin shrugged out a disappointed sigh. "You know the law as well as I Lorent. The penalty for theft from the royal coffers is death. It is just a matter of the manner in which the sentence is carried out. There is no arrangement to be made Lorent, just the severity of the punishment and the consequences." Sorkin let out a little sigh. The fact the decision never landed at his door was small consolation. He was still condemning a man to his death, whether or not he deserved it.

The door swung open, and Inquisitor Malek strode into the room with two burly questioners in close attendance. Malek cut a striking figure, tall and whip thin, with jet-black, cropped hair. His face had a hard edge like a bird of prey, his sharp nose resembling a beak and his eyes seeming to drink in all the light. In his uniform, long black high-necked dress coat, black trousers and knee-length leather boots he looked like a harbinger of doom. Appropriate given his appointed role.

"Advocate." He nodded at Sorkin, his voice dead flat and calm. Sorkin gave an almost imperceptible shudder. "Inquisitor."

Lorent looked around desperately and began to scramble underneath the table as if that would offer safe harbour. It didn't. The two questioners grabbed him roughly under the arms and dragged him bodily from the room, cracking his head on the doorframe as he struggled unconvincingly to free himself. Hopeless Sorkin supposed, but what else could you do?

"Recommendations?" Malek phrased it as a question, curt and to the point as usual.

"Well, he freely confessed, so I would recommend leniency where his family are concerned. Recovery of the stolen goods levied against his holdings?" Sorkin let the suggestion hang in the air, knowing too lenient a proposal would produce an overreaction.

"Agreed. We found no evidence to suggest any member of the family was involved or benefitted from his crime. However, a public execution by ritual beheading is in order. We must send out the right message, that this kind of crime will simply not be tolerated."

Malek's dead-flat delivery made it all the more chilling. Ritual beheading was as terrifying a death as he had ever witnessed or even conceived of. His sympathy for Lorent welled up, a little acid reflux almost making him gag. As Advocate of the Count he had the duty to pronounce sentence so was obliged to witness it.

"So Advocate, shall we see to our duty?" Malek nodded towards the door leading to the public square.

"As you say Inquisitor." Sorkin swept his hand towards the door and followed on Malek's heels, albeit unwillingly.

Word had obviously been put out by Malek and his acolytes, a good-sized crowd having gathered around the fringes of the square. Nothing like a public execution, especially an outsider and a ranking member of society to boot. One of the great joys of the commoner was to see one of their betters brought to heel.

A squadron of armed guards had been stationed behind and to either side of the execution platform, crowd control being necessary at these occasions. Things had been known to get out of hand from time to time.

The crowd jeered at Lorent as he was led out bent-backed, arms twisted cruelly behind his back by Malek's burly questioners. His eyes darted towards the platform, the execution rig set up in its centre with its wood and rope contraption looking old and worn, stained with the blood of its former victims, seemingly causing him to stumble and lose his footing. It made no difference, the questioners merely dragging him forward without breaking stride.

It always amazed Sorkin that an area so seemingly poor would have enough rotten fruit and vegetables to throw in these situations. Maybe their hardship was not as pressing as he thought. Whatever, the volleys of produce maintained their pace for a couple of minutes.

By the time they had dragged him to the platform Lorent looked a dishevelled mess, the juice and flecks of vegetable skin sliding down his face and clothes. The two questioners looped the ropes around his wrists and pulled them tight through the holes, tying them off, wrenching his arms out parallel to his shoulders, locking him rigidly in place.

"I confess my crimes. I confess my crimes." Lorent kept whimpering out his confession, over and over again. Tears poured down his face and snot bubbled out of his nose as he knelt down awaiting his fate. "I confess my crimes. I confess my crimes…" Over and over again, as if repeating the words might change his fate.

Malek looked across at Sorkin and gave an almost imperceptible nod. Sorkin bowed and stepped back from the platform, leaving the stage to Malek.

"Citizens of Darmat, this man, Overseer Lorent has been found guilty of the heinous crime of theft and profiteering. He syphoned off a considerable measure of grain, meant for distribution to the needy and sold it privately for his own gain." A great boo went up from the crowd.

"A little florid but then Inquisitors do tend to like the sound of their own voices."

"It is the judgement of the Advocate of the Count and the Office of Inquisition, that he shall be summarily executed by ritual beheading. Let this be a lesson to all who would transgress the laws of the God King, may he live forever." Amongst the raucous cheers Sorkin could hear quiet sobbing, no doubt Lorent's family. He scanned the crowd and saw a woman with two young children clinging to her, tears streaming down her cheeks. Lorent's wife and children, nothing else to do but watch. In the background Lorent kept sobbing out the same words, "I confess my crimes. I confess my crimes…"

Malek raised his hands, motioning for the crowd to quiet its jeers.

"Does the confessed have any last words?" He gestured towards Lorent, a hardly noticeable sneer on his lips.

"I CONFESS MY CRIMES. I CONFESS MY CRIMES!" Lorent screamed the words, spittle flying from his lips. A mass volley of fruit and vegetables answered his confession, a couple going astray and hitting Malek on his immaculate coat. Anger flashed across his face and he gestured to the captain of his guards, three spearmen darting into the crowd and viciously beating the perpetrator with the butts of their weapons.

Malek turned to his questioners, still irritated by events and half-growled, "Begin!"

Sorkin had no stomach for this and all he wanted to do was turn away. Protocol dictated otherwise.

One questioner put his hands to either side of Lorent's face, holding him pinned in a vice-like grip. The other pulled out a large, wickedly serrated knife and laid it on the back of Lorent's neck.

"I confess my crimes. I confess my crimes…" the words kept repeating until the questioner made his first stroke, pulling the knife across Lorent's neck, a thick stream of blood pouring out from the cut.

Lorent let rip a blood-curdling scream, his eyes wide in shock flicking from side to side in wild disbelief. The other questioner however didn't relent, his head held perfectly still.

It took about two minutes to sever his head, the relentless sawing motion mixed in with Lorent's gurgling screams of confession and the sound of bone and gristle separating under the blade. The questioner held aloft his severed head and threw it into the crowd. The mob kicked it around in some kind of grisly game, Lorent's bereft family staring disbelieving at the gruesome sight.

"So goes it with all traitors!" Malek called out the words with a certain relish that grated with Sorkin.

He hated capital punishment but had always reconciled himself with the fact that everyone knew the laws of the land, so if you broke them… Something felt different here however and he couldn't shake Lorent constantly repeating, "I confess my crimes. I confess my crimes…"

Chapter Twenty-Seven Part One:

We're in it now

The slow side-to-side motion mixed with the gentle evening breeze was soothing, almost making Jonoh fall into a slumber. A marked contrast to a year ago when all he could do was complain about riding horses and swear off them eternally.

It rankled more and more that he used to be so self-absorbed, making him shudder when he tried to reconcile himself with the person he used to be. He winced at how consistently arrogant he was, always so sure of himself and the fact that he always succeeded. The way he'd always made a big show of saying how important it was that everyone's name day was celebrated, that everyone should have at least one day that was all about them. The reality was everyday was Jonoh Shipwright day. He always won, so he always expected to win, never giving any regard to anyone else's efforts, more often than not patronising them, congratulating them for trying. He wasn't sure it was a deliberation on his part, but it came so naturally it might as well have been. But there was one thing he couldn't shift from his mind, Garic.

They had received reports from the Protectorate and had sent back their own, keeping the Elder Council informed of their progress. One report about Garic's actions at the skirmish at Seal-breaker Bay gave Jonoh pause for concern. The absolute realisation that he'd always beaten Garic only because of his gift, whether he was conscious of it or not had taken root. The extra measure of strength, pace, skill, all the little measures of extra were not something he'd ever given thought to. What he took as his natural superiority, just his exceptional self, was actually just an outpouring of his yet unrealised ability. Garic had always been better, stronger, faster. It was just that neither of them had ever realised it.

He looked back now and realised that what he saw as Garic's surly lack of grace, was actually a supreme physical specimen, producing staggering athletic results, being left dumbfounded as to why he never won. It worried him even more now that Garic knew the truth. The resentment built up must have poured out of him at some point and he pitied whoever was in firing range at the time.

He missed his friend desperately but managed to contain his personal woes. The Orphans needed his strength and his leadership, because however uncomfortable it made him the fact was that he was, by a vast distance, the most gifted among them. Learning to understand and harness that measure was another story altogether, and one he was still following.

Being with the Orphans had changed his perceptions forever. When he entered the Gift with one, some or all of them, he instantly absorbed their experience and knowledge. It added layers to his understanding, and they would hold him up, stand guard and offer him anything they had, should he need it. At times it was so overwhelming that upon exiting he would sob for ages, the wealth, strength and sacrifice of what was offered moving him beyond tears.

Then there was Shala. He had been with women before, mostly girls but some women as well. He was always supremely confident, and it created an aura that seemed to bewitch the opposite sex, but not Shala. He had to surrender himself and his ego and it was she that chose him, not the other way around, and it had made him feel vulnerable for one of the few times in his existence.

She was half a dozen years older than him and had been an Orphan in the Lawless Lands for five years. It had hardened her, making her look older than her years, her face weather-beaten, skin slightly leathered, and her lips chapped. But she was beautiful, long auburn hair, emerald-green eyes and a staggeringly alluring body. He used to think of himself as a man because he was so superior, but she made him realise just how much boy was still in him.

Now he found it hard to imagine being without her and they shared a blanket every night. It had reached a point where he doubted he could sleep without her, but one thing was certain. He had never been in love before

He was so absorbed by his own thoughts that he hadn't noticed Master Cerwin sidle up next to him. It had been at least two weeks since Sarjinn and they hadn't really spoken at all since then, but the old shadow-master had lost none of his stealth, in spite of the fact that the journey to Darmat had aged him visibly.

"Jonoh, how do you fare? It seems to me that we have not really spoken properly, for a while at least." The old Master spoke the truth, there were issues playing on Jonoh's mind.

"Master I apologise if I have appeared distant, but I am troubled by certain events. I keep going over and over them in my mind but cannot resolve them." Jonoh dipped his head and glanced away from Cerwin, still finding it uncomfortable to confront the old master.

"I did sense a certain reticence, so I gave you some time to gather your thoughts." The old master smiled his crinkly smile up at Jonoh. "But now I would like to enquire as to their nature, if you are willing of course."

Cerwin let the question hang in the air, not pressing Jonoh but letting him come to the point in his own time. Jonoh could feel the quiet lingering, almost forcing his hand, making him need to fill the gap.

Jonoh took a deep breath and sat upright, that small change in posture giving him the strength to do what he felt was needed. Still the thought of rebuking his master gave him pause, however mild the reprimand was likely to be. He turned his head, knowing that he would need to fully focus on Cerwin to get through this.

"When we had our little encounter in Sarjinn, why did you not tell me what was going to happen? At least forewarned I might have been able to steel myself." Jonoh could feel a warmth rising in his chest, his sense of indignation fuelling his resolve. "How could you leave me to face that blindly? I could feel how close I came; a shadow fell over me and I sought for the Void." Jonoh realised that his voice had risen, the words punched out with a sternness he had obviously suppressed.

Cerwin eyes were downcast as if some great weight of guilt burdened him beyond reason. "What preparation could anyone ever give you Jonoh? Whatever experience any of us gifted ever had would pale next to you. There is also the fact that we have no idea if your experiences mirror our own. You are so far beyond any of us that we have no frame of reference where you are concerned. It is akin to asking the student to take the lesson and the teacher to sit and learn." There were almost tears welling in Cerwin's eyes as he looked up at Jonoh but as bad as it made him feel it didn't override his feelings of anger.

"That is a weak excuse Master. If you had at least told me of yours or other's experiences, it may have prepared me. Although in truth I suppose there is no way of truly preparing someone for…" Jonoh's voice tailed off as he realised that the resentment he had built up over this incident was probably ill advised at best, petulant at worst. He looked away, as if looking at his master would harm him in some way.

They rode in silence for about twenty minutes, the implications of their words hanging in the air like a headsman's axe.

"There are many things in life that have saddled me with regrets Jonoh." The little shadow-master spoke with his head down, his hunched shoulders making him appear even more diminutive. "But few that have caused me more sadness than the ones that have given you pain."

The words stung at Jonoh's heart; a wave of guilt washed over him for causing this man pain. He really was like a father figure, someone he aspired to be, so wise, thoughtful and supportive. He could feel the burden that was crushing Cerwin, a feeling of responsibility as if he were the root of his trials. It always struck him as remarkable how quickly his anger would dissipate after they spoke, as if the last couple of weeks had never happened. He reached over and laid his hand on the old man's shoulder.

"I'm sorry Master, I should not lay the blame at your door. You are an honourable man and a great teacher. Without your guidance I doubt I could have realised my Gift." Jonoh felt ashamed to have brought Cerwin this low.

"Blame, responsibility, burden. There are so many words to describe my feelings Jonoh, none of which seem wholly adequate but who knew there was someone like you out there? There was no way to prepare for you, so my mistakes are born out of ignorance as much as anything else." The little master sat a touch more upright as if Jonoh's words had lifted him up.

"However, learn from our mistakes and move forwards we must, my boy. Would you not agree?" The twinkle in his eye had returned and Jonoh could not help but smile.

"I do most definitely agree Master." Jonoh smiled across at Cerwin, relieved that they seemed to have returned to normal.

"Do you know where we are Jonoh?"

"On the northern edge of the Red Desert, Master."

"That we are but do you see that standing stone up ahead?" The old master gestured off ahead of them.

Jonoh could just make out a grey object in the distance. He had to admit that however frail Cerwin may occasionally appear, his eyesight did not diminish.

"I can just about make it out Master."

"That my boy is the official border of the Kingdom of Darmat. Once we cross it to the north, we are in its territory and subject to its laws. Birds were sent before we left, so they know we are coming, but we must tread carefully." The old man looked at him sideways, eyebrow arched in a do-you-understand-me fashion. "There will be at least one Orphan there, at great risk to himself. We must tread carefully and do nothing to give him away. The Darmations are sharper than you could imagine and fuelled by zealots, so we must be on our guard at all times." Cerwin pulled back on his reins, bringing his mount to a standstill.

"They may consider the gifted to be aberrations and therefore view them as non-existent, but they are keen observers and will not miss a sign or a false step. Their aristocracy are raised to be vigilant and to notice the slightest sign of any heresy." Cerwin paused for a moment as if gathering his thoughts. "We will be granted immunity, at least that is what I hope as we are on a diplomatic mission of sorts, but we must not make any outward signs of our particular skills." Cerwin shook his head, an attempt to clear any fog that may have lingered.

As they sat there, a quiet contemplative silence settling around them, Bergin Shortspear and his small company of soldiers reined up just behind them. Bergin nudged his horse forward, coming to a stop alongside Jonoh.

"Master Cerwin, Jonoh." Bergin nodded his greeting. Jonoh grinned, Bergin's less than deferential acknowledgement being so far from the bowing and scraping individual he'd first known. It was amazing what a fight, followed by two weeks in hard country, could do to a man.

"Is there a problem Master?" Bergin directed his attention at Cerwin.

"Not a problem Bergin, more a pending decision." Cerwin's arched eyebrow had become a standard method of communication amongst their group. It was a statement with an invitation to ask another question, a wonderful way to get people to draw their own conclusions.

"What might that decision be?" Bergin always played the game, occasionally doing his own eyebrow manoeuvre as if mirroring the old man. Not out of ridicule, more an affectionate imitation.

"When do we cross into Darmat?" Cerwin smiled sideways. "Now seems as good a time and place as any."

"Then I shall organise enough provisions to see the journey taken care of." Bergin turned to his men. "Timult, gather provisions for twelve, enough to last, how many days?" He looked at Cerwin for confirmation.

"We will need at least five days of provisions to get us as far as the traditional meeting place for diplomatic guests. After that it would be difficult to say, because no one here, including myself has ever been to Dantoneen." Cerwin shifted slightly in his saddle, turning his gaze directly at Bergin.

"Dantoneen Master?" Bergin's raised eyebrow was genuine this time.

"The Golden City, capital of Darmat and the home of the Living Gods." Both eyebrows raised showed the gravity of the situation. "Also, Bergin, we only need provisions for two. It will be just myself and Jonoh making the journey."

Bergin reined his horse hard sideways, putting himself face to face with Cerwin. "I think not Master." The words came out brusquely, probably harder than Bergin intended them to land but he showed no sign of regret, holding his ground and sitting bolt upright in his saddle.

"I beg your pardon?" Jonoh nervously jogged his mount on the spot, an instinctive reaction to the tone in Cerwin's voice. No one else seemed to notice but there was an underlying threat behind it. Dangerous ground for Bergin to be treading, but credit where credit is due, he did not back off an inch. *"When did he become so bold?"*

"I will not be leaving Jonoh's side until we are back in the Protectorate or I am dead. And my men will not leave mine."

Jonoh felt almost dizzy, as if he were in a sort of fugue state. This brazenly bold young soldier was refusing to yield to a master. Not only a master but one with a great and renowned measure of the Gift. Jonoh went to interject but held his tongue. He wanted to see how this played out. He could see Cerwin step into his stirrups, rising up a fraction, his leg muscles tensing. The air around him shimmered fractionally, not that anyone else would have noticed, but still.

"You will do as commanded lieutenant. You may have command of your little squad, but you will cede to me in this matter." Cerwin was using a small measure of the Gift to pitch his voice, make it more intimidating. However, in this case it did not have the desired effect.

Bergin slowed his breathing and kept his tone flat and level, impressive considering Jonoh could feel the weight of Cerwin's words even given his talent. The rest of the Orphans had ambled up behind them, so there was quite the audience.

"Command is neither here nor there. We are not in the Protectorate and as much as you have my respect Master, you hold no rank that I am aware of, so the decision is mine. I will not leave Jonoh's side under any circumstances and my men will chose their own fate. I just happen to already know the choice they will make."

Cerwin walked his mount forward two steps, fixing his glare on Bergin, not shifting his eyes even for a second. "I cannot expend my energy looking after an extra ten lost souls Bergin. What we are doing and where we are going is fraught with peril. I do not know for a certainty that myself or Jonoh will be accepted or live for that matter. I cannot be responsible for your lives as well." Cerwin had moderated his tone, a more conciliatory, measured approach in his voice, very clever manipulation in Jonoh's opinion. It didn't hit the spot however.

"Again Master, with all due respect, you will have to kill me to stop me." Bergin had made his decision and would not be backed down, Jonoh feared for his wellbeing.

"So be it." With a final glance at Bergin, Cerwin wheeled his horse around and began to slowly walk him forward towards the standing stone. Everybody else just sat routed to the spot, apart from Bergin. Jonoh could not help but notice him almost literally deflate, like a punctured balloon.

"Thank you for your loyalty, Bergin." Jonoh nodded and smiled at the young soldier.

"Always Jonoh." Bergin nodded back. Then they all put their heels to the horses and started moving forwards. Towards Darmat.

Chapter Twenty-Seven Part Two:

All is not as it seems

"The blade whistled past his ear, the turn of his body helping him just avoid the slash. Two of the assailants lay dead on the floor but he was more and more hard-pressed by the remaining three. He had managed to cut one of them, but it did not look deep and wasn't appearing to slow him down. He got his shield up just in time to parry an axe swing from his left-hand side as the third attacker poked forward with his spear. It wasn't so much of a spear as a boar pike, but the man wielding it seemed to know what he was doing, and the point was wicked sharp. The blade slid off his leather corslet, the billhook catching on a buckle. The pikeman wrenched back, pitching him forwards, stumbling off his feet.

"He rolled frantically to his left wrenching his shield round just in time to block the downswing of the sword, but not quick enough to parry the axe. It bit into the back of his leg, making his hamstring scream. He swung his sword as hard as he could and it slammed into the axeman's leg, just above his ankle where the meat of his calf was exposed, the man going down screaming. His sword was suddenly wrenched from his grasp, embedded deeply in the axeman's leg. He heard the pike spearing towards him before he felt it, the billhook catching the top of his left eyebrow and then scraping down his cheek before flicking off the line of his jaw. It stung like buggery, but the fear drove him to keep moving, trying to turn and get his shield up before the swordsman caught him. He was too late, the edge of the blade slicing into the top of his arm, his shield sliding uselessly from his numb fingers. He tried to stand but only managed a comical shamble as he edged backwards towards the wall of

the ravine, his back touching the cool, shadowed rock. He forced himself upright, better to die on his feet, the pikeman and swordsman readying their final thrusts. He slowly went to close his eyes when out of nowhere the swordsman's head left his shoulders, while the pikeman's just seemed to explode. He slid weakly down the wall, when a scarred, war-weary face appeared in front of him, missing one ear apparently.

"'You wait there one moment my lovely.' The stranger smiled a crooked tooth smile and turned, smashing the axeman's head to pulp with his great spiked mace. He turned and walked back. 'Alright my lovely, don't you worry none, old Splitface Jack has got you.' He smiled that wonky toothed smile again. 'Who you be then?'

"'Mitter Wane.' Then all turned black."

It ended up taking only four not five days to reach the meeting point. The landscape wasn't exactly the Red Desert, but it was still very hot and arid, scrubland at best. There were standing stones the whole way, placed every mile or so and each always visible to the next. Bergin and five of his men rode on either side of Cerwin and Jonoh, providing two protective flanks, the rest working as outriders and scouts. Bergin it seemed was not prepared to take any unnecessary risks. Jonoh was staggered by the mild-mannered young man's transformation. There was real steel in him now, a certain hard, flinty courage.

The landscape had been relatively flat and featureless until the close of the third day when foothills began to rise to the west and the north. During the next day some of the hills began to climb a little higher and ravines and valleys began to appear. As dusk started to settle over the peaks the standing stones led into a valley that widened out creating quite a broad, flat plain. Pitched in the middle of it was a tent.

This was however no ordinary tent, but a vast, multi-tiered construction, as big as Red Pier Academy, the reflected lights of the sentry fires gleaming off its golden surface. Cerwin reined up, far enough away in the dusk to not be seen.

"Let us backtrack a little and make camp for the night. We will have our introductions in the daylight I think." Jonoh and Bergin both nodded their ascent, Bergin posting two guards to watch their perimeter.

They rose the next morning, a light dusting of dew covering

their blankets. It was a brisk morning as it always was in desert or scrubland. Hot during the day but usually cold at night. Jonoh had always enjoyed the morning freshness. Invigorating, it always put him in the right mood to start the day. This however was unlikely to be like any day he had ever known.

They all packed up their bedrolls and cooking implements, loading everything onto the packhorse they had brought with them. While they were all gathered round, Cerwin cleared his throat to get their attention.

"Listen to me everybody. What I am now going to tell you is vital and could be the difference between our survival or our deaths." That made every one of them prick up their ears and pay close attention.

"The Kingdom of Darmat is based on the premise that all direct family members of the royal house are living gods, immortal superior beings. There are many infractions that will be met with summary execution and whilst we may be granted some leeway in these matters, there is no guarantee that this will be the case." Cerwin swept the faces of each and every man, getting small, almost imperceptible responses from all of them.

"There are a few absolutely unforgivable actions that we must all be aware of. You will not ever address a member of the royal household directly. Only speak if asked a question and never pose a question of your own. Never make direct eye contact with a member of the household and never, I repeat never touch a member of the household or their attire." Cerwin took a breath, letting his words sink in.

"We must appear subservient and humble. There is a strict formality in Darmation society and a culture of unquestioning obedience. We cannot be seen to violate that so we will control any reactionary impulses." He fixed Bergin with a withering stare and the young soldier had the good grace to blanch and offer a bow.

"Jonoh and I will take the lead. You will need to fall in behind us and once we make our first contact just remember, heads bowed." He gave them all one last look and then they mounted up and set off for the Darmation delegation.

As they approached the final standing stone and started to

move into the valley the sight that greeted them was breathtaking. The golden multi-tiered tent was a spectacular sight to behold in bright sunlight, almost impossible to look at directly as its glare hurt the eyes. It was akin to looking directly into the sun. It had a great canopied front, two spearmen standing on either side of the entrance. On either side lined up in formation were two bodies of soldiers, spearmen all, attired in golden armour, shields, greaves, chainmail, helmets. Even their leather skirts were adorned with golden edging. The famous Golden Legionnaires, implacable foes, sworn to absolute loyalty, unwavering on the battlefield. Their armour was so burnished that it was difficult to look at them for too long as well. It was as if a part of the sun had broken off and landed in this barren valley.

On the righthand flank there was a collection of mounted men. Jonoh thought about fifty or so but it was difficult to count as they were such a mixed bag of individuals. There was no attempt to dress ranks, and no two looked alike, a more ragtag gathering of fighting men he had never seen. Mercenaries.

They had only come into sight for a minute or so when Jonoh saw a soldier in a white dress uniform signal the mercenaries on the flank. Jonoh assumed that he was an officer of some description as he had the bearing, standing bolt upright with a clear air of authority.

Three riders trotted out from the gathered horsemen and started riding towards them. Jonoh could clearly make them out now, one of them, he presumed the senior, was dressed so flamboyantly that he looked ready to appear in a costume performance. A tailed red topcoat was accompanied by a frilled white shirt, knee-high black leather boots and a wide-brimmed black hat, complete with an extravagant feather. His weapons however suggested a far more dangerous fellow than first appeared. On one side was a gnarly, weather-beaten old soldier. Thickset and heavily scarred by the looks of him and flamboyant he was not. His garb was that of a seasoned fighter, an unburnished and dinted breastplate over the top of a rough leather corslet, his attire showing the signs of age and hard use.

The rider on the other side however was different, very different indeed. He was slim and attired in a long woollen dress coat, soft-leather breeches and riding boots, obviously not a warrior. He did not carry any weapons, and his thin, slightly pinched features and pale complexion suggested he was not a native of Darmat. He had the look of a citizen of the Protectorate. Jonoh took his time, focusing his attention on this fish out of water. *"I wonder…"*

Sorkin looked at the party of riders that were approaching and felt a little stab of discomfort. He recognised Master Cerwin immediately, a little older and frailer but unmistakable. The other riders were all just soldiers, nothing remarkable there, but the young man riding next to Cerwin unnerved him. He had a haughty bearing, tall and thin but obviously in fine physical condition and his long, straight blond hair and handsome features just gave him an air of confidence. It reminded Sorkin of Darmat's royalty and what was disturbing him was that he seemed to be focusing all his attention on him. It felt like he was being scanned, as if this young man were trying to peer inside his soul.

He felt a slight itch in the back of his head, almost as if someone were trying to read his thoughts, digging around in the cloudier corners of his mind. He realised as they closed on the approaching party that the young man's eyes had not wavered, his features staying the same, immovable. Sorkin blinked and broke contact, deliberately staring down at his stirrups.

Cerwin reined in, allowing the other party to close the gap. Jonoh kept his eyes on the unarmed man, reaching out a little to see if he could get a sense of things. Suddenly the man lowered his eyes and Jonoh could feel his blocks go up. So, he was a mind-walker, and in all likelihood an Orphan. His admiration instantly grew, this was a dangerous place to be. If you were found out he imagined the punishment would be brutal and terrifying. He immediately averted his gaze, not wanting to put this person under any undue risk.

As they came to a standstill opposite Cerwin's party, Sorkin looked up, greatly relieved to see the young man's gaze averted. He felt a weight lift from his shoulders, almost literally and the sense of being pressed from without had gone as well. He looked up and made eye contact with his old master.

"Gentlemen, welcome to the Kingdom of Darmat. I am Advocate Sorkin, representative of the royal household and servant of King Lorgan." He smiled and tilted his head, Cerwin and Jonoh doing likewise. "This is Captain General Mitter Wane, commander of the mercenary army The Maimed and his Sergeant at Arms Jack Smythe." Sorkin gestured to his two companions, Smythe grunting acknowledgment while Wane flourished and extravagant bow, hat in hand.

Jonoh studied the two men closely. Their army was named well, the big welt of a scar on Mitter's face running from his left eyebrow down to his jaw. Smythe was a different story altogether, missing his right ear and with a face full of scars. It looked like it had been broken apart and stitched back together and not that well.

"Like what you see do you boy?" Smythe smiled a crooked toothed smile at Jonoh who suddenly realised he must have been staring.

Jonoh looked away, blushing at being caught in the act.

"Apologies sir, I meant no offense." Jonoh bowed his head respectfully.

"Don't worry boy, I know how pretty I am. Tis difficult not to stare." Smythe laughed, his gravelly tone making it sound like he had a mouth full of stones.

"Don't mind old Splitface Jack, he's a real sweetheart once you get to know him." Wane's languid style matched his appearance, Jonoh did not think he had ever seen anyone so laid back.

"I am Master Cerwin, this is Jonoh Shipwright, and this is our honour guard, commanded by Bergin Shortspear." Cerwin waved his hand across his group by way of introduction. Jonoh noticed that he had shortened his honourific, probably for the best, all things considered.

"If you would follow us, we are to escort you to your audience with Prince Lor." Sorkin wheeled his horse, gesturing for Cerwin and company to follow. Cerwin nudged his mount forwards, the rest of his party following close behind.

Sorkin found it a little discomforting that Cerwin had not used his full title, as if he were holding back for want of causing an incident, or perhaps he wanted to keep his agenda shrouded. Who knew? Still, it gave him pause, any subterfuge just making his own perilous situation feel less and less secure. What was concerning him more was that Jonoh Shipwright, the great prodigy was here. Why?

He trotted to the front of the riders to walk next to Wane. He felt a real need to limit his contact, his paranoia rising up in his throat, like a bad case of acid reflux. He needed a moment or two to steady himself.

"Are you all right Sorkin?" Wane glanced across, a look of genuine concern marking his features.

"I am fine Mitter, just a bit of indigestion. I am not accustomed to the conditions or to outdoor living." He offered a wan smile in return.

Wane reached across and gently patted him on the leg. "Worry not Sorkin, you are safe with me and it won't be long before we can both enjoy the comforts of palace life." He smiled at Sorkin, letting his hand linger for a moment.

Sorkin felt trapped, his paranoia knowing no bounds, so much so that now he thought Wane might be coming onto him. *"Surely not, this man is a warrior."* Sorkin tried to compose himself, from safe and secure yesterday to feeling like he could be exposed any moment on all the things he'd fought so hard to hide. He took in a deep breath and turned to look Wane in the eye.

"Thank you Mitter, I am flattered by your friendship and look forward to more comfortable surroundings." Although thinking about it, rooms in the royal tent were hardly austere.

Wane turned his most charming smile on Sorkin. "More comfort and a little privacy I hope." Wane slowly turned his horse back towards Jonoh and Cerwin, glancing back over his shoulder. Sorkin shivered.

Jonoh had been absentmindedly going over things in his head when he looked up to see what looked like a personal exchange between Sorkin and Wane. Wane slowly turned his mount back towards them, taking the briefest of moments to glance back at Sorkin. Was there a relationship between the two of them? That could muddy the waters in all kinds of ways. Wane slowly sidled up to Jonoh, turning his horse to walk alongside him.

"So young Master Shipwright, whereabouts in the Protectorate are you from?" Wane's languid nature seemed to extend to his speech, relaxed and without any real emphasis. His whole persona spoke of ease of thought and action. From what he had seen so far it was hard to imagine him in combat, but his array of weapons told a different tale.

"Main Harbour." Jonoh wanted to keep his responses as contained as possible, at least until they had found their feet.

"Main Harbour, eh? Inside the mighty jetties. If I hadn't seen them for myself, I don't think I would have believed the stories. Magnificent achievement really, and those Silver Shield boys. Well, if I had a hundred of them, I'd set up my own kingdom. Fierce would be an understatement." Wane smiled to himself.

"You've been to the Protectorate?"

"In my youth, longer ago than I'd care to admit. I visited Appledore in Westfall. Beautiful country, rolling hills, green orchards, picturesque towns and villages, and the girls. Well, I would have stayed if only I could have plied my trade there." He leaned back in the saddle and let out a rich, warm laugh, full of fond memories. "I also visited Falconer's Rest, Hoarwine, although that far north in Partia was a little too cold for my taste. I even went as far as the Whitecaps, although like most never got across the border. Would still like to see Snowbard for myself before I die." He smiled his charming smile and gave Jonoh a little nod.

"It would seem you have me at a disadvantage Captain General. I am not anywhere near as well travelled as you." Jonoh tried to sound as gracious as he could and in truth was finding that he instantly liked this man.

"Call me Mitter please, I find formality clouds the truth. Better to be open and free from the off." And there was that charming smile again, Jonoh imagined that the Captain General did not struggle where the ladies were concerned.

"Mitter of course and young Master Shipwright is a little too stiff for me, I'd prefer Jonoh."

"Jonoh it is." He flashed that winning smile and pulled out a couple of apples from his coat pocket. "Care for one?"

"Thank you, yes." Jonoh felt completely at ease with this man, and they chatted like old friends as they slowly rode towards the great tent.

Sorkin didn't hear him but Cerwin had crept up alongside him, shadow-master indeed. They were just far enough off the rest to not be heard.

"Young Sordel, it is good to see you again, despite the circumstances." Cerwin kept his head forward and down, the brim of his hat covering most of his face. "We may not get another chance to talk freely, and I will not risk exposing you with a mind-walker exchange." The old man's voice was clear and concise whilst almost whispered, a rare trick if you could pull it off.

"I fear the time to reveal myself is almost upon us, although I will admit to being scared out of my wits." All Sorkin could think of was the penalty handed out to his kind and how much worse it would probably be for him, seeing as how far he had risen. The Darmations would see it as the ultimate betrayal.

"The game is changing Sordel, the players in an almost constant state of flux. We cannot afford to lose the advantage we have with you so high in the God King's favour. You must stay where you are and keep your true identity secret."

Sorkin visibly shrank down, the weight of his fears having lifted, a little half-smothered sob escaping his mouth.

"What would you have me do Master?"

"Do as you have been doing all these years Sordel. Be our eyes and ears and keep us appraised of all we need to know. Also try to exert whatever influence you can towards assisting the defence of the Titan Gate. We are doing all we can, but I think the chances of holding against what is coming are slim at best." The old master's forehead creased tightly, the pressure he was feeling apparent for all to see.

They had almost reached the tent, Jonoh having lost track of their movements, being so engrossed in conversation with Wane. Sorkin and Cerwin had stopped just ahead of them and Sorkin had turned in the saddle to speak to their little group.

"Gentleman. If you would be so kind, we will continue on foot from here." Sorkin dismounted and wrapped his reins around a hitching post, just in front of the assembled legionnaires. Cerwin followed suit as did the rest of his company, while Wane and Smythe wandered back to the rest of the gathered mercenaries.

"Master Cerwin, Jonoh. Gentlemen, may I introduce General Kaif." Sorkin extended his hand towards the officer who had walked out to meet them. Jonoh thought he cut an imposing figure in his dress whites, tall and in excellent condition for a man of his years with close-cropped grey hair and just a few small, gilded hints of armour. All gold of course.

"It is an honour to greet you." Kaif gave a rigid, perfectly observed bow to Cerwin and Jonoh.

"The honour is ours General." Cerwin mirrored the old soldier's courtesies, Jonoh quick to do the same.

"If you would follow me Cerwin, Jonoh. General Kaif will see to the comfort of your men."

Cerwin nodded his assent. "Bergin, wait for us and please extend our courtesies to our gracious hosts."

Jonoh noticed that Bergin had tensed slightly when told he would not be going with them as if he intended to protest. Thankfully Cerwin's words seemed to take the tension out of his shoulders.

"General Kaif." Cerwin faced the old soldier and offered a bow, returned in kind. Jonoh could see the mutual respect and sensed that they would end up in conversation at some point.

Sorkin gestured for them to follow and walked towards the Golden Tent at a brisk pace.

It was a staggering sight up close, three tiers, the material not just gold but adorned with what seemed like hundreds of little vignettes playing out across its surface. The canopy extended about twenty feet from the entrance, perfectly shadowing the carpet that led there. The carpet of course was gold. They walked through the entrance and Jonoh could not quite believe what he saw. The floor was polished oak, perfectly flat and pristine. There was a wooden ceiling, he assumed supporting the floor of the second tier and at least four corridors running off in different directions. There were obviously a whole array of different rooms adjoining the corridors, the whole construction was dizzying in its complexity. Sorkin pointed at the set of steps in front of them that led up to a cloth of gold entrance. Standing on either side were two golden spearmen, Jonoh assumed legionnaires, who turned grasping the corners of the door flaps and lifting them. They stood stock still, not moving a single muscle, not even flicking a furtive glance. Impressive discipline indeed, Jonoh was beginning to understand why they had such a fierce reputation.

As they stepped through, what they saw dwarfed anything else they had witnessed up to that point. It was a vast audience room with a raised dais, topped with an ornate golden throne. There were murals all around the perimeter, some telling stories of great battles, others celebrating the tales of the gods. Sorkin ushered them towards a table, resplendent with a feast, fruits, pastries, wines, sweetmeats, just about everything you could dream of. It was set below and slightly off centre from the dais as protocol dictated and there were four ornate chairs placed behind it, all facing the throne.

"Gentleman, if you would kindly take your seats." Sorkin pulled a chair out and ushered Cerwin to sit down. Jonoh followed suit, sitting just to Cerwin's left. It was a clever seating arrangement, meaning you would have to turn and tilt your head upwards to look at the throne, diminishing the chances of looking the living god in the eye. Subtle but effective.

"Gentlemen, I do not know if you are aware of protocol, but you must stand when his Highness enters the room. Heads bowed and eyes in the direction your seats are facing. No direct eye contact and no direct questions." Sorkin raised his eyebrow, waiting for a response. Cerwin and Jonoh nodded their assent.

For all its magnificence Jonoh could not help but feel that it was just a show, a façade to cover the truth, that these were just people, not gods.

They sat for what felt like an age, being kept waiting, to make a point. Everybody knew who held the power.

Then out of sight, Jonoh could hear movement, the shuffling of feet, people finding their places before the show began. Jonoh smiled to himself, in a strange way really looking forward to whatever was coming. Then the trumpets rang out and the procession started.

First to enter behind the dais were two legionnaires with golden trumpets, blasting out a fanfare, letting all know a god was arriving. Then there were four beautiful young girl slaves, naked apart from white cloth, cinched around their waists with thin gold ribbons. In their hands were golden bowls, filled with rose petals, which they strewed on the floor. Following behind was a golden palanquin, being borne by six brawny slaves, curtain shut so that the occupant was hidden. In any other circumstances Jonoh would have quipped about the over generous use of gold but he knew well enough to hold his tongue.

The palanquin was laid on the ground with deliberate care and four more Golden Legionnaires stepped forward, two taking point in front of the curtains, the other two grasping the curtains corners and lifting them aside.

Not looking directly would have little impact on Cerwin or Jonoh's ability to see, and the sight was not one either would want to miss. Prince Lor himself was an unremarkable-looking fellow, not short but not tall with mousey brown hair. He was not handsome but was not ugly, just an average-looking young man. However, his attire was breathtaking. He wore snow white linen breeches and shirt, both beautifully highlighted with gold thread, mountains and skyline depicted on the shirt, while the breeches spoke of rivers and vales. He wore a dazzling cloth of gold cape, fastened at the neck with a heavy gold-roped chain. His pure white gloves were adorned with stunning rings, rubies and emeralds glittering reds and greens. His crown topped it all, the sun and the moon meeting at the front, the gold so polished that it shone of its own volition.

He stepped down from the palanquin, all eyes averted, and walked up to the throne. A gaggle of house slaves shuffled along behind him, some looking to clear any stray piece of detritus, others ensuring the hem of his golden cloak was not dirtied by touching the floor. He sat on the great throne and swept his cloak over the arms.

"Advocate Sorkin, if you would be kind enough to make the introductions." Jonoh thought his voice mirrored his appearance, average.

"Gentleman, you are honoured to be in the presence of His Highness Prince Lor, heir apparent to His Majesty King Lorgan, a living deity from whom all mortals must avert their gaze." Cerwin and Jonoh mirrored Sorkin's bow, making sure not to look directly at Lor.

Jonoh knew that he and Cerwin could see everything with no need for line of sight. Jonoh could not help but notice the little sneer on Lor's face as Sorkin made the courtesies. He sensed a spiteful, wilful character, not one that was likely to cede any ground. His expectations of success diminished by the moment.

"Highness may I introduce Master Cerwin and his apprentice Jonoh Shipwright, here representing the Protectorate." Sorkin offered another bow whilst sweeping his arm in Jonoh and Cerwin's direction.

"Welcome to Darmat gentleman, please be seated." Lor leaned against one of the throne's ornate arms, chin resting in his hand, all the time with his gaze fixed on Cerwin.

Sorkin felt the weight of the situation, the quiet tension building. He was uncomfortable enough as it was, his woollen dress coat as always itchy, rivulets of sweat rolling down his back, the dampness making his clothing even more aggravating. All he could think was that the next few moments would set the seal on how this meeting would pan out.

"While we are always happy to receive visitors and observe the courtesies, I am keen to find out the reason for your arrival." Lor sat a little more upright, his gaze still fixed on Cerwin.

"We have detailed reports of a great incursion from the east your Highness. A force called the H'daree have conquered the Green-lands and driven the citizens of Turan and Minari from their cities and into the Titan Pass." Cerwin paused to let the implication land.

"We are well furnished with reports of our own Master Cerwin. Those godless fisheaters lack the courage to defend themselves and have, in all likelihood, been driven off by bandits. It would seem probable that the Brotherhood of the Golden Hand have sought vengeance at long last." Lor dismissively waved his hand. "Events in that little backwater are not our concern, unless there is something we have not yet been told." Lor raised his eyebrows as if inviting a reply.

"There is much that we have found out your Highness." Cerwin was deliberately holding back. It was a good strategy as far as Jonoh was concerned, small pieces of information were much easier to explain or justify. However the risks with someone as volatile and self-centred as Lor were great.

"Please elaborate Master Cerwin." Jonoh could not help but feel uncomfortable at the exaggerated emphasis Lor put on the word 'master'. It felt as if this was a kind of set-up, almost as if he were baiting a trap. Cerwin seemed to just ignore it and move forwards.

At that very moment General Kaif entered from behind the throne, taking station to Lor's left-hand side, a step below him of course. He turned slightly to his own right and stood looking directly at Cerwin and Jonoh. Jonoh could not help but tense up, the feeling of an invisible noose tightening was inescapable.

"I assure you your Highness that this is not the actions of bandits. It is an incursion on a vast scale, hundreds of thousands of disciplined, well-organised soldiers have completely overrun the Green-lands, capturing Minari and Turan. We have reason to believe they are amassing an invasion force and plan to do so via the Titan Pass." Cerwin continued to observe the courtesies but Jonoh could hear the subtle inflection in his voice. He was trying to exert some subliminal influence on Lor.

Sorkin's stomach roiled, nervous discomfort almost overwhelming him. He fought to control it and showed no outward sign of his struggle, but he could feel the tension in the room, as if it were teetering on the edge of a cliff. One small nudge was all that was needed.

"Master Cerwin, I am intrigued. Where exactly do you gather your assurance from? How is it that an envoy from the Protectorate, far to the west has better intelligence than us? We are in most regards almost neighbours with the fisheaters." Lor held out his hands, shrugging his shoulders with a sarcastic indifference. "Why would you seek an audience with Darmat unless you are seeking aid in order to secure a foothold in the east? A base at the Titan Gate for instance? I would also ask where this mighty force suddenly appeared from? Out of thin air?" Lor leaned back in his throne, a mean-spirited little chuckle issuing from his mouth.

"The H'daree come from outside of the Known World your Highness. They have discovered how to traverse the Great Storm Curtain and invaded via the Bountiful Isles, overwhelming the defenders before they had any chance to mount an effective defence."

Lor snorted in disbelief, shaking his head and leaning aggressively forward on his seat.

"Utter nonsense and heresy to boot. There is nothing on the other side of the Great Storm Curtain, no life of any kind. And how is it that you come by such detailed intelligence, regardless of how ridiculous it is? You use your honorific Master Cerwin but what exactly is it that you are master of?" Lor's words were spat out angrily, his cheeks flushing red with anger.

"I am Master of Shadows your Highness, and my intelligence comes from brave, selfless souls who are prepared to pay the ultimate price in service of the common good." Cerwin snapped out his response, his fingers turning white as he grasped the arms of his chair.

"So now we come to it. You are a spy and have a network no doubt across the Free Territories? Well, Darmat is not a free state Master Cerwin and there is a price to pay for espionage." Lor's voice suddenly became flat and completely level, years of training coming into play.

Jonoh was trying to take in all the implications and weigh the possible consequences when he felt a bristle. It was only for the tiniest fraction of a second but the air around Cerwin shimmered.

Sorkin felt his bowels almost summersault, the fear of the retribution that would follow making him feel like vomiting. Cerwin had shimmered for the tiniest of moments, his anger triggering his Gift.

Lor craned forwards, grasping the arms of his throne, his eyes squinting, focusing solely on Cerwin. Kaif took a step forwards but stopped in his tracks at a small, almost imperceptible hand signal from Lor.

"This audience is at an end, gentlemen, as is your stay in Darmat. You will remove yourselves from our land immediately and never return. There is a price to pay for your actions. Please learn the lesson, for it will not land so lightly should you ever enter our kingdom again." With that Lor stood up and swept his cape with a flourish, exiting the audience room behind the throne, his retinue of slaves and servants scurrying after him.

Kaif strode forward, ushering Cerwin and Jonoh to exit via the way they had entered.

Jonoh was flustered, everything had happened so quickly, and yet so little was said. Lor and Kaif had obviously received training and were able to perceive Cerwin's shimmer, but how and why? There were no gifted in Darmat, or were there? Were they hunted down, were there some in hiding? What price would they too have to pay? Too many questions and it would seem no time to ponder them, at least not here.

They exited the tent to see their honour guard surrounded by Golden Legionnaires, hemmed in by spears.

"You will leave now, and this will remind you never to come back." Kaif gestured to the side and Jonoh's heart sank. Bergin's severed head sat on a spike. His mutilated body parts strewn on the floor around it.

Sorkin turned and threw up.

Chapter Twenty-Eight:

Exodus

The valley floor was inescapably hot, the only relief coming when the Pass would take a slightly northerly course, the shadows created giving a hint of cool. Torbin found himself yet again shaking his head in disbelief about the sheer size and regularity of the Pass. It occasionally veered by a degree or so north to south but was pretty much on a straight line, and the walls were vertical and sheer. Literally carved out of the mountains, astounding.

Whoever had undertaken this amazing feat had even made water wells every ten miles. Not just any old wells but ones that were bored into the rock, so deep you struggled to hear the splash at the bottom if you dropped a stone in.

It was two days since they had set off, him, Tivosi and his guard plus two extra horses each, loaded with as much food as they could carry, swapping out every now and then to try to stay as fresh as possible. Jadson was bringing a small fleet of flatbeds, some towed by horse, the rest pulled by oxen, but they would be falling behind by some distance.

His little band had a fair amount of food with them and were travelling at a fair clip, but it would hardly scratch the surface of thirty thousand refugees. And it was not as if that were the only problem. How in Andhonar's name were they going to house and feed this many people? They had supplies but they would dwindle very quickly, so he had taken a selection of Jek's foot soldiers from training to go and start fishing the Great Silver Sea, splitting them in two and sending the second party to hunt the vast forests that bordered the Titans as they made their way north. He could only hope that they were successful. Much depended on it.

He had kept his contact with Candor restricted but on the few occasions that they had exchanged he'd felt the weight of his worry. He knew that they were spread out and that holding them to their course was unbelievably difficult, and he knew that not everyone was going to make it.

Candor stopped and turned around. The sea of weary faces made him want to lay down and close his eyes, shut it all out as if it were just a bad dream. There was no escaping this however, so he just took a deep breath and set himself to the task. It was at that very moment that he caught Marye's voice floating above the bustle. He'd always acknowledged that she was in charge, now it seemed that everybody else did too.

She was going from group to group, berating those not doing enough, encouraging those that were struggling. She was a natural leader and more and more, people sought her out for advice and help, the latter of which she had in small supply.

She looked up and spotted Candor, immediately striding towards him, lifting her skirts to allow a speedier outcome.

"When in the blazes are your friends going to show up?" She stood inches from Candor, barking out her words, hands on hips, all red-faced and angry.

"They are coming as quickly as they can my love. It's a long way from the Gate and they have a lot of provisions to organise and move." Candor smiled, a weary effort granted, but then everything was tinged with tiredness. They had been on the move for days and dared not stop in case the H'Daree were on their tails.

"If they don't hurry up many more will die. We lost twenty overnight, mostly elders but there were three children amongst them." Marye's eyes were welling up, the strain of trying to hold things together beginning to really bear down on her. "If we don't get supplies soon, many and more will perish Candor. We are running out of time." Her shoulders began to bob up and down, mirroring the sobs that escaped her lips.

Candor pulled her in close, hugging her tight, letting her cry herself out. She pulled back, wiping her eyes on her shabby blouse and straightening her clothes.

"Maybe it's time to ride out and meet them? Take some of the horses and try to get back that much quicker?"

"It will mean that we'll have to uncouple some horses from the carts. It will slow us down considerably." Candor offered the argument, but it was weak as an infant and he knew it.

"What difference would it possibly make now?" Marye looked up at him wide-eyed and full of doubt. "If we don't do something now, we'll leave a trail of corpses in this Pass." She stepped back, took a deep breath and pulled herself up to her full height. Not very high. but it showed she would not be put off.

"Go now, while there is still some hope left."

Candor swept her up in his arms, kissing her hard on the lips, and put her down, nodding his assent.

He turned and strode back to the wagons, collecting Rory and Stannard along the way. They uncoupled two horses each, accompanied by a few weak protests and moans, and set off at the gallop towards Torbin and hopefully salvation.

"If I can just last until Torbin gets back to us, then I can rest and maybe recover. Maybe."

Torbin's frustration was growing by the moment. They needed to push, but with the load they expected their horses to carry, couldn't run the risk of exhausting them. It was like being on both sides of an argument, knowing you were right on both counts so ending up stuck in the mud, unable to make a decision.

"Guido, we have to move faster, or we may end up getting there to find a giant pile of dead bodies." He could hear himself, impatient at best, snappy at worst. It just irritated him even more.

"You can push it and ride ahead Torbin, but the packhorses won't survive it, and I doubt my mount would make it halfway." Tivosi's horse looked as if its back were ready to snap and it was already lathering badly.

"Torbin, things are getting desperate here. We lost twenty people overnight and our food supplies are almost gone. Myself, Rory and Stannard are coming to meet you with a spare mount each. We will load as much in the way of provisions as we can carry and get back to our people, hopefully that much quicker. How far into the Pass are you?"

Candor's voice was calm and measured but Torbin could sense

the underlying distress.

"We are near to halfway Candor and pressing the horses as hard as we dare. The main bulk of the provisions are a way behind us though, all being pulled on flatbeds, by horse and oxen. It will be a number of days yet until they can reach you." Torbin had a solution in his mind already. *"We'll have to slaughter the horses and save the cattle you have when we reach your people and wait on the rest of our party to catch up. That should see everyone fed with some to spare."* The thought buoyed him up for a moment, but only a moment.

"We had the same thought, but it would make us sitting targets. If the H'Daree follow up they would catch us cold, and no one would survive." Torbin could feel the stress that Candor was under, and it seeped into his own emotional well. It instantly dragged him down, making his limbs feel heavier.

"If they come now, it wouldn't make any difference anyway. It's not as if you could outrun them or fend them off. We will have to take the chance my old friend and trust to fortune. We will be with you soon Candor, hold fast."

With that Torbin put his blocks up, the strain leaking slowly out of his system, making him regain a certain sense of freedom, the constraints lifting. He slowed his pace for a moment, sitting upright in the saddle and shaking the sense of hopelessness out of his body.

"Are you all right Torbin?" Tivosi had trotted up next to him.

"Yes Guido, thank you my friend. However, I think it's time to throw caution to the wind and ride as fast as our mounts can manage. As faithful and steadfast as they've been, once we reach Candor and his people they will become food." Torbin gave Tivosi a look that told him all he needed to know.

"Then let us hope the H'Daree are not in pursuit. I am not ready to face my glorious death today, not on an empty stomach anyway." Tivosi leaned back and let out a roaring laugh, clapping Torbin on the back, very nearly dislodging him from his horse.

Torbin had heard plenty of gallows humour during his life but never met anyone who used it as comfortably as breathing. Tivosi was unique but he found himself ever more reliant on this great bear of a man, and ever fonder of his company.

They put their heels to their mounts, Tivosi and his guard

racing down the Pass at breakneck speed.

In less than twelve hours they rounded a slight bend in the Pass to see three horsemen galloping towards them. A real sense of joy welled up in Torbin to see his old friend Candor, alive and well, looking a tad thinner maybe, but healthy, nonetheless.

The two parties pulled up and dismounted, Torbin and Candor to the front, both falling into a relieved embrace.

"It's good to see you well, my old friend." Torbin grasped Candor's forearms, a broad smile beaming out. "Let me introduce Guido Tivosi, Captain of Jadwar Sun-blessed's household guard and a loyal and true friend."

Tivosi stepped forward and grasped Candor's hand.

"It is an honour to meet you. We have all heard of Candor Blackheart, scourge of the Brotherhood of the Golden Hand." Tivosi inclined his head in salute.

"The honour is mine Captain Tivosi, your reputation precedes you and I can see it is well merited. Thank you and your men for risking so much for my people." Candor gave a small bow in response and the two men stood still for a couple of seconds, holding each other's gaze in a moment of respect.

Tivosi introduced his men and Candor did likewise with Rory and Stannard.

"How far back to your people Candor?" Torbin walked his mounts towards the well, feeling fortunate indeed that they had met right on top of one. Their horses were blowing and heavily lathered having been pushed so hard.

"Less than a day's ride Torbin, but time is of the essence. We must get back." Candor's anxiety was spiralling, a vein on his forehead standing out, whilst sweat cascaded down his face.

"Take what you and your men can carry, we'll follow behind as soon as we can. Our horses are blown and desperately need a rest. The least they deserve is a drink and a nosebag, bearing in mind what's in store for them." Torbin rubbed his mount's nose as he hoisted a bucket up from the well.

Candor nodded. "We'll see you when you get there my old friend." He turned and went to get Rory and Stannard who were locked in laughing conversation with Tivosi's guard.

"Have you given any more thought to what we will do with so

many thousands of refugees Torbin?" Tivosi had walked his horse over to the well and when he put a bucket of water down it drank as if its life depended on it. If only it knew.

"Well, it will be a non-argument if we fail to hold the Gate. If by some miracle we do throw them back then I think the Gate itself would act like a city, but rather than laid out on the ground, just on top of each other. Like a city in the sky." Torbin shrugged his shoulders. "But in the meantime, they will have to bivouac behind the wall. Candor says that he has about fifteen hundred men capable of bearing arms, so that at least is a point in our favour." Torbin stood stock still, the enormity of his task weighing heavy on his shoulders.

"Fifteen hundred you say? Well, that is good news Torbin, we may yet survive this." Tivosi put his giant hand on Torbin's shoulder, his beaming smile meant as a reassurance, but still feeling slightly terrifying.

Tivosi's guard took turns in feeding and watering their horses, giving them a brush down as well. The difference was notable straight away, the mounts standing more upright and looking far less burdened.

Torbin and Tivosi sat down in the shade, backs against the wall of the Pass.

"Tell me truthfully Guido, what chance do you believe we really have?" Torbin gnawed on a strip of dried meat, occasionally adding a few dried fruits into the mix.

"Well, if what Candor said is true and we make it back to the Gate without incident, that extra fifteen hundred could really turn the tide. It would give us a genuine working reserve, so plugging the gaps would be a great deal easier." Tivosi seemed to get a little more animated as he set to the task. "Leave an extra two hundred to guard the main gate, along with say three hundred of Jek's best. Five hundred men in that confined space with say fifty archers amongst them could hold against a vastly bigger force. Done properly, it could even turn their numbers against them, and the murder holes would wreak havoc."

"I don't think that the main attack will be made on the ground Guido. I think they will assault the upper levels." Torbin sat with his head lowered, not despondently but more in contemplation.

"Candor told me about the assault on the twin cities. They had these siege engines that they adapted to cover and snuff out the fire pits that were laid out. And snuff them out they did. Not only that, but they created a solid firm footing for their soldiers to attack from. They are ingenious and well prepared, and they take their time." Torbin shook his head, the thoughts he was having obviously causing him to fret. "They are not in any rush Guido, there is a certainty about their actions that is the most worrying thing about them. They act as if they know it's merely a matter of time. When they come, they will be fully prepared and have all they need to launch their attack."

"I do not doubt that for a moment Torbin. But I would point out that they don't know what we will have in store for them, and no one can prepare for the unseen or the unknown. We will give them something new to think about and we fight for something that they don't understand." Tivosi's eyes widened, a hard-set grin fixed in place.

"What would that be Guido?"

"Freedom."

The sun had begun to set by the time they set off, meaning that the Pass's floor was swathed in shadow, offering relief from the day's heat. The horses seemed in much ruder health, a good feed and a rest allowing them some crucial recovery time. They were passing through the heart of the Titans now, the height of the Pass's walls verging on the unbelievable, in places thousands of feet high, towering above them.

"Have you considered the possibility that the H'daree could come while we wait for the rest of our supplies to arrive, Torbin?" Guido had trotted up alongside Torbin, as ever catching him by surprise. *"How does he do that?"*

"I have Guido, but it doesn't seem to fit their pattern. At every moment since they landed, they have reached out to Candor, letting him know that they are coming. It seems to be a major part of their strategy, putting fear into their enemy before they attack." Torbin shrugged his shoulders as if not at all convinced by his own argument.

"That's a little thin Torbin. Maybe we should consider holding back enough mounts to make a withdrawal should they come. It would damage our cause if we lost you." Tivosi cast his eyes down as he spoke as if ashamed of the suggestion.

"I would have thought that it would present you with the perfect opportunity to have your glorious death? Why would you want to avoid it?" Torbin raised his eyebrow whilst looking sideways at Tivosi. He instantly regretted it.

"I did not mention anything about me leaving." Tivosi growled out his response, fixing Torbin with a grim stare.

Torbin knew that he had dug a little too deep. Tivosi had limits and he was pushing his luck. However now was not the time to back down.

"I will not stop anyone leaving that does not want to stand Guido, but we have a choice. Watch people perish in front of us or feed them, get them on their feet and all walk out together. I will not leave until the last person that can travel is up and moving." Torbin turned his head to look Tivosi square in the face, a far more daunting task than most would ever have to endure.

"And I will be standing in front of you, so that you can see for yourself what I mean by a glorious death." Tivosi had deliberately lowered his tone, keeping his voice flat and low. It made Torbin almost shiver with fear, but he held his nerve.

"Then let us get to it." Torbin barked back his response, putting his heels to his mount and galloping off down the Pass. Tivosi sat stock still for a moment, as if uncertain how to respond, then urged his own horse forwards, his men following his lead.

It was dawn when the refugees came into sight. From a distance it was difficult to judge their numbers but as Torbin approached it became clear that they numbered in the tens of thousands, the scattered formation spreading out as far as the eye could see. They were moving but it looked what it was, slow and greatly laboured.

As he reined in his horse, Candor stepped forward from the bustling crowd. The look on his face was strained and he looked as if he had aged years. Hardly surprising Torbin supposed, but he was still a little taken aback. Candor had never exactly looked young, weather-beaten was the description that best fit. Now however, it looked as if the woes of the world were etched into his skin.

"Good to see you, my friend." Torbin clasped Candor's forearm, his friend responding in kind.

"Torbin, it is good to see you as well." Candor's smile was tired, forced out as it was with a strained effort. "Guido, you and your men are most welcome." Candor greeted the party with a genuine warmth.

"Thank you Candor, it is good to see you, my friend." Tivosi inclined his head in greeting, dismounting, closely followed by his men.

"What is the plan Torbin?" Candor turned his attention back to Torbin.

"I think we should concentrate on feeding people, Candor, and doing our best to treat people's ailments whilst we wait for the rest of our company to get here." Torbin put his arm around Candor's shoulder and led him away from earshot.

"I think we should slaughter most of the horses first and keep the cattle for pulling carts, we will need them. We have twenty fully loaded carts being pulled by cattle loaded with food and medical supplies and another twenty horses. We need to do an honest assessment of people's conditions and decide who we can and who we can't save." Torbin didn't want to cause any alarm, hence the conspiratorial stance.

"We have lost people already Torbin. A number of elders have passed and been left where they lay. Add into that the injured from the battle and some of the younger children, then you can start to understand the general mood. It may be difficult to get anyone to leave those still alive behind."

"Whatever happens Candor we will have to make camp here, get some spits up and running and wait for our relief. Food, water and rest will put us in a much stronger position." Torbin patted his friend on the back, a weak effort at reassurance but all he had.

"What if the H'Daree come Torbin? We'll be like newborn cattle, easy prey for predators." Candor could not lift his shoulders anymore. The sheer weight of responsibility holding them down, or was it something else?

"That is a risk we'll have to take Candor. At some point we would have to stop, assess and make decisions. If they were coming, I believe you would know because that seems to be their way. In any case I don't believe it would make any difference if we were stationary or on the move. At least set in place we can organise our rear to be made up of our remaining forces and then make a stand. Either way I don't believe we would survive." Torbin took a breath. "I don't want to die in this empty place Candor. I want to die an old man, in my bed surrounded by my loving family. That is a wished-for future, this is our reality, and we must give ourselves the best chance to survive."

Candor turned his tired eyes to Torbin, any argument that was left in him draining away.

"I have little to nothing left Torbin. I will bow to your leadership here, but I will need you to do what is necessary as I can hardly stay awake, let alone organise anything." Candor smiled weakly, a slight sway seeming to affect him. It was only then that Torbin noticed the dark patch on the side of his jacket. He reached across and lifted the front up, Candor offering no resistance. Underneath his shirt was blood-soaked and loosely bandaged, the crusted blood sticking the material to his pallid skin. *"No wonder he looks so ill."*

"Guido!" Torbin called out urgently and Tivosi responded, sprinting over to his friend.

"Guido, Candor is wounded." Torbin's voice cracked a little.

"LENNY!" Tivosi's shout almost hurt Torbin's ears, but it got a swift response.

Lenny White was one of Tivosi's chosen, nearly as big as the man himself but not quite, who was? He was a lot younger, good-looking with a crop of jet-black hair and a scruffy beard. More a case of unshaven, but such dark hair that it looked more of a beard than most men could manage. That wasn't what made him stand out as much as the fact that he was a true son of Sarjinn, and not from the aristocracy. And however unlikely it seemed he was one of two trained medics that Tivosi had picked for his company.

"What's up boss?" As soon as he opened his mouth, where he came from was obvious.

"Candor's carrying a heavy wound." Torbin looked across at Tivosi. "How did we not spot this earlier when we met in the Pass?"

"He was holding himself together for as long as he needed Torbin. Now we are here he could finally let go."

Just as he said the words Candor collapsed to the ground, Tivosi just managing to catch him before he hit the floor. Blood began to seep from his wound turning his shirt dark red and forming a little pool on the ground.

"For fuck's sake, 'e's bleeding like a stuck pig. 'elp me get 'im over to the wall, in the shade. Boss, get me bag from me saddle and organise some blankets an' water. Double quick now." Despite being his commanding officer, Tivosi didn't blink but just jumped to it.

Torbin and Lenny carried Candor's prone body to the shade of the wall and set him down on the floor, Lenny peeling away his jacket and shirt whilst struggling to pull off the encrusted bandage. The wound looked deep and red raw.

"It's infected Torbin. We need to get 'im some fluids and a little cheyro if 'e can 'old it down. It'll 'elp lower his temperature and make sleep a little easier. All we can do is keep 'im 'ydrated, stitch 'im up and make sure 'e eats somethin'."

Tivosi came running up with a waterskin, Lenny's medical bag and some blankets. They laid a blanket down and let Lenny start to get to work.

Tivosi put his hand on Torbin's shoulder. "I am sure he will make it Torbin, he is a strong man and full of life."

"Thank you, Guido, and I apologise if I was short with you earlier, it's just the stress gets to me on occasion."

"Think nothing of it Torbin, it's a commander's prerogative."

"CANDOR!" A scream came from the mass before them, people being shouldered apart as a short red-headed woman came rushing towards them, skirts bundled up to allow her to run that much faster.

Torbin stepped across her, grasping her by the shoulders.

"Marye?" it was half a question and half a greeting.

Marye slapped him hard across the face. It stung more than he'd care to admit to.

"WHAT HAVE YOU DONE TO HIM!" the words roared out of her mouth, spittle showering Torbin's reddened face.

"Nothing Marye, we are just tending to a wound he already had. If we hadn't got here, I'm not sure how much longer he would have lasted." Torbin kept his hands on her shoulders, the tension in her body making it feel like grasping hold of stone.

She twisted sharply, pulling away from Torbin's hold. She

turned square on, hands on hips and stared him directly in the face. For a moment she reminded him of Tivosi, the kind of steely resolve that was genuinely scary.

"What do you mean, 'a wound he already had'?" She may have been small, but she stood her ground like a warrior, not prepared to back down an inch.

Torbin instinctively took a half-step back.

"He came to greet us then collapsed. It was only then I noticed that he was bleeding from the side. I cannot believe that I didn't notice anything earlier in the Pass but for whatever reason he deliberately kept it quiet."

"He always insisted on tending his own wounds. He insisted that it was nothing to worry about. 'Just a scratch' he said." Marye's shoulders sagged as her head dipped. She began to cry, rooted to the spot. Torbin felt so awkward and uncomfortable but forced himself forward, wrapping her in a hug. For a brief moment she went to jerk away but then just sunk into his chest, arms grabbing on for dear life while sobs wracked her body.

They stayed that way for a couple of minutes while her tears slowly abated. Then she dropped her arms and stepped back, looking up at Torbin with reddened eyes.

"We are doing everything we can for him Marye. We will look after him I promise you that." He gave a wan little smile. It felt wholly inadequate, but it was the best he had to offer.

She wiped her eyes on the sleeves of her blouse and cleared her throat. Torbin thought she was quite pretty, but realised instantly that it was inappropriate.

"You must be Torbin then." She had completely composed herself and once again fixed him with her stare. Impressive.

"Yes Marye, I only wish we could have met under better circumstances." Torbin offered his inane smile again. "Please tell me what your most pressing needs are, and we will start to attend to them."

"Well, we have the walking wounded and those of failing health towards the back of the crowd. They will need attending to first, then we will need to look to feeding everyone. We are almost out of food." Without realising it, Marye had become a leader for the refugees, somehow turning into the person people turned to.

Torbin could sense a great well of strength in her.

"Marye, we have wagons loaded with provisions on their way, but they will be a couple of days behind. The plan is to slaughter the horses as the oxen you have will be better suited to pulling the carts. Our men will take care of things and get some spits going. In the meantime, we have two field medics with us, and they will do what they can for your ill and wounded." Torbin hoped he was coming across as sincere and caring but was so used to dealing with rough and ready soldiers that he worried that it may not seem genuine. "Would you show us the way Marye?"

She stood there, hands on hips, running her eyes over him, as if making her judgement. She turned inclining her head in the direction she wanted them to follow.

"Good enough."

"Lenny, grab your gear and get a couple of the chaps to come with us. Guido, I could use your help as well."

"Of course, Torbin. Lenny, jump to it." Tivosi barked out his orders, Lenny calling over his medic colleague to tend to Candor. He grabbed up his supplies and shouted across to two of his fellow guards, the three of them following their strange little column, led by the diminutive Marye.

Candor felt his senses dimming. He caught snippets of conversations, nothing more and as he drifted into unconsciousness, he saw Torbin and his men walking away, following Marye.

As night settled, Torbin sat with his back against the wall of the Pass, a couple of well-roasted ribs sitting unattended on a plate next to him. He looked out across the mass of people, all huddled around what looked like hundreds of fires. Sparks and embers flittered up into the night sky, making it almost feel like a celebration or a feast day.

Then he heard it, a little four-stringed fiddle by the sound of it. It played a wistful, melancholy jig, tugging at the heartstrings. A couple of soft-skinned drums began to sound out a soft, percussive beat, perfectly underpinning the yearning melody. Across the floor of the Pass, other instruments from other campfires joined in, creating an almost orchestral feel. Lutes, strange-sounding woodwind instruments that he couldn't quite place, and over it all a small army of the four-stringed fiddles, all coming together, lifting up to the sky, entreating the gods.

Then the voices rose up, everyone seeming to know their role, harmonies rising into the night sky. At first, he found it hard to isolate the words, but they were full of angst and regret. The chorus however was as clear as fresh river water.

"When the Grey Ocean beckons it is time to go home
Home to your loved ones, who are waiting for you
Peace will be with you, you are never alone
To be with your family, who will embrace you."

The whole Pass seemed to fill with song and as he looked out across the fires couples were on their feet, clinging to each other in a slow, swaying dance. It was as if they knew this could be their last moment together, their last chance to say I love you. Torbin could feel his eyes beginning to water a little, the unbridled emotion just pouring out in all directions.

Tivosi sidled over and sank down next to him.

"Beautiful, is it not my friend?"

"Yes, it is." Torbin turned his head, not wanting to show his tears.

"We are here Torbin, and we have not tasted defeat yet. I say we celebrate life and embrace every bit of joy it has to offer. Come my friend, join me." Tivosi got to his feet and extended his hand to Torbin. "We only have one life, let us enjoy it."

Torbin took Tivosi's hand, stood up and together they walked towards the fires, the people and the music.

Chapter Twenty-Nine Part One:

What you do not see

The smells were familiar but at the same time, just slightly off. Her head banged, as if someone were bashing away at a big kettle drum, whack, whack, whack, just a relentless pounding. She could feel the pallet that she was lying on, some sort of sacking stuffed with straw, little stalks poking through the material to scratch her.

The memory of what had passed was hazy, the noises and smells of battle all crashing around in her mind. Music, she could recall snatches of music, but not anything she could remember hearing before. It didn't seem complete, almost as if it was fighting with itself, all different sections of the orchestra wanting to be heard first. No not first exactly, more, loudest. Through it all, the power of steel pressing forward, demanding to be heard, then the pain.

Her leg throbbed intensely, feeling almost as if it were on fire. Then the noises started to coalesce, slowly separating into discernible patterns. People talking, moaning, objects being moved from place to place, even the sounds of flames flickering.

She could hear snippets of conversations, and one phrase seemed to be constantly repeated, *Kare Karaliene*. She had no idea what it meant but could hear it being whispered in private conversations, a mixture of reverence and fear clinging to it.

Everything seemed to swirl around her with no fixed point, just random thoughts and sensory input, but nothing to fixate on, as if she were adrift in time. *"Where am I?"*

Then little scraps of memory began to return, out in the Great White, a great battle and the giants wrapped in steel. Screams filling the air, desperate souls trying to save… now fear started to creep through her, the fear of opening her eyes and seeing the truth.

That was it, that was what she'd forgotten. *"Open your eyes, Marisa."*

She squinted her eyes, the light however low felt like looking directly into the sun. She tried to lift herself on her elbows but lacked the strength. She laid still and just turned her head, trying to make sense of what she saw.

It was a long, low-roofed room, with pallets on either side, each one that she could see filled with a body. What began to occur to her was that none of the pallets were simply for sleeping, this was a hospital. Incredible, a fully equipped hospital the like of which she had only ever seen in the Protectorate.

To the right a large alcove was filled with seats surrounding small braziers, people packed in shoulder to shoulder, some eating and drinking, some just sitting and resting.

One stood out from the rest, a big man, shoulders slumped forwards, head down, not communicating with anyone. She could feel his pain and it made her wince, a certain familiarity making it difficult to look. Then she realised that she knew this man, Bodger.

"Bodge." She tried calling out, but it just came out as a scratchy whisper. As she went to try again, a huge shadow enveloped her, like being swallowed by a mountain.

"Marisa Longspear, it warms my heart to see you awake and back with the living." Urdhoa loomed over her, a look of genuine relief etched onto his craggy features.

"Urdhoa, it is good to see you." She strained to lift her arm, just managing to grasp the great Wastelander's forearm. The effort made her feel slightly dizzy and Urdhoa could sense it.

"Rest Marisa, you have just woken after eight days asleep. Your body has endured, and you must rest. All will be revealed when you are stronger." Urdhoa held a bowl of warm liquid up to Marisa's mouth, it tasted a little acrid. "There, go to sleep Marisa, you will be well soon enough." He cradled her head, gently laying it back on her pillow. The room began to swim, slowly swirling around in her mind.

"But what about Bod…"

Marisa awoke with a start. She pushed herself up on her elbows, delighted that at least some of her strength had returned. She was still lying on the same pallet, but someone had obviously been tending to her as things smelt quite fresh. Looking up and down the long room there were people being tended to everywhere, nearly all of the pallets being full, plus the walking wounded milling around, filling their time with conversation.

She swung her legs over the edge, a slight dizziness almost making her fall back, but surprisingly it did not last long.

Urdhoa ambled up to her pallet before she had a chance to slide off onto the floor. He had a concerned look painted on his face, as if he was contemplating some great matter and struggling to find an answer.

"What's wrong Urdhoa?" Marisa's voice lifted an octave, a little flicker of concern floating into the air.

Urdhoa kept his head down, eyes fixed to the floor. Marisa could not remember seeing this giant of a man ever looking so nervous.

"Marisa, many were lost in the battle on both sides. Cralie Longspear did not survive her injuries. I am sorry Marisa." Urdhoa kept his head down, as if there was something irresistibly interesting stuck to the floor.

Marisa's breath caught in her throat, tears welling in her eyes. She joined Urdhoa in staring at the floor, breathing out hard to try and gain control of her emotions. She sat still, looking down for what seemed like an age. Finally, feeling like she had mastered her reaction, she looked up.

"Urdhoa, what was the final butcher's bill?"

"We lost over forty warriors Marisa, Urdlin and Andmar amongst them." The great Wolfs-head gentis chief kept his gaze fixed to the floor, his shoulders rising and falling in little ripples, too proud to openly show his grief.

It was a punch to the stomach before you had time to recover from the last blow. Marisa stood and instinctively pulled Urdhoa into an all-consuming hug, pulling in tight and sharing his tears.

"I am so sorry for your loss my friend; they were both brave men who fought with great honour. Urdlin paid a great price for his mistake and did your gentis proud."

They stood still, holding each other for a few minutes, both taking comfort in the embrace. Urdhoa stepped back, holding Marisa by the shoulders and took a deep breath, his tears soaking his beard and making it droop slightly.

"Where is she Urdhoa? I would very much like to see her." Marisa's words caught in her throat. She found herself having to fight the urge to weep, all of this information at once was almost overwhelming.

"I will take you to see her of course but others of your warriors have had to endure injury as well Marisa, although they are all doing well and are being attended to."

"What has happened to who?" Marisa had regained her composure somewhat, her eyes, red and puffy the only indication of her grief.

"Marta Swortsword has lost her right arm and Garic Carpenter has broken his left arm. Jevon Hand-axe and Barri Swortsword are relatively unscathed, but I worry for Barri's wellbeing. He has been almost mute since it happened, sitting in silence away from others."

"Barri will take this hard. He had a special relationship with Rat, sorry Cralie, more like brother and sister than fellow squad members." Marisa would deal with everything in good time, but for the moment needed to get up to speed.

She realised that she wasn't even aware of where they were.

"Where exactly are we Urdhoa?"

"We are in the Kaimas of the Snow Eagles, Marisa. They came out of their hiding places during the battle and helped turn the tide. They also captured the last Snowbard warrior as he sought to flee." Urdhoa had a little grin on his face, if Marisa didn't know better, she'd have called it smug.

"Why would they come to our aid? The tribes are not exactly enemies but not friends either. And as for the Protectorate? Well, I wouldn't expect a warm welcome. What am I missing Urdhoa?" Marisa looked at the great chief with a look of genuine confusion on her face.

"They are answering the call Marisa, as will all the Children of the Wilderness. Prophecy fulfilled cannot be ignored." Urdhoa smiled benignly at her, as if he felt a certain sympathy for her.

"What prophecy? What are you talking about?"

"The Kare Karaliene."

"I have heard people whispering that, but what does it mean?"

"There is an ancient prophecy Marisa that a great warrior, the Kare Karaliene, will be sent to us by the Great Maker. She will come in our hour of need, not of our people, when a great invader will try to crush us, and lead us to victory. All the Children of the Wilderness will rally to her call and she will spend eternity sitting at the right hand of the Great Maker, at the end of days."

Marisa stood stock still, mouth open, absolutely aghast at what she was hearing.

"Are you mad? You cannot possibly be suggesting that I am this prophecy brought to life?" Marisa let out an involuntary guffaw, turning her head to the side as if covering up a cough.

"It is not just me Marisa, word has spread, and the tribal chiefs are gathering and heading here as we speak. You may not believe but prophecy must be fulfilled." Urdhoa looked directly at Marisa for the first time since she woke, an earnest but hard look fixed to his face.

"What do you mean the tribal chiefs are gathering? The tribes fight each other do they not? Is that not a basic part of your culture?" Marisa stumbled slightly over her words, as if she had no confidence in what she was saying.

"That has always been our way Marisa, but all Children know the prophecy, and all will gather to see it fulfilled."

Marisa's head swam, a moment ago she was waking up to the aftermath of a battle and now she was a figure from legend, the saviour of a nation. She had to give herself time to focus.

"Urdhoa, I need to see my people, Crailie first and I need some time to take in what you are telling me."

Urdhoa nodded and offered her his arm, helping her down from her pallet. She winced at the stab of pain through her leg, taking a small stumble forward until she found her feet.

He walked her away from the dormitory, exiting through the back of the room. She briefly glanced over her shoulder down the room towards Bodger. She'd see him soon enough.

Urdhoa led her down a corridor, turning left halfway down,

stopping at a doorway covered with a reed screen. He pulled it aside and for a moment time stood still. There were about forty raised pallets, each of them with a corpse wrapped in white linen, faces serene and perfectly cleaned. All were big men, true Children of the Wilderness, warriors cut down in their prime and in the centre, almost in a place of honour, was Rat. Marisa felt her leg throb, pulsing out a reminder of what they had sacrificed. She stumbled a little but Urdhoa was there to catch her arm.

They picked their way through the other pallets until they reached Rat. Urdhoa stopped, head bowed to allow Marisa a moment. It was then she realised that Urdlin and Andmar were laid on pallets flanking Rat. She tried to hold on but the tears came anyway. She went to Urdlin and Andmar first, leaning in and placing a kiss on each of their foreheads. She stood by Rat for what seemed like an age, hand on her forehead before kissing her gently and turning on her heels.

"Let's go see the others." She took Urdhoa's hand and walked back to the dormitory.

She walked slowly through the room, passing pallets with men in various states of health, some up on their feet, some still unconscious. All who were awake though bowed their heads in acknowledgement, some whispering or mouthing "Kare Karaliene." There was a level of reverence that made her feel very uncomfortable, so much so that she found herself deliberately avoiding eye contact.

About halfway down the room they stopped next to two pallets. On one of them, Fugly lay stock still, her chest rising slowly, breathing a little laboured. Next to her stood Garic, arm strapped to his torso, bruising running up his arm and across his neck, cuts and nicks marking his face.

Marisa stepped towards him and lent in, wrapping her arm around his shoulder and kissing him gently on the cheek.

"It is good to see you up and about." She smiled at him and looked sideways at Fugly.

"She's doing okay Marisa. She had a little infection, so they've got her sedated while their herbs do their work. She's on the mend but obviously not quite complete." He cast a sideways glance at Fugly's missing arm, not quite knowing what else to say.

Marisa lent across and gave Fugly a peck on the forehead.

"Let's leave her in peace for the moment, let her heal. Where's Bodger?" She looked back to Garic whose head dipped a little.

"He's not injured Marisa but has hardly said a word since the battle." Garic nodded over his shoulder towards a small alcove with a brazier, Bodger sitting with his back to them, shoulders slumped.

"Okay, give me a minute, would you?" Urdhoa and Garic nodded their ascent and Marisa limped over and sat down next to Bodger.

"Hey Bodge, how are you?" She nudged up next to him and put her arm around his shoulder.

"She's gone." He looked up, his eyes red and rheumy, a look of utter devastation on his face. Marisa had never seen Bodger show any real emotion, let alone be on the verge of tears. It nearly broke her heart, so she just smiled and gave him a squeeze.

"I know Bodge, I'm so sorry. We are all heartbroken."

Bodger just stared at her for a moment then buried his head in her shoulder and wept, his shoulders shuddering violently as he let all of his emotions out at once. Marisa just sat there, wrapping him in a tight embrace, letting him get it all out.

She sat there for what seemed like an age when she felt a tap on her shoulder.

"Urdhoa needs to talk to you, let me take over here." Garic gestured over his shoulder where Urdhoa stood patiently, head dipped in respect. The mood of the whole room was sombre, no one wanting to raise their voices or disturb the silence.

Marisa stood up, Garic sliding onto the seat next to Bodger, the pair of them just sitting quietly.

"Marisa, the Snow Eagles have the Steel warrior bound and locked in a cell" Urdhoa nodded towards the far end of the room.

"Take me to him Urdhoa."

He led her out of the dormitory and down a corridor. There were many doorways leading to rooms of all shapes and sizes, activity happening in all of them. It still amazed Marisa that so much was going on and that so many people lived inside each Kaimas. The Protectorate vastly underestimated the size and sophistication of the Children. It was a culture far more advanced than they ever realised. They exited the corridor and stepped into a large round area, more corridors branching off in numerous directions.

Stood in the middle was a group of clansmen, at the front a man of a size with Urdhoa, a great feathered headdress making him appear even bigger.

"Marisa, this is Andlan, chief of the Snow Eagles."

"It is an honour to finally meet you, Marisa Longspear." The great warrior bowed to Marisa, his retainers following suit. She could hear some of them whispering 'Kare Karliene' but put it to the back of her mind, however much it rankled.

"We have the Steel warrior secured in a cell. We have waited for you to question him. We have not been able to get any information from him." Andlan looked a little ashamed, as if he had somehow let her down.

"Then please take me to him."

Chapter Twenty-Nine Part Two:

A dish best served cold

The heavy wooden cell door creaked open slowly. It was pitch black, no light or windows to be seen, the dark musty smell assaulting the senses, the acrid nature of it itching the back of the throat. Two of Andlan's men stepped forward with lit torches, placing them in the sconces, slowly spreading a dull light around the room.

It took a couple of seconds for Marisa's eyes to adjust, and then there he was. Stripped to the waist and bound wrist and ankle, the surviving Snowbard warrior was on his feet and even in his reduced condition, clearly ready to sell his life for a high price. Andlan's men took no risks, lowering their spears at the prisoner's torso, corralling him into the corner of the cell.

Marisa took her time to assess the man. He was big, probably as tall as Garic but more heavily muscled as you would expect for a man of his age. He had straw-yellow hair, piercing blue eyes and heavy stubble. His wounds had been tended to, or at least cleaned and bandaged but he looked rough and unkempt, as you would expect, having spent many days locked away in darkness.

Marisa watched as he tensed his shoulders, finding his balance so that he might shoot forward and try with what little he had to cause some damage. He stared intently at her, teeth gritted, malevolence personified. She couldn't help but admire his commitment and determination to continue the fight, but Rat was dead and at the very least she needed to find out why.

"Andlan, may I?" Marisa pointed towards one of his men,

motioning at his spear.

"Of course." Andlan nodded at the man, who stepped forward, offering his spear to Marisa.

Marisa nodded a thank you and used the spear as a crutch, hobbling forwards towards the grimacing prisoner. She motioned the two spearmen guarding him to move backwards in order to stand square in front of him, just a few feet away. She smiled at him, watching for any reaction, any kind of movement. She saw him tense his muscles, leaning back against the wall in order to help him spring forward.

At the exact moment he readied to spring, she whipped the spear round in a dizzying arc, cracking into his ankles and making him fly sideways, a half-shriek, half-grunt escaping his lips. He tried to right himself but Marisa stood over him, the point of her spear resting on his throat.

"Do you want to die pointlessly in the dark, mountain man? Forgotten and unreknowned, no glory to your line?" Marisa laced her words with disdain, deliberately taunting the prone warrior.

"Would you offer an alternative, little girl?"

"How dare you dog! This is the Kare Karaliene!" One of the spearmen cracked him round the back of his skull and stepped back as if to skewer him.

Marisa whipped her spear back to block his thrust,

"Stop, please stand down my friend." Marisa took half a step back, free palm up in a gesture of peace.

The mountain man shuffled along the cell wall, moving away from the angry spearman, getting himself back to his knees, a trickle of blood running down his forehead and dripping slowly onto the floor.

"So, this is how it goes for bound prisoners here?" He spat on the floor, pushing himself to his feet against the wall. He glared at everyone before him but gave Marisa an extra helping. "The young men who rallied to our cause told us of the legend. The great warrior queen, the Kare Karaliene, she who will lead you to victory. And you people believe this little gutter rat, is she?" He leaned his head back and let out a throaty laugh, closely followed by two hefty whacks to the head as both spearmen answered his taunt.

"Please, leave him." Marisa again stepped in front of the two spearmen, hand palm up. "Peace my brothers, peace." The looks on their faces, having the Kara Karaliene refer to them as brothers was priceless. Or at least it would be given different circumstances, but back off they did.

"You will not be struck again while I am here." She glanced at everyone else in the cell, making her point as clearly as she could. All nodded and stood back. "Your treatment is a kindness compared to the punishments you dealt out to any dissenting voices. How many young Children of the Wilderness did you execute?"

"As many as were deemed necessary, as in any military campaign."

"So, this was a campaign then? What was your goal? Why are you here, mountain man?" Marisa felt some progress here, if she could just keep goading him into giving away more information.

"What is your name girl?" He had got himself upright again and stood holding Marisa's gaze.

"Marisa Longspear. What is yours, mountain man?"

"Magnus Ivarsen. It is good to make your acquaintance Marisa Longspear." He smiled his answer, and she couldn't deny his attractiveness, tall, athletic and handsome. In another life maybe.

"And you Magnus Ivarsen, I wish the situation was different, but I offer you the respect of warrior to warrior. So, why are you here?"

"I apologise for belittling you Marisa, I saw you fight, and it was like nothing I have seen before. All in Snowbard have heard of battlesong but there are few who have ever witnessed it. I sense that you are struggling with it, as if you are unaware." The conversation had flipped in a heartbeat, a sense of cordiality that felt almost inappropriate, seemed to have settled in.

"Thank you for your courtesy and kind words, but I repeat my question." Marisa pushed to keep the conversation on topic.

"There are many prophecies in many different cultures Marisa. The time of reckoning is at hand and Snowbard has its part to play. This is just a feint, a test, the first of many to come. The world is changing, and we will take our place at the top table." He smiled at Marisa, a look of deep self-satisfaction on his face. It was infuriating.

"What does that mean?" Marisa tried to keep her delivery flat and even, not to show any frustration or emotion. Ivarsen though had that same look of self-satisfaction on his face, almost as if he was the only person who really wanted to be in the room.

"You will get nothing more from me Marisa. It is what it is, and you will win, or you will perish. My role is over, it is only the nature of my end that is to be decided," He beamed out a smile, as if he was as happy as a man could be. Frustrating and unsettling, but Marisa knew he would say no more.

"Your end will not be decided by me Magnus Ivarsen, you are not my prisoner." Marisa turned to leave, Andlan's men closing ranks behind her, spears levelled at Ivarsen.

"Do you believe in your cause Marisa Longspear? Truly believe, or are you doing what you believe to be the moral choice? These people believe in you in a way no one from the Protectorate can." Ivarsen rolled his eyes, a little chuckle escaping his throat. "The arrogance of the Protectorate, equality and fair treatment for all. This is not reality, strength is required to lead, not everybody has something worthwhile to contribute. I believe that I will go to my ancestors, in the halls of the mountain gods, whatever my end. But I need to die on my feet." His words carried a pinch of desperation.

"Marisa Longspear, will you advocate for me? I only call for a warrior's death, the Children of the Wilderness used to believe in this rite. Even if I win my contest I will still be put to death, but I have one last chance of battle and the possibility of dying on my feet. If there is someone who will face me." Ivarsen was on his feet and had stepped forward, pressing his chest into the spear tips, little rivulets of blood running down his toned stomach.

She walked out of the cell, followed by Andlan, Urdhoa and the rest of the Children. She really couldn't explain it but felt compelled to argue Ivarsen's case. In part she wanted to see if she was right about something, but there was a risk.

"Andlan, Urdhoa, I know I have no rights here and my words may not carry much weight, but I would like to propose that we grant Ivarsen his wish." She tried to land the request gently but realised that the sting for the two leaders may be too much to bear.

"Marisa, your words carry far more importance than you could possibly know. More and more, we believe you to be the Kare

Karaliene but what you ask is indeed much." Urdhoa spoke first and Marisa could sense his discomfort, this was not his Kaimas.

"Andlan my brother, please forgive me for speaking first, but also for carrying on." Urdhoa bowed to his fellow chief. "Marisa, I have lost my son and many young warriors from my tribe and Andlan lost a son leading the attack from behind. He was killed by Ivarsen, wielding a sword of dread. We need our vengeance; we need him to die in pain and fear." Urdhoa had not seemed this agitated since she first met him, when she was the invader.

"I honour your losses and I am devastated to hear that you lost your son Andlan. But let me put forward a scenario that may solve all our problems. I believe that I have someone who would relish a duel to the death with Ivarsen, and I can assure you that he will make it painful."

The ground was swept clean, a great rope laid in a circle, about fifty feet in diameter. The floor outside the rope was packed full, in places three or four deep, the anticipation of the contest being an event no one wanted to miss. Everyone stood at the edge had a shield, all locked in place forming an impenetrable wall of wood and metal. Once the combatants entered the circle, only one would leave on their feet.

The room was the great meeting hall of the Snow Eagles, a place that sweated history from its walls, tribal councils, feast days, weddings between tribes, every conceivable kind of event. At the top of a small stand, sat the throne of the Snow Eagles, Andlan sitting resplendent in his feathered headdress and robes of the virsininkas.

On opposite sides of the circle the shield-wall opened, and the combatants entered. On one side Magnus Ivarsen strode forward, boos, hisses and insults showering down on him. On the other side Barri Swortsword barrelled forward, a look of dark, angry vengeance painted to his features. When she asked Bodger, he nearly bit her hand off, so eager was he. She told him it was only a hunch, but if she'd told him he was facing the greatest warrior in history it wouldn't have made a difference, he'd still want to kill him. Both were armed with a shield, spear and a shortsword sheathed at their waists. There would be no soul blades here.

Andlan stood to his feet and motioned for silence. "This is a death match, only one will leave the circle. Begin!" He clapped his hands and a cacophony of noise filled the great hall.

Marisa sat to the right-hand side of Andlan. She would have preferred to hold a shield but knew she would be more of a liability.

The two men circled each other, the occasional prod of spear being easily turned aside on the others shield. Marisa knew Bodger's quality and that his focus would be keen because of Rat. However, there was no denying Ivarsen's ability. His footwork was smooth as molasses, his forms obviously practised, his movement and shapes as good as she had seen.

Suddenly Ivarsen leapt forward, shield up, spear darting over the top, clipping Bodger's shield rim, the tip of his spear just touching the top of Bodger's ear. He beamed a smile, drawing first blood, confidence infusing his every move. It didn't last for long, however.

"Is that the best you've got boy? Then you are proper fucked," Bodger snarled, the first time his facial expression had changed since he entered the circle.

Bodger took a half-step back, feigning surprise and instantly Marisa knew what was about to happen. Bodger gave a fraction of ground and Ivarsen stepped into it with a solid spear thrust, just as Bodger changed his balance, switching his weight from one foot to the other, whipping his spear round the outside of Ivarsen's shield, opening up a great gash down his thigh.

Ivarsen quickly hobbled backwards, crouching, trying to squeeze as much of himself behind his shield as he could. The look on his face told Marisa all she needed to know, he knew he was lost, without his soul blade not quite the great warrior he thought he was. As she suspected, all of the Snowbard warrior legends were to do with the blades, not skill. She would have bet on any, and all her squad against any warrior in the Known World, and now she had her proof.

A great roar went up in the hall and Bodger went to work, the look on his face never changing. He toyed with Ivarsen, almost like death by a thousand cuts. Marisa watched with pride, knowing that this was the best way for Bodger to exorcise the ghosts that were haunting him, although they would probably never fully leave him.

It had been going for half an hour, Bodger could have finished it numerous times but was luxuriating in keeping Ivarsen on his feet, Marisa knew that a wounded animal was at its most dangerous when cornered. Ivarsen was covered in cuts and puncture wounds, some no more than scratches, others far more significant. Blood was trickling down his arms and torso, soaking his breeches dark red. Marisa almost admired his courage and his stamina, almost but not quite.

"Bodge, end it!" she shouted above the din, everyone in the hall baying for blood. Bodger moved with impossible speed, feinting left, going right and then switching back left, Ivarsen having committed a desperate thrust. Bodger pinned his spear to the floor, stamping it halfway up the shaft so that Ivarsen had only a useless piece of wood in his palm. Marisa couldn't help but admire his persistence as he rolled under Bodger's thrust, pulling his shortsword as he scrambled back to his feet. It was all to no avail however as Bodger drove his spear under Ivarsen's shield and straight through his thigh.

Ivarsen collapsed to his knees, trying desperately to raise his sword to parry. Bodger was already in motion, slashing down at Ivarsen's sword hand, slicing deep into his wrist.

Ivarsen let the sword slip from his ruined hand and Bodger jumped behind him, grasping a handful of his hair, pulling his head back.

The crowd roared their delight, the noise almost blocking out Marisa's thoughts.

"Marisa Longspear, I..." Bodger slid his sword across Ivarsen's throat, opening it up, no more words only a cascade of blood pouring from his neck. Bodger flung his lifeless corpse to the side and raised his hands to accept the adulation of the crowd.

"You are the most skilled warriors I have ever seen Marisa. There is much we could learn from you." Urdhoa turned to Marisa and Andlan leaned in conspirationally, the three of them almost head to head.

"We want you to stay with us Marisa, take your place amongst the tribes. We believe in you; we believe you are the Kare Karaliene and we believe you are the fulfilment of prophecy." Andlan nodded his agreement.

This was ridiculous, she had a life in the Protectorate, friends and colleagues she couldn't leave. There was no way.

"I cannot stay my friends. I have a life, a home and people who rely on me. You cannot ask me to just give everything up and leave it all behind. I hardly know you people, not really." It was such a mad idea that it just all seemed like some sort of fever dream. Was she even awake?

Then she started to hear it, having been so distracted by the conversation.

Bodger stood like a god in the middle of the circle, sword raised above his head.

"Kare Karaliene! Kare Karaliene!" The whole crowd was chanting, all looking towards her, rapturous looks of hope in their eyes.

"I don't know, it is much to consider."

"KARE KARALIENE, KARE KARALIENE!" It had turned into a roar, Bodger lifted onto the shoulders of the crowd, pumping his arms up and down in time with the chants, almost orchestrating them.

Marisa stood up, gesturing for the crowd to be quiet, wanting to be able to speak.

"KARE KARALIENE! KARE KARALIENE! The noise would not abate, the sight of Marisa standing just acting as incitement.

She looked around the faces, all of them filled with hope, not just hope but belief and at that moment she knew she would stay.

She turned to Urdhoa and almost shouted in his ear in order to be heard above the din.

"What do I have to do to become part of the gentis?"

"One thing only Marisa. You must talk to the Great Maker."

Chapter Thirty:

Dangerous liaisons

The journey back to Dantoneen had been slow and labourious. There were no summons from Prince Lor along the way and Kaif had been busy overseeing the legionnaires. Mitter Wane had approached him on a couple of occasions, no doubt out of genuine concern, but he had made his excuses and kept his distance. He had always reconciled himself with the violence he had witnessed previously, as part and parcel of Darmation life, but Bergin was different. He was a citizen of the Protectorate and a fellow countryman. The excessive violence of the act had taken his breath away and he feared that his reaction may raise questions.

Sat on his balcony, looking out across the gardens, he tried to breath in the fragrances as if that may replenish his spirits. He stood up and stepped forward, leaning on the rail, staring out across the Great Silver Sea. The fishing skiffs spread out like an armada, nets being cast from the rails, fishermen hauling in the day's catch.

There was a knock at the door, Matoc shuffling quickly across the floor to open it, head down, not daring to look the messenger in the eye. The man pushed the door with a hard shove, apparently irritated by the length of time the old slave took to open it fully. Matoc stumbled backward, the bottom of the door almost cracking his toes as he tried to avoid injury.

Sorkin frowned but said nothing, walking into his living quarters, hands clasped behind his back, eyebrows raised in inquiry.

"Inquisitor Malek requests your presence." The messenger was all formality, attired in formal dress whites, lined with gold braid, appropriate for a Herald of the Crown. He held a silver tray with a small scroll, tied with a red ribbon and sealed with a wax stamp. Sorkin followed protocol picking it up, breaking the seal and unravelling the scroll. It said exactly what the messenger had announced, but established courtesies were what they were.

"Please, lead the way." Sorkin strode after the messenger, fixing the buttons on his dress coat as he walked.

He always disliked spending any time with Malek. The man was a zealot, never seeing beyond his duty and following its consequences, regardless of the outcome. Sorkin had always felt as if the man relished administering punishment, especially the capital kind. The memory of Overseer Lorent made a little bile rise up his gorge. He managed to swallow it back, the acidity biting into his throat.

He took none of his usual joy when walking the corridors, eyes down paying attention only to the carpet and the heels of the herald. They had been walking for a few minutes when the herald turned right down a sub corridor, stopping outside a beautifully ornate door. It was the first hint of opulence that Sorkin had noticed.

The herald offered a perfunctory bow and turned on his heels, marching back the way he came. Sorkin knocked on the door.

"Enter." The dead flat tone as ever made Sorkin almost shudder with discomfort.

Sorkin opened the door and stepped into Malek's office. It was a sight to behold, mirrored panels adorned the walls, completely encompassing the room, creating various images of the person stepping in, as if you were seeing all aspects of yourself. It was whispered that was indeed Malek's intent, leave nowhere for anyone to hide. A vast golden, crystal chandelier hung from the ceiling, spreading little diamonds of torchlight around the room. Malek himself sat in what was a relatively plain, straight-backed chair, bolt upright, just adding to his hawkish appearance. The desk he sat behind was more in keeping with the rest of the office. It had more carvings than most throne rooms.

"Advocate Sorkin, thank you for attending so promptly. Please take a seat."

"Thank you, Inquisitor. How may I be of assistance?" Sorkin smiled, gently lowering himself into the seat offered.

"It would appear that there has been an administrative error."

"Have I failed to complete any duty? Incorrect paperwork perhaps? Although sitting here I cannot for the life of me think of a situation where that may have occurred." Sorkin chose his words very carefully, any invitation from the inquisitors Office was potentially fraught with peril. Even incomplete or incorrect paperwork could be deemed fraudulent and due the severest of penalties.

"No, nothing on your part Advocate. Interesting though, that your thoughts instantly stray in that direction." Malek tilted his head back a touch, looking down his beak of a nose, almost using it as a rangefinder.

"I find a degree of caution lends itself meetings of this nature. None of us are perfect after all, Inquisitor." Sorkin offered a gentle smile in return, not certain it covered his nerves, but, given the circumstances, the best he could offer.

"Caution is always wise, but not necessary here." Malek's smiling response was unnerving as always. "It would appear that an error was made during the investigation of Overseer Lorent."

A cold shiver ran down Sorkin's back, the fear of hearing Malek's words fixing him rigidly in place.

"It would appear that certain documentation was forged, or altered at least. Upon further investigation it would seem that Lorent was in fact innocent." Malek steepled his fingers, as if inviting Sorkin to respond.

Sorkin sat there, images of Lorent spinning around his mind, falling to his knees, begging mercy and finally confessing. Not just confessing but shouting out his guilt. Why would he do that?

"How was this not discovered earlier? How did you let this slip through the net?"

"Do you suggest that I carry out these investigations personally Sorkin?" Malek had sat forward, looking like a cat ready to pounce on unsuspecting prey.

"No, of course not Inquisitor, an unfortunate slip of the tongue, please accept my apologies. It is just a bit of a shock as I was the one who joined you in condemning this poor man to death."

"He condemned himself Advocate. I cannot remember a more fulsome confession in my entire career, shouting 'I CONFESS MY CRIMES, I CONFESS MY CRIMES'. It did not leave a great deal of room for doubt." Malek had sat back, any offence taken apparently brushed aside.

Sorkin slumped back in his chair, head in hands, the weight of this pressing down on him.

"This is not your fault Advocate so please do not burden yourself with blame. I have always found you to be thorough and professional in the execution of your duties." Malek seemed to be attempting a show of empathy. It was even more unnerving than his usual waspish attitude, but Sorkin, for once, simply didn't care. A darkness was descending in his mind, like pulling the shutters closed.

"To help salve your conscience we are searching for his wife so that we can return his property to her and it has been agreed that the state will provide her with a stipend in order to see to her comfort." Malek rearranged some papers on his desk, for the first time in Sorkin's memory looking a little uncomfortable. "Rest assured, those responsible will be hunted down and punished. As for the investigators that erred, they have been admonished." Malek looked for but got no response from Sorkin.

"Thank you for your attendance Advocate Sorkin. Good day." Malek looked back to his papers and began to read from the top of the stack.

"Thank you, Inquisitor." Sorkin pushed himself out of the chair and exited the room, pulling the door closed behind him. As soon as it was shut, he bent forward, hands on his knees, heaving in great gouts of air.

He shambled back to his rooms, head down, that sense of despair welling up inside of him. He opened the door, barely noticing Matoc slowly approaching.

"Can I offer any service Master?" The old slave bowed his head, standing stock still and waiting for an answer.

"No, thank you Matoc. I just need some peace and quiet." His wan smile was the best he could manage, the effort to admonish Matoc about his formality just escaping him.

The old slave bowed, shuffling backwards, before turning to

leave the room.

Sorkin stood rooted to the spot. He looked around the room, all the things that he had spent so long acquiring, symbols of his elevated status, held no meaning. The grand dining table and ornate chairs, the great display cabinet, full of objet d'art, statuettes, gifts from state visits, all of it seemed hollow.

He went to walk out onto the balcony, then decided he did not want to be seen, so flopped down in his favourite longchair. It offered no comfort, the guilt at his complicity in an innocent man's death was investing his very being, as if someone had taken a piece of his soul, his essence, in payment of his crimes.

Pictures of Bergin and Lorent were flooding through his mind, the more he tried to put them aside, the more they pressed to the front of his thoughts. The finality of it stabbed at him, the impossibility to atone sinking him further into darkness.

It suddenly occurred to him that Lorent was not what he thought at all. He remembered feeling irritated by the man's grovelling, thinking at the time that he should show some dignity in the face of the inevitable. On reflection he was probably one of the bravest men he had ever met. If he hadn't confessed his family would have been condemned, either sold into slavery or summarily executed. As terrified as he was of the sanction levelled at him, he chose to face that horror. That was why he was so vocal, the last chance to at least give his family a hope of freedom and a future.

He didn't remember hearing a knock at the door, or Matoc answering.

"Sorkin, I heard the news. How are you?"

Mitter Wane stood at the arm of his chair, a comforting hand resting on his shoulder.

He thought about getting up, but he simply couldn't hold to the formalities.

"Apologies Mitter, but I would not be good company for anyone at the moment." He could hear his words, sullen and self-serving, but he just didn't care.

"Let me decide what I consider to be good company. Right now, I think you could do with some of this and an ear to listen to your woes." Wane had two patterned glass bottles in his other hand.

"I'm not much of a drinker I'm afraid." Sorkin stayed where he was, a more pitiful looking sight he couldn't have made if he tried.

"All the more reason to practise, how else does one improve?" That alluring, cheeky smile worked its charm, Sorkin in spite of himself grinning and sitting up.

"What is it? Something sophisticated by the look of the bottles." Sorkin feigned interest.

"Well, I am glad you ask Sorkin. These are two of the last ever bottles of Minari pear brandy." Wane had a slightly smug, 'how clever am I' look on his face.

Sorkin went to ask how he came by them but decided against it. Holding on to the façade of joviality was testing his reserves of will.

"I appreciate what you are doing Mitter, honestly I do. I just don't know that I can engage in conversation. Really I would like some quiet time." Sorkin was trying as hard as he could to remain polite and not snap. Also, there was a tinge of self-preservation, as offending a mercenary with the reputation of Wane was littered with risk.

"Then we will quietly drink together, and conversation be damned." Wane smiled that winning smile and Sorkin conceded with a weary nod of the head.

Wane went to the great display cabinet, picking two glasses from the shelf. He sauntered back to Sorkin and sat on the couch opposite, pulling the cork from the first bottle with his teeth, spitting it onto the balcony. Sorkin resisted the temptation to go and pick it up. He may as well leave Matoc something to do.

Wane poured two very healthy measures and held one out to Sorkin.

"To all our mothers, may they live forever!" He downed his glass in one long swig. "Ahhh! That'll wake you up in the morning!"

Sorkin didn't really understand what he was saying, some sort of soldiers toast he assumed. He went to down his own glass and spluttered halfway through, some of the brandy coming out through his nose. It burnt something fierce, an acidic taste that grated at the back of his throat. Wane laughed at the sight, holding his hands up in mock apology. Sorkin girded himself, took a deep breath and sank the remaining half. It stung, but less the second time and surprisingly a nice warm glow flowed through him, throat to belly. He smiled and offered his glass back to Wane.

"As you wish my friend." Wane poured two more measures, both of which went down in one this time.

Sorkin was feeling much better all of a sudden, the alcohol pumping through his body, filling him with a certain sense of abandon.

"So how did you hear, Mitter?"

"When serving a term of service in Darmat, it pays to establish friendly relations. On occasion a little silver or gold can keep you informed. However, for now I will keep my sources close to my chest." A flash of that smile and all of a sudden, Sorkin felt like he was in a conspiracy.

"It doesn't really matter how I know, does it? I heard and was concerned for you." Wane leaned forward and offered a comforting smile. "From what I have seen of you so far, I just assumed you would take this hard." He paused for a second as if debating his next words. "I do not wish to be presumptuous, but I worried that you would feel some blame in this. It is not your fault if others make mistakes Sorkin. From what I understand you merely followed the law and executed your duties."

Sorkin sank his third glass and laughed a laugh laced with irony.

"Executed my duties. How very appropriate. Do you want to know the truth Mitter?" He arched his eyebrows at the Captain General.

"Why not? Friends share with each other, do they not?"

"While I hate violence, I was more irritated at the time. I was irritated by the heat, the amount of my time it took up and lastly, to my everlasting shame, by what I saw as this man's lack of dignity. This brave selfless man and all I could offer him at the end was indifference." Sorkin had poured a fourth glass and threw it back like an old soak.

Wane joined him, hissing as he sank it in one.

"If you had known the truth, would you have acted the same?" He was clever, no doubt there.

"Doubtful but would I have risked my own safety? No. My

behaviour is reprehensible none the less, such scant regard for another's life. Is this what I have sunk to?" Sorkin's chin had dropped to his chest, the weight of the guilt swimming in alcohol, proving too difficult to overcome.

Wane stood up and sat himself on the end of Sorkin's longchair. He placed his hand on Sorkin's shin.

"Sorkin. Sorkin, look at me."

He looked at Wane. He had a soft, gentle look of concern on his face. He could feel him reaching out, trying to provide what solace he could.

"I have met many people in my life. Men and women, kings and paupers, murderers and healers. There is nothing set in stone in this life other than being true to yourself. The reason you are feeling as you do is because you are a good and gentle soul, caring for humanity is at your core. It is not your fault when acts of violence or evil are committed, you are not responsible."

Wane put his hand on Sorkin's cheek, gently cradling his face. Sorkin turned his head and instinctively kissed the palm of his hand. He instantly jerked back, the realisation of what he had just done suddenly dawning on him.

"Please forgive me Mitter, I have had too much to drink and forget myself." He tried desperately to backtrack, the punishment for this behaviour in Darmat was a death sentence.

He stared straight down, afraid to meet Wane's eye.

To his surprise, Wane shuffled up the chair taking Sorkin's face in both hands and gently kissed him on the lips.

"You should never forego any of life's pleasures."

Chapter Thirty-One:

Love in the dust

The shape of her hip was one of the most beautiful sights he had ever seen. He knew he was in love with her, but it scared him, as there was a real risk one or the other of them could die. Either way, he could not imagine being without her. The thought of her occupied most of his waking hours and seeing her once they'd cleared the Darmation border was the only thing he could ever imagine lifting his spirits.

They had ridden back from their so-called diplomatic mission in almost total silence, Cerwin staying apart from the rest of the group, head bowed in what would have seemed to most people to be contemplative prayer. Jonoh knew better. The little shadow-master blamed himself for Bergin's demise, his flash of the Gift bringing the violent reprisal. Deep down a part of Jonoh blamed him too, at least in part, but that was a thoughtless, childish part. No one could possibly know it would happen, and the speed with which it did happen pointed to some sort of preplanning. It was executed in minutes, to exit the tent and witness that bloodbath gave nobody any hope of reacting with anything other than shock.

Cerwin's last comment was to suggest Timult take command of Jonoh's honour guard in Bergin's absence. Jonoh had tried to convince them all to return to Sarjinn and take ship for the Protectorate, but to a man they insisted on staying by his side.

Shala gave a little shudder, stretching her arms out like a cat. She rolled over, facing Jonoh and gently stroked his cheek. "Good morning my love." Her smile made his heart flutter. This must be love, because at that moment he couldn't imagine anywhere else he would rather be. In a tent, on a rocky floor, in the endless dust of the Red Desert's caravan route. Just perfect.

She shuffled over and wrapped him in an all-enveloping embrace, pulling him in tight, flesh pressed on flesh, almost as if they were one entity. At moments like these he didn't want to be anywhere else, lost in the instant, happier than he had ever been.

She pulled back a fraction, gently brushing his forehead with her lips.

"Would you like some breakfast?" That beaming smile just melted him.

"You stay where you are gorgeous, I'll get it for us." He sat up, pulling on his breeches in the same move. He grabbed up his shirt and wriggled into his boots, leaning down and kissing her before he exited the tent.

With all the Orphans gathered, their tents spread out like a small town, morning campfires already lit, bacon, eggs and beans cooking away. He'd become fast friends with another Jonoh. He was from Stonebard, a mason by vocation and somehow had lived amongst the Murgan without being killed. It was an impressive feat, few were allowed to do anything other than trade in the Grass-lands, so to make a life there and be accepted was remarkable. He had explained that the Murgan had a three-tiered society, warrior, worker and slave. He had been accepted as a worker, or *Kaihoko* and adopted by the Brahim clan. Everyone knew of the Brahim clan, mainly because Bloodspear was one of the most renowned warriors in the history of the Known World.

"It was easier for me as they don't really have any stoneworkers in the Grass-lands, so I was quite the commodity." Jonoh Mason always had an upbeat attitude to things, with that ability to make a disaster sound like the greatest opportunity you could ever hope for.

His tent was pitched opposite Jonoh and Shala's and he was already cooking breakfast, with a kettle of cheyro on the boil as well.

"Morning number two."

"Morning number one." Jonoh Mason, responded, a little chuckle accompanying their little in-joke. It made it less confusing for themselves and others, and gave them a unique bond which they both appreciated. They always called each other one and two now, the first friendship Jonoh had had of that kind since Garic. Nicknames and poking fun at each other being the basis of it, something that he had really missed over the last year.

"Up nice and early today two. Bad night's sleep." Jonoh took a little spoon of beans. Bowing to make them eatable. He smiled at number two, grinning his approval. "Mmmm, you'll make someone a nice wife one day."

"You'd know. How is Shala by the way?" They both giggled, even though Mason was about ten years older that Jonoh, he still retained that schoolboy humour.

"Oh she's amazing my friend." Jonoh beamed a smile, talking about Shala always made him happy.

Mason reached across the campfire, patting Jonoh on the shoulder, a smile of genuine happiness on his face. "Good for you my friend. Two plates I assume?"

Jonoh smiled his assent, pouring two cups of cheyro and adding a little honey to take the sharp edge from it.

"Have you spoken to Master Cerwin at all?" Jonoh proffered the question, almost a little nervous about the reply.

"No one has, one. He's pitched his tent right on the sentry line, as far away from everyone else as possible." Mason looked away from Jonoh, the subject being a sore spot for the Orphans. Even with his blocks up, every one of the Orphans still felt the pain and sorrow that emanated from him.

Jonoh took the two plates offered, balancing one on his forearm, two cups of cheyro in his other hand.

"Thank you number two; I will see you later." He turned grinning and walked gingerly back to his tent, thinking he must look like a circus performer, trying to balance so much at once.

"Breakfast is served," Jonoh called out, having no hands free to open the tent flap.

Shala popped her head out, pulling the tent flap around her, obviously still naked. She flashed her alluring smile, beckoning Jonoh in with a flick of her head.

"Now that looks lovely. I assume number two was on cooking duties?"

"He was and I told him that he'd make someone a wonderful

wife one day." Jonoh chuckled away to himself. "He suggested I already was." This made him laugh out loud, Shala joining in.

They ate their breakfast in relative peace, Jonoh casting little furtive glances at Shala, still not convinced that he was actually with her. When they'd finished, he took the cutlery and crockery out to the washpot, cleaning and drying them, placing them back in the racks.

He went back to his tent, slipping through the flap, tying it off behind him. He turned around and there was Shala, head propped up on one arm, alluring smile on her face.

"Care to join me in a little morning exercise my love?" She pouted out a sensual smile, a little lick of the lips accompanying it.

It took Jonoh a matter of seconds to remove his apparel, flopping down next to her, kissing her passionately, losing himself in her allure.

After they had finished, they laid on their backs, heaving in great gulps of air, beads of sweat covering their bodies. She always left him breathless but never more so than when they had finished making love. He turned his head and just soaked her in, her perfect form rising and falling gently, tiny little rivulets of moisture running down her ribs.

"Shala. I am going to find Master Cerwin. I do not like the way he has isolated himself and I need his guidance. I know I am meant to be some sort of leader but I am not yet ready. Will you come with me?"

"You know I will Jonoh, although I'm not sure how much use I will be. Strategic planning is not really a part of my skillset." She brushed loose hair covering his eyes to one side and laid her head to rest on his slowly rising chest.

"It's you I need Shala, not your expertise. You calm me, help me find my centre. You occupy every moment of my thoughts but strangely at the same time you help me focus on the problem at hand. I don't know how but I've come to rely on you in all things."

She lifted her head and looked him straight in the eye. "I would not be without you Jonoh. Where you go, I will follow." She craned her neck and kissed him gently on the lips. "Let's get to it then."

It took a while to find Cerwin, he had secreted himself as far from sight as he could and no one knew or were prepared to say where he was. He had pitched his tent to the south of the camp, just in the shade of a little hillock, its shadow obscuring his presence.

He sat in its shadow, hunched up with no fire or any sustenance apparently. Shala had insisted on bringing some food and a cup of cheyro, as always proving to be right.

They walked over to the shadow-master and Jonoh could never remember him looking so browbeaten, appearing to look every bit of his age. Not one hundred and eighty-seven exactly but more of an old man than he ever imagined possible.

"Master." Jonoh called out gently, worried that if he startled him he may break.

"Ah Jonoh, how are you my boy? And I see you have brought a special surprise with you. How are you, my favourite girl?" Even in his diminished state, his charm never eluded him.

Shala leaned over the old shadow-master, reaching out to hug him. It brought a warm, contented smile to his face, something she seemed to do for everyone.

"I brought you some food and a little cheyro."

"I find my appetite is not what it once was." He offered a wan smile, but it looked what it was, weak.

"I insist, you must eat to keep up your strength." She gently placed her hand on his cheek, letting him know in no uncertain terms that she would brook no argument.

"As you wish," he conceded, picking up a piece of bacon, teasing it with his teeth, whilst drinking some cheyro. He seemed to perk up a little, Shala did that to people.

Jonoh sat on the floor opposite the old man, leaving it a few minutes for him to consume some food.

After a few minutes he cleared his throat.

"Master, we have missed your counsel and we must push on. I assume you have been keeping up to speed with the information coming in from Torbin Pale-skin?" Jonoh got straight to the point.

"We may not arrive before the enemy, so we must be prepared. There is also the question of the refugees. Given the state of relations with Darmat, I hardly think they'll be prepared to accommodate thirty thousand new mouths to feed." Jonoh looked at the shadow-master.

Cerwin looked downcast and ashen-faced, the guilt still burdening him. "I do not think that my judgement is as sound as I once believed it to be Jonoh. You will need to start taking some of these burdens on your shoulders now, regardless of your youth."

"I will do so Master as and when I need to, but your guidance will still be needed." Jonoh had a little bite to his words, a degree of impatience infusing them.

It seemed to shake Cerwin out of his misery, a look of embarrassment painting itself to his face. He sat a little more upright and his face seemed to regain a little of its colour. The pallor seemed to almost disappear before their eyes, a little spark returning to his eyes.

"My apologies Jonoh, Shala. I have been so consumed by my own guilt and misery that I forgot why I was here. Torbin has already posited a plan to settle the Green-landers in the Titan Gate's barracks. Whoever they cannot fit will need to bivouac in its shadow." All of a sudden Cerwin seemed to warm to his task, his thoughts spilling out in a flood.

"Darmat does not lay claim to the land east of the Great Silver Sea so the Green-landers could settle that. However an accommodation of some kind will need to be reached if they intend to fish. Darmat does consider the Great Silver Sea to be sovereign territory, so some form of tax is bound to be levied." The old man sat forward, chin in his hand as if that helped his thought processes.

"We will need to act as a bolster to their forces, reinforcing at the front line, where our skill at arms will be of most uses. In any siege it is necessary to launch the odd sortie, offer a counter for the enemy to deal with. Given the resources available I think the responsibility may well fall to us."

The old man almost sprang to his feet, the contrast to just a few minutes ago seeming impossible. There he was however, on his feet and beginning to pace, hands clasped behind his back, an intense set to his features.

"You were right Jonoh, we need to push on and we need to do it now." Cerwin closed his eyes and Jonoh heard his words in his mind. Instructions for all the gathered Orphans to pack up the tents and gather all the supplies they had. Cerwin was calling for an instant muster and there would be no stopping until they reached the Titan Gate.

"I must ask your forgiveness Jonoh. My rashness cost Bergin his life and my atrophy since we returned has cost us time we cannot afford." Cerwin stood in front of Jonoh and proffered a little bow.

"You do not owe me anything Master. The burden you carry has already proved beyond me, or we would not be having this conversation. You are a great leader and you are trying to take everyone's worries on your shoulders." Jonoh placed his hands on Cerwin's shoulders and offered a reassuring smile.

"Thank you, my boy. Right, no time to dawdle, we must move now." Cerwin turned to Shala.

"Thank you, Shala, you honour me. Could I ask you for a moment alone with Jonoh?"

"Of course Master. Jonoh, I will see you back at the tent." Shala turned and set off at a run back to the campsite.

Jonoh turned to Cerwin, a slight look of concern of his face.

"What do you need to talk to me privately about Master?" Jonoh and Cerwin walked slowly around the foot of the hillock, staying out of sight and hearing range of anyone else.

"Jonoh, we are going to defend the Titan Pass but we must be ready for all eventualities." Cerwin looked up to him, almost as if he were trying to gauge his feelings.

"What do you mean Master?"

"We have to consider all possibilities. At what point would our losses be too many? Do we fight to the last in some kind of glorious final stand or do we need to be prepared to negotiate or possibly even surrender?" Cerwin had stopped, placing himself directly in front of Jonoh. The conversation had flipped through one hundred and eighty degrees in a matter of moments and for the first time ever Jonoh doubted the words coming from his Master.

"Why are we even talking about negotiation or surrender. If we don't hold the H'Daree at the Gate, they will have free and unfettered access to the Known World. They could attack in any direction and roll over the Free Territories, picking every nation off, one at a time." Jonoh's surprise poured out of him. He made no effort to mask it.

"There are larger questions Jonoh, and you are at the centre of everything. Your death would be a loss from which we could not recover. A negotiation cannot be summarily dismissed." Cerwin was speaking the words but Jonoh did not feel the truth of it. It was as if he was withholding something and the discomfort it was causing Jonoh was making him lose his composure.

The way Cerwin went from despondency to invigorated, energetic leader in a matter of seconds didn't sit right. Something was awry but he couldn't put his finger on it. Jonoh felt caution for the first time ever in his master's company and he didn't feel safe sharing his doubt with anyone.

"As you say Master. Maybe we should put these concerns aside for the moment and concentrate on the task at hand?" Jonoh found himself having to disseminate his thoughts for fear that Cerwin may pick up on them.

"Yes, of course Jonoh, quite right. I will pack up my kit and see you back on the trail." Cerwin offered his wrinkled smile, apparently not having picked up on his worries.

Jonoh watched the little shadow-master walk away. It pained him deeply that he felt this pang of doubt, but he could not ignore it. More than at any point since his snap, he felt isolated, with nowhere to turn. He wished that he was wrong and tried to hold to the belief that it was a real possibility, but deep inside the thought would not go away.

"What is he hiding?"

Chapter Thirty-Two:

Hope endures

"Thank you, Lenny. For once I can actually say I owe my life to somebody and really mean it." Candor laughed, the first time he'd been able to do so without pain since the spear thrust had parted his skin.

"You're welcome me old cocker. Bit of luck, you gettin' back to 'ealth just in time to organise firty fousand refugees." Lenny White put his head back and roared out a laugh, clapping Candor on the shoulder before riding ahead through the Gate.

Candor was well enough to sit up in his flatbed, he was ready to walk in truth, Lenny's ministrations having worked miracles. For such a seemingly rough and ready individual he had remarkably skilled hands. The infection and its accompanying redness had gone, and the stitch work was as good as Candor had ever seen. He felt nearly ready to get back to normal, although a little stiffness persisted. To be expected all things considered.

All the refugees were flooding through the Gate, but thirty thousand would take a bit of time. Torbin had sent a rear-guard of three hundred infantry out into the valley. There had been no contact with or sign of the H'Daree but Torbin wasn't taking any chances. The man who led them had shot him a baleful glare, but hadn't stopped to say anything. He was a big, fierce-looking chap and his men obviously looked up to him, snapping out 'Yes sirs!' to any command he gave, all jumping to his commands without question. They looked well drilled, just what was needed for the coming fight.

He carefully slid off the flatbed, a little stab of pain in his side, but nothing compared to the pain he'd been dealing with. Torbin and his officers were directing traffic, those men that had fought and survived the H'Daree attack being separated out and billeted with the rest of his forces on the ground-floor barracks. Marye was at the centre of activities, moving the ill and wounded to the field hospital they had set up in one of the old dining blocks. He felt a well of pride watching her go to work, nobody questioning her directions.

Torbin had allocated the ground-floor barracks at the northern end of the Gate and all the rooms above them, reaching to the floor below the first embrasures. It would not accommodate all thirty thousand, but they had plenty of tents to set up along the treeline at the foot of the mountains. Not a perfect solution but one they could work with.

Torbin stood inside the Gate, Tivosi by his side. The stream of refugees seemed to go on forever,

"This is going to stretch us Guido. We really need Candor on his feet so that we can assign duties to his people. At the moment it's just a giant crowd, we need to find out who can do what. We need carpenters, smiths, builders, cooks and anyone with a skill set to work." Torbin contained his frustrations, offering smiles and welcomes to the Green-landers as they filed through the Gate.

"Let's get everyone in first Torbin." Guido looked over Torbin's shoulder and a smile crossed his face.

"What is it Guido?"

"It looks as if your wish is coming true my friend." He nodded towards the reason for his optimism.

Torbin turned to see Candor walking gingerly towards them. He didn't look fully healed but considering the state he was in when they met in the Pass, he looked hale and hearty indeed.

"Candor my friend. It is good to see you looking so well." Torbin pulled him into a light embrace, scared to hug him so hard, lest he cause further injury.

"You too my friend. Good to see you as well Guido." Candor grasped Tivosi by the forearm in a happy reunion.

"Candor, I'm delighted Lenny worked his magic."

Candor lifted his shirt to show them both the healing wound.

"I have to give him my thanks Guido. I owe him my life after all."

"Nice work on the stitching as well. For a big, common lout, he has a light touch when it comes to putting people back together again." Tivosi laughed, while Torbin simply nodded his accord.

"Do you feel well enough to get involved Candor?" Torbin asked the question, knowing with reasonable certainty what the answer would be.

"Absolutely Torbin, what did you have in mind?" Candor put on his serious face, keen to be busy at least.

"I need you to select all the artisans and craftsmen you have. We need to start taking steps to provide for your people and provide all and any support to the defence that we can."

"Leave it to me Torbin. With Marye's help we will have our people ready by the end of the day." Candor nodded his agreement, keen to get to it.

"Marye is quite the lady, Candor. If there's been a better natural leader, I am yet to meet them." Torbin was genuine in his praise and Candor could see that.

"You should see her at home. I don't get away with anything." Candor gave a sheepish grin and Tivosi a roaring laugh.

"I will get to it straight away. It's nice to be useful again." He turned and headed towards Marye, glancing back over his shoulder. "I will see you both later."

Torbin watched him go, happy to see his old friend looking so much better.

"So when are you going to broach the subject of Jek then?" Tivosi raided his eyebrows in query.

"Let's leave that for the next strategy meeting Guido. Once everyone is through and things are settled down a little, we will call the officers together. Do you want to bring a second, just so that they are up to speed?" Torbin asked the question without saying 'In case we lose you', but Tivosi was a soldier, he understood.

"I'll bring Lenny. I think he's shown his colours." He nodded at Torbin, getting an approving dip of the head in response.

Torbin had called a strategy meeting in his tent, all officers in a command position in attendance. Terror ambled in looking full of himself. Torbin hadn't seen him since they had gone to help the Green-landers. He'd become the defenders' mascot, spending his time being fussed over by everyone but it would seem particularly Jadran. He sat himself down next to the young Lhossan officer and Torbin felt a little pang of jealousy.

He had set a circle of chairs, enough to accommodate all of them. Candor had brought Stannard and Rory along, Jadran and Jadson were Torbin's own command staff and Tivosi had Lenny White by his side. The last to enter the tent was Jek, the only reminder of the pitiful figure he'd cut when they first met him being the rat brand on his left cheek.

"Welcome Jek. You know everyone here apart from Candor, Rory and Stannard. They are the officers commanding the remaining Green-lander forces." Torbin waved his hand towards the empty seat.

Jek stood still rather than taking his seat, an aggressive set to his stance, staring dead-eyed at Candor.

"Candor Blackheart, the scourge of the Brotherhood of the Golden Hand." He spat the words out, not even trying to hide his enmity.

Jek stayed where he stood, almost shaking with rage. Torbin suddenly realised that he hadn't taken into account the level of hatred someone born to the Brotherhood would have for Candor. The Battle of the Shifting Sands was a horrifying and bloody loss for them. The tension in the tent was rising to boiling point, everybody sat forward, waiting for the inevitable explosion.

Suddenly Jek lurched towards Candor, fists balled, ready to strike. Candor went to get up, no spring available to him, but before they came into contact, Tivosi flew out of nowhere, crashing sideways into Jek, knocking him to the floor. Terror growled out a warning, his hackles rising, but a hand from Jadran placed on his shoulder made him settle back.

"Well that's something I didn't think I'd see."

Jek struggled, trying to wriggle free of Tivosi's grasp. He was a big man, but not big enough. Tivosi held him pinned tight, his vice-like hold offering no room for movement.

"Let go of me, you fuckin' great ape. I'll fuckin' kill 'im!!" Jek's invective spat out of his mouth, verbal darts, full of venom. Tivosi held him fast, pinning him to the floor with his great muscled bulk.

"Jek! This is not the time for this. You must put aside your anger, we have bigger enemies to deal with." Torbin stepped forwards, palms up in peace.

"'E burnt thousands of me people in their ships. They tried t' surrender and 'e burnt 'em anyway!" He continued to struggle, hatred burning in his eyes, spittle flying from his lips.

"Lenny, get a few of your boys in here and put him in the brig until he cools down."

Lenny got up and left the tent, returning with three more of Tivosi's guard, big men all. Tivosi stood up, whispering something in Jek's ear, before handing him still struggling over to his men. They walked him out of the tent, still spitting angry jibes at Candor.

"I am so sorry; I should have thought about that and prepared a little better." Torbin spluttered out his words, a little shaken by the events that had passed in a flash.

"It was my actions that brought that about Torbin. I had no idea that you had any citizens of the Brotherhood. Their hatred for me is deep, a blood feud that will only end with my death." Candor leaned forward, head in his hands. He'd only just arrived and this was his contribution, the cause of division and anger.

"I know about vendetta Candor. Bloodspear has had a death marker on me for years. I killed his son and he nearly avenged him. I would be dead but for Tivosi and his men but I was doing what I thought was right, defending my home. It is difficult to see it from the other side, I will talk to Jek after he's had some time to calm down," Torbin looked at Candor with as much empathy as he could muster, Candor offering a weary tilt of his head in return.

"Okay, let's get back to business. Welcome everyone, Candor could you give us an accurate disposition of your people?" Torbin ceded the floor to Candor.

"Well, we have about fourteen hundred armed men. They are not really trained but all of them fought and survived the H'daree, so they have shown their grit. They will stand and fight again, happy to be surrounded by such hardy comrades I am sure." Candor nodded his acknowledgment to his peers.

"We are glad to have you with us Candor. Will you cede their command?" Torbin had to ask the hard question.

"Of course Torbin, we have to fight as one, not separate forces." Candor did not hesitate.

"We will give them as much training as time allows, but you have just met my sergeant at arms. Can you suffer them to be under his command?"

"I will if you can broker some kind of peace between us."

"Thank you Candor." Torbin was moved by his friend's humility, sacrificing his pride for the greater good.

"Can I ask why you appointed him as sergeant at arms Torbin?" Jadson rarely spoke up, so it took Torbin a little by surprise.

"I have a better idea. I think most people here would acknowledge that Guido Tivosi is probably the fiercest warrior here? No offence to anybody else." Torbin glanced across at Jadran and Cerwin.

"None taken." Jadran gave a little wave of his hand, as if the question should never have been asked.

"Guido my friend, would you care to give us your assessment?" Torbin ceded the floor with a gentle nod.

"Well, let us see. The Lhossan militia are expert at fighting from an elevated position, in confined spaces. A natural consequence, bearing in mind the architecture of Lhossa. The Golden Legions are implacable enemies, disciplined, resolute, fanatically loyal, their lockstep phalanxes nearly impossible to break. The Protectorate infantry is superbly trained and bolstered by the network of mind-walkers in their squad system, always able to relay orders in an instant." Tivosi sat forward, hands on his knees, really warming to the task. "The Murgan fight on horseback and on foot as many here know." He looked up at Torbin, Jadran and Jadson, the memory still obviously vivid for them all. "But when on foot are fierce and quite frankly scary. They fight as if in an enraged trance, but they have no discipline, much like the Snowbard ravagers." Tivosi looked around the chairs, letting his words settle, giving everyone a moment or two to think about things.

"To be a Brother of the Golden Hand means you are born to the life. You spend nearly all of your life on the deck of a ship and that is where you learn to fight. They learn to fight in tight formation, regardless of the conditions. Have any of you tried keeping your feet on the deck of a ship being tossed in a storm?" Tivosi looked up from under his eyebrows. "Think about that for a moment."

"Maybe we should dig out in front of the Gate and flood it?" Jadran looked about his peers. Everyone broke into great guffaws of laughter.

"By Andhonar's ghost, we needed that."

"Right gentleman, we need to discuss dispositions. Myself and Guido have put the following plan together, but if anyone has any objections or suggestions, now is the time. This is a forum my friends, and you are all here of your free will, so speak up if you feel the need." Torbin scanned the room, looking everyone in the eye. All nodded their agreement.

"We will place five hundred infantry at the entry gate. The tunnel is nearly fifty feet deep, so their numbers should count for little if they actually breach the Gate. Three hundred of Jek's best and two hundred of yours Candor?" Candor inclined his head.

"We will leave fifty archers in the gatehouse. They can deploy the boiling oil if they break through, those murder holes may be asked to live up to their name. Dropping the portcullis must be an absolute final measure. We will need to try to keep the Gate clear in order to launch sorties. If we do so we will need to lead them on horseback, the initial shock should disperse at least their front lines, so I'll give you one hundred Orphans as soon as they arrive." Torbin took a breath, partly to gather his thoughts but also in case anyone had something to say.

"Alright, the first embrasures are where we expect the brunt of the attack to land."

"Really? One hundred and fifty feet in the air when there is a gate at ground level?" Jadson, merely voiced what many were thinking.

"I know it sounds mad, but think about it. The only entrance is a twenty-foot high and wide three-foot-thick oak gate, banded with iron. It leads through to a tunnel nearly fifty feet deep and barely a foot wider, covered from above by murder holes, which would rain down all kinds of terror. A force of a fraction of the attacking strength could hold them almost indefinitely and the cost of lives would be unthinkable, even for the most fanatical of enemies." Torbin had their attention now.

"The first embrasures are at one hundred and fifty feet, and there are over one hundred of them. Candor will tell you that they are an extremely sophisticated enemy, with siege equipment I have never heard of, and numbers almost beyond imagination. They will come and when they do they will be prepared and capable." Torbin had stood up and was beginning to pace the circle. "If we are to hold them, we must be prepared to face an onslaught the like of which the Known World has rarely seen, at least not in recorded history." He didn't realise it, but he was shouting and gesticulating at everyone, like an angry schoolmaster berating his students.

He stood stock still in the middle of the circle and put his hands out, palms up in a gesture of peace. "I am sorry my friends, I should not raise my voice to you."

"If we can't 'andle a little shoutin', we're gonna be fucked when they start chuckin' spears." Everybody burst into fits of laughter, any tension leaking from the tent.

"Bless you Lenny."

Candor was new to this group, but could already feel the bonds, the camaraderie was obvious to anyone with eyes. He knew that before anything else that he had to make things right with Jek.

The laughter petered out, Tivosi patting Lenny on the back, White being the only person he'd seen take it without showing any signs of discomfort. He could see why Tivosi chose him as his number two.

"Anyway, we are going to station the bulk of our forces, fifteen hundred men, the balance of the Orphans and Jadran's militia included at the first embrasures with a two-man operating crew every other slot to fire our secret weapon." Torbin broke into a beaming smile. "They are not the only ones with a few tricks up their sleeves."

"Shaloh, would you please come in?"

From the back of the tent, the master smith entered carrying one of his artillery crossbows. He set it up in the middle of the tent and explained its function to everybody there, Torbin, Tivosi and especially Jadran, standing there with conspiratory grins on their faces. By the time he was finished he was treated like a conquering hero, everyone crowding in to congratulate him and slap him on the back. As he left the tent Torbin could swear he looked a foot taller.

"I thought you'd like that." Torbin beamed, the atmosphere in the room was flush with positivity.

"Right the last disposition is the top of the wall. Jadson you will take one hundred and fifty men, all with bows and defend the top of the wall on either end. We cannot discount any possibility here gentlemen, even them scaling the peaks in numbers and trying to flank us from above, whilst you are up there, you can rain a storm of arrows onto them. Fired from that height they will come down vertically, not as easy to shield against as arrows on a normal trajectory." Torbin looked to Jadson, who bowed his agreement, delighted to have his first proper command.

"The remainder of our forces will form a reserve, plugging gaps when they appear."

"In the meantime we need to get pits dug across the Pass's floor, fill them with spikes and caltrops. I will need everyone to join the effort, we will not man our posts until the enemy arrives. We need hunting parties, woodsmen and carpenters to start chopping down trees and making arrow shafts, spears, shields. Can we all get to it gentlemen?" Torbin stood and everybody understood that the meeting was over.

Everyone left the tent to set about their tasks, all apart from Candor.

"I need to go and see Jek Torbin. I must put this right, or at least convince him to put it aside, if only until this is done." Candor's shoulders were slightly slumped and Torbin couldn't tell if it was because of this or his obviously reduced physical state. Nonetheless he completely agreed with his friend.

"I'll take you to the brig." Torbin ushered his friend from the tent and headed in the direction of the brig.

The Gate's shadow cast its wings across the mouth of the Pass, covering everything in shade. At least until the sun flew directly overhead in the middle of the day. As they walked Torbin glanced about and noticed Lenny White sauntering over to a group of ladies. Out of all the people here, they seemed the only ones without purpose. They all fluttered their eyelashes and acted coy around Lenny, Torbin had noticed that he had that effect on most women. He looked across at Candor, raising his eyebrows as if to say 'What's that all about?'.

"Ladies of the Silk, plus Lenny. What do you expect?"

"Ahh, of course." Torbin just nodded and quickened his pace towards the brig.

It was far larger than Candor expected, twenty barred cells in a block on the first floor, right at the end of the Gate. Only one had the barred door locked. Jek pacing up and down like a caged animal. Torbin went to speak to him first, so Candor stepped back, staying just out of sight. He couldn't really catch all of the exchange but it was heated, and it took at least ten minutes before Jek lowered his voice and seemed to calm down.

Torbin walked slowly out of the cell block, gently placing his hand on Candor's shoulder. "I've done my best."

Candor walked past Tivosi's guards until he reached Jek's cell. Jek was stood, arms folded, a baleful glare on his face.

"I need to talk to you Jek." Candor extended his hands, palms up in a gesture of peace.

"What? About all o' my people that you murdered?" A twisted little grin fixed to his face. Nothing friendly there.

"The Brotherhood was invading my homeland Jek and we had to stop them. If they'd captured the Bountiful Isles they would have taken the deep water harbours and taken control of the Grey Ocean. It's no secret that the Brotherhood's great floating city cannot be sustained forever and that they want land to settle." Candor took a deep breath, knowing he had to find a way to make some kind of peace.

"I was a much younger man back then, more hot-headed and rash. I felt we had to make a statement, ensure that the Brotherhood didn't ever attempt an invasion again. Looking back I could have done things differently." Candor was tiptoeing along, desperately trying to find a compromise. It wasn't working.

"What? Like not burning 'em alive in their ships. You burnt 'em to the water line an' put t' the sword all those that tried t' escape. Would you 'ave done that differently?" Jek had pressed up to the cage, his knuckles white, hands grasping the bars as if he felt he could rip them from the walls.

Candor knew he had to change tack. "Jek, what is coming will be the end of everything we know, unless we hold them here. To do that we need every able-bodied soul to do what is needed, and we need you more than most. I need to put my men in your charge and they will never follow the man that killed me." He breathed in again, taking a full measure of air, closing his eyes and centring himself. "We have to put any enmity aside until this is over. If we both survive I promise you satisfaction, if that is what you still want."

Candor held out his hand and Jek put his through the bars, grasping it tightly and nodding his assent.

"'Till after."

Candor turned and slowly walked out of the cell block, motioning on his way to Tivosi's guards to set Jek free.

Torbin reached the southern end of the Gate and looked up to see Jadran, Tivosi and Shaloh Torm huddling together, discussing something of great import by the look of things. He ran up the stairs to the forge and made his way over to the little group.

"Torbin, welcome. We could use your insight as Tivosi and myself are having a friendly disagreement about the allocation of resources." Jadran ushered Torbin into their tight-knit conspiracy.

"Please, enlighten me." Torbin absentmindedly scratched an itch on his nose, looking at Jadran to start.

"Well, Torm informs us that he is running out of metal to forge." Jadran paused for a moment.

"Okay, and?" Torbin held his gaze for a second, impatience almost creeping in.

"Well, I believe that we need to consider how best to allocate people. We have no miners in our numbers but there are some amongst the Green-landers. They have been mining ore on the far eastern Titans for generations. There are also fishermen, hunters, carpenters, farmers, woodsmen. I am sure you get my point." Jadran held his tongue for a moment, but as no one spoke decided to plough on.

"We need to allocate some resources to these kinds of tasks now, but Guido believes that we should put every able-bodied man to the task of defending the Gate, at least until the battle is over." Jadran took a breath, a little red-faced for having hogged the floor quite so much.

"I understand both arguments my friends and I believe you are both right. As you know I have already asked Candor to set his people to various tasks and to separate out his skilled workers. However when the time comes it will need every hand to the pump." He nodded to both Jadran and Tivosi, as if to say, 'That's it for now.' "I think it deserves further discussion but for the moment we need to look to our disposition. Shaloh, what is the state of things where armaments are concerned?" Torbin looked to the master smith who, as always, seemed a little uncomfortable addressing those that were his betters only weeks previously.

"We have made fifteen hundred banded shields and spears Torbin, and about five thousand arrows. We found a carpentry workshop with benches, and unbelievably some tools still intact on the second floor. There were a couple of experienced fletchers in the Lhossan muster, so we put them to work and they are making shafts for arrows and spears as we speak, as well as feather fletchings. It would seem there is an abundance of wild turkeys in the forests." Torm looked about as if seeking approval or permission to carry on.

"How about swords and billhooks?" Torbin prompted Torm to continue.

"Well there are two billhooks per embrasure and so far, about two hundred swords. The problem is, as Jadran stated, a lack of metal to work. Also swords take much longer to forge and the folding process is difficult and time consuming." Torm lowered his head slightly as if expecting a rebuke.

"You are doing magnificent work Shaloh and many will owe you their lives by the end of this." Jadran and Tivosi voiced their agreement, patting the smith on the shoulder in reassurance.

"Well gentlemen, I believe we are in good shape. Jadran and Tivosi's forces are already well-armed, and Candor's people seem to have rescued much of their arms and armour. The Orphans will be well equipped so I believe we can arm every fighting man with some to spare." Tivosi joined the others in patting Torm on the back.

"Keep forging for as long as you can Shaloh my friend, but just spear and arrow heads from now on."

Torm nodded and left them, walking backwards with a

deferential dip of the head. It was getting better but Torbin supposed it would take longer still for most of the Lhossan slaves to adjust to freedom.

"Can I ask you both to start seeing to our positions? There are a few things I need to take care of."

Jadran and Tivosi both nodded their accord, Tivosi absolutely beaming at the prospect of battle. As much as he'd grown close to the great bear of a man, he still frightened Torbin, but in a good way.

"At least he's on our side."

He looked over his shoulder and saw Candor descending the steps from the brig and making his way over to one of the cooking fires. He descended the steps from the forge and started to make his way towards Candor. The hustle and bustle taking place reminded him of Market Square in Lhossa, the buzz of activity creating an atmosphere, almost giving it a life of its own.

He could see Candor clearly, sitting on a stool next to a cookfire, big kettle pot bubbling away, steam rising into the air. As he got close, he could see Candor was sitting with Marye, they were holding hands and sharing a moment, her caressing his face, him leaning in to kiss her tenderly on the lips. He thought about turning round, not wanting to disturb them when Marye caught sight of him. She stood straight up, hiking her skirts and marching purposefully towards him.

She stopped and placed herself right in front of him, hands on hips, a stern set to her face. He stopped stock still, unconsciously leaning back a fraction, not wanting to receive another of her stinging slaps to the face.

Suddenly she burst into a beaming smile, almost leaping off the ground to throw herself around his shoulders, squeezing him tight in an all-consuming hug. She pulled back a fraction, giving herself room to plant a kiss on his cheek.

"Thank you for all you have done for my people, and especially my Candor." She held his face in her hands, tears welling in her eyes, her smile shining through it all. "Bless you Torbin Pale-skin. I will leave you two to talk." And with that she planted another kiss on his cheek and marched off see to whatever needed seeing to.

As she walked away a small herd attached itself to her, asking questions, seeking instruction. She was a leader all right, one of the most natural ones Torbin had ever seen.

He sat next to Candor on Marye's vacated stool.

"She is quite something." Torbin said it matter of factly, as if everyone accepted it as true.

"That she is Torbin."

"You're a lucky man my friend."

"I know."

Torbin was happy for his friend but felt a certain angst, his heartstrings being plucked, the absence of Jadzia causing a little melancholy.

He didn't realise that he was sitting with his head slightly bowed, lost in thought. Candor reached across and put a hand on his shoulder.

"Missing your lady? Jadzia wasn't it?"

"Yes my friend, I am. Especially when I see what I miss right in front of me with others. But please ignore my maudlin nonsense, I don't mean to bring you down. I genuinely could not be happier for you Candor." Torbin looked away, wanting to hide his embarrassment.

"Thank you Torbin. You will see her soon enough; I am sure of it." Candor gave his shoulder a little squeeze.

"Do you want some stew? It's pretty good. They're still using the horse, but in fairness it's kept quite well."

"Thank you, that would be good." Torbin realised he hadn't eaten since yesterday; his rumbling stomach had been trying to remind him all day.

Candor got up, and dipped two wooden bowls in the stew, a little of it slopping over the sides as he turned back to the stools.

"Here you g…"

"Torbin Pale-skin, Candor Blackheart, Jonoh Shipwright and all mind-walkers gathering at the Titan Gate hear us. We are the H'Daree and we are coming. We offer you this one opportunity to lay down your arms and acknowledge our supremacy. Join us and you will be spared, defy us and you will all perish."

Candor dropped the bowls, stew splashing up his breeches. He looked across at Torbin, who ran his hand over his face, signalling to put their blocks up. Torbin could feel what Candor had told him, that they communicated as a group but with one spokesman at a time, any one of them able to pick up the conversation from where it had ended. You never knew who that would be.

"We must engage them Candor, find out any information we can that may be of use. If they have any weaknesses, any chinks in their armour, we must look for them. Let's try not to provoke them overly, keep them engaged for as long as we dare."

"We will not surrender to any invader. You are not welcome here, and you will find us hard to dislodge. We are dug in and we are ready for you." Torbin tried to keep it defiant but without being too provocative, keep them engaged.

"Ahh, the great Torbin Pale-skin, the Great Defender. We know who you are and we salute you. You dismiss our offer but we fail to understand why. All of the lands outside of your 'Known World' are now H'Daree. We have banished hunger, poverty and war; at least behind us. We seek only the H'Dar, paradise if you will, the birth right of humanity. But humanity cannot reach its goal unless all are united, all march together. We will crush any who hold us back and continue the fight until what is left of mankind are together. Then we shall ascend."

Torbin could feel the truth of it. This wasn't so much a religious fervour or dogma, it was more like a moral certainty, a commitment to a tenet, one that overrode everything else. They weren't bragging, just telling an absolute truth as they saw it, and they genuinely couldn't understand why anyone would resist.

"Your beliefs are not shared here. This is a world of varying nations, independent from each other, and all will resist you and drive you back into the sea." Torbin tried to sound resolute but he could sense the derision coming from the H'Daree.

"Like the Green-lands and the vaunted twin cities of Minari and Turan? Their pitiful resistance lasted a matter of hours when put to the test. We ran them off their lands like unwelcome squatters, their efforts to withstand us swatted away like flies. I hope you have a little more to offer than butchers and bakers with sticks. We were looking forward to some exercise ha-ha!"

The laughter rankled, cutting close to the bone and before he could counsel him, Torbin watched as Candor exploded with rage,

"We had enough to bring down your little wall of energy though, did we not? I would say that the hundreds of H'Daree left for dead on

the streets of Minari and Turan speak to a different picture. You treated it like a game, but you forced a whole nation from its homeland, killing everyone in your path and then belittle that loss? There is a price to pay, and no matter how long it takes, one day you will pay it!"

Candor screamed out the words in his mind, his anger overwhelming him.

The response was no less dark, a flat malevolent tone responding to his words.

"Candor Blackheart, for you there will be no mercy. You killed our brother, one of The Chosen, and for that the penalty is execution. We will find you and make you suffer the most agonising of deaths for your blasphemy. We will avenge his death and wipe all memory of you from the face of the world. There will be no place for you or your loved ones to hide." The words came out flat and level, ominous in their lack of emotion, matter of fact; just another task to accomplish.

Torbin knew that nothing said would change a thing now.

"Then we will meet you on the field and watch your army smash itself to death on our walls. We await your pleasure." Torbin laced his thoughts with as much malice and threat as he could muster. The pieces were in play now and there would be no turning back.

"We are coming and there will be no mercy and no escape. We are the H'Daree, we are bound by glorious purpose and led by the All Father's guiding hand. He returns to the lands of his ancestors and will not be denied. Our time is at hand and all that rise against us will be ground to dust!"

Torbin and Candor did not need to raise their blocks. They both knew with a certainty that they would not hear from the H'Daree again until they were at the Gate.

Chapter Thirty-Three:

Drawing close

"We are coming and there will be no mercy and no escape. We are the H'Daree, we are bound by glorious purpose and led by the All Father's guiding hand. He returns to the lands of his ancestors and will not be denied. Our time is at hand and all that rise against us will be ground to dust!"

Jonoh reigned in his horse, turning to look at Cerwin. Neither of them had spoken, trotting aimlessly forward whilst they listened to the exchange. They both looked around at the Orphans and realised that they had all been under the same spell.

They dismounted. Looking a little befuddled, it took a moment or two for them to find their bearings.

"We are close to the Gate now Jonoh, only a day or so's ride away. Let us make camp and give ourselves a little time to think and rest our minds." Cerwin turned aside, leading his mount to a little copse of trees, tying it off. He didn't say anything, just wandered off, head bowed in private contemplation.

Jonoh walked his own mount over and tied it off next to Cerwin's. He unloaded the feedbag and looped it over his horse's head, doing similarly for Cerwin's. It wasn't like the old man to forget to tend to his mount, not like him at all. He really did look like he had he weight of the world on his shoulders.

Jonoh could understand the distraction. The mind-walker contact was powerful. It may only have been a single voice but there was a multitude behind it, almost as if it was many speaking as one, but all interchangeable. They were sophisticated and determined. It wasn't a religious belief but more a conviction; a moral certainty and they would not be gain-said. There would be no negotiation. They knew this already but getting that sense of implacable certainty, that immovable resolve, just confirmed it.

Jonoh sat cross-legged, with his back against the tree trunk, leaned his head back and closed his eyes. He heard her and didn't need to open his eyes to know who it was.

She stroked his hair, running her hand down his face, leaning in and placing a gentle peck on his lips.

"How are you lover?" She slid down the tree next to him, resting her head on his shoulder.

"A little winded, metaphorically at least." He opened his eyes and offered her a wan smile. By Andhonar's ghost she was beautiful. "Do you think everyone heard?"

"By the way everyone suddenly went silent and started mooching about I would think so,"

"How do you think they knew my name? Not Cerwin, but me. Him I'd understand but how could they know about me? I'm not exactly renowned, a famous warrior or anything really. It doesn't make any sense, not unless someone is passing information. The other possibility is far more frightening." Jonoh stared off into the middle distance, not seeming to focus on anything.

"What other possibility?" Shala furrowed her brow, preparing for a blow, as if she was worried about the answer.

"That one of our number is responsible. We have to accept the possibility that there is a traitor in our midst. How much do you know about our Orphan friends?" Jonoh felt a little awkward asking the question, but knew he had to ask it.

"About as much as I know about you." She looked a little defensive for the first time, it made him feel instantly guilty, and a little hurt.

"Really?" Jonoh couldn't hide the sting. He couldn't ever hide his feelings from her.

"Well not really, but you know what I mean. What do any of us really know about each other? If you start to think that way, we have over five hundred suspects." Her wide-eyed look was all he needed to see.

"I know, but at the moment I feel that you are the only person I can trust."

"What do you mean? Surely you don't have any doubts about Master Cerwin?" Shala's defences seemed to intensify, for the first time feeling to Jonoh as if she was measuring her words with him. It made him feel very low, but what choice did he have?

"Have you not noticed changes in him? His moods seem to swing wildly, from manic enthusiasm to hangdog despair. He's not the same person I knew. He has always been my rock, now I feel as if I am carrying him more and more." Jonoh knew that there wasn't exactly solid proof of any misdeeds but he couldn't help that itch in the back of his mind.

Shala sat forward, arms wrapped around her shins, in a little bubble of contemplation.

"I hadn't really given it any thought. I just assumed it was a natural reaction to what happened with the Darmations. He blames himself for Bergin's death and the fact that any chance of support from Darmat was ruined." She sat back a little, looking as if a sudden realisation had dawned on her. "Are you saying that there was some kind of deliberation at work?" She glanced sideways at Jonoh, trying to hide how shocking the thought was. She failed miserably.

"Now you can see what I've been struggling with. The thought of it sends shudders down my spine, and as unlikely as it is, I have to consider it." Jonoh sighed out, as if an exhalation of breath would set the world to rights. It didn't.

"The more I think about it, the more it concerns me." Jonoh paused, weighing up the risks of what he was saying, but it didn't stop him saying it. "He was the one who warned us for the entire length of our journey there, to be careful and reserved in everything we said and did." His breath deepened, almost hyperventilating, as if scared he would run out of air. "And yet he lost his composure very quickly. There was no provocation that prompted it, not really. Prince Lor was arrogant and dismissive, but he didn't exactly poke the bear. I haven't sat down and thought about in any real detail because it happened so fast." Jonoh shook his head, trying to free himself of such dark thoughts. "But there just doesn't seem to be any justification for it. None that I can think of anyway."

"Nobody's perfect my love. Anyone can make a mistake."

"That's true, but not someone of Cerwin's skill and experience, especially as that was why we were there. Add that to all his warnings and I just don't know." Jonoh shifted, sitting cross-legged, sideways on, encouraging Shala to do the same. She did.

"Have you not noticed a marked change in him since we came back?" Shala looked him in the eye, a gentle little nod confirming that she had.

"It's like a mixture of mild paranoia, as if he's trying to mask something. Then there's the extraordinary shifts in temper, switching in a moment, turning through one hundred and eighty degrees in a heartbeat." Again a moment of hesitation. "I can't read him anymore. It's almost like he's deliberately blocking me. I'd never felt the need to look, but it's something I have felt once before, albeit with a different person." The more he thought about it, the more it bothered him.

"You're the only person I feel I can fully trust, but we cannot alert him. Just continue being the lovely, affectionate person you have always been to him." Shala smiled warmly, a slightly wan smile accompanying her assent. "Also, I could be wrong, and this might just be false speculation on my part. We must tread carefully."

Shala leaned forward and held him in a gentle embrace. He pulled her in more tightly and they sat there for a while, taking comfort in each other.

After a little while, Jonoh kissed Shala goodbye, the pair of them arranging supper together and walking slowly back towards camp hand in hand before Jonoh pulled away to go and seek out Cerwin.

Jonoh walked for a little while, the landscape on the northern edge of the Red Desert being dotted with scrubby copses of mean, small trees. He found Cerwin sitting at the base of one, hat pulled down over his eyes, shutting out the world around him.

The old man tipped his hat back, revealing his face. Jonoh thought he'd never seen him look older. It was as if the strain of whatever it was he was going through, was beginning to suck the very moisture out of his wrinkled skin.

"Are you feeling all right Master?" Jonoh sat down next to him and gently laid a hand on his shoulder. In spite of everything he still had a great well of affection for the old shadow-master.

"Thank you Jonoh, I find myself a little drained but I am feeling a little better. I apologise if my behaviour has been a touch confusing recently. I have needed a little time to shake off certain doubts and take a look at myself and my actions." Cerwin had a look of genuine regret and sorrow. It tugged at Jonoh's heartstrings but at the same time made him feel a little defensive. It was as if Cerwin had read his emotions and keyed into his doubts. He kept his counsel and did not respond, just offering a small nod.

"I cannot forgive myself for my outburst at the parley with the Darmations." He leaned forward, putting his elbows on his knees, clasping his hands and looking at his feet. It looked like a conscious effort to control his emotions but still caused a little tickle at the back of Jonoh's mind.

"I keep going over and over it in my mind. How did I let my guard down; allow myself to be goaded by that puffed up little peacock? And Bergin? I was growing so fond of him. He was developing into a fine young man, and an admirable leader. The thought of him plagues my thoughts, and that is a large part of the reason I have withdrawn a little. I am not sure I trust my judgement anymore." The old man's head dipped even further, the weight of his guilt seeming to make it heavier and heavier.

Jonoh gently shook Cerwin's shoulder making him sit a little more upright and look at him.

"We are all fallible, all capable of mistakes. You were bearing everyone's burdens, mine included. You have brought us this far and we will still follow you." Jonoh pushed his doubts aside, the grief apparent on Cerwin's face making him feel a great well of sympathy.

"It is not me we should follow anymore, it is you. I know the burden of leadership fills you with doubt, but you are ready my boy. It is your time to stand up and be what you are. The most gifted of his and probably any other generation. Everything you have practised and experienced in the last year have led you to this point. You are ready, and all here will follow your lead." Cerwin fixed him with a heartfelt look.

Jonoh's face could not hide his bewilderment, he was not

prepared for this.

"I know my moods have been shifting, like autumn weather, but what happened has cut me to the quick. I think if I had undertaken something like this a hundred years ago I would have coped admirably, but at my age now? I will always be beside you should you need my advice but I have to take a lesser role now. I am a Master of Shadows after all so that is where I will be best placed I think."

Cerwin's words felt so earnest and genuine that he wanted to believe him wholeheartedly but knew a pinch of doubt was still necessary. The timing of it, just what he wanted to hear at the moment of his greatest doubt?

The look of angst on Cerwin's face made him put it aside for the moment and he reached out and pulled the old man into a hug, and for once Cerwin did not resist.

They took their time walking back to the main camp, the afternoon sun blazing overhead but just starting its descent.

They reached the first cookpot, Shala standing there stirring the pot, laughing with Jonoh Mason and a few of the other Orphans. Cerwin threw Jonoh a little sideways look from under the brim of his hat.

"You have found yourself quite the girl Jonoh." His impish little grin creasing his wrinkled face.

"Oh I know Master." Jonoh flushed a little red, pulling his hat slightly forward to cover his embarrassment.

"Jonoh, Master Cerwin." Shala called out, passing the ladle to Jonoh Mason and trotting over to them.

She planted a kiss on Master Cerwin's cheek, giving him a little squeeze, the old man giving her a little coy chuckle in return.

She turned away from him and wrapped her hands around his shoulders, kissing him passionately. She laid her head on his shoulder and whispered into his ear, "Is everything all right my love?"

"Yes darling. I may have been mistaken but let's wait and see."

"As you wish."

"Come Master Cerwin, Jonoh. Let us eat." Shala ushered them over to the cookpot, stools laid out around it. Jonoh Mason handed out bowls of stew to all who were there, everyone sitting down, sharing food and comradeship. The mood felt really upbeat, despite what they all knew they were marching toward. There was a sense of tight community that Jonoh had never experienced before, a sense of togetherness drawn closer by who they were. Orphans all, mind-walkers, gifted and for most of their lives alone and living in secret. Now they were in the open and all together and the feeling was intoxicating.

For the first time in what seemed like an age Jonoh saw Master Cerwin relaxed, laughing and joining in the banter. It gave him a sense of comfort and pushed those negative feelings to the back of his mind.

Cerwin got up, having a little stretch, yawning his contentedness.

"Jonoh, would you be so kind and escort me back to my tent?" Cerwin smiled out his invitation.

"Of course Master." He leaned across to Shala, giving her a light touch on the lips. "I won't be long darling."

She gave him her most alluring smile. "Looking forward to it sweetheart," giving his buttock a nice squeeze as he turned to follow the old shadow-master.

Apart from the odd sentry there was no one about, everyone having broken for food.

"Jonoh, I did still want to talk to about something." Cerwin walked, hands clasped behind his back, pace nice and leisurely, taking his time as if wanting to place his words carefully.

"Please Master, continue." Jonoh matched his pace, enjoying the quiet peace that seemed to settle at evening time everywhere he had ever been.

"We spoke about it previously, but I feel the need to broach the subject again."

"Please Master." Jonoh felt a little knot in his stomach, fear about what was going to be said.

"There is still the issue of alternative strategies. With what we are facing we must accept the possibility that we cannot win." Cerwin spoke gently. It felt to Jonoh as if he was trying to sound like he wasn't pushing a particular agenda. Once again hackles went up in Jonoh's mind.

"I don't understand why you would bring this subject up now

Master, just as we are about to arrive at the wall. Why put any kind of doubt in my mind. We have spoken so many times about the vital nature of this mission. Has it become any less important for us to hold them at the Gate? Are you suggesting a fall-back strategy? Darmat is no longer an option and as far as I'm aware no one has approached the Murgan for support." Jonoh tried to keep his response level but he could hear the agitation in his own voice.

"I am suggesting that we have not attempted any negotiation with The H'Daree, or considered how to protect you if things go ill." Cerwin had stopped walking and stood his ground. It seemed as if he wanted to force the argument, here and now.

"Negotiation? Are you being serious? What potential for negotiation have the H'Daree given anyone up to this point? Surrender or conquest is the nature of their negotiation." Jonoh's frustration leaked out, his inability to control his annoyance blatantly obvious.

"We have to consider all possibilities Jonoh, plan for all contingencies." If Jonoh didn't know better he'd have thought Cerwin was begging.

"I will suffer the same fate as everyone else willing to give their lives to defend the Gate, Master." Jonoh turned and strode back towards the campfire and the solace of Shala's company. He did not look back.

"Jonoh!" Cerwin called out, a touch of desperation in his voice but Jonoh would not be swayed, the disquiet in his mind adding to his urgency.

He reached the cookfire in minutes, gently clutching Shala by the elbow and leading her out of earshot.

"Listen my love, my worries have not been assuaged. There is something off, something different about Master Cerwin. I still can't get a read on him, no sense of emotion or feeling. I've always been able to get a sense of how he was set mentally and I've never had to search for it, it just accompanied our exchanges. I know that sounds vague, I really do, but know I find myself reaching and it's just a blank. It's as if he's put a wall up and all he seems focused on is finding a way out of what's coming. For me at least. It makes no sense." Jonoh moaned out a feeble breath, at a loss how to proceed.

"Then you must keep your own counsel Jonoh, and the rest of us will follow you." Shala stood on her toes, gently kissing his cheek.

"Keep my own counsel."

Chapter Thirty-Four:

The walls are closing in

Wane left quietly, cracking the door and looking carefully before he sneaked out, a furtive glance over his shoulder the only goodbye Sorkin needed. He laid still, his chest rising and falling slowly, keeping his breathing quiet, almost frightened that if he made any noise he'd be found out.

Found out. The fear hit him like a wave, a sense of nausea overwhelming him. He doubled up, heaving over his bedsheets, unable to make it as far as the chamber pot under his bed. What had he done? Had anybody seen Wane leave? Had anybody seen him arrive and not leave the same day? What about Matoc? Could he trust his silence? He knew the consequences, everybody did, it was common knowledge. Public execution, and given his station and the sense of betrayal it would generate, probably a long drawn out public execution. He went to throw up again, mainly bile this time, having emptied his stomach the first time.

"Master." Matoc's voice accompanied by a knock on the door.

"Matoc, give me a moment." His voice was scratchy and nervous sounding. His head spun a little as he went to get up, a little sideways stumble only stopped by the bedpost.

"Why did I drink. What was I thinking?"

He grabbed a robe off the changing screen and half-walked, half-staggered to the door, pulling it open, trying to show a little dignity. He failed miserably.

"Master, is everything all right. May I be of assistance?" The old retainer stared down, not breaking protocol, awaiting Sorkin's response.

"I found myself a little overcome with some kind of brief malady. I'm ashamed to say that I have soiled my bedsheets Matoc." Sorkin mirrored the old slave, too embarrassed to look up for fear of seeing any look of disappointment in his face.

He needn't have worried.

"Leave it to me Master. I have drawn you a bath and there is fresh water and juice in the living area. Would you like something to eat? Something light maybe Master? Just some pastries, nothing to cause your stomach any further issues?"

Matoc stood still, eyes cast down, awaiting his Master's consent.

"Thank you Matoc, what would I do without you?" Sorkin regained a little of his composure. "What did you witness last night?" He blurted the question out, instantly regretting it.

"Nothing of any note Master. Nothing that your humble servant would ever talk to anyone about." He kept his head bowed, still waiting for permission to get about his duties.

Sorkin felt a little weight lift from his shoulders, he should have known that he could rely on him.

"Thank you old friend, as always." He gave the old man a gentle squeeze on the shoulder. Matoc smiled taking it as approval to carry on. He scuttled into the bedchamber and began gathering up the sheets. Sorkin walked over to his bathroom, sliding out of his gown and lowering himself into the ornate golden bath, the water just hot enough to bear.

He laid there, sliding under the water, eyes closed, immersing himself completely. The thought of Wane caused him to smile and shudder at the same time. The last time he'd been with a man was when he'd accompanied Prince Imber on a slave-buying negotiation to Lhossa, finding time to visit a pleasure house. It gave him some relief but was clinical, as pretty and perfumed as the young man had been. He'd been a slave and was doing what he had to in order to survive. Wane was a completely different case in point.

It was wonderful, so passionate and sensual. He wasn't sure he'd ever felt like that and it frightened him. He was scared that he wouldn't be able to hide his feelings, worried he'd give himself away. If Kaif and Lor could spot a fraction of a second when Cerwin brushed the Gift, could they not sniff out a dalliance between two men? To lay with a man broke a cardinal law and was punished mercilessly, but add in who it involved and you'd be looking at a showcase. It scared him even more because Wane would be considered risqué at best, indiscreet at worst and any indiscretion could cost him his life.

He climbed out of the bath, feeling physically clean at least. As he stepped on the reed mat his head began to thump. He suddenly remembered why he chose not to drink anymore, the enveloping headaches, dry mouth and roiling stomach. A brief pleasure for a lot of discomfort, still not worth it in his opinion.

Matoc had laid out a change of clothes for him, short-legged underwear, loose linen trousers and an open-necked silk shirt. Perfect light airy clothing, just what he needed given his reduced state. He wandered out onto his balcony to find that Matoc had laid out a breakfast spread. Iced water in a long-necked glass ewer, fruit juice, honeyed milk and a small selection of sweet pastries. Exactly what was needed, a spirit-lifting selection.

He poured himself a glass of honeyed milk and sat there nibbling on a pastry, taking it slowly, hoping his stomach would start to settle down. He looked out across the beautiful gardens and found himself wondering if he'd seen that particular gardener before. Was he a gardener? Was he there to spy, catch him in the act? Well one thing was certain, his paranoia wasn't going to leave him anytime soon.

He resolved to control himself in future, no more wallowing in self-pity, certainly no more drinking. He may have got away with it this time so there was no need to push his luck. The morning sun, sea breezes and aromatic scents wafting across his balcony were remarkably effective, his head clearing and his mind settling. If anyone had seen anything he would have been summoned. He stretched out, shaking the stress out of his body. Straighten up and do not take any more risks.

There was a knock at the door, breaking his train of thought and making him sit suddenly upright.

Matoc shuffled across the living area from the bedchamber,

opening the door, head bowed.

A Herald of the Crown entered, the usual formality observed, rolled, sealed scroll on a silver platter.

"You are summoned by General Kaif." The herald stood, all stiff formality.

"Please, give me a few moments to dress appropriately." Sorkin signalled Matoc to get a dress coat and some shoes.

"Can I get you something while you wait? A drink maybe?" Sorkin made the offer just as the herald turned on his heels, walking out and stationing himself in the hallway. He couldn't help but notice the look of distain on his face, as if being made to wait was equivalent to a slap in the face.

Matoc scurried across the room, soft leather slippers and a full-length woollen dress coat in his arms. He lent over slightly, allowing Sorkin to lean gently on his shoulder as he slid on the slippers. He pulled on the dress coat and made for the door.

"After you." He gestured to the herald who took off at a rapid pace, not quite trotting but at a very good clip.

He didn't have any time to think why he'd been summoned, probably a good thing, no point worrying about it. If it was anything serious he felt sure that he would have been arrested, not called for.

The herald marched down the corridors, past the turn for Inquisitor Malek's office and further into the bowels of the pyramid. Sorkin buttoned his dress coat as they walked, something he was becoming quite adept at. They continued for a few minutes until the herald stopped outside a double-doored entrance. He offered Sorkin a perfunctory bow and turned, walking back the way he came.

He knocked on the door. "Come in," General Kaif's deep voice boomed out.

Sorkin opened the doors and walked in, his breath catching in his throat. It was a large, relatively unadorned room, with a sizable, decorated table in the middle of it. There were three chairs on his side of the table, with a golden throne on a slightly raised platform on the other. Sat or rather slumped on one of the chairs was Wane, General Kaif stood behind one of the other ones, looking as if something was offending his nose. He really did not care for Wane at all.

"Advocate." General Kaif nodded acknowledgement.

Sorkin had gathered himself quickly. "General Kaif, Captain General Wane." He dipped his head to both men and stood where he was in anticipation.

The doors on the backside of the room suddenly swung open, two Golden Legionnaires standing to either side holding them open. Kaif prostrated himself and Sorkin dropped to one knee, head bowed. He glanced sideways and saw that even Wane was kneeling, head down, showing a real sense of respect.

Two beautiful, full-breasted female slaves entered, naked apart from thin golden belts, bowls of deep-red rose petals in their hands. They scattered them liberally and then stood to the side of the throne, behind them King Lorgan entered the room, looking every part the warrior king of renown.

"Leave us." Lorgan ushered the slave girls and legionnaires from the room and sat on the throne. He didn't care for finery in the same way as his son. His white trousers and shirt were more practical, still ornately embroidered with gold but with more of a soldier's cut. He had a shortsword sheathed at his waist and a small non-pretentious golden circlet on his head. It was his footwear that spoke to his character, old worn, leather riding boots, comfort not appearance driving his choice.

"Gentlemen, please sit." The three men all took their seats, meticulously observing protocol, eyes averted, waiting to be invited to speak before opening their mouths.

"Please, let us put aside formality while we are here together. Kaif my old friend, how do you fare?"

"I am well Majesty and it is an honour to be in your presence once again."

"So much for dropping the formality then." Lorgan let out a belly laugh, Wane and Sorkin joining him. Kaif, however, could just not escape a lifetime of worship and obedience.

"Sorkin it is good to see you." Sorkin bowed his head.

"You honour me, Majesty."

"And Captain General Mitter Wane. Your reputation precedes you. I thank you for your service." Lorgan nodded in Wane's direction, Sorkin catching the look of shock and disgust on Kaif's face.

"Majesty." Wane gave what for him would be considered his most formal bow. As Lorgan had said, so much for dropping formality. Hardly surprising though, not only was he the God King of Darmat, he was also a warrior of great fame.

"Gentlemen, you were all part of the diplomatic meeting with the Protectorate's representatives, although it appears my son's version of diplomacy was somewhat lacking. I need your honest assessment of what is happening to the east. It concerns me greatly that the threat seems to have been summarily dismissed." Lorgan waited for a response. "Kaif my old friend. What are your thoughts?"

"Majesty, I find it difficult to offer an opinion after a lifetime of service. My duty is to implement the royal house's orders, I am not sure my opinion has any value."

"It has value to me, old friend. What is said here will stay here." Lorgan leaned forward, his demeanour making it clear that he required a more fulsome answer.

"Majesty, my own operatives tell me that this incursion, these H'Daree are a real threat. They have already landed many tens of thousands of troops and completely over run the Greenlands. They are sophisticated and well prepared, having found a way to traverse the Great Storm Curtain points to their abilities." The old general took a breath, still uncomfortable offering his opinion. "They have deep water anchorage on the north side of the Bountiful Isles and have captured Minari and Turan. This is all observed from a safe distance, none of my agents have successfully infiltrated their numbers, but it appears they are preparing a vast force. I can only presume they plan to attack the Titan Gate and if they capture it they will have free rein to strike out at will." Kaif stopped, nervous that he may have said too much.

"Thank you my old friend. Captain Wane, would you please offer me your insight?" Lorgan turned to the mercenary.

"Majesty, I would echo all that General Kaif has told you. Tactically it would seem they follow a pattern. Overwhelm with numbers and then dig in, secure their internal lines and build up another, fresh, crushing force and move to the next objective. They do not seem like risk-takers, but meticulous planners." Wane stopped, nodding respect to Kaif. To Sorkin's surprise, Kaif reciprocated, a small nod being the first time he'd ever seen the old general acknowledge Wane.

"Advocate? You were at the meeting were you not?"

"Majesty, I do not share the expertise or insight of my colleagues but the representatives of the Protectorate seemed extremely eager to press these points. I have agents of my own and they have confirmed a lot of what has been said here. Also it would appear that the entire remaining population of the Greenlands have removed to the Gate, somewhere in the region of thirty thousand people." Sorkin slightly inclined his head, ensuring no direct eye contact was made.

"Thirty thousand? I am no fan of these godless fisheaters but that's only, what, half of their population?" Lorgan gripped the arms of his throne, a look of shock briefly settling on his face.

"I believe their losses have been fairly catastrophic, Majesty. Not to mention the loss of their ancestral lands." Sorkin felt the shock, never having put it into words before. It made it feel more real.

"Gentlemen, what are your recommendations?" Lorgan sat back, not so much relaxing as slightly slumping, trying to absorb the impact of what he'd just heard.

"Majesty, whatever else happens, the Gate must be held. If it falls they will be able to funnel armies through it and strike out in any direction they choose. If they are contained in the Greenlands they have no other way of successfully invading. There is no other route through the Titan mountains and the Brotherhood of the Golden Hand control the southern seas. They must be held and at some point countered, driven from the Known World." Kaif snapped himself short, again worried that he may have overstepped.

"I concur your Majesty, they must be held at the Gate." Wane nodded his accord.

"I defer to my colleagues your Majesty. I cannot find fault with their logic."

"It is something of a shame that my son took an undiplomatic approach to the Protectorate's diplomatic mission. Allies will be required if this threat is to be repulsed." Lorgan sat for a moment, chin in his hand, going over his thoughts while the three men sat in anticipation.

"Gentleman, let me think on it. I will call for you all soon." Lorgan stood up, knocking on the doors. The two legionnaires opened them, heads bowed in reverence, the flower girls taking up position in front of their king, spreading petals as they moved off.

As the door closed Wane slumped back in his chair, a loud exhalation of breath signalling his relief. An audience with the God King was a rare honour but also full of tension, always having to be switched on, certain mistakes being potentially fatal.

"So gentlemen, what do we make of that?" Wane voiced what they were all thinking.

"I believe that we need to see to our dispositions Captain General." Kaif nodded, turned on his heels and strode out of the room. Sorkin thought that was the most polite he had ever seen him act towards the mercenary. Some may have seen it as a mark of respect.

Sorkin suddenly felt completely exposed, all the nerves and doubts he'd felt upon waking closing in on him. His stomach turned, making him feel nauseous again. A little bile rose up, stinging the back of his throat. He swallowed it down, composing himself.

"Don't look so worried Sorkin, some secrets are meant to be kept." Wane offered him a warm smile as he untangled himself from his chair, leaving the room with a little flourish of his hat.

Sorkin sat down, taking a moment to himself, a little dizziness almost unmanning him again. How had he complicated things so badly? Putting himself in peril was something he didn't do, risk taking not being a part of his nature.

"Don't ever drink again."

Chapter Thirty-Five Part One:

Hard choices

The snow gusted almost horizontally, the wind howling and whistling, adding its own voice to proceedings. The smoke billowed dark grey, up into the sky, until swallowed up by the Great White, flames glowing orange and yellow, flickering hard from side to side, battling with the wind for dominance.

They had made the journey back from the Snow Eagles' Kaimas and Urdhoa had asked Marisa to let them put Rat on the pyre with all of the Wolfs-head tribe's warriors who had perished in the battle. She asked the rest of the squad and they agreed to it. The Children believed that the passage to the afterlife would be walked with whoever you were sent off with, so Rat would not be alone. They had placed her at the centre of the pyre with more than thirty warriors, Urdlin and Andmar flanking her, a place of great honour.

They all stood around the pyre, Garic and Skin to either side of her, Fugly with her remaining arm wrapped around Breda, him hugging her tightly in response. Bodger stood slightly apart, closer to the pyre. Marisa was worried he might get burnt, for a second concerned that he might throw himself on top to be with Rat. He had that look of bereft despair, totally lost.

The whole of the Wolfs-head tribe had come out to pay homage, at least two thousand as far as she could tell. They all swayed slowly, side to side, a low, humming chorus drifting into the night sky. Their numbers were beyond anything Marisa thought possible and if repeated across the Great White, pointed to a strength nobody knew existed. It made her more certain of her decision.

They all stayed there for hours, the Children included, standing in respect until the pyre began to collapse and the flames abated. Everyone began to file back into the Kaimas, the Great White already beginning to swallow all evidence of the funeral.

Urdhoa had set aside a small room for the squad, giving them some privacy to mourn amongst themselves. He had made it clear that they were welcome and wanted by everyone in the tribe but Marisa appreciated the thought. They needed to talk and she didn't expect it to go well.

There was a table in the middle of the room, plates of food, sweetmeats, roasted potatoes and drinks in clay ewers spread across it. They brewed what Marisa thought was a more than acceptable ale, and their spirit was like fire water. Urdhoa had told Marisa that they fermented it from potatoes, bulves vynas, and it stung the throat going down, making one's eyes water, invariably with the nose running to create a hot salty afterburn.

The Children respectfully left them in peace, Urdhoa being the only non-squad member to join them. They all sat in relative silence, drinking and remembering their lost friends. Marisa broke the silence, trying to explain as best she could what she planned to do. As expected it was not received as well as she hoped.

"Are you fucking serious!" Garic jumped up, grabbing his chair by the back and smashing it off the wall. It came apart, little scraps of wood flying around room.

"Calm down buddy." Skin was the first to react.

"Oh I might have known you'd stick up for her. I s'pose you're staying as well?" Garic shot him an acid look.

"Not that it's any of your business Newbie, but I'm going home when this is all over." Skin may have been small but he wasn't interested in backing down.

Urdhoa and Bodger went to rise from their seats to intervene, Marisa ushering them back with a slight wave of the hand. Garic stood there, fists clenched, the cords on his neck standing out.

"Please tell me you're not buying into this Kare Karaliene shit? You're not the fulfilment of fucking prophecy Marisa, you're an officer of the Protectorate!" Garic angrily spat the words out. "You've forgotten who you are, and where you came from." He was very drunk, at least half a dozen cups of bulves vynas having been consumed. He staggered and drunkenly bumped off the wall, shoving Marisa away before untangling his feet.

Bodger stood up, despite Marisa motioning for him to stay seated.

"C'mon Newbie, calm down and let Marisa talk. It's a shit day for everyone." He held his hands out, palms up, trying to get Garic to settle down.

"Fuck off and mind your own business Bodge!" Garic went to step to Bodger, obviously spoiling for a fight. Marisa stepped in between them, peace-making foremost in her mind, but also thinking that she would knock him on his arse if he carried on.

"Garic, calm down, you're drunk and talking shit. That's an order soldier!" Marisa went nose to nose with him, refusing to cede any ground.

Garic gave a grimacing smirk, teeth bared, then threw his hands in the air, turning to drunkenly storm out of the room. "Fuck the lot of you then."

Fugly went to follow him but Marisa cut her short. "Leave it Marta darling. I'll go, the rest of you just relax, eat drink, cry, talk, whatever it is you need to do." She smiled at them all, realising that her revelation was affecting everyone. She found it hard to believe that she would ever love a group of randoms as much as she loved all of them.

Marisa walked out of the room, just catching sight of Garic exiting the end of the corridor, stepping outside in the freezing winds, no warm weather gear on. She grabbed a big fur coat, not prepared to step outside and freeze her arse off. She walked outside, the snow and wind dancing with each other creating a wall of white. It was difficult to see anything, but there he was, stood with his head on his chest, his shoulders jumping up and down. He was crying and it broke Marisa's heart. She walked over and stood in front of him, expecting another tirade, but he just slumped into a hug, weeping quietly on her shoulder. She wrapped him in a hug, pulling the coat around them both.

They stood there, not talking, just holding each other for ten minutes. It felt like an age to Marisa, not wanting to be the one to break the quiet.

Garic lifted his head, gulping down deep breaths to try and get his sobs under control.

"I am sorry Marisa. Losing friends in battle is as hard a thing as I've ever gone through, but losing you for no reason, especially today is too mu…"

His head sunk into her shoulder again, the sobs not having their time yet. Because he was such a behemoth, she sometimes forgot just how young he was. She was probably his first true love and she loved him back with a passion, but she knew she had to do this.

They stood there for a while, waiting for him to gather himself. Marisa stepped back, reaching up and wiping his eyes with the back of her hand.

"C'mon, let's go back and join in, Rat deserves that of us." She smiled affectionately at him. "Plus it's fucking freezing." He put his head back and laughed and they walked hand in hand back into the Kaimas.

"I'm sorry everyone, just got a bit carried away." Garic stood there, head dipped, too ashamed to look anyone in the face.

Fugly got up and ran over to him, hugging him one-armed, but as tightly as anyone ever could. He rested his face on the top of her head, planting a kiss. Bodger, Skin, Breda all joined in, Urdhoa holding back, obviously feeling a little on the outside. As they all pulled apart, Garic walked up to the hulking tribal leader and wrapped his arms around him.

"Please forgive me Urdhoa, I meant no disrespect." Garic kept his head down in apology. Urdhoa put his hand under his chin, lifting it up so that he could look him in the eye.

"You owe me nothing young Garic. You lost a member of your family whilst fighting for mine. We owe you a debt that will never be forgotten. The Wolfs-head tribe will always hold you in honour and stand beside you." Urdhoa bowed his head and at that moment there was hardly a dry eye in the room.

It broke the tension completely and they revelled into the early hours of the morning, crying, laughing and drinking until they all finally passed out, the release being what they all needed.

They had decided the night before to head back, Urdhoa sending a dozen warriors to see them back to Partia. It was a duty sought after by all, the twelve chosen puffing up like peacocks, as proud as anyone could ever be.

There were tears and embraces, and the Wolf-shead tribe came out en masse to salute the warriors as they left. But leave they did and Marisa stood there for what seemed like an age, long after they had disappeared from sight, not wanting to lose the feeling.

Urdhoa walked up behind her and placed a gentle arm around her shoulder, her dipping her head onto his chest. "Come Marisa." They walked slowly back to the Kaimas and out of the teeth of the Great White.

They had packed everything they'd need for the trek north. Urdhoa was not going but rather Chetta, the diminutive Spirit Raiser plus six warriors to carry their supplies. Marisa worried for her, as tiny and frail looking as she was. She just didn't see how she could survive the hardships of the journey. She couldn't have been more wrong. It was Chetta who set the pace and at times, Marisa struggled to keep up. It didn't seem possible, especially as the furs she had to wear to defeat the cold looked like they weighed more than her.

The further north they headed, the colder and more severe the conditions became. The snows blew in blizzards so thick that you could hardly see a couple of feet in front of you. It got so bad, they had to rope to each other in order to stay together. The temperature kept dropping, getting so cold that Marisa worried that they would all freeze whilst they walked. The hood of her coat was pulled so tight that all that was exposed was her eyes. *"Who'd have thought your eyes could get so cold?"* She struggled on, flagging but resolute, staying the course because what else was there.

She was plodding forwards, head down, eyes nearly shut when suddenly everything went quiet, or more accurately silent. The only noises she could hear were the crunching of snowshoes and the breathing of everyone else. Her own breathing nearly roared inside the hood, so she pulled it back with her gloved hands. She'd been warned not to do so, because in these low temperatures frostbite could take in seconds and the first thing it bit into were your ears.

What she saw seemed impossible. She rubbed her eyes,

blinking furiously, trying to reassure herself that she wasn't hallucinating. The heavens were clear, pitch black, with thousands upon thousands of stars littering the sky. It was beautiful and breathtaking; the like of which Marisa had never seen in her entire life. Her warm breath still plumed out of her mouth, like great gouts of steam, but the wind and snow was gone, replaced by a still, cold, clear evening. The landscape was flat and white, snow as far as the eye could see, no breaks on the horizon.

Apart from the great triangle of black, almost perfectly symmetrical, sitting in the middle of the great plain of white. The moon sat just above it, showering white light on it sheer sides, making it look like a beautiful black jewel floating on a bed of clouds.

Marisa stood stock still, slack jawed, just staring at the majesty of the view. She shook herself from her dazed state, looking behind her. All six of the young warriors had stopped in their tracks, the same slack jawed look on each face.

She turned her head to see Chetta with a little impish grin on her face, enjoying everyone else's reactions. She'd obviously been here before.

"Let's to it then." Chetta barked out an order, snapping everyone out of their paralysis. Her voice almost echoed, seeming to roll across the snow and bounce back off the mountain. Marisa ambled up to her, a look of amazement still painted to her face.

"The Makers Mountain. This is where you will make your journey Marisa Longspear. If you are the Kare Karaliene then this is where you will find the truth of things." There was a timbre of melancholy, just a touch of foreboding about Chetta's voice, or was it just her imagination. Marisa shook her head, trying to snap out of it, there was a task to complete and she intended to see it done.

They got within about one hundred feet of the mountain when Chetta called them to a halt.

"We will make camp here and only myself and Marisa will go any further." No one argued with her, all accepting her authority, without question.

The six warriors set about pitching tents and setting up a cookfire. Marisa recognised one of them, Urdhan, who had stood with her in the line at the Battle of The Snow Eagles.

"How are you Urdhan?"

"I am well, thank you. It is an honour to make this journey with you." He was so deferential, as if he was afraid to speak out of turn. It irritated Marisa, but she understood it what with all the fuss being made about her and who she was meant to be,

"You do not need to stand on ceremony with me Urdhan. I saw you fight in the line and it was my honour to stand with you." She smiled at him and it seemed as if he grew in front of her eyes. He flushed red, trying to turn his head away, not knowing where to look. She was finding this strange mixture of pride and deference difficult to adjust to.

"Please Urdhan, don't feel as if you cannot speak to me freely. I am just like any other person."

"I mean no disrespect Marisa Longspear, but you are not. You are The Kare Karaliene." He dipped his head, his inability to not show deference outmanning him.

"That is not decided yet my friend. Let's wait and see." She reached out and gently patted him on the shoulder, trying to reassure him.

"Even if you are not Marisa, I still saw you fight. I have never seen a more terrifying warrior, so from my point of view if you are not The Kare Karaliene, life would make little sense. I argued for this duty, as did my fellow warriors. We are resolved to follow you regardless." He kept his head up, the absolute conviction in his eyes made Marisa's chest fill with pride. She stepped to him, wrapping him in a warm embrace, whispering in his ear, "You honour me. Now introduce me to your friends." They had all seen the exchange, and all stood open mouthed, not quite believing their own eyes.

Urdhan introduced her to each of them, and she hugged them in turn, thanking them for their loyalty. Once she'd finished, she walked over to Chetta who was sitting cross-legged in front in front of her tent.

"Look Marisa. This is the reason you are here."

Maris turned to look, the six young warriors all slapping each other on the back, animated and delighted that The Kare Karaliene had treated them so.

Once all was set, Chetta got up ushering Marisa to follow her, but not before telling the young warriors to go no further, no matter what they heard. They stopped at the foot of the mountain, in front of a dark cavern.

"Your time has come Marisa. This journey is yours and yours alone. No one can come with you and no one can help you. Everything is not what it seems, but everything is an absolute truth. You do not realise but an epiphany awaits you, the realisation of an absolute truth and you cannot turn away from it." The little spirit-raiser held Marisa's hands. "Hopes and fears will confront you, regrets will try to pull you from the path. Remember this, that there are many paths to enlightenment, it is not just the Gifted who see."

Marisa didn't understand what Chetta was saying, but rather than asking she burnt her words into her mind, repeating them over and over.

"You must drink this." Chetta held up a cup of dark liquid, the smell was pungent but it didn't taste as bad as it smelled, a hint of liquorice infusing it, even though it stung the back of her throat.

"Now you must remove your clothing."

"But it's freezing. I'll die of exposure before I get ten feet." Marisa couldn't hold her tongue.

"You go to see the Maker as he brought you into the world, naked, hiding nothing. It is the only way Marisa. Trust me, he will not let you come to harm."

Marisa stepped out of her clothes, her skin goose-pimpling, all the hairs on her arms and legs standing proud. She wrapped her arms around herself, running on the spot to try to stay warm.

Chetta gestured for her to enter the cave and her arm suddenly wobbled as if it was made of rubber. Marisa walked forward. Looking over her shoulder to see Chetta wobbling from side to side, phasing in and out of sight, the snow and campsite flickering in and out of vision. She turned back, sucked in a deep warm breath and stepped into the cavern.

Chapter Thirty-Five Part Two:

Everything is not as it seems

She stepped forward but there was no floor, no walls, no ceiling. Why would there be? Smoke swirled all around, or was it mist? Was it vapour? Did it matter? A myriad of colours pulsed in and out, all of them grey, all forming shapes, nearly recognisable then not, swirling around and around. The corporeal didn't matter here, everything was real, permanent, then gone in a wisp, never having been.

Faces formed, so near, so close. They drifted in and out of thought, smiling and benign, snarling and malevolent, everything crystalising into little vignettes, sharp and defined, then drifting into smudged dirty drawings, never really settling.

She reached out her hand and the vapour wrapped itself around her, solid and unrelenting, like being grasped by a multitude of hands. She breathed slowly and deeply, smoke diving deep inside her, filling her lungs with emotions, lives lived, people's histories. She breathed out and instantly forgot all she'd just learned.

The smoke let go of her arm and danced in front of her, teasing her, promising something, but she didn't know what. At the edges of her vision she saw faces that she thought she recognised, but as quickly as she whipped her head round, they were gone, dissipating into the mist.

Frustration pressed in on her, nothing substantial to hold onto, just suggestions, hints. She carried on walking but there was no direction, no forward or backward, no up or down, just possibility.

Hints of voices called out, so much familiarity, people she'd loved, those she missed, calling out to her with messages. She could hear them all clearly but couldn't hear a word. Yet more frustration, *"How do I hear? What do I do?"*

She reached forward with her hand, the swirls of vapour letting her nearly touch them, but just pulling away at the last second, almost laughing at her, not letting her in on the joke. She shook her head, waves of vapour surging away from her, pulsing back at the same time.

She stopped still, whatever still was, holding herself, wanting it to come to her. She breathed slowly, evenly, and just waited. In front of her strands of smoke began to coalesce, forming a shape, something familiar. It started to look like a person, someone she knew, someone she loved. A nervous anticipation flushed through her, making her shiver in apprehension. Tall and slim, with a dark cloak, hood pulled up, partially hiding their face.

Marisa instinctively pulled back, trying to give herself room to escape. There was nowhere to go.

The figure lifted their arms, clutching the hood in their hands. Marisa felt a bolt of white fear course through her body, fixing her to the spot, unable to move. Her breath stuck in her throat, too scared to inhale. *"Who are you?"*

The hood fell backwards, the reveal making Marisa gasp. *"Tommec!"* She began to weep, the sense of shock, mixed with unbridled joy swamping her. Through her tears she reached out, desperately wanting to embrace her old friend. Her fingers just passed through the figure, smudging the mist, while it simply reformed behind her.

"Marisa, I am not here, you cannot touch that what isn't. I am a message; you must listen and understand. This is the only time this will happen, your one chance."

"Chance for what?" Marisa found her voice, although it sounded as if it was coming from elsewhere.

"You heard the song Marisa. The door was open but you couldn't walk through. The melody was there for you to hear but all you heard was discord, clashing instruments fighting each other when all they want to do is play the same music. You have the key but instead of unlocking the door you stand facing away, full of anger and resentment. It is not you that is being singled out but your arrogance stops you seeing." It was Tommec's voice and for the first time the loss tore a hole in her heart, a feeling of emptiness almost making her collapse.

"I don't understand Tommec." Her words whimpered out, drifting weakly into the smoke, worthless and without conviction.

"In your heart you know the truth. You cannot let anger rule you. It is not always about you."

Marisa shook her head. What was she doing? She felt the truth of his words, cutting through her like a hot knife through butter. She felt her anger rising up, trying to impose itself, overwhelming her like an actual enemy, determined to cause her injury, standing in her way. She threw her arms out, a great gout of energy flying away from her, pulsing into the ether. She collapsed to her knees, sobbing at the enormity of the revelation, epiphany indeed.

She pushed herself to her feet, a breathless relief mixed with a huge coruscating flood of angst investing every part of her being. She felt exhausted, totally spent.

"Is that it, have I passed the test?"

"Test? I am not here to test you Marisa. I am not here at all." As he spoke he began to flicker in front of her, a warm smile, full of love, a fraternity the last thing she saw as he disappeared into the mist.

She wept, the sense of loss and confusion leaving her wanting. Seeing Tommec again flooded her with emotions, ones she had fought her whole life to suppress. It felt like a test, whatever he said. She tried to regulate her breathing, the vapor investing her being, flowing through her in waves of colour, completely filling every last nook and cranny. She could feel it at the tips of her fingers, on her lips, tasting of everything and nothing. She looked at her arms and they seemed to be pulsing, iridescent, tickling the skin, filling her with warmth.

She continued onwards, not exactly walking forward, more just a case of moving further in, searching for whatever was waiting. The mist continued to dance about her, sometimes just randomly floating, sometimes seeming to call her on, offering a direction.

Something was there, floating in the mist, a dark, sinister presence. Marisa felt a cold fear pulse through her entire body, a cold sensation covering her from head to foot. Whispers swirled around her, little hints of dark deeds, negative and malignant.

She began to see faces in the smoke, filled with pain and anguish. She thought for a brief moment that she recognised some of them. But how could that be? A surreal sense of foreboding crept along beside her, tapping her on the shoulder as if to remind her. But remind her of what? Her mistakes, her indiscretions?

All of a sudden a vision appeared in front of her, stopping her in her tracks. A hulking warrior stood tall, but something was wrong. His face was sliced off, as if severed clean by a sword stroke. She tried to back off but didn't move, caught in the moment as if manacled to the spot. She looked around, desperately seeking a way out. She glanced at the floor, the man's severed face staring up at her, one eye blinking. "What are you?" It mouthed the question, looking back and forth between its own standing body and Marisa.

She screamed but no sound came out. The face and the body drifted away into the mist, as if it had never been there. Marisa remembered the Battle of the Snow Eagles, a memory forming in her mind, blood and screams rushing through her head. She wanted to escape but knew she had to carry on.

She walked for what seemed like an age, the smoke growing darker and thicker, closing in on her, making moving feel more and more testing. Then another figure began to form in the mist. Tall and broad, clad in steel with a huge double-headed axe in his hands. Haftor Thorsen stood there, his faced chiselled from granite, poisonous intent oozing from every pore.

"Little girl, did you think our dance was done?" He smiled, a grim, harsh set to his face.

"I don't understand. You are dead." Marisa whimpered out her response, terror almost overcoming her.

"Do you think that I don't know that? I feel the death blow over and over. I relive it and will do so through all eternity. And yet you cannot remember a thing, can you? So pathetic, gifted this great prize but too afraid to own it. A coward, hiding in the dark recesses of your pitiful little mind." Thorsen tipped his head back, a throaty, sinister laugh escaping his mouth.

"Shut your mouth! You are not here; you are not real!" Marisa found some courage, fuelled by anger and frustration, screaming her defiance at the apparition before her.

Thorsen laughed, mocking her opposition. "You do not know who you are or what you should be. Just a little girl lost, hiding behind a lie, too frightened to step forward and grasp her destiny. You do not deserve your award, you are unworthy." Thorsen growled out his words, a look of disgust on his face. He lifted his great axe above his head, roaring his battle cry. He swung it straight down at Marisa's head. She crouched down, instinctively covering her head with her arms, eyes squeezed tightly shut waiting for the death blow.

Nothing happened. She slowly stood up, opening her eyes, but Thorsen was gone, sucked back into the vapour. She began to shiver, the air around her growing colder, the mist getting darker and darker. It was almost black now, all light being sucked into the gloom, nothing escaping its clutches.

In front of her an arm began to form. It was dark, grey and lifeless. Its skin seemed to be on the verge of rotting, as if it was recovered from the grave, reanimated just to torture her. Its digits flexed, open and closing, trying to inject some essence into it. It formed into a fist, its index finger hooking, beckoning her forward.

Realisation hit her like a hammer, all of the air sucked from her lungs, her throat so tight she simply couldn't speak or breath. *"This cannot be real. The Beckoner is just an old maid's tale. It's not real, it's not real."* She closed her eyes, trying to shut the screaming voices out.

"Marisa Longspear, it is good to meet you." The voice was so loud, louder than anything she had ever heard. And dark, dripping with venomous intent, taunting her, enjoying itself. "You have sent me so many souls Marisa, time and again doing my work for me. I feel that you should be rewarded for all your efforts." The voice sneered, derision lacing its words, a dark malicious intent filling the air, almost touching her skin, imbuing her with horror. Its touch felt like decay, the smells floating around her stinking of rot, almost making her retch.

She shivered, cold terror flowing through her like a river, but somehow she found her voice.

"What do you want of me?" It was a weak, reedy response, but she felt a little strength return to her. She stood tall; chin stuck out defiantly.

"What do I want? I want nothing Marisa Longspear, I simply

am. Do you imagine that I am a person, an entity? I am death, undeniable, inevitable and not open to negotiation. I am and always will be, the one unquestionable consequence of living. I am the balance, the payment and everyone must meet the price." A low, rumbling chuckle filled the space, swirling round Marisa's being, brushing her skin, making her tremble.

"Then we will meet one day." Marisa forced the words out even though it nearly made her gag. There was a taste to her words, vile and acrid. Forcing them out was akin to expelling poison. It gave her courage.

"We will indeed Marisa, we will indeed." She could sense the smile, the little 'I know something you don't know' smirk behind the words. "Would you like me to tell you when it will happen? I know the day and time. For me it is no length of time, a mere click of the fingers. You pitiful creatures cling on so desperately to your meaningless existence. I could save you the trouble, take you with me here and now." Dark laughter pulsed toward her, carrying a stench with it. The hand grew, bigger than a person, opening up as if to pluck her out of reality.

She cowered down, all her defiance lost, an overwhelming rush of terror flowing over her.

Suddenly a great flash of light blasted the darkness away, the great hand disintegrating in front of her eyes, the mist reforming, white and warm. She stood back up, her shivering abating, warmth washing over her.

A gentle orange, yellow-tinted ball of light formed in front of her. It felt reassuring, full of affection and goodwill. She had the impression of being wrapped in a warm fluffy blanket, safe and secure, like being swaddled as a baby.

"What do you seek Marisa Longspear?"

"That voice, I've heard it before. With Urdhoa and Chetta, back at the Kaimas." It made no more sense than the Beckoner, but she could not deny the absolute truth of it. The voice of God. Although she felt safe, secure and loved, it was the most terrifying moment of her life.

"I do not know for certain. Do I have a purpose? Am I the Kare Karaliene?" Her voice sounded thin and anaemic, barely audible over the noise in her head.

"Would it gratify you to know that you have a role to play?" The voice was so loud that it felt enough for the whole world to hear, but there was no malice in it. Just a certainty, not punishing you for not believing, just not concerned with the irrelevant. What was, was. What will be, will be. It was simply fact.

"It would help me understand. I want to do right; I want to help." Mumbled Marisa

"You have a destiny Marisa, but it is one you must realise. I cannot tell you what will be or it will not happen." There was a warmth, a genuine concern, Marisa felt love. This somehow mattered. "You are the Kare Karaliene but the path you walk is for you to tread. I cannot guide you. But know this, you will help shape the future. Protect the weak and offer your life for anyone that needs it. Anyone. You will one day sit at my right hand, when the end of days come."

Marisa felt a great invisible hand set her on the ground, laying her down on a soft bed of grass, covering her with a blanket.

"Sleep Marisa. When you wake you will know what to do." The voice was gentle and soothing, a sense of exhaustion began to overtake her and she fell into a deep sleep.

She dreamt of Garic, being held in his arms, making mad passionate love, shuddering with pleasure when the release hit her. She dreamt that she was back in barracks, all of her squad around her, laughing, drinking, rough housing. Falling asleep in a warm drunken stupor. Rat and Tommec were there, smiling and joking, clapping each other on their backs, filling the rooms with fellowship. Urdlin and Andmar were there as well, that stoic, dry-humoured nature making her smile. It was all the things she loved and all the things she would miss but she realised having the memories meant that they would never leave her.

She woke and stretched out like a cat, sitting up and letting her eyes adjust. To her surprise she was lying on a patch of soft grass. She knew it wasn't possible, so far inside the cavern with no sunlight, but there it was. And where had the blanket come from? A little tremor ran down her body at the thought of it. Everything had been so surreal, so completely impossible, but here she was sitting in a bed of grass, covered in a blanket.

She pulled her knees up, her feet brushing against something hard. She pulled back the blanket and there was a sword sitting at her feet. It was beautiful and ornate, a golden grip and pommel, the cross-guard turning slightly upwards at the ends. It was about four feet long, a proper longsword, with two fullers, broad and beautifully weighted. She looked carefully at the grip and pommel and they had an exquisitely wrought image of a female warrior standing on a small hill of vanquished foes.

It would have filled her with awe and trepidation in a previous life, but not now. She stood up, holding the sword by her side and started to make her way out of the cavern. It was pitch black but somehow her eyes had adjusted enough for her to see her way back. She found it hard to believe how far she must have walked but it took what felt like an age to reach the cave opening.

She stepped out into the brief daylight, eyes stinging at how bright it felt. Chetta was sat cross-legged but jumped up as soon as she saw Marisa. She looked at her for a few moments, her mouth levering further and further open, a vision of awe washing over her face. She fell to her knees, forehead touching the ground, almost afraid to keep looking at her.

"Kare Karaliene. I am your servant."

For the first time Marisa accepted the words, knowing the truth of things.

"Get up Chetta please. I accept your service gladly and will always seek your advice."

Chetta got up, all snuffles and watering eyes, reaching out and grasping Marisa's free hand, kissing the back of it. She looked up at Marisa with an awestruck look of adoration, as if she was in the presence of the Great Maker himself.

"Please Chetta, I am still Marisa, still the same person. I do have one task for you that requires urgent attention though." Marisa smiled down at the modest, little spirit-raiser.

"Anything Kare Karaliene, anything at all."

"Can you get me my clothes? I'm fucking freezing."

Chapter Thirty-Six:

And so, we come to it at last

The trail turned slightly to the north, dropping into an ancient-looking woodland. The trees were gnarly and twisted, all of them standing their ground, searching for a meagre measure of sun. The trail narrowed, four horses abreast at most, forcing them into a long drawn-out column. There was barely any chatter, the canopy blocking out the sun, reflecting the sombre mood. Everyone knew what they were riding towards and none of them felt that survival was likely.

Jonoh rode at the head of the column, Cerwin on one side and Shala on the other. He exchanged glances with Shala, occasionally flicking his eyes at her, drinking in her smile. There hadn't really been any meaningful communication with Cerwin, the ground between them muddied by recent conversations. The old shadowmaster had withdrawn a little, obviously sensing Jonoh's confusion and doubt. It was the first time since they'd met that he hadn't sought his counsel and it was telling on both of them.

It took nearly an hour before the wood began to thin out a little, the trail widening, letting in a little sun. They rounded a corner, the trail meandering back in a southerly direction; the treeline coming to an end. And there it was, standing like a giant sentinel at the mouth of the Titan Pass. Jonoh lost himself for a moment, awestruck by the size and complexity of the Gate itself. There was a buzz of activity, people moving in all directions, setting about their allotted tasks, filling the Gate with life. It reminded

Jonoh of the ant farms they had at the Red Pier Academy, staircases, corridors, a whole raft of tents raised at the north end.

He snapped himself back to the moment and saw a mounted welcoming party trotting towards them. Torbin and Candor he instantly recognised, despite never having met them, that mind-walker contact giving them form. They had been in constant contact with them both and had heard all of the truncated contact with the H'Daree as well. They already knew what the defenders' dispositions were and what their own deployment would be.

There were two other men with them, one a big young Lhossan officer, dark-skinned and well built, with a cuirass decorated with a cloud motif. He was lightly armoured but carried himself with that natural soldier's confidence, ready to fight at a moment's notice.

The Lhossan officer was big but the other man was built like a fighting bull, his neck barely discernible as it disappeared into his huge shoulders. His jet-black ponytailed hair and hard-won facial scars just added to his frightening appearance, at least that's what struck Jonoh. He was probably the scariest looking man he had ever seen, clearly the renowned Guido Tivosi.

They pulled up just in front of them and Cerwin virtually leapt from his horse, nearly stumbling in his eagerness to greet their hosts. He wrapped Torbin in a warm embrace and it reminded Jonoh of the fact that both he and Candor were Orphans and his students.

Torbin was taken aback by the warmth of the old shadow-master's greeting, but moved by it nonetheless.

"Torbin Sculptor, or should I say Pale-skin? How are you my boy?" Cerwin stood back, hands on Torbin's arms, squeezing them excitedly.

"I am well thank you Master Cerwin. It is good to see you after so many years." Torbin smiled warmly, the reunion almost outmanning him.

Candor stood looking at the two men, wondering if his reunion would share the same warmth. He needn't have worried, Cerwin turning with a beaming smile on his face and wrapping him in a heartfelt hug.

"Candor Scribe, again apologies; Blackheart. It warms my heart to see you alive and well." Cerwin smiled up at his old student, obviously delighted to see him. Candor fought back a tear, his eyes very nearly welling up.

"Gentlemen this is Jonoh Shipwright." Torbin and Candor stepped up to eagerly shake his hand. "It is an honour to meet you Jonoh, the great prodigy indeed." Torbin nodded his acknowledgement.

"Thank you Torbin. What you have done here is remarkable." Jonoh was indeed impressed with what he saw. He turned to shake Candor's hand, but was confused by his reaction. Candor had stopped short, a shocked look painted across his face. He stood still, not moving, mouth open, a look on his face like he was deciding on a course of action but couldn't make his body comply.

"You are identical to them. Not a lookalike, but a perfect copy. Exactly the same." Candor shuffled back half a step, his hand going instinctively to the sword on his hip. Shala and Jonoh Mason had dismounted, the rest of the Orphans fanning out around them. They both strode in front of Jonoh, hands on their sword hilts, staring Candor down.

"Candor! What are you doing?" Torbin stepped across him, blocking his way, a look of real confusion on his face but at the same time a look of granite determination that would not be gainsaid.

Candor shook his head, as if he were trying to set loose a thought. "He is identical to The Chosen, the ones that lifted the great energy barrier. They were all exactly the same, including the one I killed." Candor's fingers had turned almost white on his sword grip, his stance slipping into a fighting form.

Torbin saw Tivosi and Jadran ease forward either side of Candor, ready to protect their friend. Tension began to mount, more and more Orphans sliding from their horses and gathering around Jonoh.

"Peace my friends, please stand down and listen to me." Cerwin inflected a still, calm tone to his voice and all the gathered Orphans eased a little, Candor included. Torbin glanced at Tivosi and Jadran, a tiny shake of the head being all they needed.

"Candor, this is Jonoh Shipwright, the most gifted of his generation, probably of all time. He has never been outside of the Protectorate in his entire life, until now. Any resemblance, whilst troubling, irrespective of how close it is, is not what defines him. He is defined by his actions, and until now they have been nothing less than commendable. We will not find answers here, and may never do, but he has done you no injury and is not H'Daree." Cerwin had stepped in front of him, nudging Torbin aside, keeping his palms up in peace.

Candor felt the breath rattling in his ears, the memory of the H'Daree raging through his mind. Jonoh was identical to their leaders, not similar but exactly the same. However with Cerwin in front of him, he began to hear and absorb the words being said and he let go of his sword, turning and mounting his horse, galloping back to the Gate.

Torbin stood, watching his friend gallop away from the group, confused by what he had just seen and heard.

"Jonoh, Master Cerwin, please forgive Candor. He is the only one amongst us to have faced the H'Daree and has had to suffer great loss. Please give him a little time. I will talk to him." The look on Torbin's face was a mix of bewilderment and earnest honesty.

"I can only imagine what he has suffered Torbin, we will not press the matter." Cerwin squeezed Torbin's arm in reassurance, turning to look at Jonoh. Stood just behind Shala and Jonoh Mason, he had a look of confused shock on his face.

"Please, allow me to introduce Jadran Greycloud, commander of the Lhossan militia and Captain Guido Tivosi." Torbin swept his arm towards his two companions, relieved to see that their body language was more relaxed, hands off the hilt of their swords.

"It is an honour to meet you gentlemen." Cerwin stepped forward, eagerly shaking their hands, starting the introductions with the rest of his band of Orphans.

Candor glanced back over his shoulder and saw everybody shaking hands and backslapping. The sight just rankled with him, unable as he was to lose the memory of The Chosen. He trotted up to the gatehouse and tied off his mount. Jek was drilling his men, mixing them in with the units made up from the slave muster. He was better than good, and he could see why Torbin had chosen him. The coordinated footwork he was teaching them was almost like dancing, so nimble and reactive, almost as if they were on the moving deck of a ship.

He stood quietly, admiring what he saw, when he caught Jek's eye, nodding respectfully. Jek called for one of his chosen subordinates to take over the drill and walked towards Candor.

To Candor's great surprise he extended his hand in greeting. "'ow d'you fare Candor?"

Candor eagerly grasped Jek's hand, unable to keep the smile from his face. "I am well, thank you Jek. Your training methods are very impressive, very much so. How are my people bearing up, any problems at all?" Candor sat on a wall. Inviting Jek to join him. To Candor's continuing surprise he did so.

"They are good men Candor. Willin' t' learn an' quick t' pick things up." Jek looked across at his new recruits, a little grin of satisfaction on his face.

"I am glad of it. I stood with them on the ramparts and in the streets when we faced the H'Daree. They are brave men but your training will greatly improve their chances. For that I find myself even further in your debt." Candor looked down at the floor, the guilt he felt about his past actions making his head feel like a great weight.

"Your debt is not t' me Candor. My rage took over, but I know you only did what you 'ad to. I honestly don't know if I'll ever get past it, but I'll not seek satisfaction from you." Jek glanced across at Candor but he couldn't return his look, head still down, the guilt a long way from leaving him. "Anyway, with what's comin', we ain't got time t' fuck about."

Candor gave a little laugh. "Indeed, thank you my friend. You give me more honour than I deserve." The blindingly obvious hit him like a wave. This man forgave him for something he had actually done, while he petulantly raged at a young man innocent of anything more than sharing others features. *"Fucking hypocrite."*

Torbin left the Orphans to their greetings, all of them eager to clasp hands with the great Guido Tivosi. He felt a little sympathy for Jadran. It was quite a shadow to try and get out from under but it just went to show that reputations really did travel. He had motioned to Jonoh that he wanted to talk and the young prodigy had nodded his agreement, the two of them wandering towards the north end of the Gate.

"I am delighted and somewhat relieved that you have all

arrived Jonoh. It will greatly improve our chances." Torbin walked hands behind his back, not quite comfortable and finding it difficult to jump-start the conversation.

"We are proud to be here Torbin, although knowing what we face, more than a little nervous." He sensed that Jonoh shared his discomfort, both of them awkwardly trying to navigate the situation.

"I will give you the full tour once your people have had a chance to rest and settle in, but I just wanted to introduce you to someone important first." Torbin relaxed a little, unclasping his hands and walking a little more freely.

They continued walking and idly chatting as they got closer to the tented gathering that had grown up at the far end of the Gate. It appeared to Jonoh that it numbered in its thousands, extending beyond the wall, skirting the treeline at the foot of the mountains.

"I should warn you in advance that it is Candor's wife we are meeting. The Green-landers don't seem to have any discernible leadership structure anymore, but she has emerged as the one they listen to and she is quite formidable." Torbin's eyebrows raised, a mischievous little grin forming as he spoke.

As they reached the edge of the camp, a diminutive, red-haired woman strode towards them, dress gathered up a little so that she didn't trip.

"Hello Torbin, who's this then?" Marye stood there, hands on hips, her customary pose.

"Marye, let me introduce Jonoh Shipwright, leader of the Orphans that have just arrived." Torbin stood aside a little and watched Marye size Jonoh up.

"Leader is it? He doesn't look old enough to shave." Marye fixed Jonoh with a withering look.

Jonoh stood mute for a moment ant, taken aback by this woman's presence, unsure of what to do.

"Miss Marye it is my honour to meet you. Torbin has told me about you. Please accept my service." He offered a little deferential bow, hoping his attempt at charm would work.

"Stand up young man, I am not your mother." She stepped forward almost making Jonoh flinch back, and hugged him close. "You are most welcome. It is a great deal for so much to be placed on such young shoulders, and it's just Marye." She winked at him and gave him a little peck on the cheek.

Jonoh flushed red, keeping his head low, trying not to show his embarrassment. "Thank you Marye."

"Have you eaten?" She grasped him by the elbow, leading him towards a cookfire just inside the camp.

"I will see you soon Jonoh." Torbin called after him, smiling at the thought of him trying to resist Marye's charms. He didn't much fancy his chances.

He looked back towards the gatehouse, off to the south, the Orphans all filing across, tying off their mounts and introducing themselves. Tivosi and Jadran would see to their billeting, it was Candor he needed to talk to. And just as he thought it, there he was walking toward him, his limp almost completely gone, Len's ministrations obviously having taken.

Torbin strode out, wanting to reach him quickly, allowing himself time to explain that he'd left him with Marye. All of a sudden he was full of trepidation, fearful that Candor may react angrily.

Candor shook himself from his thoughts and looked towards the tents, only to see Torbin striding purposefully toward him. He braced himself for an angry reaction, reminding himself not to flare up, knowing that he had amends to make. He took a deep breath and girded himself, walking as fast as he could toward his friend. His wound felt almost free of pain now, a little stiff but pretty much healed. He had much to thank Len for.

The two friends met halfway along the Gate, and stood silently for a moment, as if neither quite knew how to start the conversation.

"I am sorry Torbin. I let my anger blind me. It was an overreaction and hardly the boy's fault. I did not mean to create an issue, I really didn't. Speaking to Jek I realised how unfair I was being and I feel ashamed of myself." He shrugged his shoulders, uncertain if it was enough.

"There is nothing to apologise for my friend, we explained what you have been through and there is nothing but understanding from their point of view. There is so much to deal with here and so much to take in, that the odd frayed nerve is inevitable. I took

Jonoh aside and I have to say that he is an impressive young man. He is only seventeen after all, with the weight of the world on his shoulders." Torbin put his hand on his friend's shoulder, giving it a little reassuring squeeze.

"How is he? Hardly the welcome he and the rest of the Orphans deserved; I would like to set things right."

"Then you have the perfect opportunity. I left him with Marye." Torbin looked up from under his eyebrows, a wicked grin on his face.

Candor groaned. "Best be quick, before I get in real trouble."

They set off for the camp, laughing and joking, the tension leaking away.

Jonoh sat on a little wooden stool, a bowl of steaming stew in hand, being quizzed by Marye. He found he liked her enormously, maternal affection just oozed out of her. She bombarded him with questions about his upbringing and life in the Protectorate, amazed that family as she understood it didn't exist. She shook her head at the idea of being raised in a communal system, children all brought up together by vocational caregivers, but didn't press the matter.

"Do you have a lady in your life Jonoh?" Marye smiled at him, looking as if she had some options prepared for him if he said no.

"I do Marye." He almost stammered the words out, taken aback by her directness.

"Tell me about her."

"Her name is Shala. We met on the journey; she is one of Andhonar's Orphans." Jonoh blushed a little, unable to hide the strength of his feelings for her.

Marye tapped him on the knee, a warm, caring smile on her face "First time you've been in love?"

"Yes Marye, it is." He looked away, not wanting to reveal his discomfort. Marye giggled, placing a hand gently on his cheek.

"I am happing for you darling boy. From what I understand a little love is the very least you deserve."

Jonoh smiled across at her. She was so warm and caring, making him feel welcome and at home.

He heard a few greetings over his shoulder and turned to see Torbin and Candor walk into the camp, coming directly toward the fire. He stood up, steeling himself for possible conflict, hoping against hope that it didn't come to pass.

Candor made straight for him, head slightly down as if he was contemplating something and didn't want to reveal his intent. Jonoh stiffened a touch, shifting his weight a little onto his heels, just in case.

Candor looked up. "Jonoh, please accept my apologies. It was just a shock to see your face, but I know that I was in the wrong." He offered his hand and a deferential nod.

"Gladly Candor. I can only imagine what you have been through." Jonoh clasped his hand, shaking it warmly, a relieved smile covering his face. "Torbin, Candor, I need to talk to you both in private. If you would be kind enough to excuse us Marye?" He turned to her and she nodded.

"You do what you need to my darling." She cupped his face in her hands, kissing him on the cheek.

"Thank you." He smiled back at her, already beyond fond of this lovely, warm woman.

They made their excuses and made their way up to the first floor, finding a quiet room close to the jailhouse.

"Do you not want Cerwin and some of our officers here Jonoh?" Torbin asked the question, not quite certain why Jonoh felt the need for secrecy.

"I need to talk to you both in absolute secrecy gentlemen. Hopefully you will understand my concerns once I have told you what I feel I must." Jonoh was infested with nerves, not sure this was the course of action he should follow but feeling that it was a risk he had to take.

"Please Jonoh, the floor is yours." They all sat down on the wooden benches that rested against the walls.

Jonoh told them everything he had experienced, the painting of Curlon, the journey back with the blades, every detail that he could recall. All of his fears and doubts, the overwhelming sense of responsibility that he felt, sitting on his young shoulders like a great weight. He talked about the Elder Council meeting and the strand of events that had led them to this point, all of the experiences he had endured, the transference after his first kill still pressing down on him. Lastly he spoke, hesitantly, about the doubts creeping into his mind with regards to Cerwin. His wildly swinging moods, the incident with the Darmations, but especially his insistence on exploring alternative options.

"I can see no other option open to us than holding the Gate and throwing the H'Daree back. What other choice could there possibly be? It pains me to have this conversation without Master Cerwin but I could not see another way." Jonoh slumped back against the wall, the sheer weight of his concerns seeming to release in the telling.

Torbin and Candor looked at each other, Candor motioning for Torbin to begin.

"Master Cerwin has had a great deal to cope with, and is not as young as he once was, so I think we need to give him the benefit of the doubt for now. However what you have told us is concerning, so I suggest we keep it between us for the time being. The things you experienced are beyond us both Jonoh and I can only imagine the stress this is causing you. The implications are mind-boggling and I don't really understand what it points to. Is this part of a centuries old plan, is Curlon behind it? I remember some of my history lessons, but this is almost out of legend." Torbin paused, not quite sure what to say, or for that matter what he was saying. He looked at Candor, hoping he would step in.

"Firstly, let me say Jonoh, that I am personally honoured that you choose to share with me, especially after our rocky beginning." Jonoh nodded his appreciation, Torbin mirroring his action.

"As Torbin says, what you have had to endure is beyond either of us, but I agree that for the moment that we keep our own counsel." He took a breath before carrying on. "The situation with Master Cerwin does cause me to worry though. I agree with you Jonoh, there is no other course available to us, other than holding the Gate. Whilst waiting for the attack on Minari and Turan I endured almost endless contact with the H'Daree and listened to their history of conquest. They call it liberation, but conquest it is. They do not stop until they have won or the opposition has acceded. And winning for them means genocide, no one left alive." Candor looked them both in the eye, making sure they understood him clearly. "If we fight it will be to the end, there are no other options available."

They all sat in silent consideration, each taking in what had been said, no one wanting to break the quiet.

"When we had that final contact with the H'Daree I sensed a weakness." Jonoh was the first to speak. "It was as if it was driven by emotion, at least toward the end, not by the usual cold, focused intent. I think you touched a nerve Candor and that is something we can use."

"I hadn't thought of it in those terms Jonoh; too tied up in the emotion of it. If they can be goaded then we can draw them into making mistakes." They all grunted their accord, a little thread of hope ignited. A small advantage, but an advantage.

"Defenders at the Titan Gate, hear us. We are the H'Daree and we come. Open your doors and surrender to the inevitable. Hand over Candor Blackheart and Jonoh Shipwright and we will grant you the freedom to govern yourselves as you see fit. You only need accept our overlordship and bow before the All Father, joining us until we unite humanity and reach the H'Dar. We cannot be denied, do not sacrifice your lives pointlessly, join us or perish. All who defy us will be destroyed."

They all sat still for a moment, the shock of the contact pinning them to their seats. Then almost instantaneously they leapt up and made for the stairs, sprinting up the flights to reach the north end of the first embrasures. Torbin looked down the length of the corridor, their comrades all appearing at the opposite end of the Gate.

The three of them sprinted towards their colleagues, meeting them halfway. Cerwin, Tivosi, Jadran, Shala, Jek and Jadson were all there, surrounded by other Orphans.

"You all heard?" Jonoh directed his question at the Orphans, all nodding their acknowledgement.

"Right, Jek, Jadson, see to your deployment. Jadran, Guido, I need a rotating watch, one third strength at all times. From now on we leave no position unmanned. Let's get to it gentlemen and good luck to us all." Torbin barked out his orders, everyone snapping to their duties.

The Orphans remained and Torbin ceded the moment to Jonoh.

He stood there for a moment, looking into the eyes of his fellows, composing himself.

"We know why we are here and what our deployments are. From this moment until the battle is done, Torbin Pale-skin is in command and we will follow his lead without question. Am I understood?" He felt like a little boy, telling grown-ups what to do, but it needed to be done.

As one, the Orphans saluted Torbin, all putting their right hands on their left breasts, bowing their heads in deference. Torbin gulped, an overwhelming sense of pride filling him to bursting. Then he felt the warmth, all of the Orphans reaching out to touch his mind, swearing their allegiance.

"I thank you all and am honoured by your loyalty. You are the best hope we have of holding and much will be asked of you. I know that you will make us all proud." Torbin walked through the press of bodies, hands on his shoulders the whole way, a great flow of strength coursing through his body.

Jonoh stayed his ground, letting Torbin take his place, important that he made this connection. Shala stood by his side, both of them refraining from talking, feeling the sense of fellowship flowing out from the crowd.

Cerwin had followed Torbin and Candor as they descended the stairs, casting a brief glance over his shoulder. Jonoh couldn't pinpoint it exactly, but he had an uneasy feeling, unable to shake a sense of discomfort.

"They have given us a room down on the first floor. It's near to the forge so not exactly quiet, but it has a door and a bed. There is little we can do at the moment. Best leave them to it and take advantage of the opportunity." Shala laced her fingers through his, a coy little smile on her face.

She walked toward the stairs, pulling him along, almost tripping over his feet as he followed.

The night passed writhout much incident, just the expected nervous rattling about, everybody slightly on edge whilst absorbing the news.

Torbin had sought out Jadran and Tivosi, heading for the top of the Gate, wanting to start the day with the best view of the battlefield.

"Does something strike you as odd gentleman?" Torbin turned to his companions, peeling the skin from an apple with an old worn paring knife as he spoke.

"The clouds are not breaking on the highest mountains Torbin, and they are obscuring the sun." Jadran spoke with a slight waver to his voice. A lifetime worshipping Sardis would not wash away in one morning.

"The clouds are rolling in. If I didn't know better I'd say it was going to rain." Tivosi spoke absentmindedly, as if it was the most stupid thing he'd ever uttered.

A silence settled on them, standing still, staring at the highest peaks of the Titans, way off in the distance. The mountains all wore white and grey hats, their tips covered in great storm clouds. They were rolling forward, covering more and more peaks as they made their progress.

"Correct me if I'm wrong Jadran, but it doesn't rain this close to the Red Desert. The sun's heat always burns the cloud cover." Torbin put words to what they were all thinking, stating the obvious being the only thing he could think to say.

"That is right Torbin. Next thing you know it'll rain over Lhossa." Jadran gave a nervous laugh, trying to sound dismissive but knowing he couldn't hide his fear.

"They brought the rain before they attacked the twin cities. They are nearly upon us." Torbin turned to face his colleagues directly.

"We must deploy now gentlemen, every man to his station."

Jadran and Tivosi each gave the briefest of nods, spinning on their heels and sprinting for the stairs, descending at breakneck speed, barking at everyone they passed on the way.

Jonoh heard the commotion and jumped out of bed, rushing around the room to get dressed. Shala rolled off the mattress, following his lead, both of them fuelled by urgency. He pulled on his boots and grabbed for the door, just as Jadran came into view.

"Jadran, what is happening?"

"We are standing to, Jonoh, every man to his station. I am heading for the Gate to pass on instructions to Jek." Jadran offered a brief nod, turning and running for the stairs to the entrance gate.

He looked across from his room and saw Shalo Torm at the bellows, firing the forge up and barking out orders to his workers. Lhossan militia, Green-landers and men of the muster were all running to take up their posts, all armed for battle, shields, armour and swords fitted to every man. Torm had obviously been busy and the armament was impressive indeed. Each man was furnished with everything they could carry, and there were racks of spears and billhooks at the back of every embrasure and spare weapons at the gatehouse. They could not have been better prepared and now the test was upon them.

Candor turned to see Jadran descend the stairs at a good clip. He headed straight for Jek, so he ran over to join them.

"The Gate must be held at all costs Jek. You'll have five hundred infantry plus one hundred Orphans, mounted if necessary to defend the tunnel. If they breach the Gate the portcullis must be dropped. That will be the last chance to re-form, and hold you must." Jadran grasped Jek by the bicep, reinforcing the point.

"We will hold Jadran or die trying. Candor, have you selected your men?" Jek glanced at him, urgency now investing every word.

"I have Jek, we will rain a storm of arrows down on their heads and drop the portcullis at your command." The three men exchanged handshakes, no more words spoken, just looks of respect, their eyes wishing each other luck.

Candor climbed the ladder into the gatehouse, his forty bowmen with him, survivors of the first contact with the H'Daree. The gatehouse was directly above the Gate and its tunnel, with the raised portcullis at the back end, made from four-inch-thick rolled steel and held in place with restraining bolts. Once they were removed the portcullis would drop, isolating them from the rest of the defending forces but with the ladder hole being the only access it was a defensible position, at least for a while. He knew the risks but it was a command he had chosen and all his men were volunteers.

The gatehouse itself was only as deep as the tunnel, about fifty feet, but it extended roughly an extra twenty feet to either side. It was a tight fit for forty men, but not exactly cramped. At the front there were fifty arrow slits, some straight, some angled, offering a one-hundred-and-eighty-degree field of fire in front of the Gate, with very little risk of being hit by return fire.

They had laid supplies in, enough to last them more than a week. Candor doubted they'd need that much but better safe than sorry. He had Stannard with him as his second, a position the young man had insisted on. He looked like a boy when they first faced the H'daree, now he looked like a man, bearded and grim-faced. His blond hair had darkened, in all likelihood more due to lack of washing than anything else, but it gave him a stronger, sterner demeanour.

"Stannard, you have command. Rotate the men, twenty on, twenty off. There's no point us all sitting in this place until we have to. I am going to see Torbin and the rest of the command staff, but I will be back before it starts." He clapped the young officer on the back and descended the ladder.

Candor nodded to Jek and then bound up the stairs toward the first embrasure.

Jonoh stood with Shala, not wanting to part, the fear that this may be their last moments together gluing him to the spot.

"I have to go my darling; we all have our duties." She looked him square in the face, a look of utter love reflected in her eyes.

"I know." He pulled her close, kissing her as if his very life depended on it. He pushed her gently away. Holding her gaze for a moment longer, they both turned, her descending the stairs to join her fellow Orphans at the Gate, him heading for the first embrasures.

He glanced back and saw her pass Candor on the stairs. He was running, head down as fast as he could, no doubt following him up to talk with Torbin.

Torbin stood at the embrasure, looking out down the Pass. From there you could see for roughly three miles, before the Pass veered slightly south. It was a clear field of view and the embrasures offered them a one-hundred-and-eighty-degree field of fire, a better defensive position he couldn't imagine. He glanced over his shoulder to see Jonoh mounting the stairs, Candor just behind him.

"Jonoh, Candor, how do you fare?"

"We are ready at the entry gate Torbin, at least as ready as we'll ever be." Candor offered an apprehensive grin, covering his nerves. Torbin felt the same, nervous but not wanting to show it.

"I intend to stay here Torbin and stand with you and the rest of our force. Like everyone else I am keen to know what we are dealing with, eager to get to it. The anticipation is draining on the nerves." Jonoh wished he didn't keep stating the obvious, but what else was there now?

"Then would you command the reserve Jonoh? We will need to plug gaps quickly, respond where things are hottest."

"I would be honoured Torbin."

Torbin smiled at his compatriots, all the words spoken, so he offered none. He ambled over to the edge of the embrasure and reached out with his hand. He felt little spots of rain, barely believable but there it was.

"They are coming, and soon. We must stand to our stations." He nodded at Candor, both of them knowing that there were no guarantees they would see each other again. They stepped toward each other, embracing silently. Candor turned, squeezing Jonoh's shoulder and setting off back down the stairs, Torbin watching him disappear, a little lump in his throat reminding him of the gravity of their situation.

Tivosi had stationed himself a few embrasures along the Gate, while Jadran had chosen to take command at the northernmost point. There were mixed squads of Green-landers, Lhossans and former slaves occupying every embrasure along the length of the Gate. There were just short of one hundred embrasures, each twenty feet across with a forty-foot gap between each. Every embrasure was manned with fifteen men, the reserve spread along the length of the Gate. Jadson had taken his command on the top of the Gate, one hundred and fifty men, all with bows to defend the high flanks and rain down as much misery as they could manage on the H'Daree. The decision to not man the second embrasures was agreed by all. They would be a fallback position if the first embrasures were overrun. Jonoh's reserve was made up of Orphans, except for the ones acting as mind-walker contacts at each embrasure.

There was nothing left to do but wait.

It had been a day since Torbin felt the first drops of rain and everyone's nerves were a little ragged, the tension rising the longer they had to wait. Torbin was sat with his back against his embrasure's wall, worrying some salted pork with his teeth, eating more to interrupt the monotony than because of hunger.

It had been raining for the whole of the last day. Not light rain but torrential, vertical rain, so heavy it made it difficult to see clearly. The sun was blanked out of the sky, vast dark clouds filling the heavens, blotting out all light. It almost felt like nighttime, even though it was the middle of the day, the grim sky just adding to the darkening mood.

His mind began to wander, thoughts of Jadzia going through his head, when Terror ambled up beside him and snuggled his head under Torbin's arm. Torm had made him some armour, a head plate and a back piece, offering him some protection. Just as well, as Torbin knew there would be no holding him back once they came into contact. Torbin rubbed his chest and the great hound laid his head on his lap.

It was good to see his old friend. He'd been so tied up with organising the defence that he hadn't realised how much he missed him, but Terror was nothing if not gregarious, so having this many new people to meet had obviously kept him busy.

Terror's ears suddenly pricked up, a little growl rising in his throat. Torbin could feel a little tremor coming through the stonework. He put his hand on the wall and swore he could feel it, an almost imperceptible shudder, tiny but there.

"This is it; they are here."

He stood up, Terror at his heel, and stared down the Pass. The rain made it difficult but he saw it, the head of the snake appearing in the distance. The formations spread from one side of the Pass to the other, all bodies clad in black, making it look like a solid mass, a single entity moving inexorably forward, filling the Pass floor with its presence.

Terror barked his defiance, shoulders hunched, the tensed muscles on his body standing proud and ready.

"Battle stations!" Torbin trumpeted the order: every Orphan at every station, relaying the word. Behind him, a hum of activity started, people running to their posts, gathering armour and weapons as they went. Everyone they had capable of fighting stood to their posts, as ready as they were ever likely to be.

The body of the snake wound its way down the Pass, black and liquid in form, akin to a vast dark river; flooding after a drought. As well as the vast legions of infantry there were cavalry, great flatbed carts, stacked with something; impossible to make out at this distance.

"What the fuck are they?" Lenny White had stepped up next to him, pointing down the Pass at the carts; not so much the carts but what was pulling them.

"I have no idea." Torbin stood there, open-mouthed, looking at what didn't seem possible.

Pulling the huge flatbeds were impossibly big oxen. More akin to aurochs, twenty feet to the shoulder at the very least. Their horns measured what seemed twelve feet across, like nothing ever seen or heard of in the Known World. Great carapaces of bone covered their shoulders, skulls and upper legs. Vast yokes sat on their shoulders, tied back to the carts, pulling seemingly impossible quantities. The slow stomping of their hooves beat out a deep bass rhythm, loud and implacable, coming on with a dark purpose.

They kept coming, thousands upon thousands covering the floor of the Pass, almost more than could be counted. On and on they came, an almost inexhaustible number, endless legions with one thing in mind. Torbin felt the fear, the same fear that he knew would be running the length of the Gate, a cold shiver pouring over him, but he knew better than to show it. He stood to the very front of the embrasure, standing stiff backed and defiant. *"Let them come. Let them come!"* He sent his thoughts to every Orphan across the Gate, a picture of him smashing his spear on his shield. In moments he heard the noise picked up by everyone holding a weapon, a great cacophony of steel clashing on steel echoing down the Pass.

"Let them know who we are."

It took at least half an hour until the front of the H'Daree column stopped. It was roughly four hundred yards short of the Gate, just out of longbow range. The Pass was full, bodies of soldiers as far as the eye could see. Torbin gulped, a nervous, instinctive reaction to what he was witnessing. Their numbers seemed inconceivable, the weight of their task pressing down on him, a little voice in the back of his mind screaming, "Run you fool!"

The front battalion split in the middle, a group of hooded figures walking forward, spreading out along the length of the formations. They formed a line, more than a hundred strong, standing ominously, silently; ramping up the tension.

One of their number stood forward and craned his neck up, throwing back his hood, his fellows all doing likewise. Torbin's breath caught in his throat. It was akin to looking at one hundred or more Jonoh Shipwrights, as if one poor woman had given birth to a century of children. Impossible, but still.

"Defenders of the Gate. We salute your courage but offer you a chance to live." His voice boomed out, clear for everyone to hear, as if it had somehow been amplified.

Jonoh had stepped forward into Torbin's embrasure and stood alongside him, barely able to breathe; looking at the impossible.

"Open your gate, hand over Candor Blackheart and Jonoh Shipwright and there will be no bloodshed today. Do not and all of you shall perish." The threat boomed out, loud and implacable.

"Show them who we are!" Torbin lashed out in his mind, thumping his spear on his shield and roaring his defiance. To Jonoh's surprise, everyone with a shield took up his cry, spears and swords rattling out angry opposition once again. His heart swelled with pride, the loyalty and bravery showed truly overwhelming. Every one of the defenders were ready and determined. He didn't sense any doubt, fear but no doubt. Fear he understood only too well. He glanced at The Chosen, a look of disgust and anger descending across their faces. It made him smile. *"We are under your skins already."*

"So be it." The response was flat, matter of fact; the inflection suggesting a slight sense of boredom, as if this was always inevitable; something they had to do time and again. Jonoh however felt a different truth. They were confident but that confidence was laced with fear. They did not want this conflict, almost as if they weren't quite preprared.

A battalion of infantry trotted forward, setting up a great defensive line just ahead of The Chosen. The front row locked shields, spears thrust forward, the second and third rows lifting their shields above their heads, forming a solid metal tortoise. They were on the edge of bow range but well protected.

Candor peered out through the arrow slit, quietly looking at the H'Daree deploying. It reminded him of the battle in the Green-lands and suddenly it made sense. They'd changed their tactics to defend The Chosen when they raised their energy barrier. A clever and strong adaptation. It would be near to impossible to sneak past that mass of bodies, even for the gifted. He could see the tactic, raise the barrier, nudge forward until they are under the Gate and then deploy whatever siege engines they planned to use. He found himself regretting that they hadn't dug pits out in front of the Gate but time had not been on their side, although the memory of the great wooden platforms made him think that it would have been a waste of effort.

He stared hard at the line of The Chosen, all of them standing, arms outstretched, heads tipped back, just like before; and no one could stop them this time.

"Torbin, they are going to raise their energy barrier." Torbin heard Candor's words and made his decision. He needed to slip into the Gift to see this for himself. The last thing he did was glance at The Chosen, little strands of energy seeming to leave their fingertips, connecting them all, forming a bridge of energy.

"Jonoh, I am entering the Gift, would you take my shield and spear and look over me?"

"Of course Torbin, I will stand by you."

Torbin took a breath and slid into…

"The pain, the blinding pain, AARGHH!"

The screaming pain lanced through his body, agonising white hot shards shooting through him, piercing everything, not a single scrap of flesh left untouched. It closed around him, engulfing him in agony, and all he could do was pray for death.

Terror roared out a bark, agitated and pitching about foot to foot, not understanding what was happening, looking up at Jonoh, his eyes begging for help.

Jonoh dropped Torbin's shield and spear to the ground. Torbin was contorted in agony, his body twisting into impossible shapes, agony pressing down on his contorted features. He put his hands on him, trying to hold him still, stop him from hurting himself. He reached out with his mind and felt the agony tormenting Torbin. It was like picking up a boiling pot with your bare hands, your first reaction being to drop it, but he held to his path and stretched towards him.

The agony was all there was, engulfing everything, still looking for new parts to attack. Death was the only escape but it wouldn't release him. He wanted to sob but there wasn't time or space for anything other than the pain, then he saw it. A hand formed in the centre of the agony, outstretched, reaching for him. For a fraction of a moment he unfurled his twisted fingers and threw his hand out.

"Torbin, are you alright?" Jonoh kneeled over him, clasping his hand.

"What happened?" Torbin found it hard to reorient himself, the memory of the pain dissipating but something he instinctively knew would be with him forever.

"Look." Jonoh nodded out toward the H'Daree to see all of The Chosen lying prone on the ground, all of them twisted into torturous positions. The infantry were pulling back in confusion, covering them with their shields, trying to withdraw to a safe distance.

"Jonoh, call for the archers to loose some volleys." Torbin strained to release his words, everything still feeling compressed, like the moment of release after your bonds are cut.

Seconds later, volleys of arrows arced into the sky, hundreds loosed from the first embrasure joined by Jadson's men at the top of the Gate. They rained down on the retreating infantry, but few found their mark, shields lifted up protectively more than a match for the defenders' darts.

Suddenly the Gate lit up, bright shining runes bursting into life across the stonework. It was breathtaking to look at, symbols from a culture that no one recognised or knew, a warning from those that had built it. As mesmerising as it was, it occurred to Torbin that it was to their detriment, the advantage of the Gift negated; the peril of entering it far too great.

He raised himself to a seating position, leaning back against the embrasure's wall. The pain was gone but the recollection made him nervous, almost expecting it to jump out at him from the shadows.

"Jonoh, we cannot enter the Gift." He looked at Jonoh's face, seeing the agreement in his eyes before he had uttered a word.

"There is much we don't know Torbin. In fact let's be honest, we have no idea what just happened, but as you say, the risk is too great." He looked around him as the runes that had appeared began to fade. They left no trace as they flickered out, not even a hint of an outline, just disappearing into nothing.

"Orphans, do not use the Gift. What appeared to happen to The Chosen also affected Torbin. I have no answers but the runes that appeared on the walls seem to be a warning. It is a blow that we cannot use the Gift to our great advantage but the same is true for them." He felt their acknowledgement and also their fear, the one true advantage they felt they had, torn away from them in a moment. But he also felt their steel, accepting what was and still ready to fight to the end.

Torbin staggered to his feet, nervous and jumpy in case the pain returned. He leant on Jonoh as he did so, grateful for the assistance. "Thank you Jonoh. If you hadn't pulled me out I don't know…" His voice tapered off, the words just escaping him. Jonoh gently placed his hand on Torbin's shoulder.

"You are welcome Torbin. I sensed a small reflection of it and it felt akin to having your bones broken, but very slowly and deliberately, whilst fully awake." Jonoh gave a little shrug as if unsure of his own words, half wishing he'd kept his mouth shut.

"That's a pretty good description." Torbin coughed out a tentative laugh. "Only ten times worse."

"Are you fit to continue?" Jonoh spoke gently, trying not to insult Torbin's pride.

"The pain has passed Jonoh, although it would appear that is not the case with our friends." Torbin grinned and motioned towards the H'Daree front line, all The Chosen having been recovered, but each and every one of them laying prone and close-eyed on the floor.

"Well it would seem that it has brought us some time. Whatever their plan was it's clearly been scuppered."

"We need to stand down full deployment for the moment Jonoh, put everyone on half-watch. Would you take care of it for me?"

"Consider it done Torbin. Go and rest a while, I'll take care of things."

Torbin smiled, patting Jonoh on the shoulder as he turned to make his way down the stairs, Terror at his heels. He couldn't help but admire Jonoh, so young and unaware of what his Gift really meant, but unfailingly kind and willing to put himself in peril. Neither of them knew what he may have been risking, but he dove in nonetheless and pulled him from the fire. He was mighty glad he did, the thought of the pain making him shudder.

He passed the forge, nodding to Torm but the burly smith was engrossed in his work, hammering away at the anvil, shouting instructions to his assistants. They had landed squarely on their feet with Torm, a more skilled smith he could not remember having met. He could produce anything that required forging and his inventive mind was a blessing. He had forged bodkin arrowheads, capable of piercing most armour apart from the thickest steel plate. He smiled to himself and continued down to the Gate, when he spotted Master Cerwin, sitting by a cookfire under a tent canopy; shielded from the rain, deep in conversation with Shala.

The little shadow-master had always been a bit of a charmer and he had the pretty young Orphan eating out of his hand. She sat there transfixed by his tales, throwing her head back in uproarious laughter, clapping the old man on the back.

Jek was closer to the Gate, continuing to drill his infantry, section by section. Keeping them sharp and battle-ready. As he walked toward him, Candor descended from the gatehouse, half a dozen of his men behind him. He ushered them over to one of the cookfires, obviously taking care to rotate them out, give everyone a rest and a feed before they were called to fight.

Candor sent his men off toward the cookfire where Shala and Cerwin were sitting and laughing. He turned to go back when he spotted Torbin, giving him a half wave, so he stopped and made his way over to him.

"How are you Candor?" He reached out and shook his friend's hand.

"We are good Torbin, well provisioned and well prepared." He reached down and gave Terror a little scratch behind the ear, the great hound smiling up at him.

Candor nodded to the cookfire and they slowly ambled over, talking as they went, Terror trotting along, full of expectation that a treat would be forthcoming. Shala looked over and saw

Terror, spreading her arms wide in greeting. He bounded forward, jumping into her arms, bowling her off her stool, the pair of them rolling around in the dirt, her laughing, him growling out little happy barks.

Torbin smiled to himself. Terror had always been friendly with children but now he was making more friends than he knew what to do with. He wondered if it had something to do with all these mind-walkers gathered together in one place, that sense of comradery seeping into his consciousness.

They sat on a couple of stools and said their hellos, Shala bringing them each a cup of cheyro, honey sweetened.

"I see Jek's keeping his men on their toes." Torbin nodded towards the infantry being drilled.

"That he is. The very moment we stood down he had them drilling. My men will thank him for it if we survive the battle, but I doubt they'll show it until after." Candor chuckled, looking across the top of his cup. Rory and Brownleaf had chosen to fight at the Gate and Rory was shadowing Jek, learning as much as he could in the short time they had. He was surprised that Brownleaf had made the choice but he was insistent. "I just want to fight the same as everyone else Candor. No special treatment." So that was where he was, in the middle of the infantry, just another foot soldier.

"How do you fare Master Cerwin?"

"I am well thank you Torbin, but taken aback by what happened. How are you more importantly?" the old shadow-master turned his full attention to Torbin,

"Fine, at least I am now, although the memory of the pain still makes me wince. Lots of questions though. What were those symbols? Why did it cause such agony? Why does it affect the Gift and not mindwalking?" Torbin took a breath, stating the obvious seeming to be everybody's new favourite pastime.

"We saw the runes light up down here. It seems they completely covered the Gate from one end to the other." The old man stroked his beard. "I have never seen those symbols before and they do not seem familiar to anyone. At least no one has come forward." He gave a breathy shrug of his shoulders. "There are many things yet to be explained. Mindwalking, the Gift, these are but two things that we take for granted but have no real explanation for. I think for now we just have to accept that these questions cannot be answered."

"I have to ask Master, where do you plan on being during the battle?" Torbin tried to land the question as gently as possible but knew he had to ask it.

"I will be close to Jonoh's side as I have been. My counsel is the best thing I can offer him, along with my service of course." Cerwin smiled his wrinkled smile.

"When they attack as they surely will, Jonoh will be in the thick of things Master. Are you sure that is the best place for you?" Again Torbin felt compelled to ask but instantly realised how insulting it sounded.

"Do you think me incapable? Am I so old and frail that I cannot defend myself? Maybe you should ask the bandits who tried to rob us in Sarjinn young Master Torbin. See what they have to say on the matter!" Cerwin almost sprang up, spilling his cheyro on the floor and storming off indignantly toward the stairs. Shala jumped after him, shooting an accusatory glare at Torbin as she left.

"A bit of an overreaction don't you think?" Torbin turned to Candor, eyebrows raised.

"Not the most subtle way of asking the question."

"I see Jonoh's point. Either age is truly mastering him or his behaviour is overly erratic. Either way we need to be mindful." Torbin took a sip of his cheyro and watched Jek's drills.

Jonoh leaned on the embrasure wall looking out at the massed ranks of the H'Daree. They had all withdrawn to a safe distance and were tending to The Chosen. It had taken an age for the first of them to come out of the trance entering the Gift had put them in. They looked stunned, fragile and uncertain of their bearings. It had unmanned them but it pointed to something more interesting. Although they were as Candor stated identical, there was clearly an unspoken hierarchy, Jonoh guessed based on actual age. He surmised the eldest and most experienced was the first to recover and the rest followed, either based on age, experience or ability. Either way the first to wake seemed to be the senior, everyone appearing to defer to him.

What fascinated Jonoh was the probability that they were different ages, almost as if they were somehow manufactured from a mould. Identical, but replaceable, bred to implement not to lead.

The thought floated about in the back of his mind as he watched the great swell of activity taking place on the valley floor. The great flatbeds were being unloaded; huge pieces of metal-banded wood being laid out on the floor. Like pieces of a giant puzzle, waiting to be assembled. What unnerved Jonoh was what they were planning to construct.

He didn't hear him sidle up but he looked sideways to see Cerwin standing at his side. He hadn't lost his stealth, still able to move unseen if you weren't looking for him. They stood in silence for a while, staring down the Pass, watching the H'Daree begin to build. What exactly was still unclear.

"Jonoh, do you harbour doubts about me?" He was not expecting the question but knew he could not reveal his concerns, a niggling sense of peril sitting at the back of his mind. It still filled him with guilt to think that way but he just couldn't shake his unease.

"No Master, no doubts, just concern for your wellbeing. Please believe me I mean no disrespect, but you have been under tremendous strain and you are not as young as you once were. How many one-hundred-and eighty-eight-year-olds are still fighting in battles?" Jonoh gave a little laugh, hoping that he hadn't set the old shadow-master off.

Cerwin returned his laugh, shaking his head. "I know that to be true my young friend but I will not leave your side until this is done." His tone brooked no argument so Jonoh just offered a respectful nod. "However, I believe I owe an apology to Torbin."

"Master?" Jonoh put forward the query but Cerwin had already turned to head back toward the Gate.

He shrugged and turned back to the activity of the H'Daree just as they began to bolt a number of the flatbeds together, making an extended base. He was beginning to work out what they were doing but it would take a while to confirm. He sat down, making himself comfortable, transfixed by what he was witnessing.

Torbin finished his cheyro and walked over to Jek and his infantry. Jek left Rory to carry on the drills, much to the young Green-lander's delight. Torbin grasped his arm in greeting.

"How does the training go Jek?"

"We are ready Torbin. If they breach the Gate we'll make 'em regret it." Jek puffed up proud and determined. Torbin was more certain than ever that he was the right choice.

"If they make the Gate, what is your battle plan? What about deploying the portcullis?"

"Well me and Candor 'ave spoken at length about it. We mean t' let about a couple o' 'undred through, enough for us t' deal with before we drop the portcullis. There is a risk for those in t' gatehouse until we've wiped 'em up so we'll only have t' bare minimum in there when t' time comes."

Candor was stood at Torbin's shoulder, nodding his agreement.

"That's quite the risk for those trapped in the gatehouse is it not?" Torbin raised the question along with his voice.

"But a risk worth taking Torbin. Myself, Stannard and a couple of my best will let two hundred or so through before we drop it, enough to manage from Jek's point of view. It makes sense, two hundred less to face and a crush of them trapped in the tunnel, the numbers pressing in behind will cause carnage. We can defend the ladder entrance for as long as we need to, they can only enter one at a time after all and someone needs to place the restraining bolts after the cullis has dropped."

Candor's argument made perfect sense but Torbin didn't see why it had to be him. He simply couldn't afford to lose him.

"It's a good plan, really it is. But why do you need to see it done? We are not blessed with leaders Candor, especially those tempered in the cauldron of battle. We cannot afford to lose you." It was a good, sound argument but Torbin could see it was not one he was going to win.

"I will not abandon my men or ask them to do what I will not." Candor cut his words with an acid edge. Whatever Torbin said, he would not be changing his mind.

"Alright Candor, alright." Torbin gave a wan smile, trying and failing to cover his true feelings.

Torbin stepped back a fraction, composing himself. "I will see you after then." He held out his hand, clutching Jek and Candor's hands tightly.

"See you after my friend." Candor stepped back toward the gatehouse.

"See you after Torbin." Jek nodded and walked back to the drilling, barking out instruction as he did so.

Torbin stood still for a moment, suddenly feeling completely alone. He shook himself like a wet dog climbing out of water, looked about and headed back up the stairs.

He sat down in the first embrasure with Jonoh, both of them unable to sleep as night descended. They could make out small pockets of activity where the campfires of the H'Daree offered meagre light but it revealed little. What was revealing was the noise, hammers falling, collective grunts of many bodies putting their shoulders to the task at hand and the constant tumult of urgent labour.

As the sky lightened, morning shaking off the gloom of night, it became clear what all the activity was about. The H'daree were raising great siege engines, but nothing like anyone had ever seen or heard of. The first one was complete, work continuing on a number of others, but what they saw was awe-inspiring. At their peak they were at a height with the first embrasures, twenty feet wide, constructed from what looked like thick, metal-banded oak. From the side they resembled enormous right-angled triangles, a giant stepped ramp angled at forty-five degrees running up to the top. They were loaded on the back of the extended flatbed carts, great yolks fitted to either side at the front of the construction. Huge intricate cables hung down from the sloping ramps, giant metal loops tied at their ends. Finally there was what appeared to be great wooden sheds loaded on the ramps, cables running to the top and back down to great ratcheted cogs set at the base. Turning handles extended left and right, standing sideways from great stepped wheels, big enough to accommodate at least twenty men.

The only saving grace was that there was only enough material to construct half a dozen of these leviathans. Now they knew what they were facing and where they would need to focus their resources.

"Right, at least we know how they will attack us." Torbin stood up, stretching the night's stiffness away.

"We'll have to see what embrasures they attack and reinforce them." Jonoh yawned, the lack of sleep telling a little but there was nothing to be done about it.

"At the rate they are raising them I think they'll attack before day's end." Torbin looked to Jonoh who nodded his agreement.

"Okay then, all we can do is wait."

Candor looked out through the arrow slit, not quite believing what he was seeing. There were no embrasures above the gatehouse so he felt certain the H'Daree would revert to the traditional battering ram but as of yet there was no sign of one. He gave Stannard a little signal and slipped out the back of the gatehouse, climbing down the ladder.

Jek was sat down, breaking his fast with a cup of cheyro and some boiled bacon and beans. He had deployed about a quarter of his force, allowing the balance some time to sleep. They may not get much opportunity over the next few days.

"Did you get a look at their siege engines?" Candor poured himself a cup of cheyro as he walked over to sit down.

"I did, very impressive. But they are fightin' uphill and can only present a line as wide as their platforms allow. They'll 'ave to do it while under fire an' facin' a determined foe. I fancy our chances." Jek nonchalantly brushed it off, as if it were a mere trifle. Candor was not so sure.

"They'll come for the Gate with a battering ram, no doubt covered so that our arrows will be useless."

"Why so gloomy Candor? Y' can't go into a battle expectin' t' lose or you'll make it happen. This is the best defensive position I've ever seen. They can't get around our flanks, their main target is a 'undred an' fifty feet in t' air and the broadest front they can put forward is twenty feet wide. They will smash themselves on the walls an' destroy their army here." Candor couldn't help but be lifted by Jek's optimism.

Jek flicked what he hadn't eaten off his plate, getting up and giving Candor a reassuring pat on the shoulder, walking towards his men, shouting them out of their slumber.

Torbin and Jonoh stood anxiously watching the H'Darees progress when suddenly the rain just stopped, the clouds rolling back up the mountains and the sun breaking through, casting warmth and light all around. The cessation of the rain clearly revealed the force in front of them for the first time, detail previously obscured clearly visible.

They were hooking the great aurochs into the yolks at the sides of the siege engines. Their covering of bones augmented by back and leg armour, making them almost invulnerable. The first engine began to rumble forward, heading for the first embrasure, straight at Torbin and Jonoh. Great clumps of infantry hid in its vast shadow, shields up apart from those carrying ropes with grappling hooks. Behind them teams of soldiers carried sections of ladders, hundreds of them in total.

"BATTLE STATIONS!" Torbin screamed out his command, at every embrasure men stepped toward the front, shields locked, spears lowered. All across the Gate bowmen nocked their arrows and stood ready. The two-man heavy crossbow teams readied themselves, told to hold their fire until the siege engines came within close range. Torbin would've preferred point blank but didn't want to stretch the nerves any more than necessary.

Terror sidled up next to him, all bristling anger, head down growling out a challenge to anyone stupid enough to accept it. Master Cerwin stood next to Jonoh.

"Spread along the line and reinforce where the siege engines stop. We must hold them where they land and throw them back. I will stand where I am at the first embrasure. Courage my brothers and sisters, we are children of the Protectorate and we will stand." Jonoh gave out his order, knowing it may be his last, Cerwin stepping up beside him, almost disappearing under the weight of his armour. The wave of strength that flowed back to him was almost overwhelming, so he took a deep breath to steady himself.

The first great engine rolled slowly, inexorably forward, the two great aurochs straining; heads down, dragging the immense weight toward the wall.

The signal came for the archers to loose their arrows. Great swarms of deadly darts showered down on the advancing H'Daree. Their shields were strong but the arrows began to find more and more marks, a low groan going up from the soldiers below.

As the great engine approached the wall at Torbin's embrasure the solid metal-banded shed at the base filled with heavily armoured infantry and began being winched up the sloping ramp. The huge cogged wheels were filled with armoured men, walking the great drums round and round, winching the sheds further and further up the slope.

Torbin and Jonoh stepped forward, shoulder to shoulder, shields locked with their companions. A small nest of spears poked out over the shield rims, a dozen or so of Jonoh's Orphan reserve bolstering their numbers. The great siege engine hit the wall, the wooden shed winching up, only twenty or thirty feet short of the top. Torbin signalled his heavy crossbow team to let fly. Bolts flew from the bow, smashing into the front of the shed, causing the timber to crack, the impact ringing the ears. The wood held, the great metal bands bowing but keeping the structure together.

The shed made the top of the ramp, a mass intake of breath followed, that moment of terrible anticipation causing everything to seem to stop in space. Torbin briefly looked over his shoulder and was shocked to see Terror scrambling to the back of the embrasure, running down the corridor toward the north end of the Gate. Then the front of the shed slammed down forming a flat platform and the soldiers inside rushed out screaming their battle cries. The front lines crashed into each other, defenders digging in, holding the line, attackers charging in pulses, hit, withdraw, hit again, trying to make it to the corridor. They were mainly armed with heavy axes, big looping overhand swings crashing down on the rims of the defenders' shields. In the background the banded wooden shed began its descent, ready to ferry the next group of attacking troops up the ramp.

The contact was fierce, Torbin and Jonoh felling an attacker each, spear thrusts proving more effective than the axes of their enemies. Torbin called for a great push and they put their shoulders to it, the reserve Orphans adding extra weight. They nudged forward, slowly gathering momentum and began to push the H'Daree towards the edge of the embrasure. They realised too late what was happening, the roar and confusion of battle affecting their senses. In desperation they launched a frenzied attack, the man next to Jonoh going down, a great heavy axe embedded in his shoulder, another falling to the H'daree but it made no difference, all of the attackers running out of room. Some of them managed to cling onto the ramp, most of them falling screaming to their deaths.

Torbin sucked in a deep breath and turned to nod at Jonoh.

"Alright?" It was all he could think of to say. Jonoh nodded, lifting the body of the dead man next to him to the back of the embrasure, laying him down in the corridor. The other victim was still alive but not able to stand in the front line. Two of Jonoh's reserves stepped forward, as they did two more joined the back of the line. If they lost two people per attack they would run out of defenders quickly.

Torbin looked out the front of the embrasure. The other five great siege engines were engaged and the great cables were being used to stabilise them, stretched out tight, soldiers on ladders hammering the huge metal loops into the stone. At the same time vast wooden bracing beams were being ferried to the engines by the aurochs, raised on pulleys and driven into place by teams of big powerful looking men with sledgehammers. He had expected them to be organised but this was beyond anything he had imagined.

The wooden shed had reached the bottom of the ramp and was loading up with soldiers, ready to winch into action. He glanced to his right and saw what looked like a low-level building mounted on a couple of flatbeds. A covered ram, rolling toward the Gate. Nothing he could do about anything now, other than fight, and hope.

Candor looked out at the approach to the Gate. A long wood-covered cart was rolling toward the Gate, a huge number of infantry following on behind, shields locked, forming a tight protective wall. He had an archer at each arrow slit, all with arrows nocked, armour piercing bodkin heads levelled at the enemy. At a relatively short distance and fired flat, he hoped they would cause carnage. He reached out to the Orphans at the Gate.

"They are upon us."

He watched as they rolled the cart up to the Gate and could hear men heaving back the ram, crashing it forward into the wooden gate. They had reinforced it with thick lengths of oak, almost trunk thick, to brace the Gate from within and Torm had rivetted broad bands of iron to the inside. The ram crashed forward, the Gate shuddering, the sound of wood splintering ringing through the air. It held, but for how long remained the question.

"Right lads, let's give them something to think about. Pick

your targets and fire at will."

Almost as one they loosed their arrows, many of them sticking in shields but some crashing through. A number of H'Daree fell, shields pinned to their torsos, some hit through their helmets, the bodkin tips having done their work.

Their front lines bunched up, overlapping their shields as much as was possible, rows behind lifting their shields over their heads, forming their tortoise defence. Candor's men kept pouring on their fire, enough attackers being dropped to give the defenders belief, but the ram kept pulling back and swinging forward, crashing time and time again into the Gate. The noise of fracturing timbers grew louder and louder, the cracking sounds a sickening blow to the defenders. Candor looked down through one of the murder holes and could see one of the bracing beams already split, just a matter of time before the Gate gave.

Jonoh braced himself, right in the middle of the front line, waiting for the shed to make the embrasure for the third time. They had repelled the first two attacks but at a cost of four soldiers dead, two so badly injured that they couldn't carry on. They had not killed all of the attacking H'Daree, some of them managing to scramble back down the ramp to relative safety. The front of the shed was buckling, just holding together; metal bands bending under fire but not breaking. It was about ten feet from the top when Torbin gave the order for the heavy crossbow to let fly.

The first bolt bounced away, flying off to the side, but the second smashed through the timber, instantly killing a number of H'Daree. The next bolt missed its target, smashing into the side of the shed, wood disintegrating, splinters big and small flying through the air, the shed completely destroyed. The soldiers still alive bravely charged forward but none of them made the embrasure, all shattered as the remaining three bolts burst through them, scattering their remains over the sides of the rampart.

The defenders' shoulders all seemed to sag together. The relief of not having to come into contact again making them all breathe easy, at least for the moment.

Torbin turned to Jonoh, sweat pouring into his eyes. He took off his helmet and wiped his eyes on his sleeve. "Jonoh, we need to check down the line, see how we are set. I don't completely trust mind-walker contact in these situations, the fog of battle and all that."

"Leave it with me Torbin, I'll be back as soon as I can."

As he turned to leave and one of his reserve stepped into his place, Torbin saw the shattered shed's remains winched to the ground, discarded and replaced with another identical one. This was going to be a long day.

Jonoh ran along to the next embrasure defending a siege tower. A number of H'Daree seemed to have gained a foothold, enough forming up to make a good wall, the shed already back at the bottom of the ramp, loading up with reinforcements. He could see the defenders' line badly reduced, replacements finding it hard to reform properly, navigating the dead bodies proving arduous in such cramped space.

He heard the roar before he saw him, then a hulking figure rose up at the front of the line with a huge double-headed axe lifted above his head. Guido Tivosi crashed into the H'Darees' shields, shoulder charging, forcing a gap to appear. They tried desperately to reform, spear thrusts bouncing off Tivosi's armour, none of them composed enough to find a gap. Their faces were figures of terror, looking as if they were shaking hands with the Beckoner himself. Tivosi had a maniacal smile on his face, standing in the middle of the throng, swinging his axe as if his very existence depended on it. Four foes fell dead at his feet, the remaining H'Daree losing their nerve, desperately pulling away from him just to run into the shields and spears of the defenders. Those remaining were easily despatched, pushed out into the air, falling to their end.

Tivosi turned around, blood spattered over the front of his body. Face, armour and helmet all showing the results of his gruesome work. He saw Jonoh and made for the back of the corridor.

"How goes it Guido?"

"We are holding Jonoh but we lost our heavy crossbow in the first attack, firing team and the weapon. Both went over the edge unfortunately." He grinned, not exactly a smile but the look of someone enjoying his day.

"I will get a team from one of the embrasures not repelling. How many have you lost?"

"Seven dead, three on their way to the field hospital, Jonoh. The H'Daree are fierce buggers, brave and fanatical; a dangerous combination." Tivosi looked over his shoulder to see the shed winched well over halfway, the next set of foes well on their way. "Worry not Jonoh, we will throw them back, go do what you need to." They clasped forearms and nodded to each other, Tivosi returning to the front of the line, Jonoh carrying on down the corridor.

There were injured men and dead ones laying in the corridor at the back of the engaged embrasures, medics carrying them away as quickly as they could manage. Jonoh kept pushing forward, each embrasure where there was a siege engine were pressed hard. The facts were plain, every time a defender fell they were plugging with the reserve, but their replacements were not inexhaustible. The H'Daree however were sending fresh troops into the fray every time, and the numbers were on their side.

He covered the full length of the Gate, all the way to the north end where Jadran was marshalling the defence. Terror was stood by his side, his blood-soaked face set in an angry scowl, growling out an invitation to anyone brave enough to take him up on it. They were hard pressed, probably harder than anywhere else so Jonoh sent one hundred reserves to shore up his efforts. By the time he returned to Torbin's embrasure nearly all their reserves were committed. They had made the H'Daree pay a terrible price, great swathes of ground in front of the stonework was littered with corpses, but they kept coming on.

Torbin stepped back, gulping in air, the last attack only just repulsed but at a terrible cost. Another four had fallen and the H'Daree had slightly changed tactics, somehow managing to save troops, withdrawing earlier and managing to navigate a retreat down the ramp. He looked at them loading the next wave of troops, all of them fresh and seemingly eager. They were overloading, men bunching up behind the open-backed sheds and there were crossbow men amongst their number.

Jonoh came running in, red-faced and sucking in air; obviously not the bearer of good news.

"We are nearly all in Torbin, all we can do is defend the embrasures where siege engines are attacking. We will have to abandon the rest and to add mud to the waters the Gate is straining under the ram, it won't hold much longer. I saw Terror with Jadran. He looked like he was giving a good account of himself." He looked exactly like Torbin felt, desperate and forlorn.

Cerwin shuffled up, carrying his spear, almost engulfed by his shield; a wrinkled frown on his face.

"Maybe now is the time to consider another path Jonoh." The puppy-dog look in his eyes made Jonoh feel a tug of guilt, as if he was being an unreasonable, petulant child. He hated the way he did that.

"What do you suggest Master? I would say that unless you can magically produce more men, we are fucked!" he barked out at the old shadow-master, his patience rubbed thin. He had never used that kind of language or disrespected the old man but he felt pushed to the limit, going over the same old redundant argument.

Candor looked down through the murder holes, watching the Gate begin to bow; a couple of the iron reinforcing bands having cracked. Two of the bracing beams had split and fallen away. The Gate would not hold much longer.

"Right, everybody out, now!" His bowmen made for the exit at the back of the room, a few of them touching the portcullis on their way out, as if it were a lucky touchstone. All of them ran across the ground, sliding in behind Jek's infantry, gaining some elevation so that they could get a clear shot at the H'Daree once the Gate fell. A couple of them refused to leave, and Candor couldn't help but be moved by their courage and loyalty.

CRAAACK! The sound of the Gate splitting and crashing inwards rang across the yard. Candor and Stannard went to the back of the gatehouse and made ready to remove the restraining bolts. Dust kicked up through the murder holes, a strange silence descending upon everything, the deep breath before the plunge.

A great roar went up, H'daree infantry pouring through the Gate, fanning out to form a line. Jek had pulled his men back in a great arcing semicircle, blockading the yard beyond the exit tunnel. Candor watched as the H'Daree shifted right in tight formation, forming a defensive block around the ladder to the gatehouse. They didn't need time to work out where things were, they knew exactly what to do and where to go before they had even made it.

"Drop the cullis Candor." Shala called out, urgency in her words, almost as if she had realised the danger but too late. He motioned to Stannard and they both removed the bolts, the portcullis slamming down, two tons of steel with spiked feet, descending like a falling mountain.

It crashed down, spiked feet plunging into the holes made to fit them like shoes. The men underneath screamed, the spikes pinning them to the floor like skewered meat, the angry shouts of their comrades aimed upwards. The H'daree that had made the yard formed up in a tight defensive formation, shields locked tight, only their helmeted heads peeking out above the rims of their shields. At their rear, armoured men began to climb the ladder, swords drawn with murderous intent.

Candor and Stannard replaced the restraining bolts, securing the portcullis, locking it tightly in place. They drew their swords and stood either side of the ladder entrance, knowing that this was it, not a single soldier could be allowed to pass. The two bowmen that had stayed began firing arrows through the murder holes, impossible to miss their targets, not just fish in a barrel, but a barrel packed tight with fish that could hardly move.

Candor's breath was coming quickly, in and out like a panting dog, the peril absolutely certain. This was the vessel of his existence, the crossroads; one way forward with all the possibilities life held, the other to eternal darkness, the end of everything. It stuck him as excruciating that this much truth would be so self-evident at the moment that he may not be able to act on it.

The shed was nearly at the top of the ramp and the crossbow men had been loosing speculative bolts, forcing the defenders to hang back, not able to meet them at the embrasure's edge. Master Cerwin had stepped into the line next to him, Jonoh noticing his spear and shield were clean, his sword and stiletto dagger still sheathed.

It was evident that they would not be able to hold a shield-wall for many more attacks; they just didn't have the numbers. If it came to it, they would have to go hand to hand, where the metal met the meat. If only they could use the Gift, if only.

The shed shuddered to a stop, the front screen crashing down, H'Daree troops pouring out, screaming their battle cries. They crashed into the shield-wall, spears smashing on shields, swords slashing down, men dropping, some dead, some wounded, screaming in pain. It didn't matter, all that did was winning, driving them back, making them pay the blood price.

"Together." Torbin nodded at Jonoh and the two of them dropped their shoulders and shoved forward with all their strength. The H'Daree's line split and they both drew their swords together. The H'Daree lost their cohesiveness for a brief moment, it was all they needed. Torbin cut down two men in moments, the rest of them stumbling back nervously toward the embrasure's edge. He glanced sideways and could not quite believe what he saw. Jonoh was moving like liquid, his every stroke fluid, every move so precise, avoiding contact by the merest of margins, the thickness of paper. H'Daree were falling to his every swing and stab of his sword, looks of terror and shock fixed to their faces, the moment of their death leaving them in stunned confusion.

A shield poked up through the ladder hole, Candor and Stannard hammering down on its rim, splitting it down the middle, the soldier behind it desperately trying to raise his sword to block any blows. He was too late. The next H'Daree shouldered his way past the corpse of his fellow, shoving with his shield. Behind them a shower of crossbow bolts flew up through the murder holes killing one of his bowmen and hamstringing the other. He desperately hacked at the new shield, pulling out a dagger from his belt, stabbing around the side, feeling the satisfaction of it plunging into flesh, tearing it free and seeing the man fall away only to be replaced by another determined face.

A shortsword flashed out, clipping Stannard on the shin making him jump back instinctively. He landed on a murder hole and Candor watched the bolt tear out through his leather jerkin, blood cascading into the air.

"Noooooo!" Candor launched a frenzied attack smashing the next two H'Daree to attempt the entry but he could not sustain it. The first man made the entrance, getting his shield up well enough to block most of Candor's sword thrusts. As he managed to get around his shield another two H'Daree had breached the top of the ladder, locking their shields together allowing their fellows to gain entry. Candor fought with a frenzy, spittle bubbling from the corners of his mouth, the veins on his neck looking like they were going to burst, but it was all to no avail. They had gained too great a foothold, lining up in a shield-wall lockstepping forward, forcing him back.

He retreated to the arrow slits, picking up his one surviving comrade and sitting him down against the wall. They locked eyes, the certainty that this was their final moments dawning on them, not being able to find the words.

"It was my honour Candor." The man leaned into the wall, propelling himself bodily at the advancing wall of wood and metal, making it buckle for a moment but being despatched by at least half a dozen blades nonetheless.

They advanced toward him, tight lockstep holding them solidly together. No way out. For a brief moment it seemed as if all the events of his life lit up, like a vast wall of memories. They were on him now, the wickedly sharp points of their blades only inches away. In the background he thought he could hear Jek screaming his name, imploring him to hang on but his time was up.

He felt the first blade push into his skin, a sharp stinging sensation as the flesh parted, the metal sliding in feeling cold, as if made of ice. He felt it scrape his ribs, the noise was like a carpenter rasping a rough piece of wood. The second and third blades hit simultaneously, one going in through his belly button, tearing slightly upwards, the other into his inner thigh, making the muscle bunch up so tightly it stung. Two more blades pressed in and he stared at the metal penetrating him, stealing his life. He snatched a breath, difficult to do, the noise of his blood pumping out of him filling his ears, so very loud.

"Torbin, tell Marye I love her."

Torbin heard Candor and felt him go. Rage overcame him and he tore recklessly into the remaining H'Daree, ignoring his own wounds, cutting them to ribbons, standing over their ruined bodies, gasping in great gouts of air. He stood to the front of the embrasure and roared out his anger, the H'Daree that had managed to withdraw to the safety of the ramp cowering away, hands over their heads as if in danger of being struck down.

Jonoh walked over the corpses laying on the floor and placed his hand on Torbin's shoulder. He span round, teeth gritted like a wounded tiger, knuckles white on the pommel of his sword.

"Peace Torbin, it's Jonoh." He glanced over Torbin's shoulder, the next shed already being winched up the ramp. Torbin's glazed eyes seemed to refocus, recognising friend from foe and regaining some measure of calm.

"Candor is gone Jonoh, and we've lost the gatehouse." Torbin's eyes watered, the realisation hitting him like a falling boulder.

"I am so sorry Torbin, he was a good man. I'm afraid that is not all though Torbin. Two of the embrasures have been breached and the H'Daree have a foothold. We have withdrawn to the corridor and are making a stand but we have committed all of our reserves. We cannot throw them back; we simply don't have the numbers."

They looked at each other, that moment of realisation that this would be their end passing between them. Jonoh felt a strange sense of serenity, no fear just a certainty that he was where he was meant to be. Whatever came to pass was as it should be.

"Jonoh my boy, please listen to me." In all the commotion he'd forgotten about the little shadow-master. Even after the ferocity of the last contact his weapons remained undrawn, sitting on his sword belt. The shed was winching its way back to the top of the ramp, very nearly there.

"Master Cerwin, now may not be the best moment." Jonoh turned, sword in one hand, spear in the other. There were too few of them left to form a wall so they would have to attack them as soon as they stepped forward.

"Jonoh it is not too late. You could give yourself up, they may yet spare everyone else. Candor has passed, it is only you they really want." Cerwin was pleading with him, a desperation in his voice that shocked Jonoh. The shed was almost there.

"There is no time now, we stand here. How would you know what they want?" Jonoh snapped out angrily no longer concerned about the old man's feelings, just irritated by his nonsensical bleatings. "Either draw your weapon or withdraw. There are no other choices."

The front of the shed fell forward when Jonoh felt it, a pinch in his side, something that shouldn't be there. He looked down at his side and saw Cerwin's liver-spotted hand touching his ribs, the handle of his stiletto dagger pressed against the gap in his armour.

"I'm sorry my boy, you leave me no choice."

He instinctively snapped, falling into the Gift, somewhere safe and welcoming. The white light surrounded him, flowing through his body and consciousness, lifting him high, free from the worries of the corporeal. It was like the Void's brighter, bigger sibling, everything available; as if it wouldn't be? There were no requirements here, just an invitation to step forward, walk through the door. He looked sideways and pulled Cerwin's hand back, removing the blade. As it exited the sinew, cartilage, veins, arteries, muscles, every single piece of flesh or matter healed itself, no scar of any form visible on his skin. He irritatedly flicked him away towards the melee of bodies.

Everything outside of his little bubble was stuck in time, swords swinging, bolts suspended in mid-flight, contorted faces; snarls fixed on mouths, blood and sweat spinning off into the air. But it was all irrelevant, one tiny moment in time. If it wasn't happening, didn't exist, what possible difference would it make? There was only the light, the invitation. The runes were a key to the next level of existence, a welcome not a warning; enter without agenda. A door held open, only no one understood the language. He went toward the light but something held him back; something tied his mind to this reality.

"Ahh, that's it." He smiled, happy that he had done his part, sending them the key before he left.

Torbin was flung backwards, away from the embrasure's edge, his back slamming into the corridor's wall. He looked to where Jonoh had been standing, a bright white ball of light filling the air. Master Cerwin was thrown bodily into the H'Daree at the top of the ramp, knocking them over like skittles, bowling down the ramp, gathering bodies like moss on a rolling stone.

Then it hit him, a great shining white light flowed through him, connecting him to all the Orphans still standing. It was the key to open the door, a final offering from Jonoh Shipwright. The Gift would be their saviour, walking in the light to turn back the darkness.

He suddenly returned to the now, the blinding white sphere where Jonoh had been, gone. In its place a great spherical hole in the stonework. The top twenty feet of the ramp had disappeared, wood shattered, bands of iron warped and twisted, sticking into the air like arthritic fingers, the shed vanished, soldiers scrambling back down the ramp.

The portcullis was raising, the H'Daree in the tunnel having recovered their dead to the rear, all formed up, shields locked, looks of revenge for their dead comrades creasing their features.

Jek had pulled back his men, forming up in line, shields locked, grimly determined. Shala had saddled up along with the rest of the Orphans and was readying herself for the charge when she heard a noise behind her. She turned and saw a great dust cloud rising from the old path through the woods. Out of the swirling dirt a great press of mounted, armoured warriors were charging toward the Gate, all of them dressed in mismatched armaments. She realised straight away that this was The Maimed, the mercenaries Jonoh had told her about. At the head of the cavalry was a man dressed so flamboyantly that she thought he'd do well on the stage. She rode straight at them, turning her horse to ride alongside the colourful leader.

"Captain General Wane I assume."

"It is indeed my lovely. We come to offer assistance." He smiled that smooth-as-molasses look and she thought immediately that Jonoh's description could not have been more accurate.

"You are most welcome and just in the nick of time. The H'Daree have made the Gate and raised the portcullis. We are making a last stand but if you will ride with us I believe we may yet turn the tide." She smiled across at him and he gave her a playful wink.

"I am your servant, if you will lead the way."

Shala sent a mind-walker message to her comrades and charged towards the Gate.

Jek got the message, roaring defiance at the gathered H'daree who had poured out through the end of the tunnel, the portcullis withdrawn into the gatehouse. His formation feinted a charge, splitting in the middle and pulling away on either side leaving a channel, twenty feet wide, matching the tunnel exit.

Moments later Mitter Wane's mercenaries crashed into them, led by a screaming Shala, riding them down and bursting out into the massed hordes of the H'Daree. They poured out through the

Gate scattering the lines of the H'Daree, enemies breaking before them, instinctively turning to run.

Torbin struggled to his feet, winded and sore, still reeling from what he had witnessed. Around him the surviving defenders in his embrasure were slowly regaining their composure, looks of shocked relief on their faces. He shuffled forward to the ruined front of the embrasure and looked across the field of battle.

A great arrowhead of cavalry was pouring through the Gate, tearing into the H'Darees' front lines, a sea of black troops rolling backwards, desperately trying to escape. A smaller group of mounted soldiers wheeled left and began attacking the siege engines. He was sure he could see Shala at their head, roaring her defiance, disappearing and reappearing from view, cutting down great swathes of enemy soldiers. It was the one hundred mounted Orphans that had been part of the Gate's defence, dropping in and out of the Gift, felling the H'Daree like stalks of wheat at harvest time.

He looked along the front of the Gate and saw H'Daree troops being dropped in bunches, scrambling back down the ramps, falling to invisible blades, tumbling from the ramps, all in total disarray. All apart from the next engine along, Tivosi's embrasure.

He turned and made for the corridor, running toward Tivosi's embrasure. "On me!"

As he and his small retinue made it to Tivosi's command the defenders were backed into the corridor, formed up tight, the clashing sounds of blades on shields ringing through the air. He shouldered his way forward, weary but determined faces stepping aside to let him through. The remaining H'Daree were packed into the embrasure, having gained a foothold simply unprepared to give it up.

It wasn't a stalemate exactly but Torbin could sense that things were teetering on a knife edge. If they could establish a solid foothold, the H'Daree could still win the argument, on sheer weight of numbers if nothing else. They lacked nothing in terms of courage and they had obviously been relentlessly drilled to defend against gifted opposition.

Suddenly a great battle cry went up from the back of the corridor and Torbin saw him, charging the massed ranks, great double-headed axe cutting a deadly gap through the H'Daree. Guido Tivosi roared forward, Lenny White and another of his chosen guard at his back, smashing through the shields, forcing their defensive wall to split. The H'Daree were powerless to resist him, some actually being trampled underfoot, as if run down by heavy horse. Then out of nowhere Tivosi used a shield to leap into the air, landing about six feet down the ramp, right into the heart of the attackers. Bodies scattered all around him, desperately trying to avoid the mad axeman, some turning and trying to escape back down the ramp.

"Noooo GUIDO!" Torbin cried out as Tivosi tumbled sideways from the ramp, half a dozen H'Daree joining him in the deadly descent. The tide had turned completely, the remaining H'Daree being cut down or pushed off the edge, the ramp emptying onto the battlefield, some being cut down by the marauding Orphans.

He ran back to the stairs by the first embrasure, running down toward the Gate. Jek was there with about one hundred men, holding the rear while the rest of his force poured through the Gate, following the cavalry and engaging the H'Daree forces that had been isolated by the charge.

Jek looked across and saw Torbin, saluting him, a grim, hard-set grin on his face. Torbin nodded, his breath coming hard making his chest heave up and down, the noise of battle muffled by the tunnel. He leaned forward, hands on knees, giving himself a moment. Just a moment to gather himself. Then he heard it, the unmistakable sound of a great body of soldiers on the march. He turned back to look toward the woods at their back and his breath caught in his throat. The Golden Legions marched through the woods, their white-suited officer at the head of the column.

Torbin grabbed a mount and rode straight at them, pulling up short and raising his hand in salute.

"Greetings my friends. I am Torbin Pale-skin, commander of the defence of the Titan Gate." He heard himself say it, embarrassed by how pompous he sounded, but couldn't think of anything else to say. It almost felt like a dream, the one where everything you wanted comes to be, at least until you woke up. He closed his eyes, rubbing them and then opening them again. *"Definitely awake."*

The white-suited officer came to a halt, raising his right arm and making a fist. The Golden Legions stopped instantly, snapping to attention in perfect unbroken formation. Their reputation was well founded, disciplined and pinpoint in their movements.

Torbin trotted up beside the officer, his bright white uniform, pristine and gold-braided, truly a Darmation soldier.

"His Majesty King Lorgan sends his greetings and offers you the services of the Golden Legions. I am Colonel Kafir, and I am your servant. How may we assist you Torbin Pale-skin?" The Darmation officer offered a formal nod, perfectly observing protocol.

Torbin offered his hand, the slightly shocked look on Kafir's face not stopping him from accepting it.

"I accept your offer gladly my friend. We have driven them back but lack the numbers to press our attack, Colonel. We need to engage them and keep them on the run." Torbin smiled, realising that in his blood-soaked state he must have been a sight to behold. As he released Kafir's hand a little wave of guilt washed over him, blood staining the perfectly white gloves of the Darmation officer.

"If you'd care to follow me." Torbin reined his mount around, pointing it at the Gate and rode back toward Jek. He glanced back, watching Kafir raise his blood-stained hand, the signal instantly answered, the Golden Legions marching purposely forward.

He reached Jek, dismounting before his horse had stopped.

"Let them through my friend and hold the tunnel entrance." Torbin looked over to the ladder hole into the gatehouse, dead H'Daree littering the ground around it.

He looked at Jek, not wanting to do this alone.

"Torbin, can I come with you?" Jek asked the question, eyes down, not sure if he had overstepped the mark.

"Please my friend, I am not sure I can do this by myself." Torbin gestured for Jek to follow him, which he did, leaving Brownleaf to look to their dispositions. Torbin made the bottom of the ladder as the first ranks of the Golden Legions trotted through the Gate tunnel, quickstepping it. He looked back toward the woods and saw them still pouring toward the Gate, at least five thousand as far as he could make out.

He turned, taking a deep breath to steel himself. As he reached the gatehouse floor he slowed, taking in all that he could see. Young Stannard laid on his back, a bloody hole punched through his leather jerkin, a wide-eyed look of shock on his face. There were a couple of dead H'Daree and two bowmen, one of them with so many stab wounds, he looked like a human pin cushion. Then he saw him and the tears welled up, dripping down his cheeks and rolling down his chapped lips, sharp and salty. He fell to his knees, head bowed, shoulders shuddering up and down uncontrollably, the weight of grief hitting him like a hammer.

Candor was sat against the wall, blood having poured out of so many stab wounds that his skin almost looked grey. It looked more like a savage revenge attack rather than a battlefield death. Torbin wept, Jek kneeling beside him, shedding his own tears, the pair of them taking a quiet moment amid the tumult of battle, saying goodbye to their friend.

They left the gatehouse saying nothing, Jek calling half a dozen of his men to help him clear the bodies, Torbin ascending the stairs, needing to clear his head and look at the battle that was still raging in the Pass.

He reached the first embrasure and looked down at the Gate. The H'Daree had been driven from the Gate and were pouring back up the Pass, corpses littering the ground like a great black carpet, thousands upon thousands dead on the field. The Golden Legions were pressing forward in disciplined lines, the black-clad H'daree running before them. The cavalry were continuing to press but the shock of the initial charge had slowed and a melee battle was beginning to form.

About half a mile up the Pass a great line of H'Daree, about ten deep, had spread from one side to the other, gaps allowing their comrades to withdraw. The Orphan cavalry had managed to down a number of the great aurochs but the rest were through the line, tramping back up the Pass with the rest of the retreating army. It was almost a rout but even now Torbin could not help but admire their discipline, knowing that the rear-guard they had formed would hold long enough to let them escape. Brave men all who knew this was a death sentence.

"We must eliminate their rear-guard but not pursue any further." Torbin could feel the murderous rage that had built up in the Orphans, but he could see what they couldn't. the H'Daree were defeated but even with their catastrophic losses they still had a vast

force retreating, too many to completely eliminate. Regrouping and taking care of their own dead and wounded was the only course of action. He descended the stairs and mounted up, riding out to see Kafir and inform him of his decision.

In the weeks that followed, a pall of gloom settled on the survivors of the battle. A number of great piles of dead H'Daree were stacked about a mile up the Pass and burnt in mass funeral pyres. The thick black smoke hung in the air for what seemed like an age, the smell of burning meat filling the atmosphere, making everyone pull cloths across their faces. Torbin had to tell Marye about Candor, and he hadn't seen her for days, the loss hitting her like bolt of lightning.

A representative of Darmat had turned up, Advocate Sorkin, to establish a diplomatic presence and discuss trade and taxation issues. It was hard work, dry and outside of his purview but Marye had reappeared, strong and steadfast, representing the interests of all that remained. He felt a little sorry for Sorkin, knowing that a fight with Marye would be one he couldn't possibly win.

He left such matters to those best disposed to deal with them. He had walked to the top of the Gate to get a little peace, nodding at the sentries posted and sat with his back against a wall, closing his eyes and breathing in the air. It smelt cleaner up there and more serene. Terror wandered up and sat down next to him, nudging up and giving him a look full of understanding. How he always knew what to do was beyond him, but he did.

His head was full to overflowing with questions. What had happened to Jonoh, Cerwin and Tivosi? There was no confirmation about any of them, no reports of death, no sightings. Would the H'Daree come again? Would the Darmations aid in the continuing defence of the Gate?

What rankled most was the absence of certain things. Why would a force as accomplished and capable as the H'Daree launch an attack on a defensive position as strong as the Titan Gate without any kind of artillery? No catapults, no Scorpions and what he couldn't get past, no fire? Who would launch an attack like that without fire arrows, fireballs? It made no sense.

Epilogue:

Time to face the fire.

The one thing they never prepare you for is the smell. Not the body odours, made worse by the sweat of exertion. Not the release of bowels by the dead or dying. No, it was the smell of blood, tangy and metallic, so much so that it stuck to the top of the palate and no amount of liquid would wash it away. It formed a memory in the mind that never left you, rising up like a wraith, haunting your thoughts.

It shouldn't have been his responsibility anyway; he was after all only secondary. If primary hadn't been killed in that little skirmish outside the twin cities he would be still. He had never expected it after all, being stuck as secondary for decades, never being elevated to the top position. Too impetuous, being reactive rather than proactive. At least that was what he was told, but circumstances changed all that.

They should have waited to attack the twin cities once they had won the Bountiful Isles. The mantra was clear, conquer, secure, reinforce and then meticulously plan; waiting until everything was prepared, every single aspect had been addressed. Then and only then did you move to the next objective; the power to overwhelm. The fact that this was instilled into every one of The Chosen was simply matter of fact, something beyond debate.

However, Primary had decided otherwise, believing quite rightly that it would be a simple task to run the Green-landers from their homes. The intelligence reports had told them that their main force, the Water Spears, were based on the Bountiful Isles and all but a handful had been eliminated in the initial attack. They had little to no way of withstanding an assault but the longer they waited, the more chance there was of them organising a much more robust defence.

It had been so easy, less than an hour to completely overwhelm them. He had followed protocol perfectly, especially in the aftermath of Primary's demise. They had stopped, secured, populated the twin cities and began the building programme, instituting all the processes required to move forwards. It was a textbook operation and the resistance so pitiful that it made sense to move quickly, hit them before they had a chance to organise properly.

The reports had told them that they had only managed a ragtag collection of mismatched soldiers to defend the Titan Gate, so few that they should be able to sweep them from the field. He would have ordered the advance immediately, but even he wouldn't be so rash as to attack a five-hundred-foot-high defensive fort without siege engines. He was convinced that would be more than sufficient to overrun their little band of defenders, which was why he hadn't bothered constructing any artillery. That and the fact that it would have caused even further delays. Impetuous indeed. If only he'd had catapults, ballista, fireballs, the tide would have undoubtably turned, and who could have known that they would have manufactured artillery of their own?

The most unexpected and confusing event was that suddenly the defenders were able to use the Gift, whereas all it did was cause carnage amongst his own. Why had they not used it earlier? Was it a ploy to lure them in, cause maximum casualties? There was just no time to react, the tide had turned so quickly.

They had assembled an overwhelming force, over one hundred thousand strong. It should have been enough, he should be standing atop the Titan Gate, triumphantly waiting at the top for the arrival of the All Father. Instead he would be waiting with his head hung low in shame with tens of thousands of devotees left for dead on the battlefield.

Everyone knew the histories, the last time that the H'Daree had lost a battle was against the Safar. Now the Titan Gate would go down in infamy alongside the slaughter at the Fields of Gold, a story told to children as a cautionary tale, the reason preparation was now key to everything they did; the power to overwhelm.

He found it incomprehensible that people still fought them. Candor had all the information, knew the facts. What they brought was an end to poverty and hunger, an end to war; at least behind them. A society of plenty, where everyone was valued, everyone was protected and everyone was driven by the same goal. The unification of the human race, the Ascension of humanity, the next step forward. Why fight the inevitable? Why strive to stand against that which was a benefit to all? So much unnecessary bloodshed; so many people sent ahead as a vanguard, made to wait for the rest of humanity to join them. Then there were all those that were consigned to eternal nothingness, robbed of the chance due to ignorant doctrine.

But the worst of it was the missed opportunity to capture the great defiler, the abomination, Jonoh Shipwright. They all knew the importance of it. If they captured him the conflict would have an inevitable conclusion, the rest of the Known World rolling over and playing dead. He was the key, the only thing that gave the deluded nations of the so-called Known World any chance or hope of resisting.

The Known World? The arrogance of these people, as if their little piece of the planet was the be all and end all of existence. They had no idea that there was anything outside of their quaint Storm Curtain, some of them believing that the Known World was all there was. Uneducated, superstitious savages. The thought of it angered him, how dare they question the will of the H'Daree.

Now all that was left was to wait. He knew the consequences of his actions but he no longer feared the outcome, he would be glad for it all to be over and done with, the weight of the responsibility pressing down on him. No one would look him in the face because there were no words to say.

"My son, I am here and I await your presence."

His breath stuck in his throat, as it turned out he did still have fear in his soul. The rest of The Chosen reined in slightly, keeping a little distance as if in fear of catching a disease. The All Father had come.

www.ingramcontent.com/pod-product-compliance
Lightning Source LLC
Chambersburg PA
CBHW061342190726
48288CB00005B/1564